Kakuriyo
Bed & Breakfast for Spirits

5

Art by

Waco Ioka

Original Story by **Midori Yuma**
Character Design by **Laruha**

CONTENTS

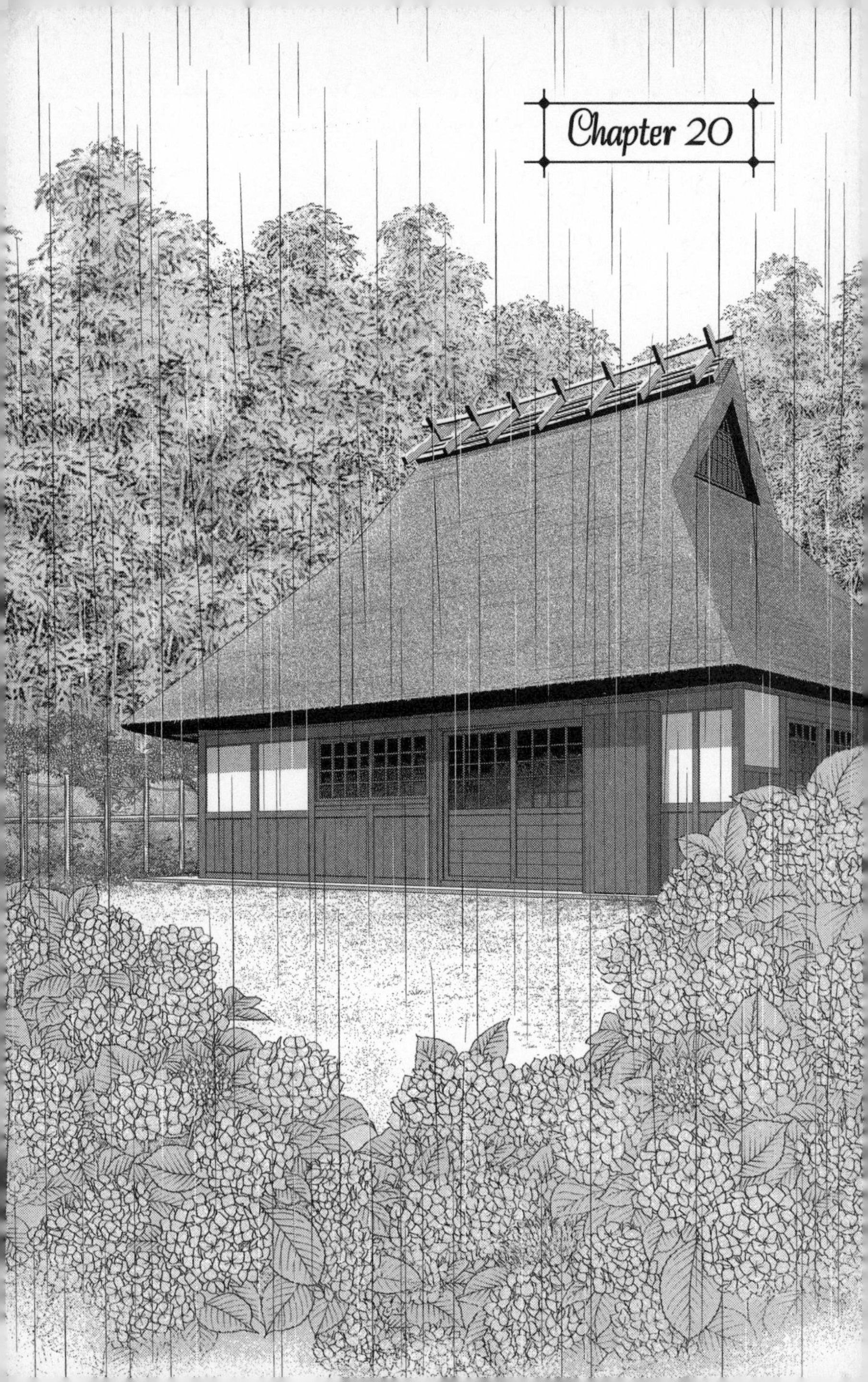
Chapter 20

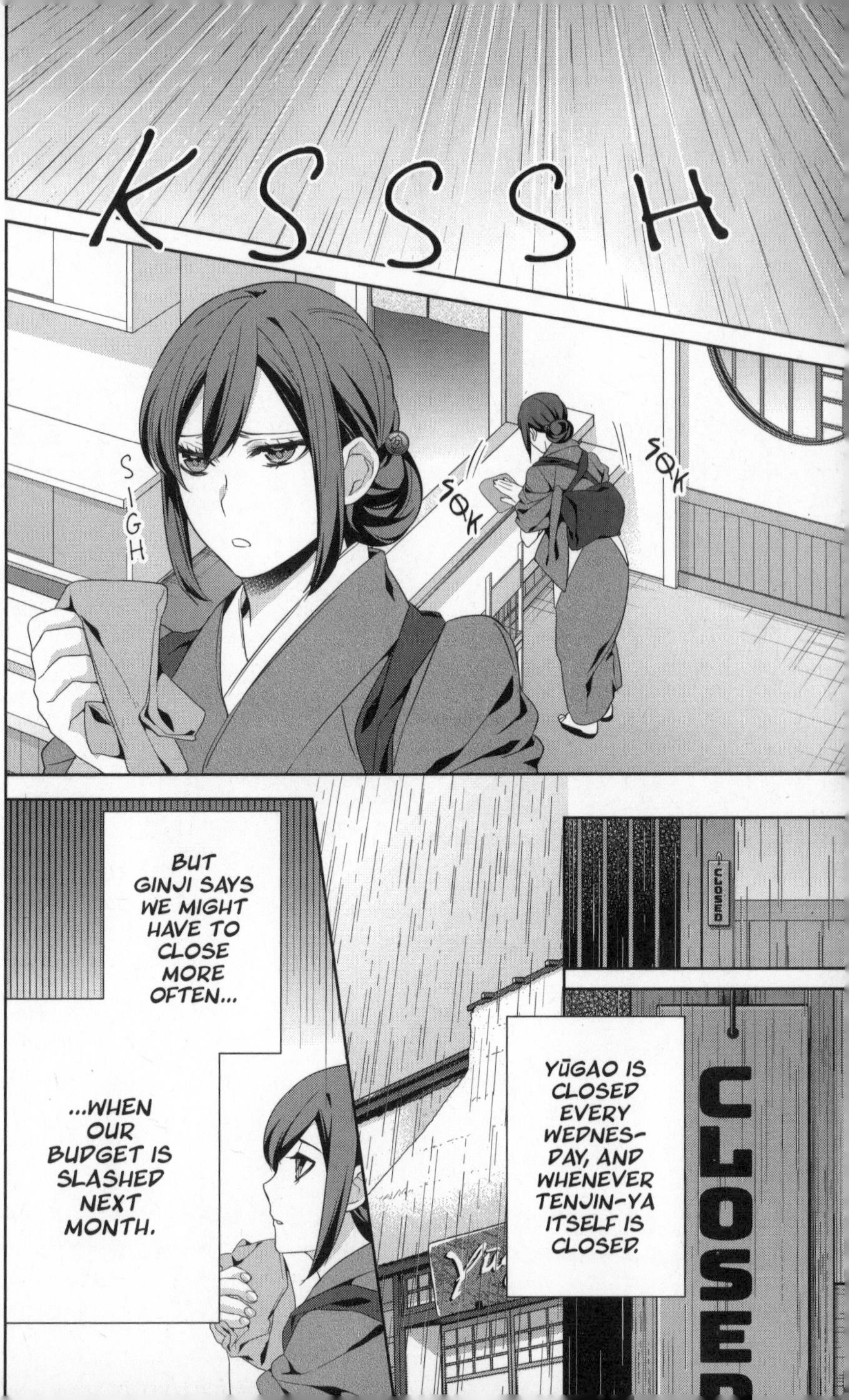
KSSSH
SQK
SQK
SIGH
CLOSED
CLOSED
YŪGAO IS CLOSED EVERY WEDNES-DAY, AND WHENEVER TENJIN-YA ITSELF IS CLOSED.
BUT GINJI SAYS WE MIGHT HAVE TO CLOSE MORE OFTEN...
...WHEN OUR BUDGET IS SLASHED NEXT MONTH.

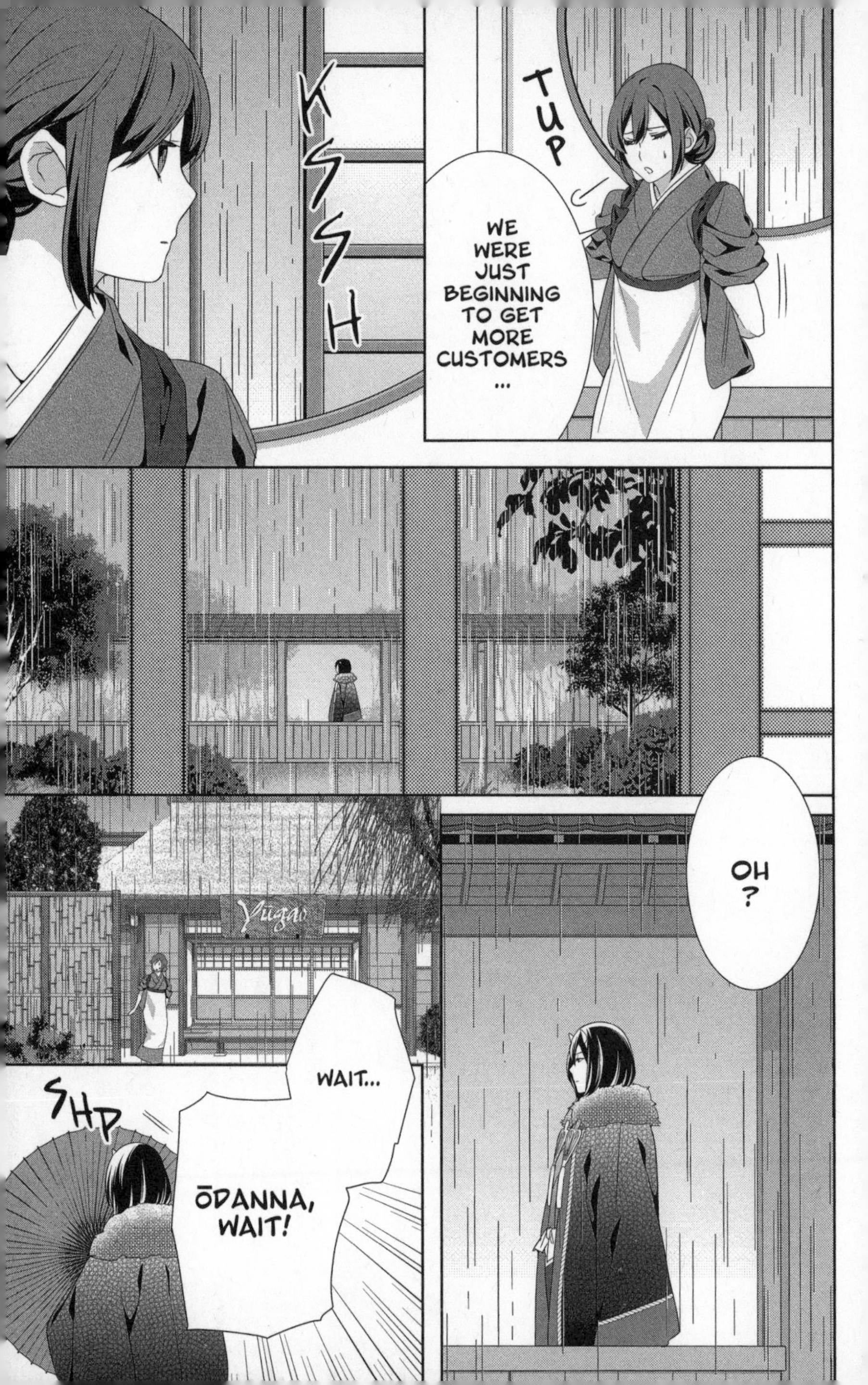
TUP
WE WERE JUST BEGINNING TO GET MORE CUSTOMERS...
KSSH
OH?
Yūgao
WAIT...
ŌDANNA, WAIT!
SHP

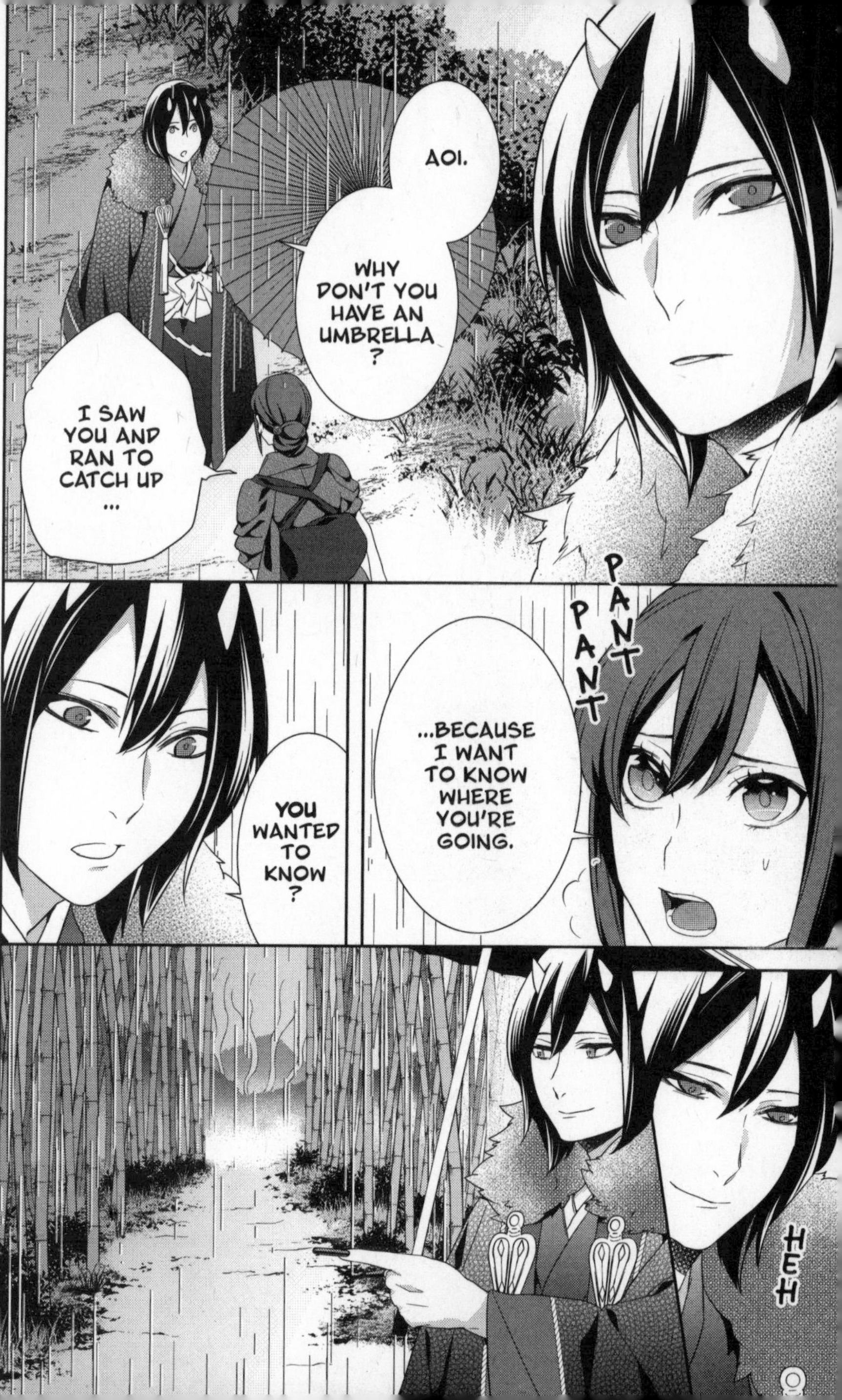
AOI.
WHY DON'T YOU HAVE AN UMBRELLA?
I SAW YOU AND RAN TO CATCH UP...
PANT PANT
...BECAUSE I WANT TO KNOW WHERE YOU'RE GOING.
YOU WANTED TO KNOW?
HEH

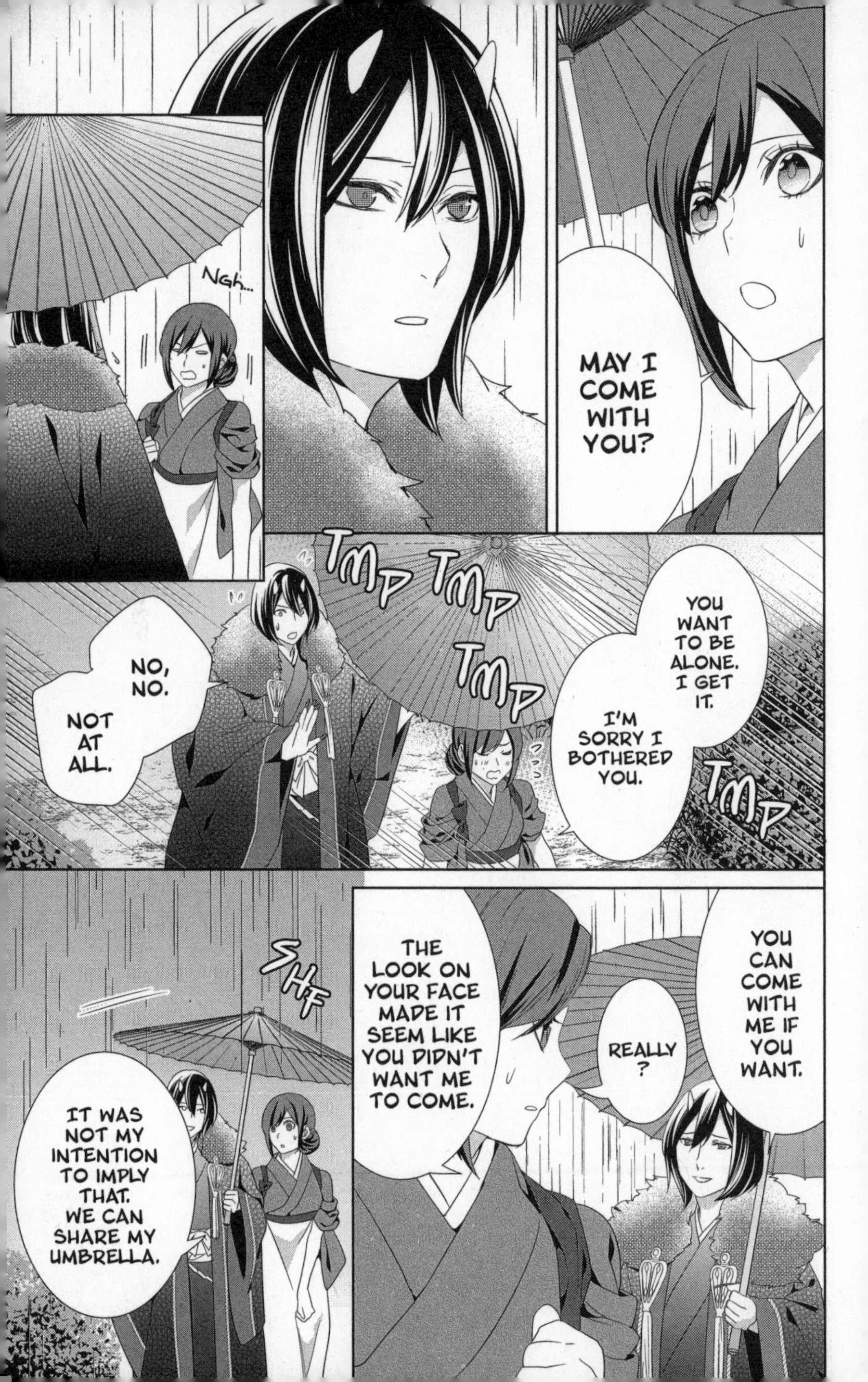
MAY I COME WITH YOU?
Ngh...
YOU WANT TO BE ALONE. I GET IT.
I'M SORRY I BOTHERED YOU.
TMP TMP TMP TMP
NO, NO.
NOT AT ALL.
YOU CAN COME WITH ME IF YOU WANT.
REALLY?
THE LOOK ON YOUR FACE MADE IT SEEM LIKE YOU DIDN'T WANT ME TO COME.
SHF
IT WAS NOT MY INTENTION TO IMPLY THAT. WE CAN SHARE MY UMBRELLA.

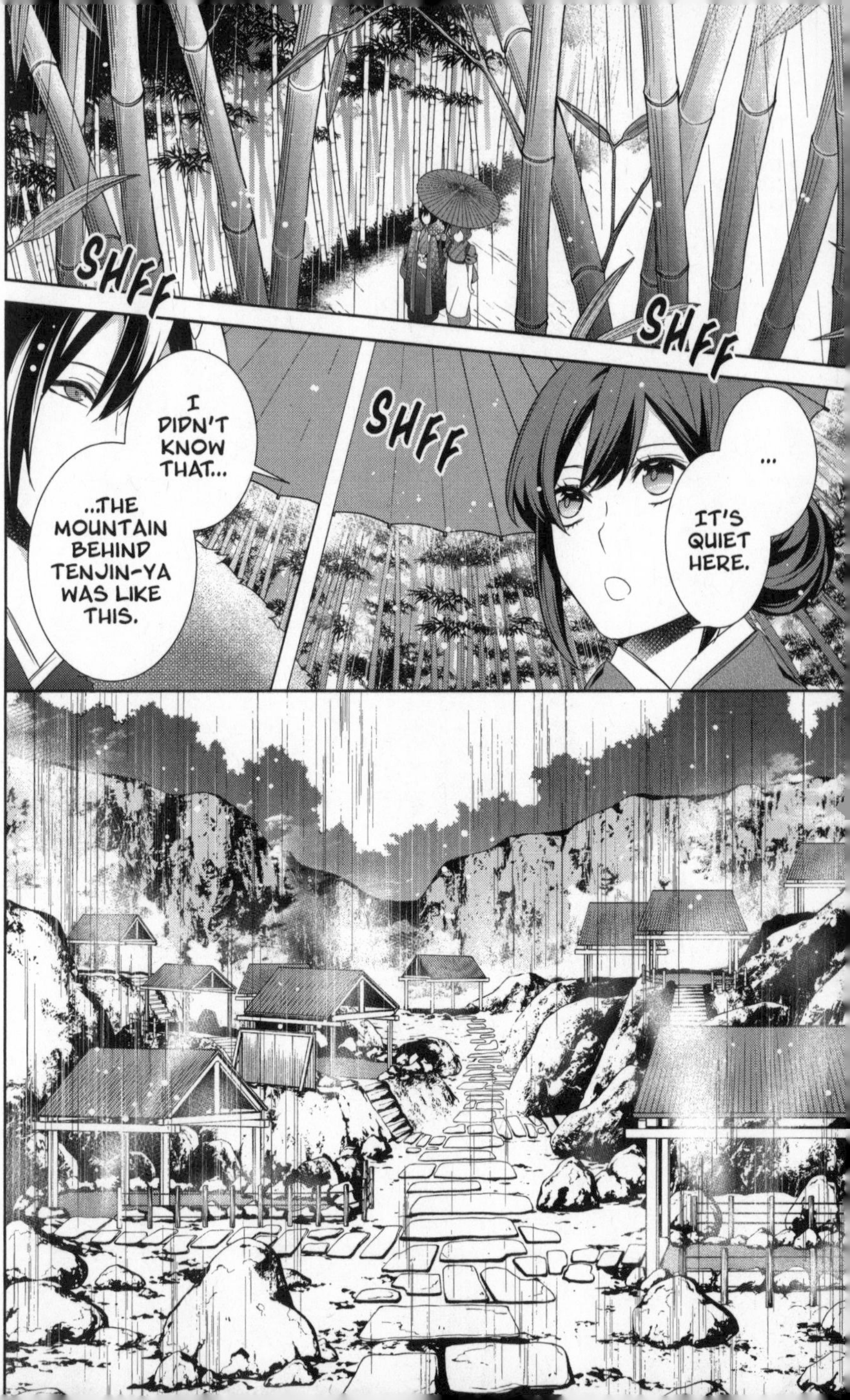
SHFF
SHFF
...
IT'S QUIET HERE.
SHFF
I DIDN'T KNOW THAT...
...THE MOUNTAIN BEHIND TENJIN-YA WAS LIKE THIS.

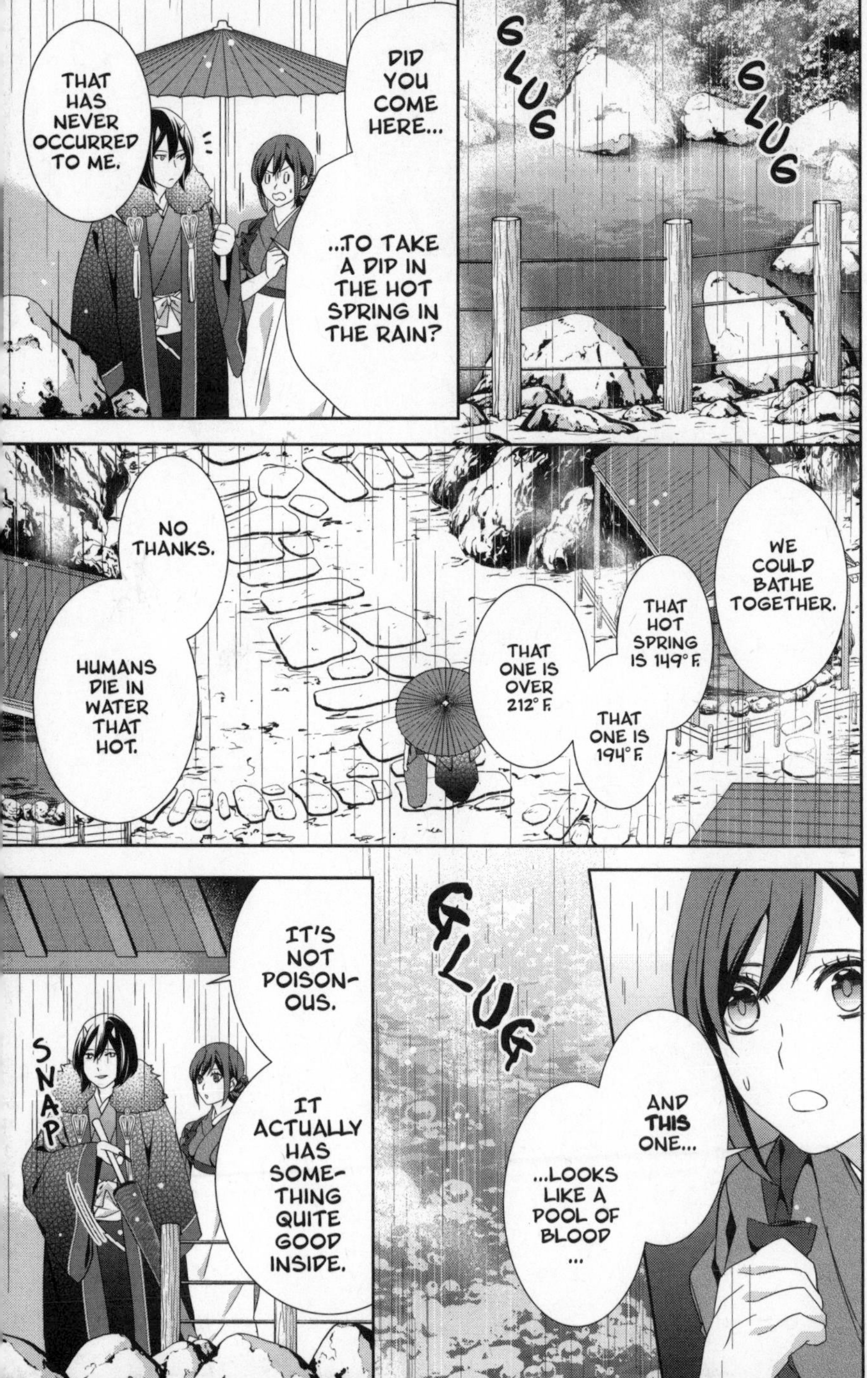
GLUG
GLUG
DID YOU COME HERE...
...TO TAKE A DIP IN THE HOT SPRING IN THE RAIN?
THAT HAS NEVER OCCURRED TO ME.
WE COULD BATHE TOGETHER.
THAT HOT SPRING IS 149° F.
THAT ONE IS OVER 212° F.
THAT ONE IS 194° F.
NO THANKS.
HUMANS DIE IN WATER THAT HOT.
AND THIS ONE...
...LOOKS LIKE A POOL OF BLOOD ...
GLUG
IT'S NOT POISON-OUS.
IT ACTUALLY HAS SOME-THING QUITE GOOD INSIDE.
SNAP

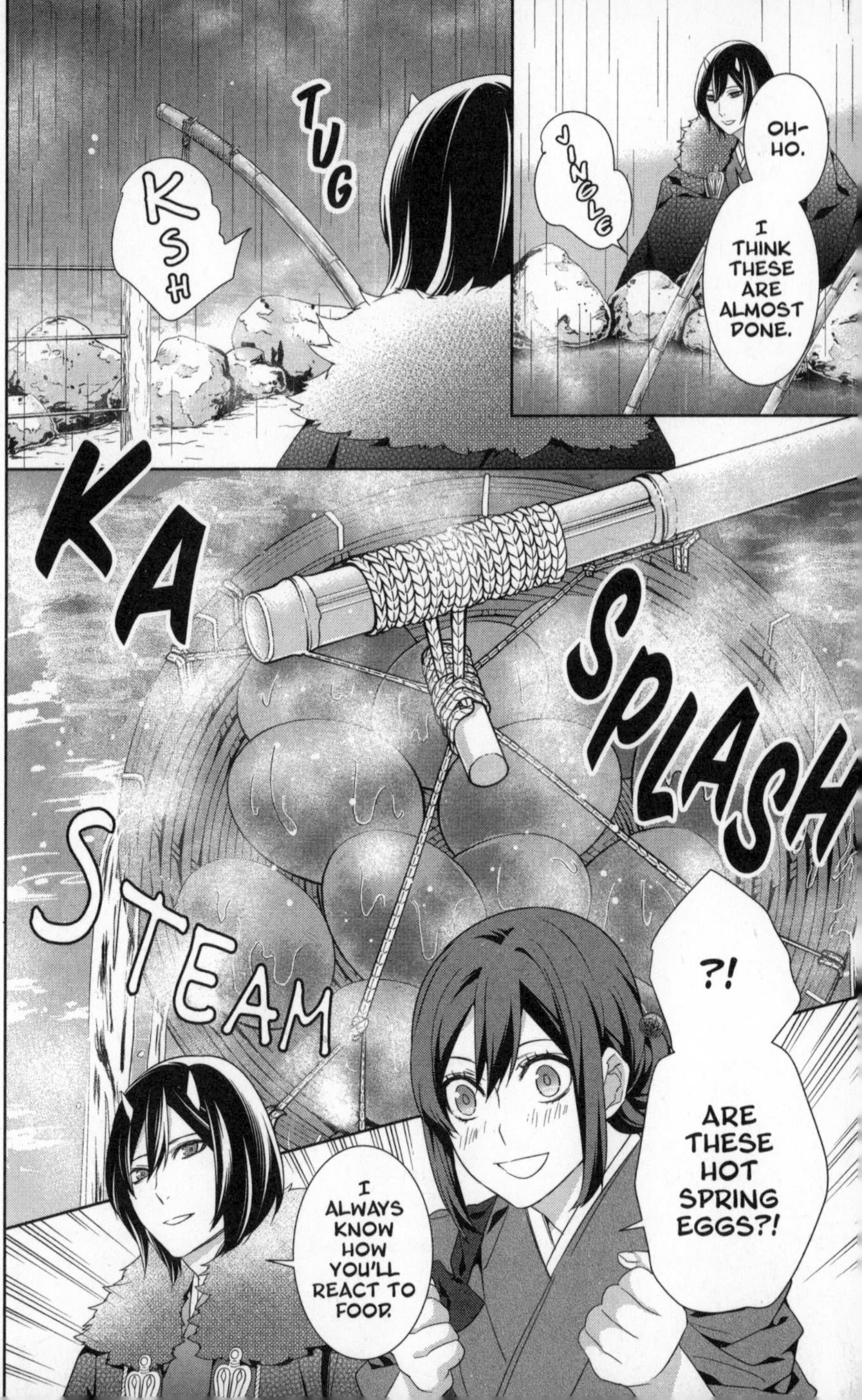
OH-HO.
I THINK THESE ARE ALMOST DONE.
JIGGLE
TUG
KSH
KA
SPLASH
STEAM
?!
ARE THESE HOT SPRING EGGS?!
I ALWAYS KNOW HOW YOU'LL REACT TO FOOD.

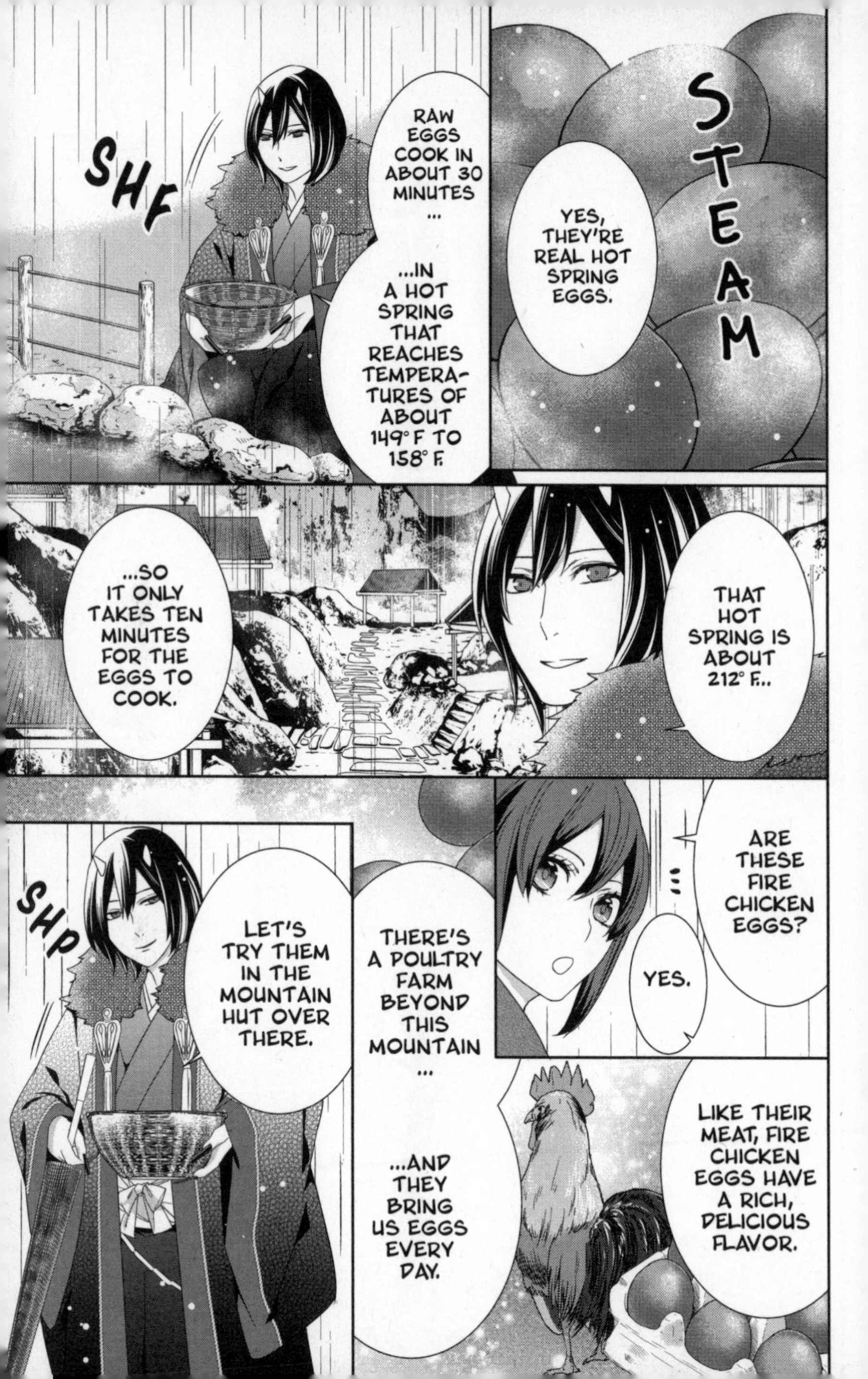
STEAM
YES, THEY'RE REAL HOT SPRING EGGS.
RAW EGGS COOK IN ABOUT 30 MINUTES ...
...IN A HOT SPRING THAT REACHES TEMPERA-TURES OF ABOUT 149° F TO 158° F.
SHF
THAT HOT SPRING IS ABOUT 212° F...
...SO IT ONLY TAKES TEN MINUTES FOR THE EGGS TO COOK.
ARE THESE FIRE CHICKEN EGGS?
...
YES.
LIKE THEIR MEAT, FIRE CHICKEN EGGS HAVE A RICH, DELICIOUS FLAVOR.
THERE'S A POULTRY FARM BEYOND THIS MOUNTAIN ...
...AND THEY BRING US EGGS EVERY DAY.
LET'S TRY THEM IN THE MOUNTAIN HUT OVER THERE.
SHP

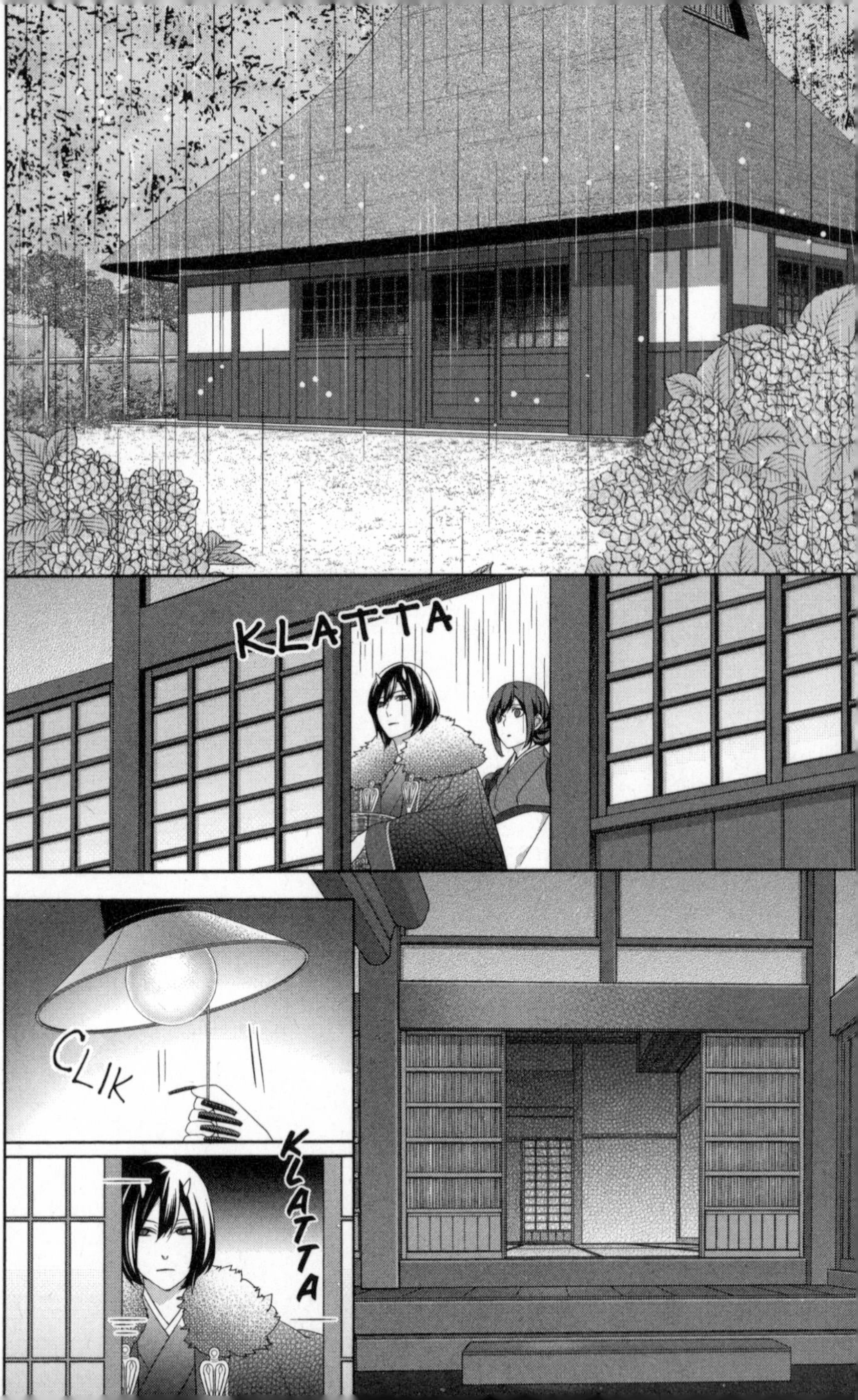
KLATTA
CLIK
KLATTA

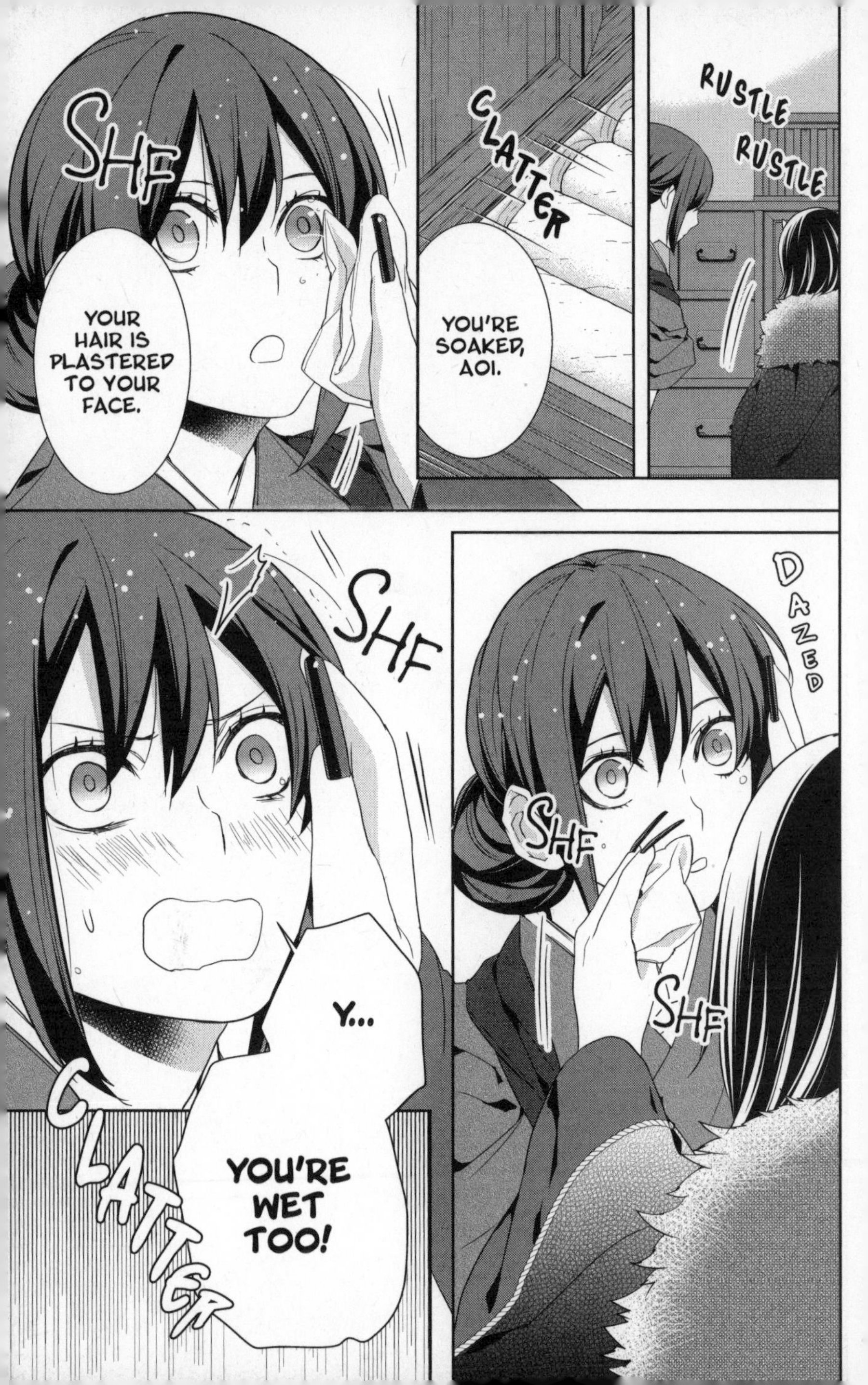
RUSTLE
RUSTLE
CLATTER
YOU'RE SOAKED, AOI.
SHF
YOUR HAIR IS PLASTERED TO YOUR FACE.
DAZED
SHF
SHF
SHF
Y...
YOU'RE WET TOO!
CLATTER

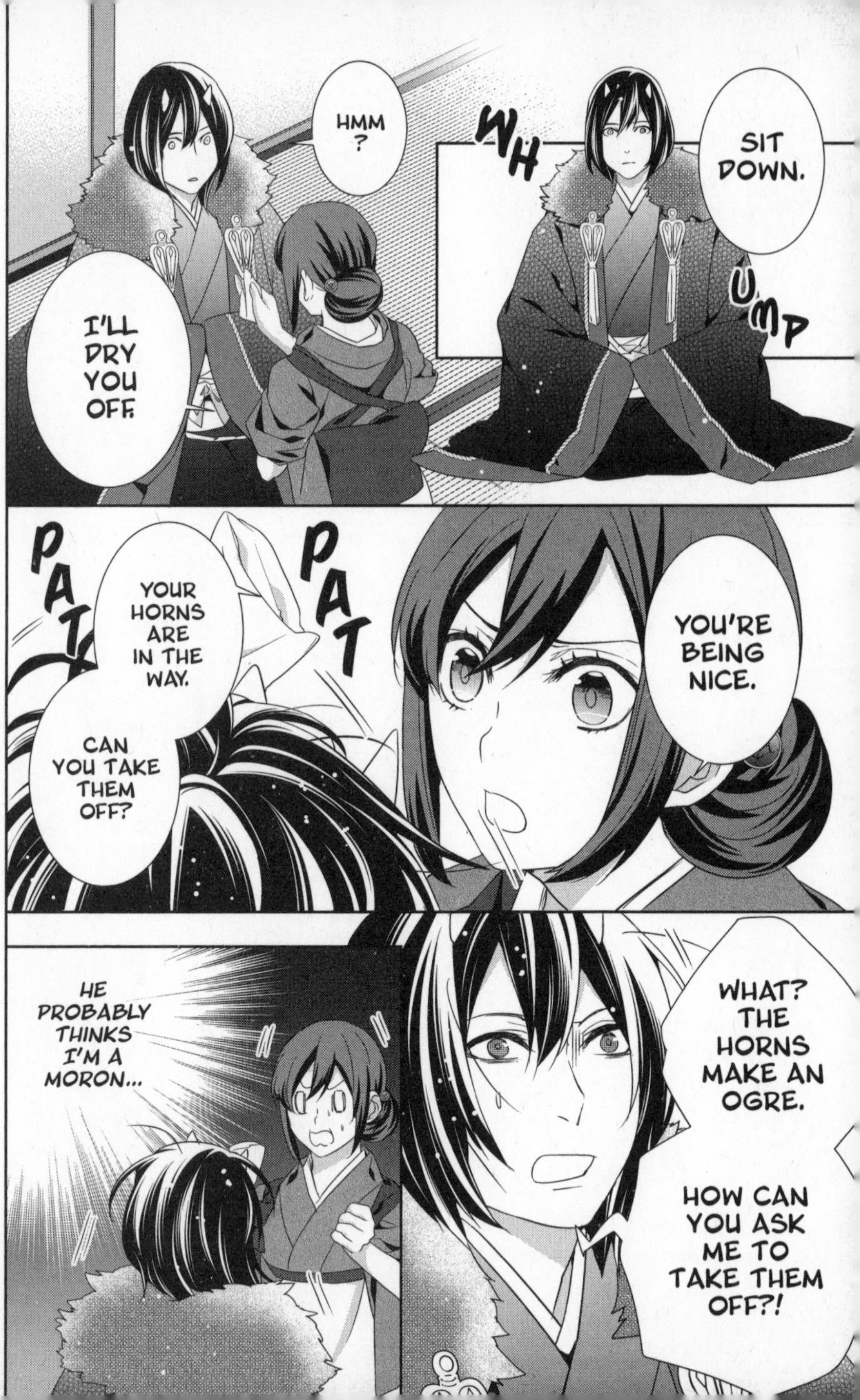
SIT DOWN.
WH UMP
HMM ?
I'LL DRY YOU OFF.
YOU'RE BEING NICE.
PAT
PAT
YOUR HORNS ARE IN THE WAY.
CAN YOU TAKE THEM OFF?
WHAT? THE HORNS MAKE AN OGRE.
HOW CAN YOU ASK ME TO TAKE THEM OFF?!
HE PROBABLY THINKS I'M A MORON...

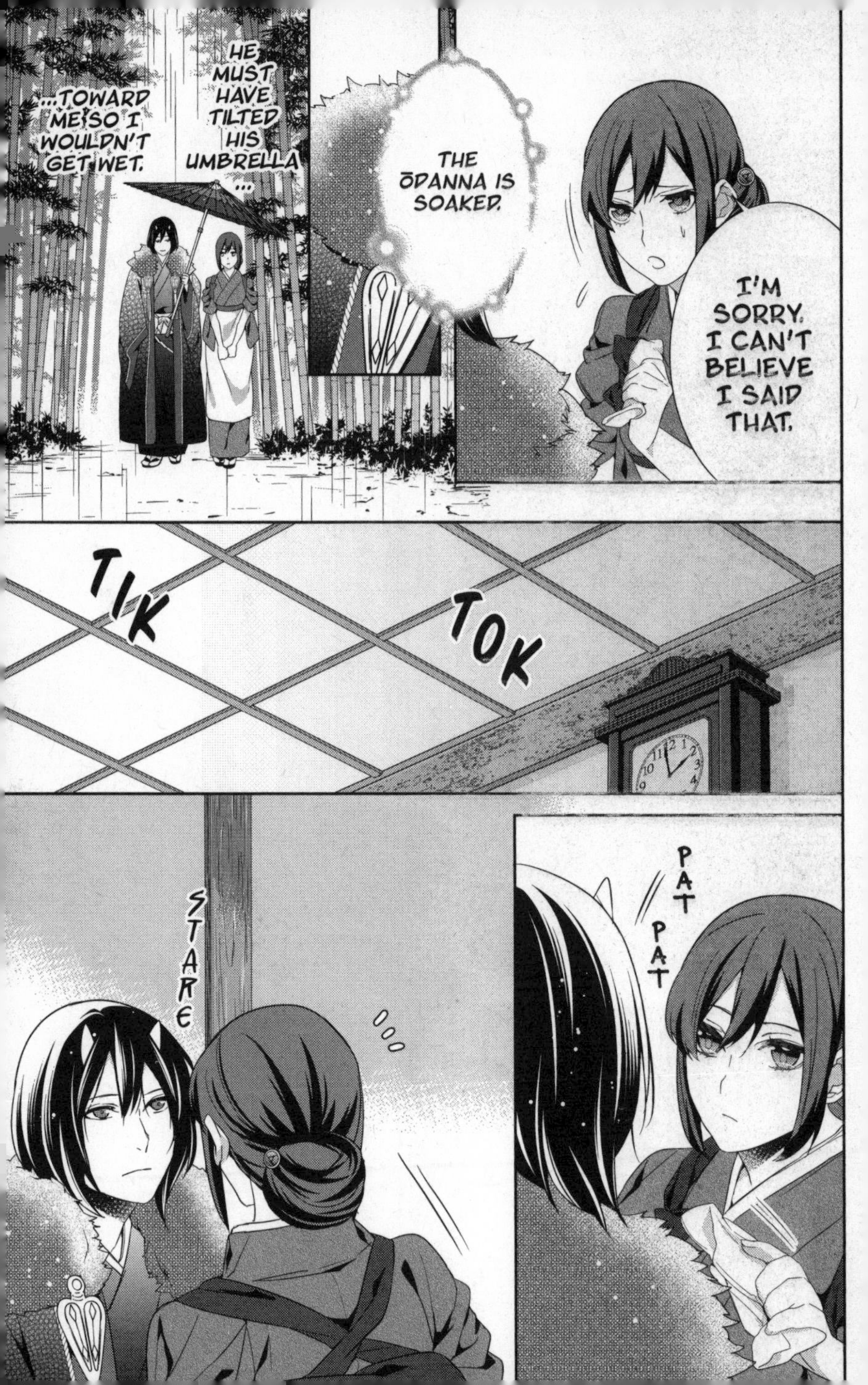
I'M SORRY. I CAN'T BELIEVE I SAID THAT.
THE ŌDANNA IS SOAKED.
HE MUST HAVE TILTED HIS UMBRELLA ...
...TOWARD ME SO I WOULDN'T GET WET.
TIK
TOK
PAT PAT
STARE

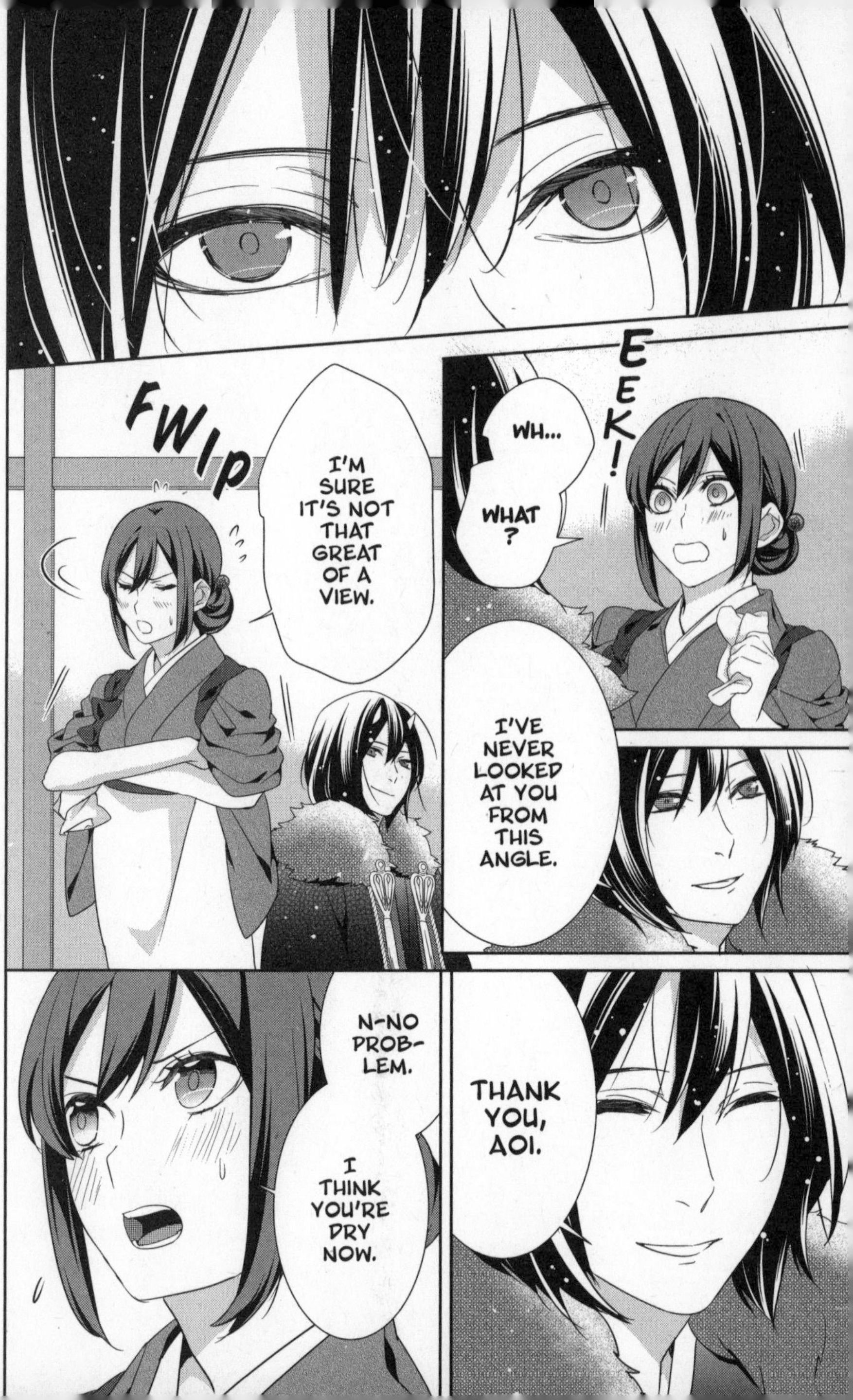
EEK!
WH... WHAT?
I'VE NEVER LOOKED AT YOU FROM THIS ANGLE.
FWIP
I'M SURE IT'S NOT THAT GREAT OF A VIEW.
THANK YOU, AOI.
N-NO PROB-LEM.
I THINK YOU'RE DRY NOW.

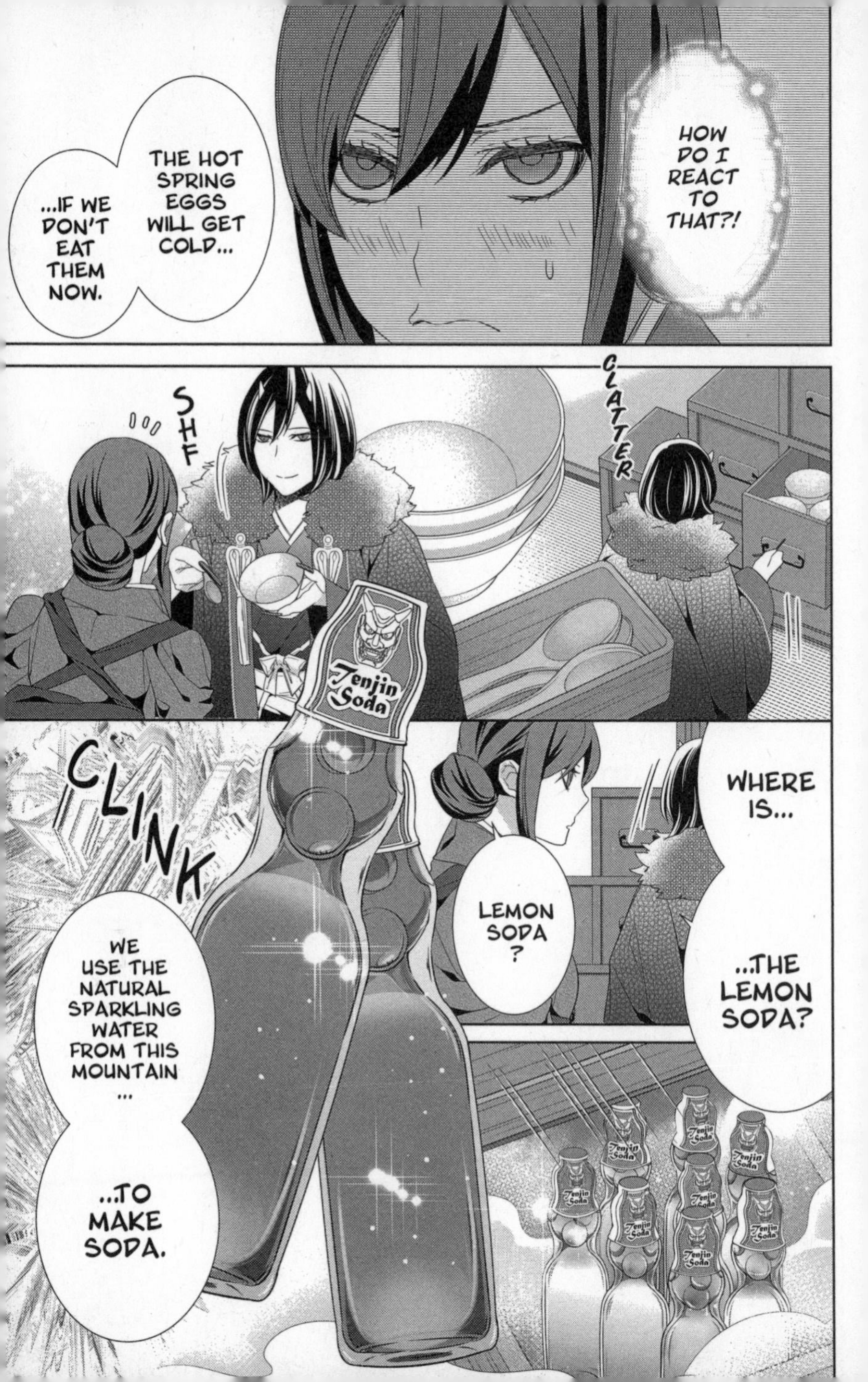
HOW DO I REACT TO THAT?!
THE HOT SPRING EGGS WILL GET COLD...
...IF WE DON'T EAT THEM NOW.
CLATTER
SHF
Tenjin Soda
WHERE IS...
...THE LEMON SODA?
LEMON SODA?
CLINK
WE USE THE NATURAL SPARKLING WATER FROM THIS MOUNTAIN...
...TO MAKE SODA.
Tenjin Soda

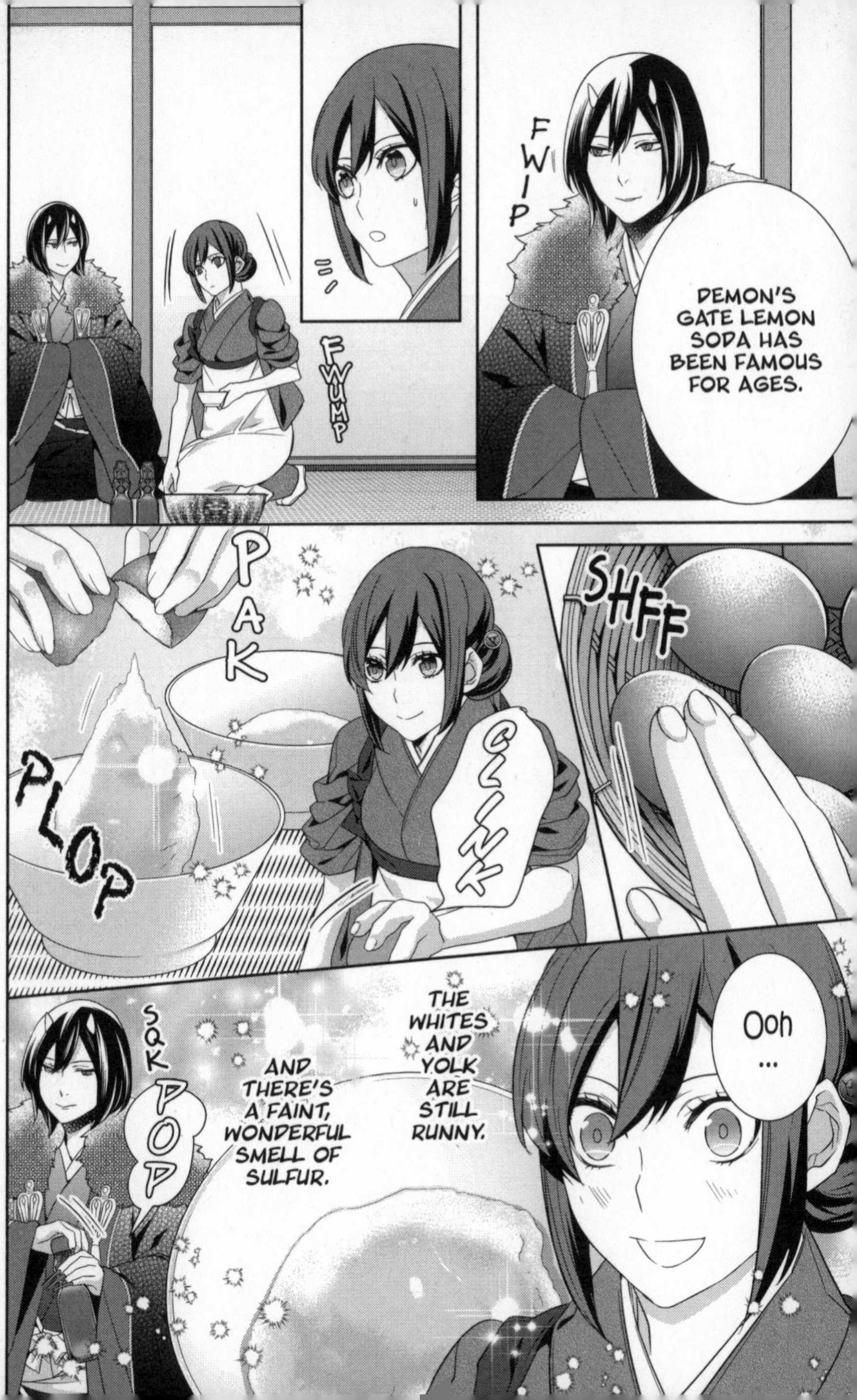

DEMON'S GATE LEMON SODA HAS BEEN FAMOUS FOR AGES.
FWIP
!!
FWUMP
SHFF
PAK
CLINK
PLOP
Ooh ...
THE WHITES AND YOLK ARE STILL RUNNY.
AND THERE'S A FAINT, WONDERFUL SMELL OF SULFUR.
SQK
POP

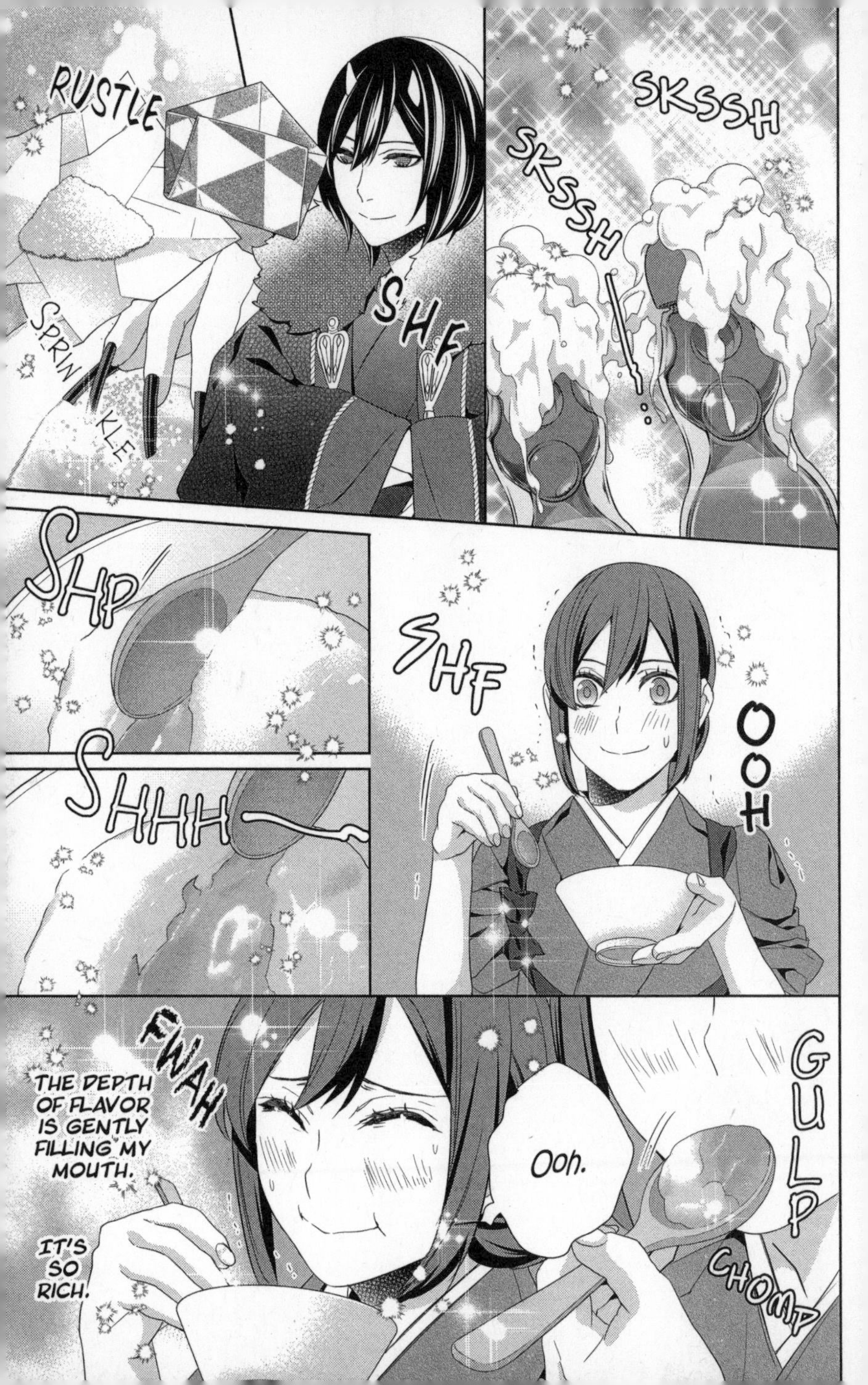
SKSSH
SKSSH
RUSTLE
SHF
SPRINKLE
SHF
OOH
SHP
SHHH
GULP
CHOMP
Ooh.
FWAH
THE DEPTH OF FLAVOR IS GENTLY FILLING MY MOUTH.
IT'S SO RICH.

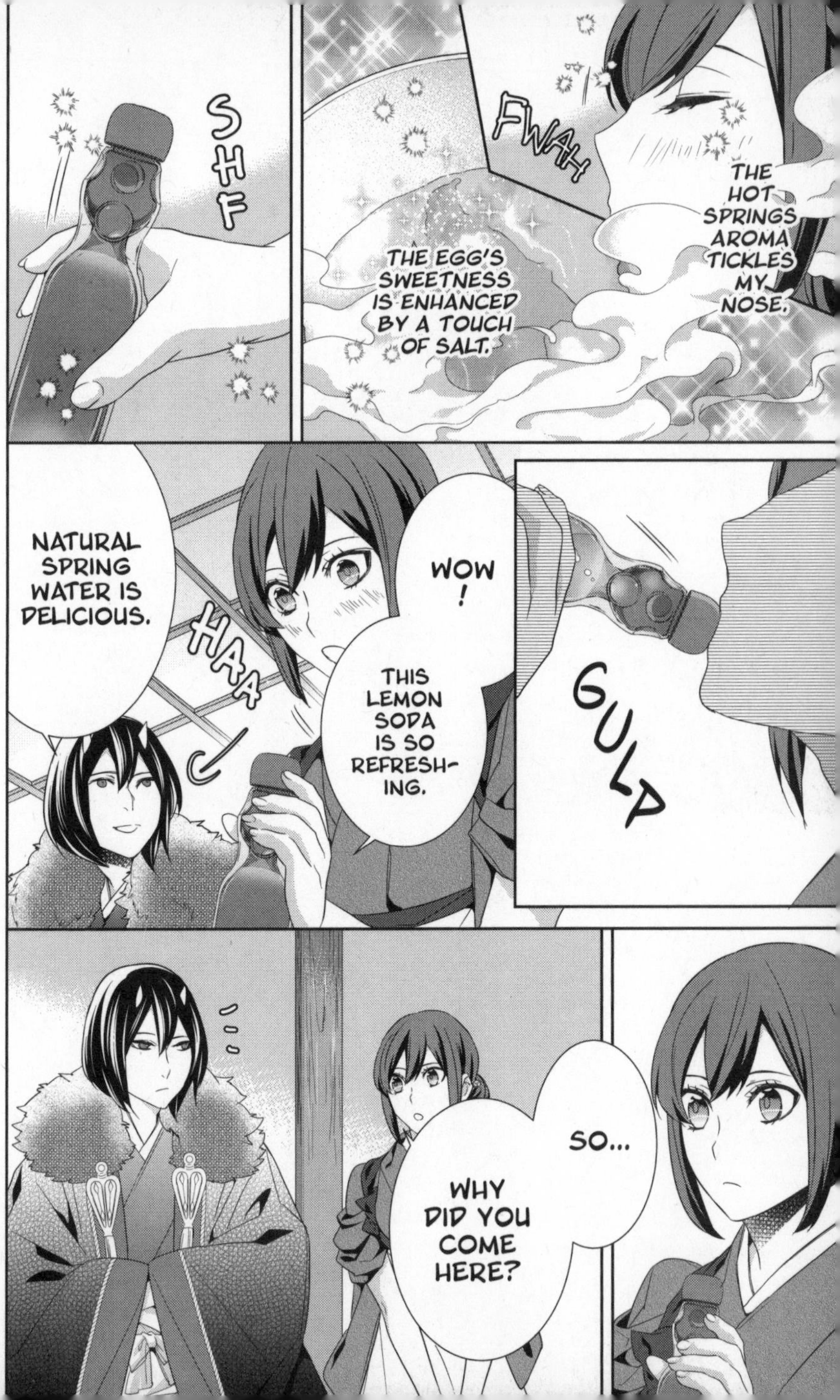
THE HOT SPRINGS AROMA TICKLES MY NOSE.
FWAH
THE EGG'S SWEETNESS IS ENHANCED BY A TOUCH OF SALT.
SHF
GULP
WOW!
THIS LEMON SODA IS SO REFRESHING.
HAA
NATURAL SPRING WATER IS DELICIOUS.
SO...
WHY DID YOU COME HERE?

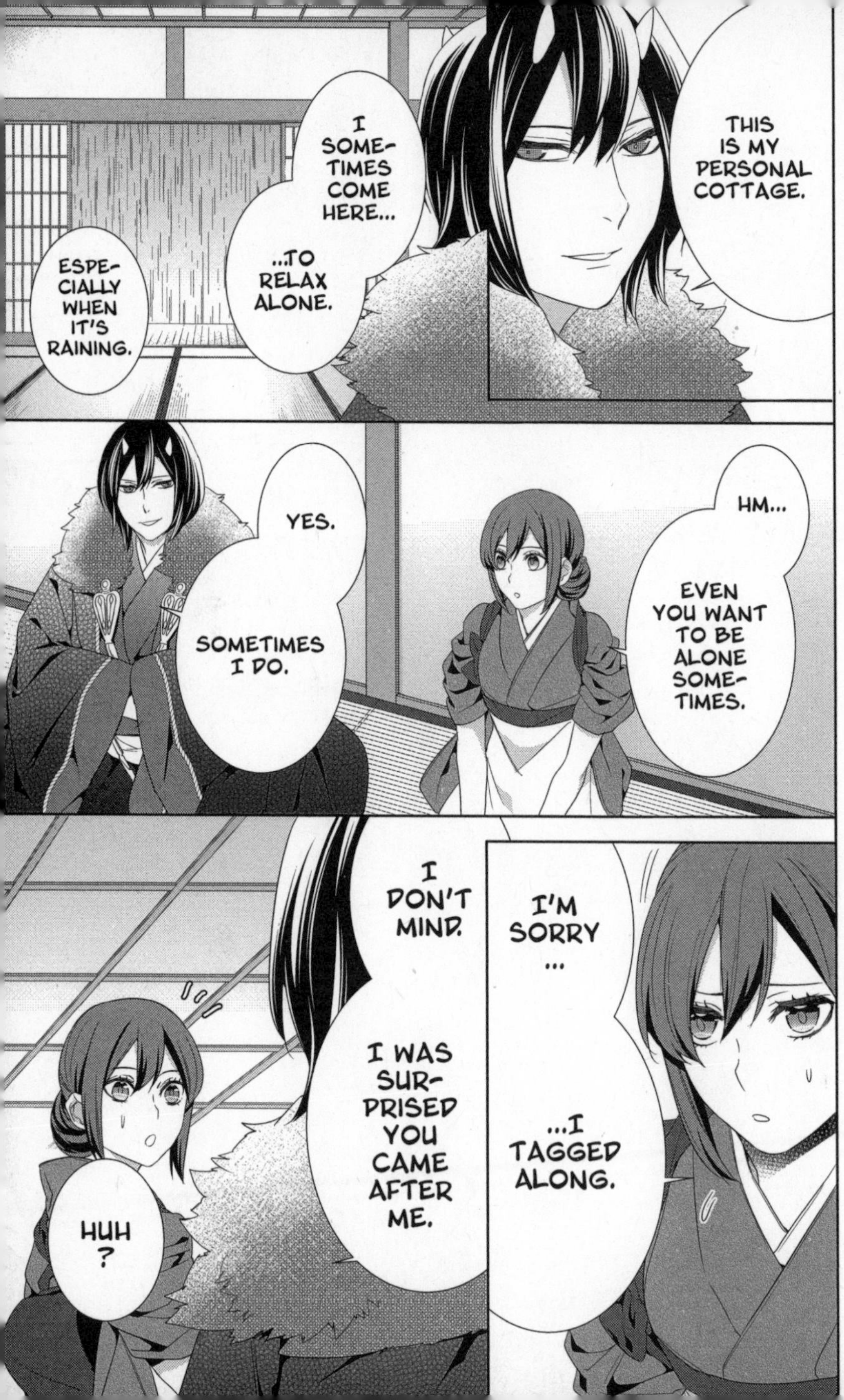
THIS IS MY PERSONAL COTTAGE.
I SOMETIMES COME HERE...
...TO RELAX ALONE.
ESPECIALLY WHEN IT'S RAINING.
HM...
EVEN YOU WANT TO BE ALONE SOMETIMES.
YES.
SOMETIMES I DO.
I'M SORRY ...
...I TAGGED ALONG.
I DON'T MIND.
I WAS SURPRISED YOU CAME AFTER ME.
HUH ?

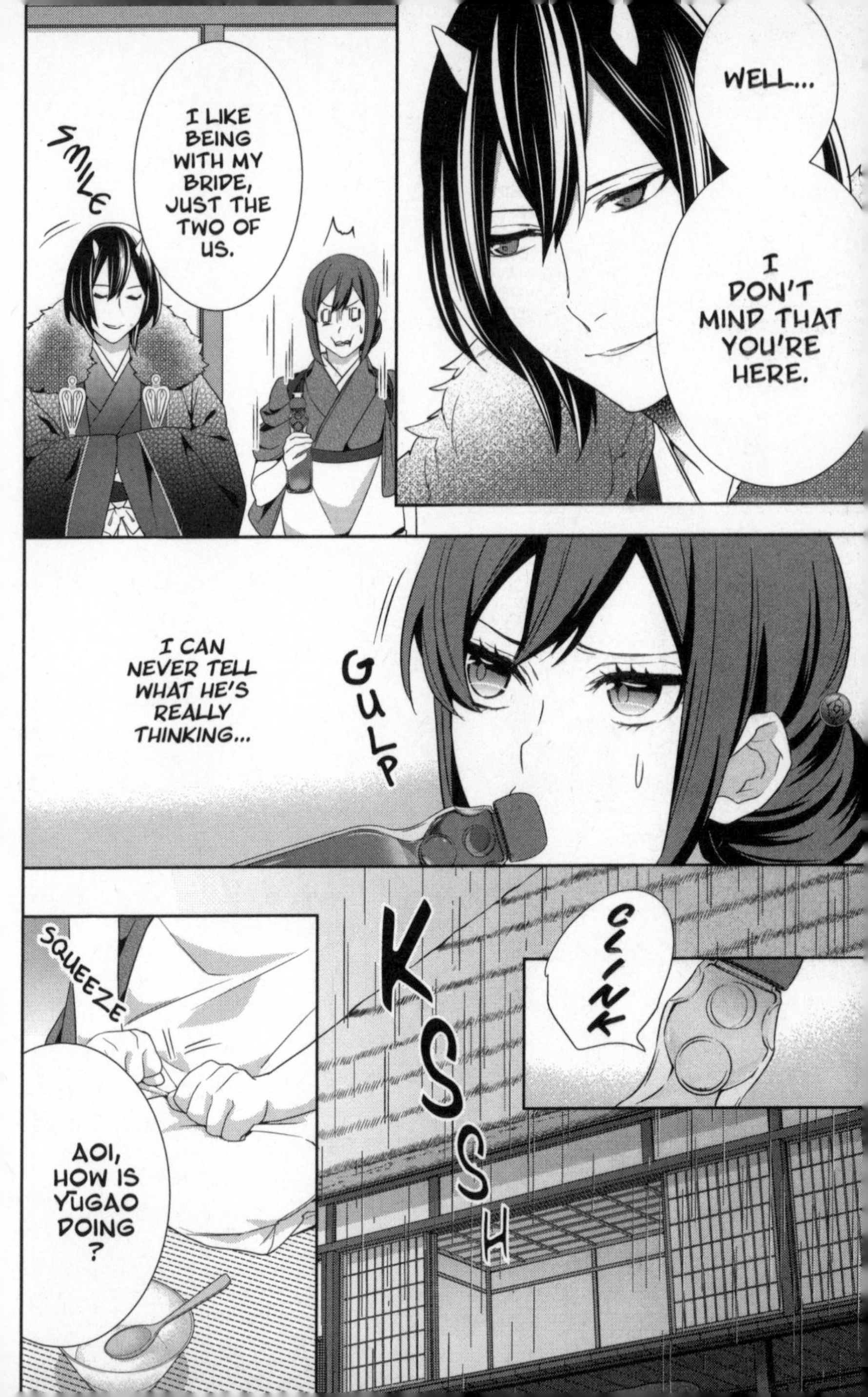
WELL...
I DON'T MIND THAT YOU'RE HERE.
I LIKE BEING WITH MY BRIDE, JUST THE TWO OF US.
SMILE
I CAN NEVER TELL WHAT HE'S REALLY THINKING...
GULP
CLINK
KSSSH
SQUEEZE
AOI, HOW IS YUGAO DOING?

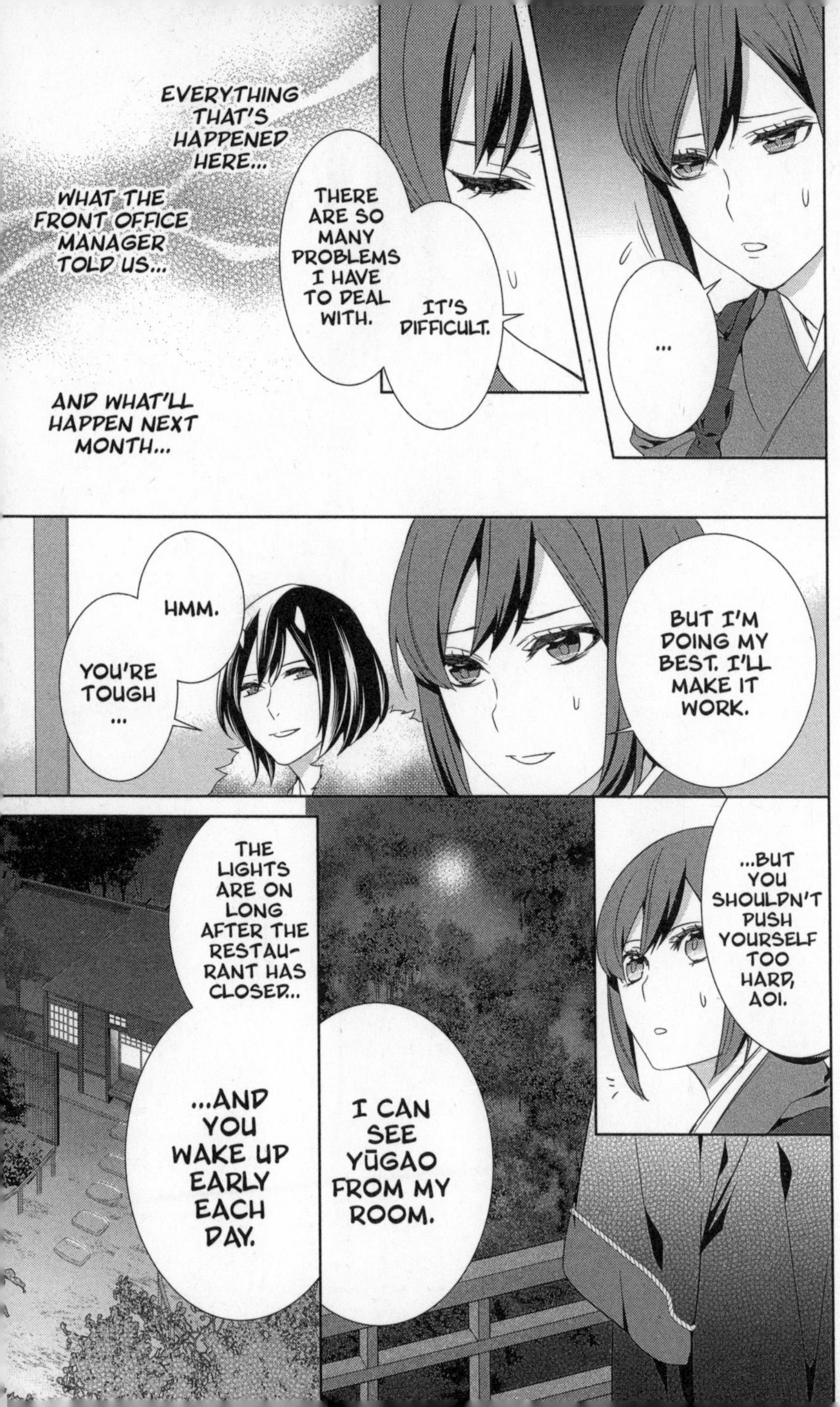
...
THERE ARE SO MANY PROBLEMS I HAVE TO DEAL WITH.
IT'S DIFFICULT.
EVERYTHING THAT'S HAPPENED HERE...
WHAT THE FRONT OFFICE MANAGER TOLD US...
AND WHAT'LL HAPPEN NEXT MONTH...
BUT I'M DOING MY BEST. I'LL MAKE IT WORK.
HMM.
YOU'RE TOUGH ...
...BUT YOU SHOULDN'T PUSH YOURSELF TOO HARD, AOI.
I CAN SEE YŪGAO FROM MY ROOM.
THE LIGHTS ARE ON LONG AFTER THE RESTAU-RANT HAS CLOSED...
...AND YOU WAKE UP EARLY EACH DAY.

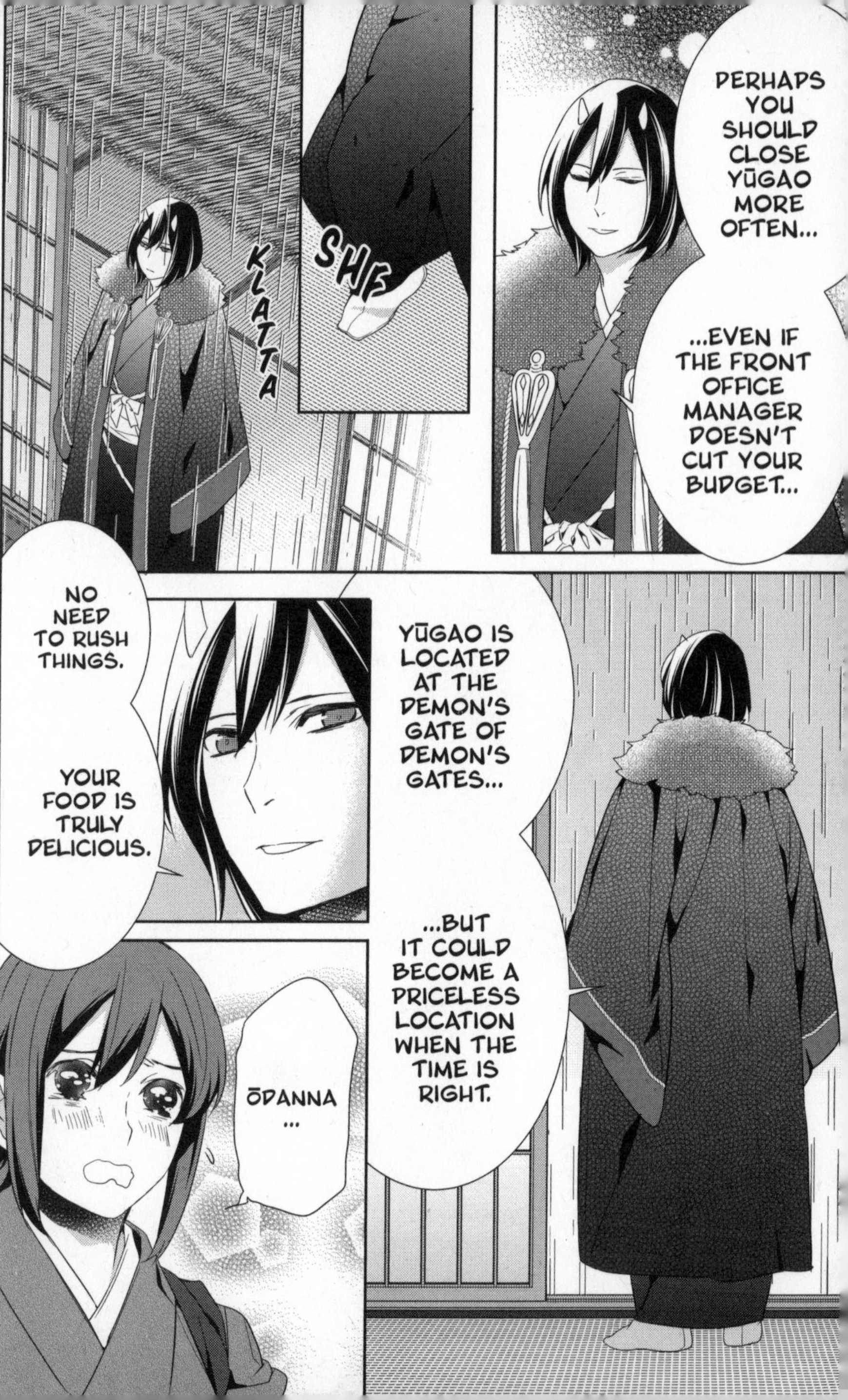
PERHAPS YOU SHOULD CLOSE YŪGAO MORE OFTEN...
...EVEN IF THE FRONT OFFICE MANAGER DOESN'T CUT YOUR BUDGET...
SHF
KLATTA
YŪGAO IS LOCATED AT THE DEMON'S GATE OF DEMON'S GATES...
...BUT IT COULD BECOME A PRICELESS LOCATION WHEN THE TIME IS RIGHT.
NO NEED TO RUSH THINGS.
YOUR FOOD IS TRULY DELICIOUS.
ŌDANNA ...

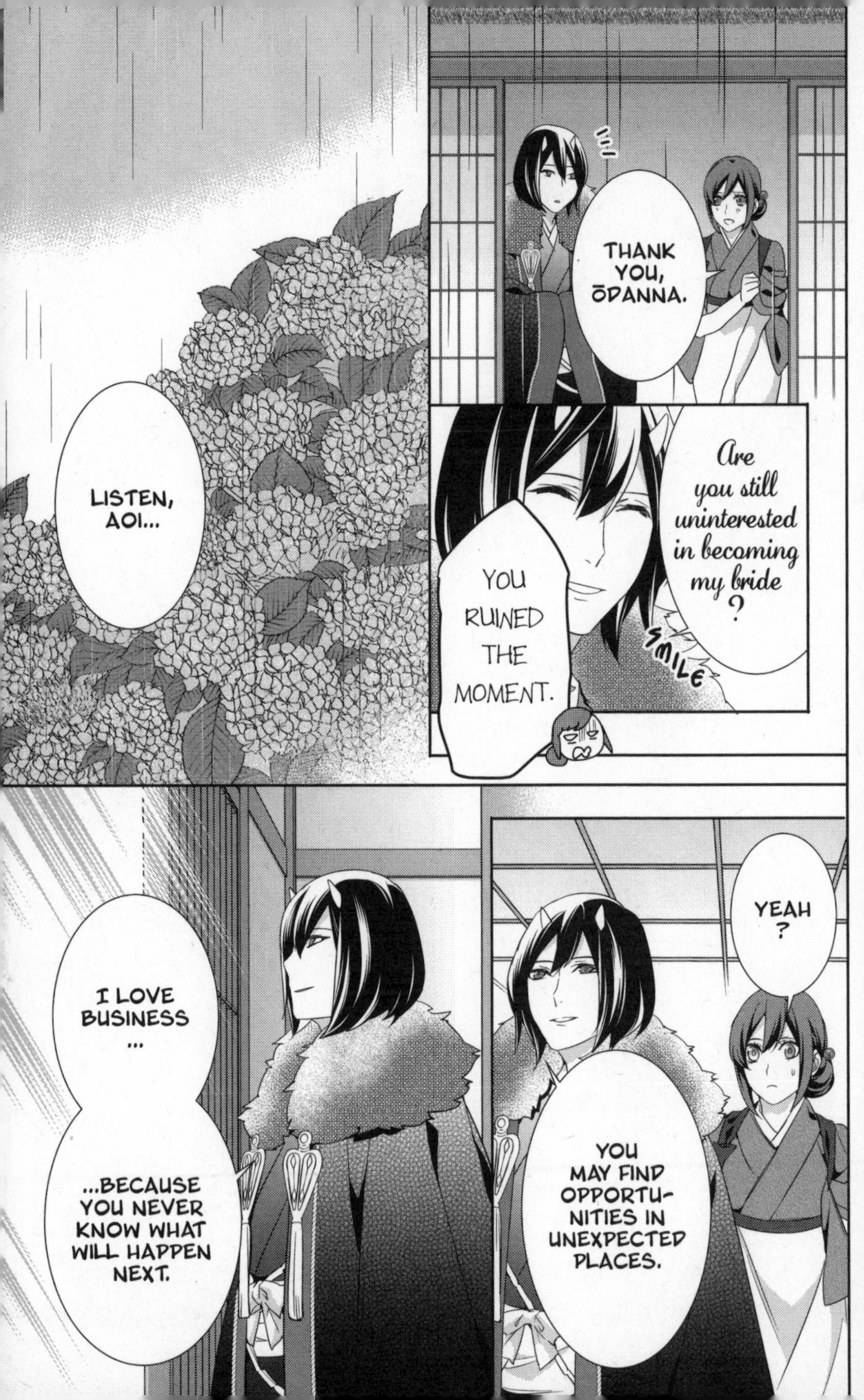
!!
THANK YOU, ŌDANNA.
Are you still uninterested in becoming my bride?
SMILE
YOU RUINED THE MOMENT.
LISTEN, AOI...
YEAH?
YOU MAY FIND OPPORTUNITIES IN UNEXPECTED PLACES.
I LOVE BUSINESS...
...BECAUSE YOU NEVER KNOW WHAT WILL HAPPEN NEXT.

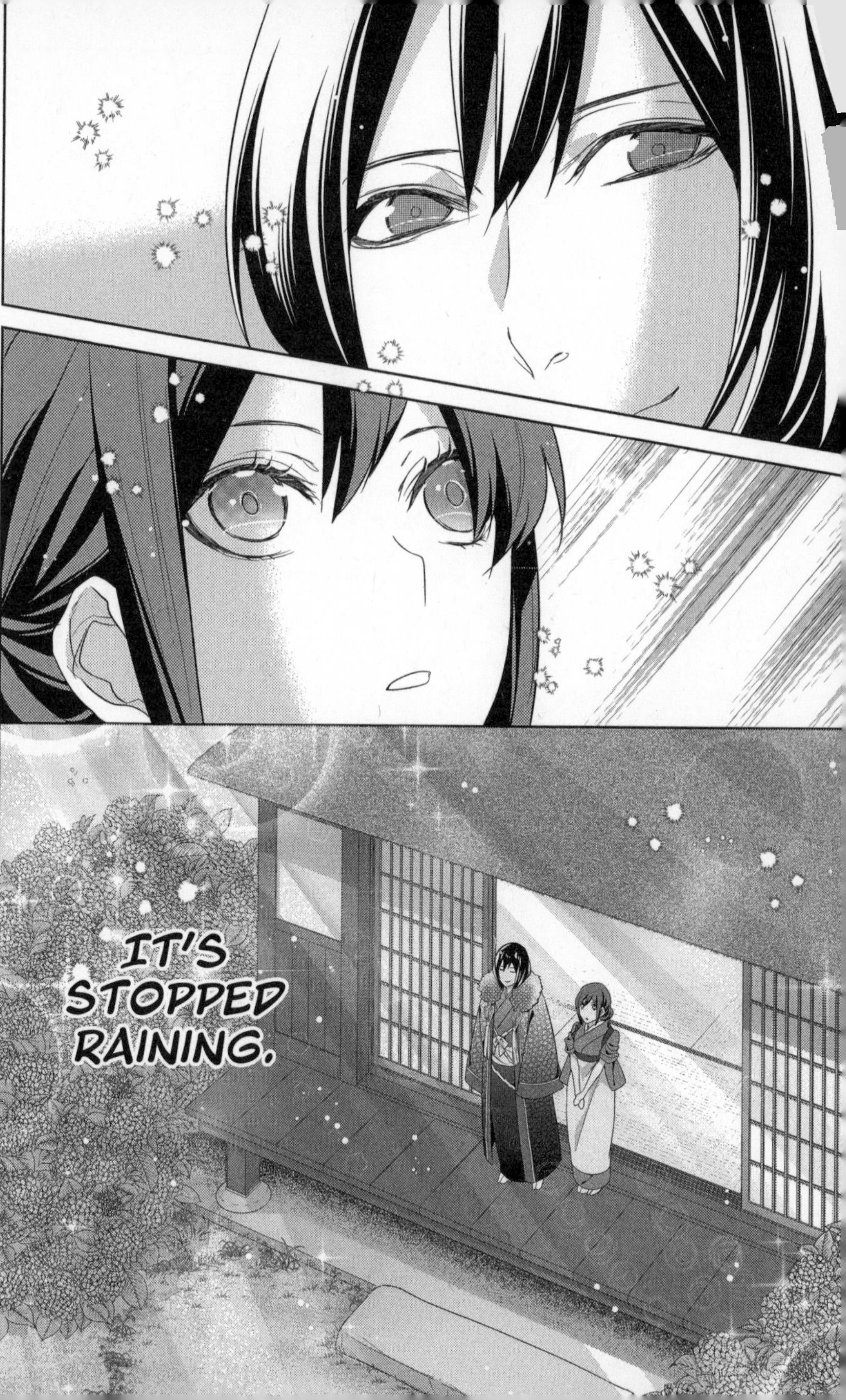
IT'S STOPPED RAINING.

Kakuriyo
Bed & Breakfast
for Spirits

Kakuriyo
Bed & Breakfast
for Spirits

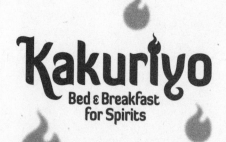

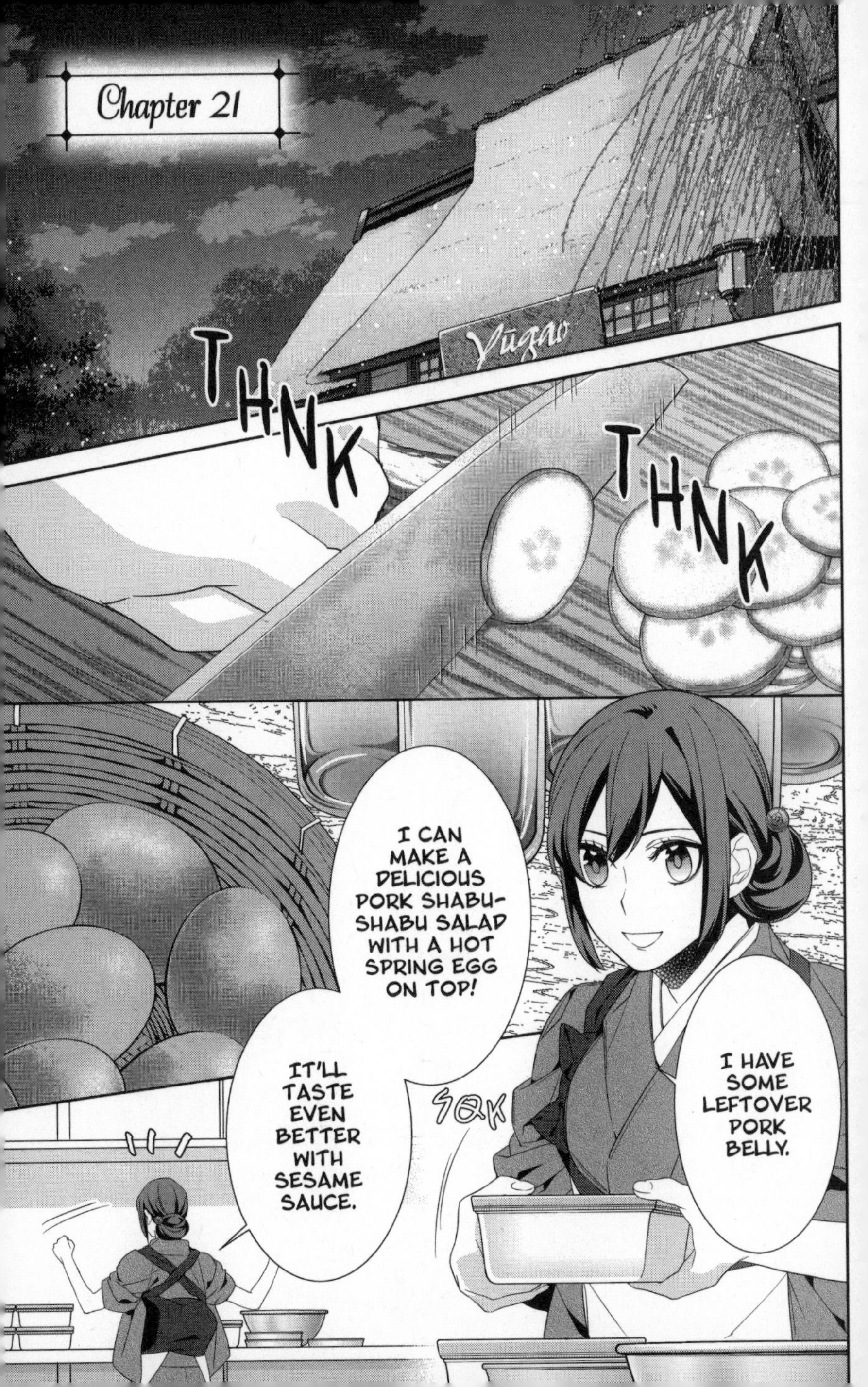
Chapter 21
Yūgao
THNK
THNK
I HAVE SOME LEFTOVER PORK BELLY.
I CAN MAKE A DELICIOUS PORK SHABU-SHABU SALAD WITH A HOT SPRING EGG ON TOP!
SQK
IT'LL TASTE EVEN BETTER WITH SESAME SAUCE.

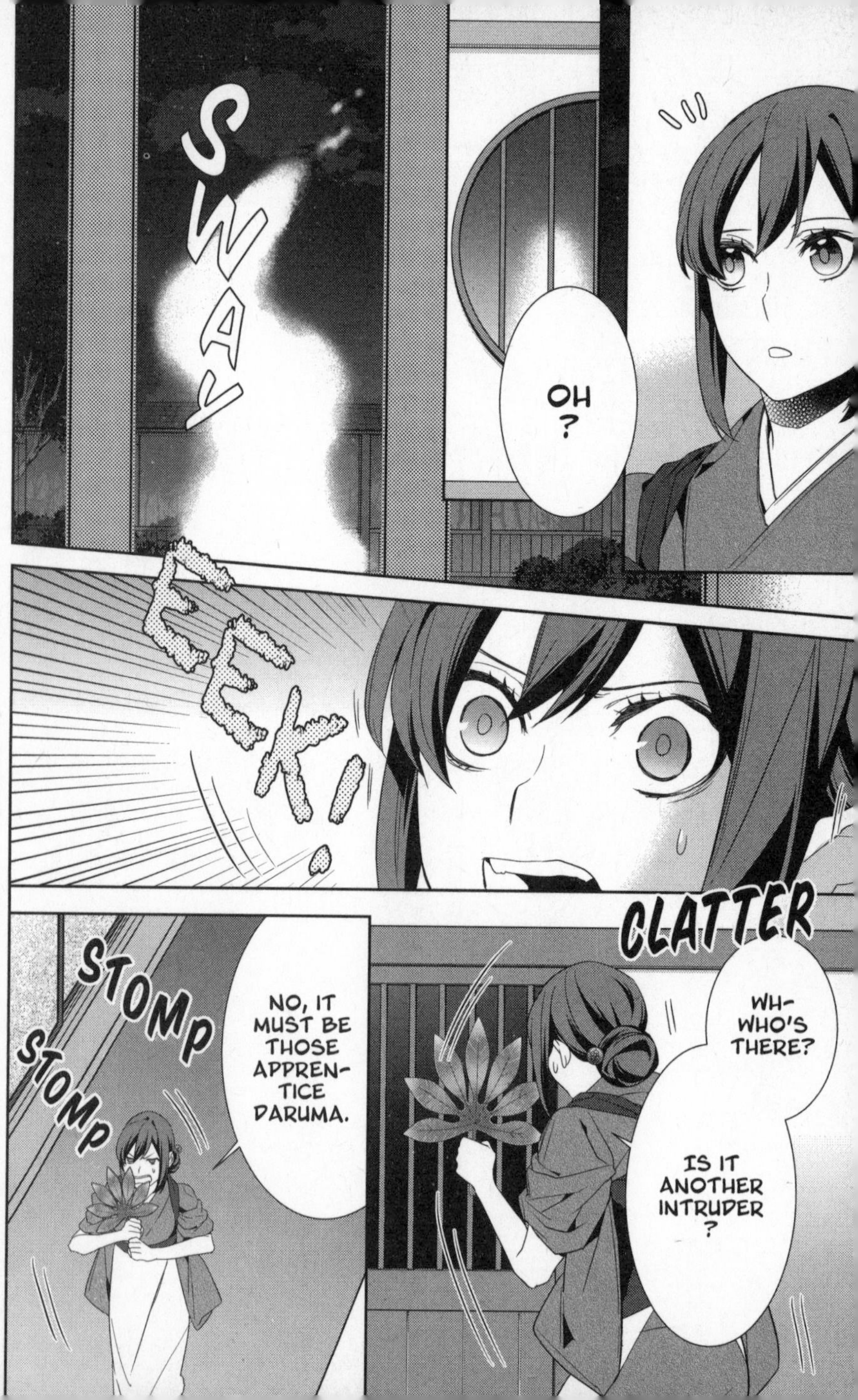
OH?
SWAY
EEK!
CLATTER
WH- WHO'S THERE?
IS IT ANOTHER INTRUDER?
NO, IT MUST BE THOSE APPREN-TICE DARUMA.
STOMP
STOMP

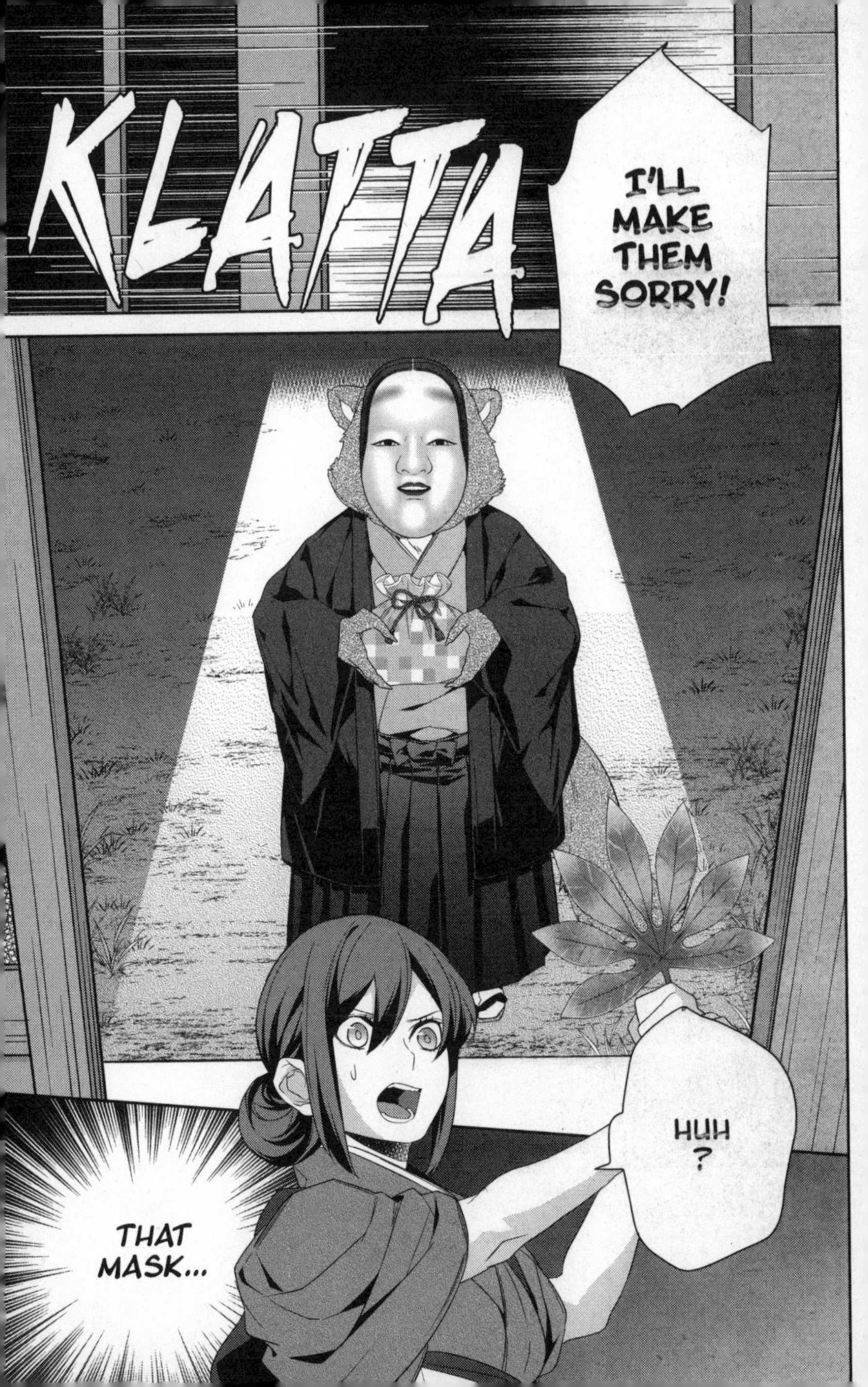
I'LL MAKE THEM SORRY!
KLATTA
HUH?
THAT MASK...

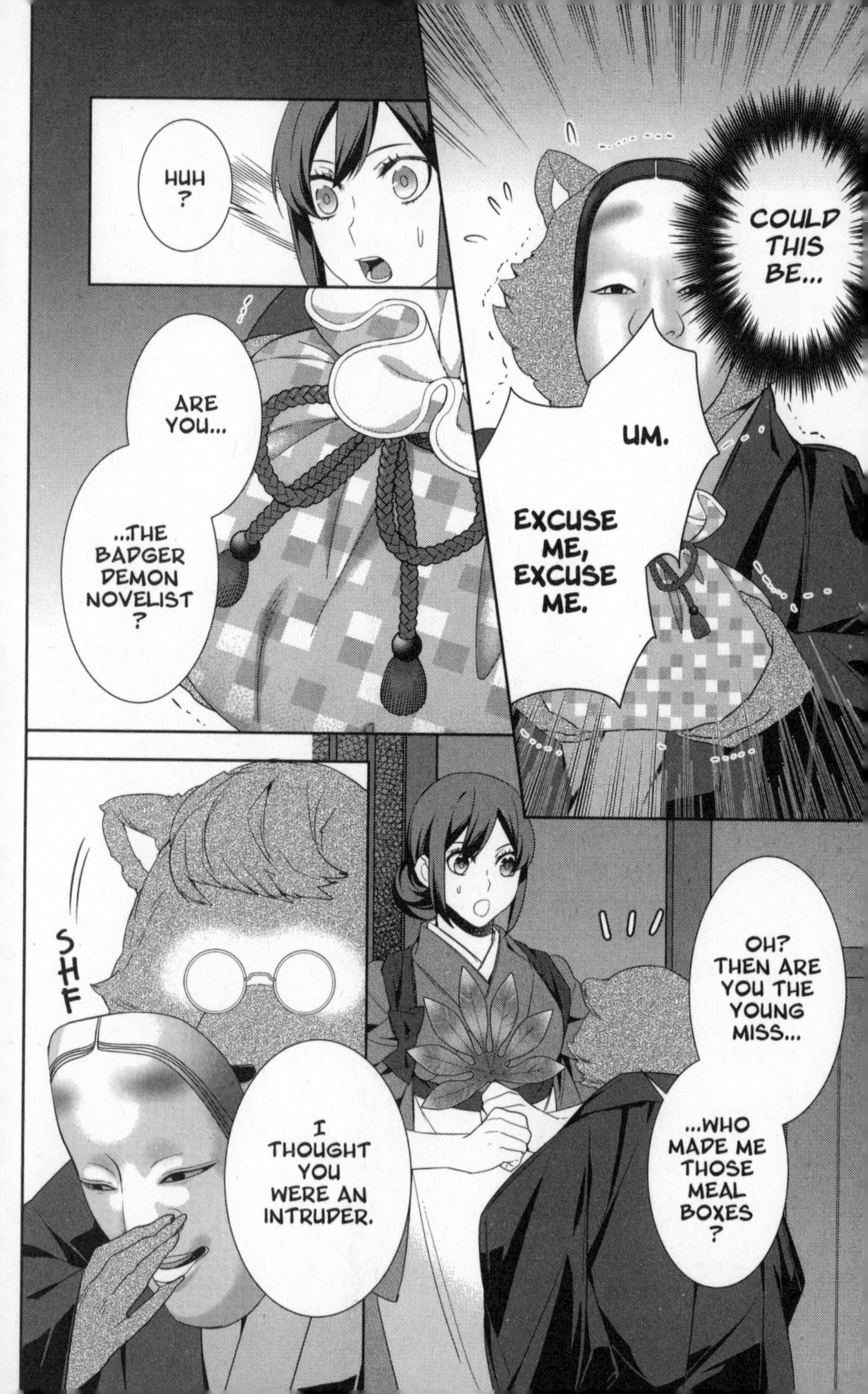
COULD THIS BE...
UM.
EXCUSE ME, EXCUSE ME.
HUH?
ARE YOU...
...THE BADGER DEMON NOVELIST?
OH? THEN ARE YOU THE YOUNG MISS...
...WHO MADE ME THOSE MEAL BOXES?
I THOUGHT YOU WERE AN INTRUDER.
SHF

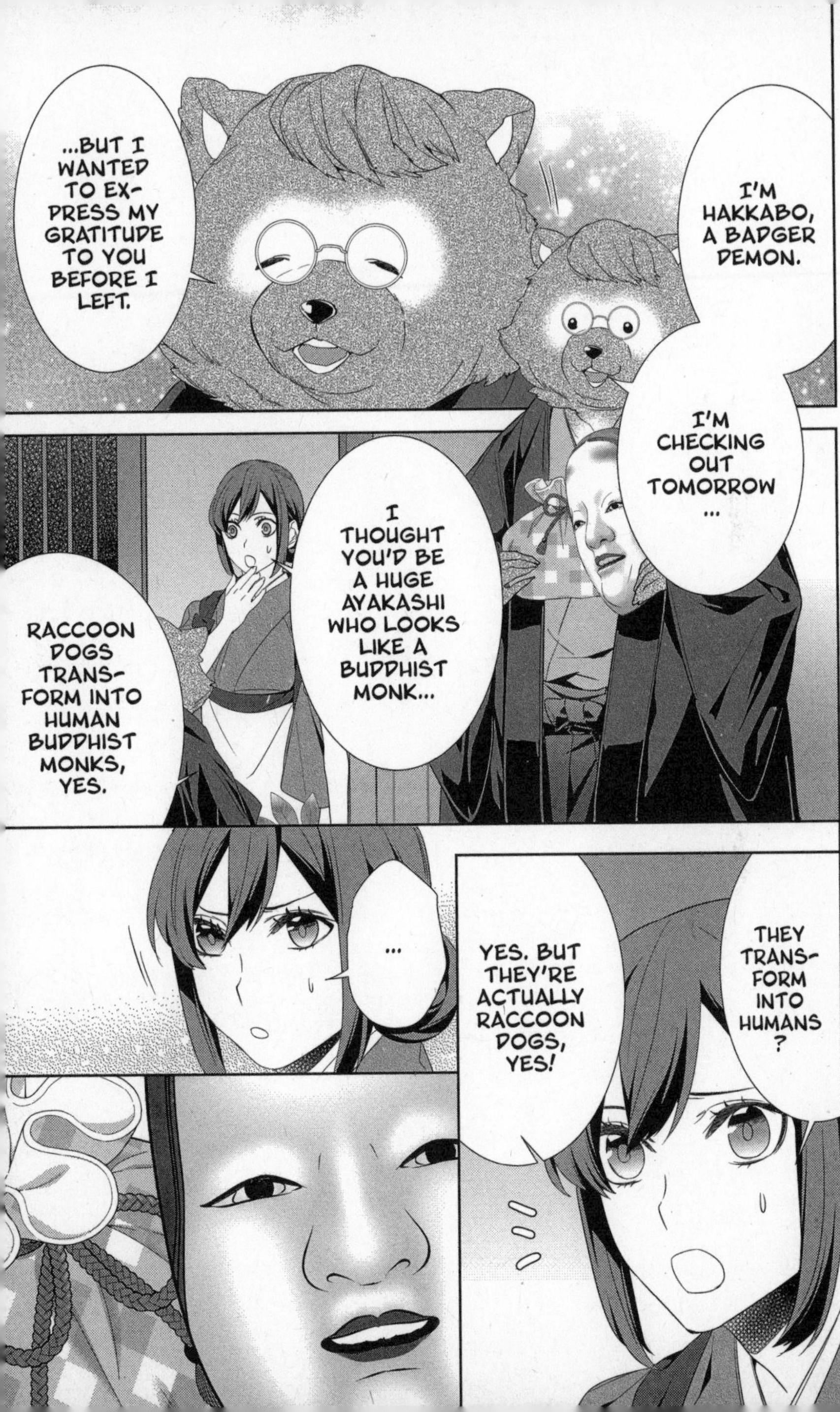
I'M HAKKABO, A BADGER DEMON.
I'M CHECKING OUT TOMORROW...
...BUT I WANTED TO EX-PRESS MY GRATITUDE TO YOU BEFORE I LEFT.
I THOUGHT YOU'D BE A HUGE AYAKASHI WHO LOOKS LIKE A BUDDHIST MONK...
RACCOON DOGS TRANS-FORM INTO HUMAN BUDDHIST MONKS, YES.
THEY TRANS-FORM INTO HUMANS?
YES. BUT THEY'RE ACTUALLY RACCOON DOGS, YES!
...

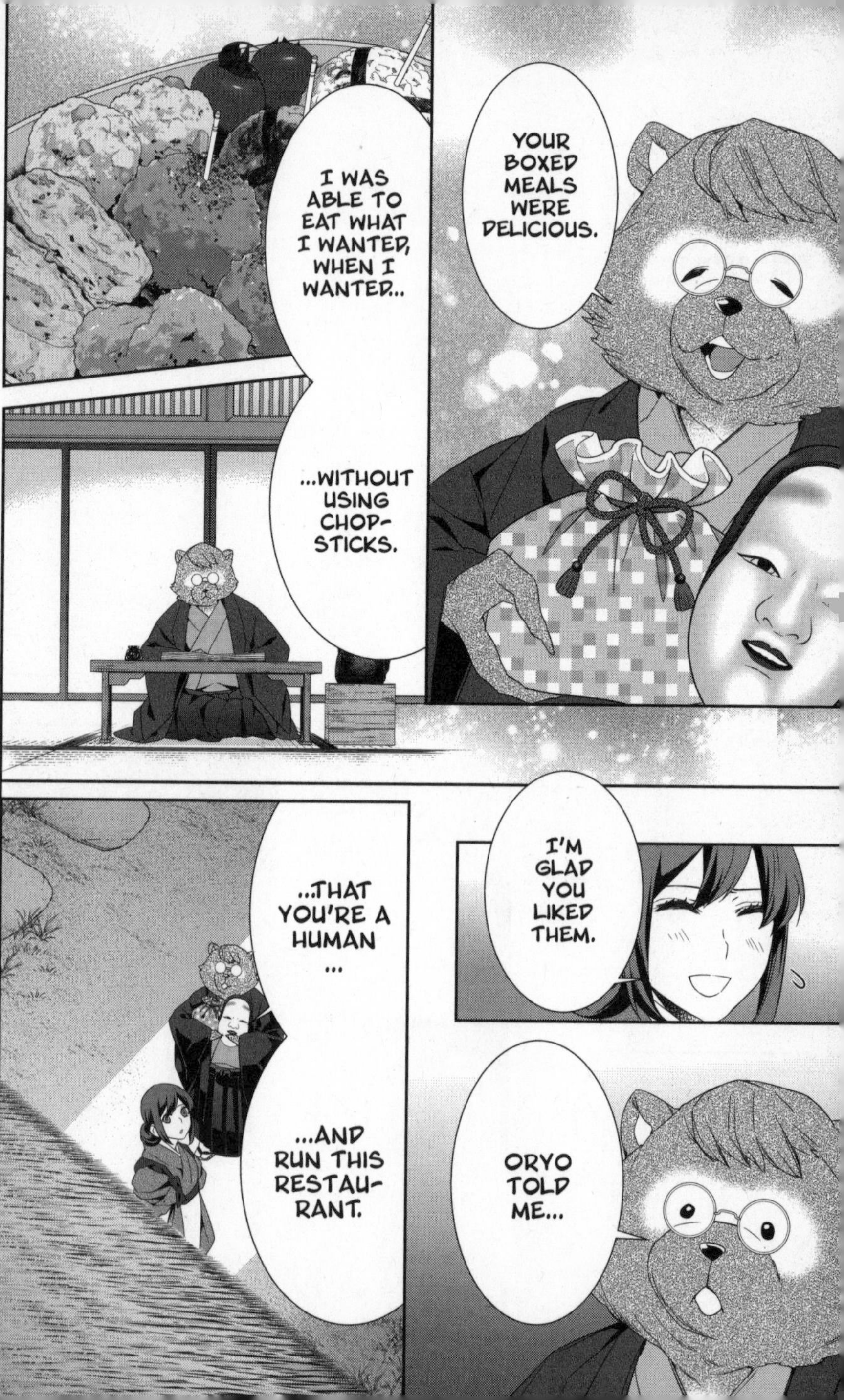
YOUR BOXED MEALS WERE DELICIOUS.
I WAS ABLE TO EAT WHAT I WANTED, WHEN I WANTED...
...WITHOUT USING CHOP-STICKS.
I'M GLAD YOU LIKED THEM.
ORYO TOLD ME...
...THAT YOU'RE A HUMAN ...
...AND RUN THIS RESTAU-RANT.

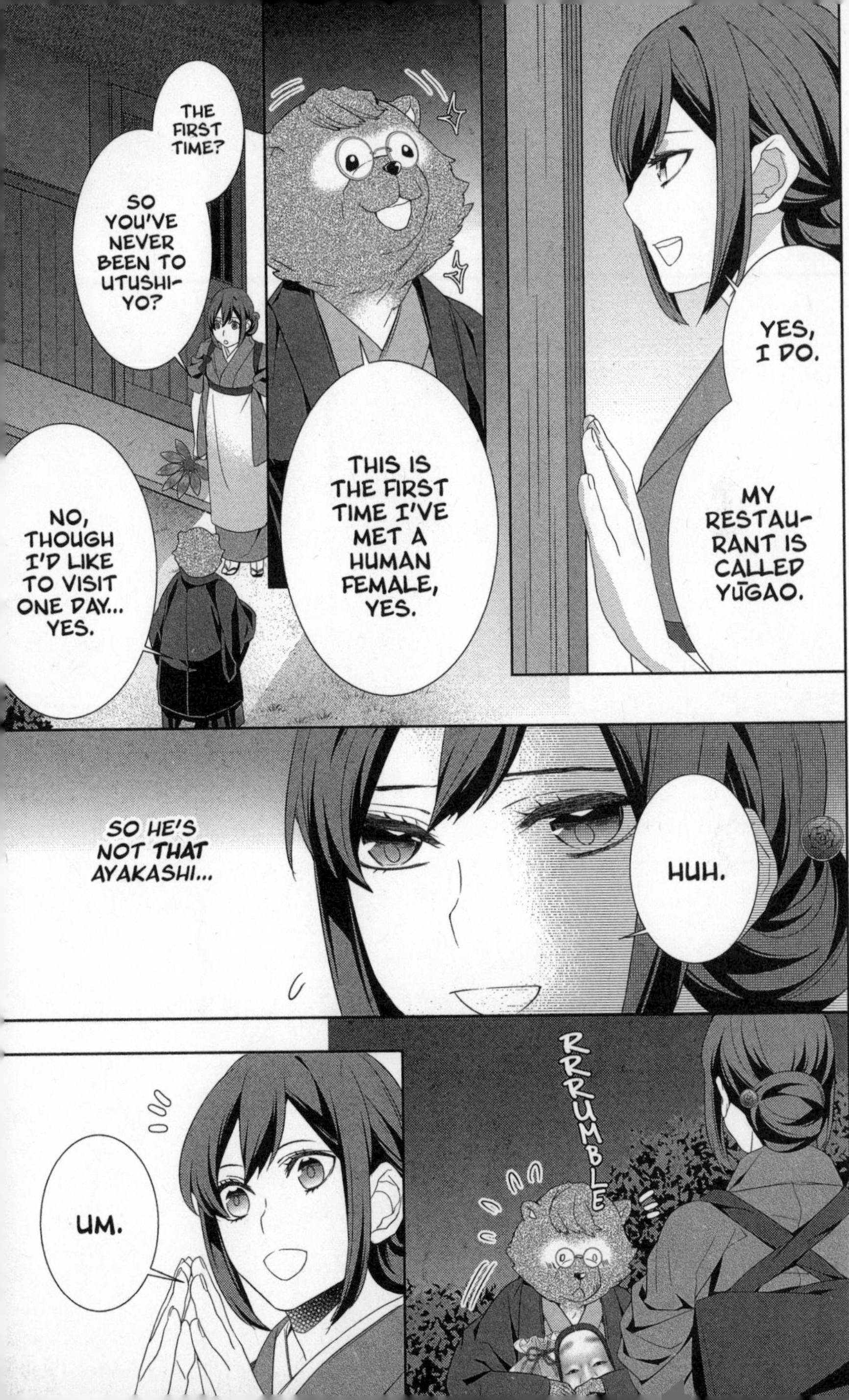
YES, I DO.
MY RESTAURANT IS CALLED YŪGAO.
THIS IS THE FIRST TIME I'VE MET A HUMAN FEMALE, YES.
THE FIRST TIME?
SO YOU'VE NEVER BEEN TO UTUSHIYO?
NO, THOUGH I'D LIKE TO VISIT ONE DAY... YES.
HUH.
SO HE'S NOT THAT AYAKASHI...
RRRUMBLE
UM.

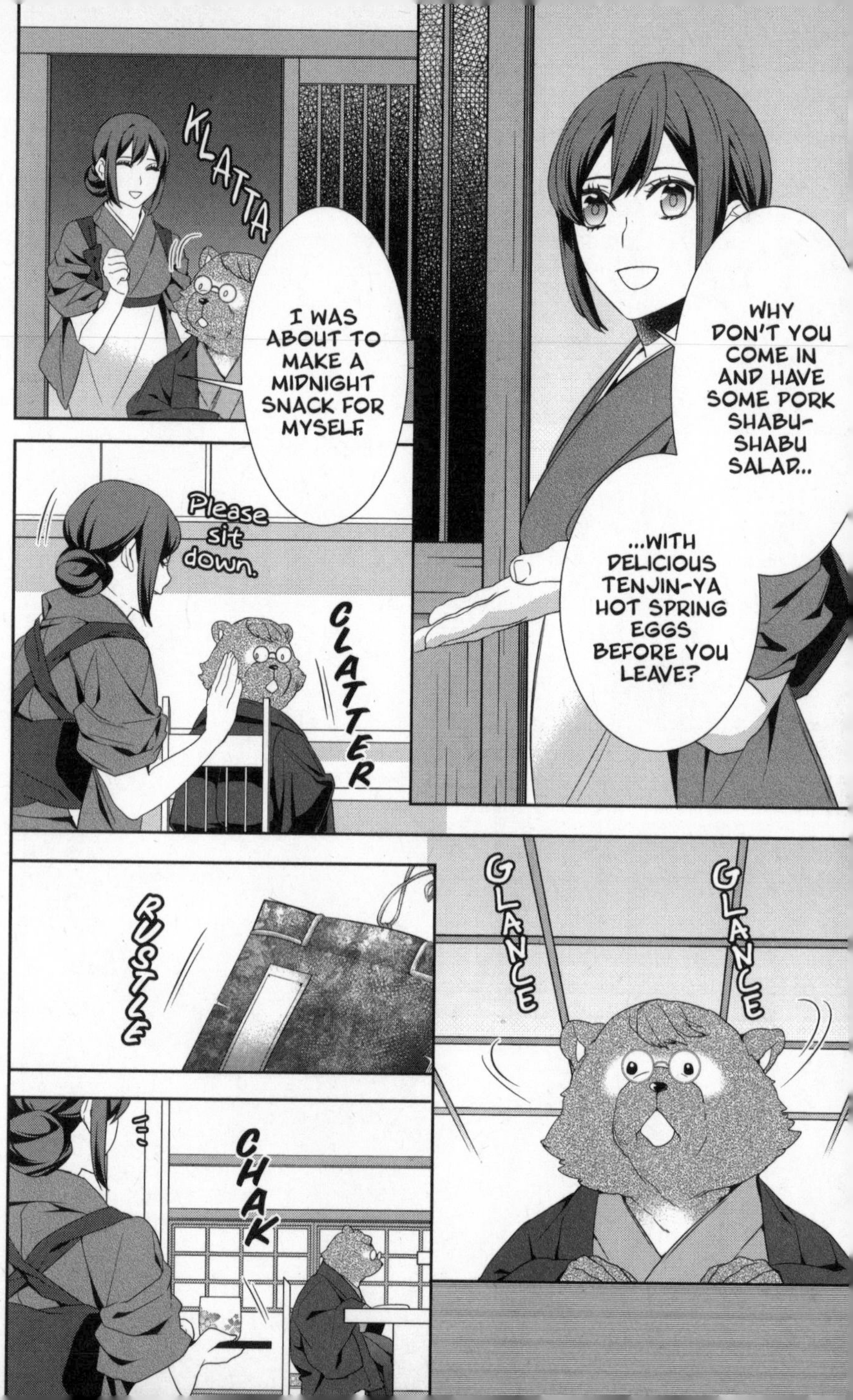
WHY DON'T YOU COME IN AND HAVE SOME PORK SHABU-SHABU SALAD...
...WITH DELICIOUS TENJIN-YA HOT SPRING EGGS BEFORE YOU LEAVE?
KLATTA
I WAS ABOUT TO MAKE A MIDNIGHT SNACK FOR MYSELF.
Please sit down.
CLATTER
GLANCE
GLANCE
RUSTLE
CHAK

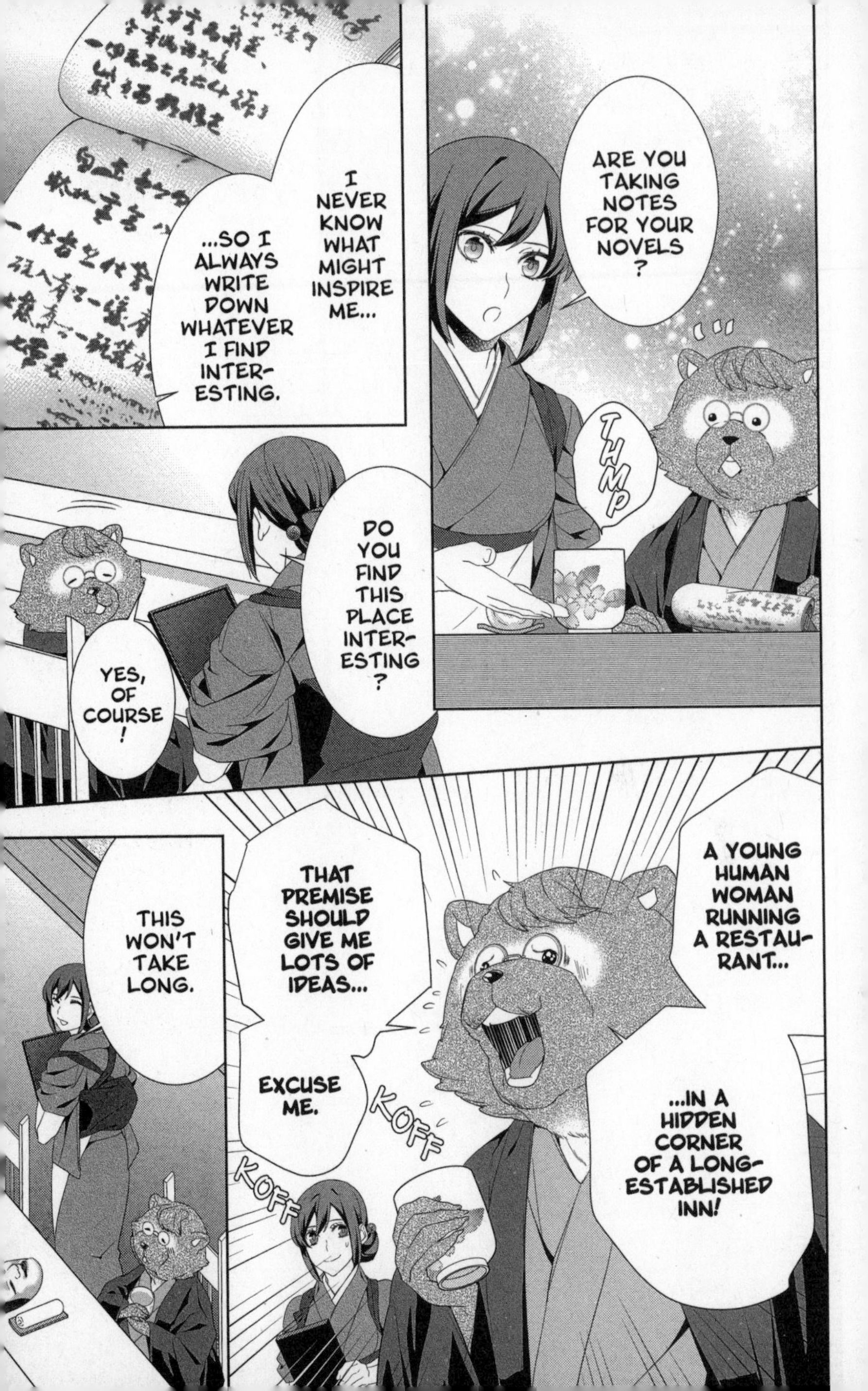
ARE YOU TAKING NOTES FOR YOUR NOVELS?
THMP
I NEVER KNOW WHAT MIGHT INSPIRE ME...
...SO I ALWAYS WRITE DOWN WHATEVER I FIND INTER-ESTING.
DO YOU FIND THIS PLACE INTER-ESTING?
YES, OF COURSE!
A YOUNG HUMAN WOMAN RUNNING A RESTAU-RANT...
...IN A HIDDEN CORNER OF A LONG-ESTABLISHED INN!
THAT PREMISE SHOULD GIVE ME LOTS OF IDEAS...
KOFF
KOFF
EXCUSE ME.
THIS WON'T TAKE LONG.

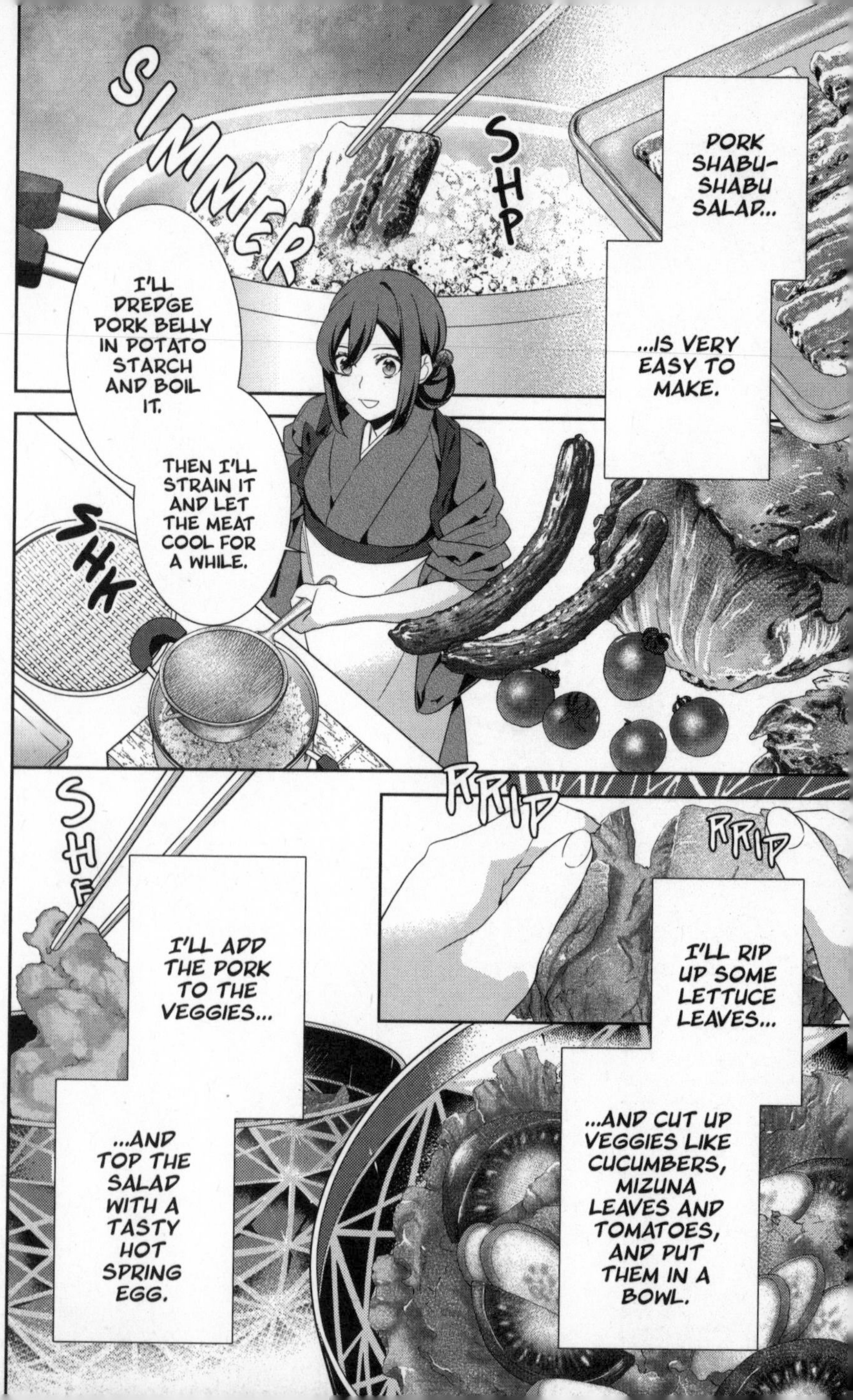
PORK SHABU-SHABU SALAD...
...IS VERY EASY TO MAKE.
SHP
SIMMER
I'LL DREDGE PORK BELLY IN POTATO STARCH AND BOIL IT.
THEN I'LL STRAIN IT AND LET THE MEAT COOL FOR A WHILE.
SHK
RRIP
RRIP
I'LL RIP UP SOME LETTUCE LEAVES...
...AND CUT UP VEGGIES LIKE CUCUMBERS, MIZUNA LEAVES AND TOMATOES, AND PUT THEM IN A BOWL.
SHF
I'LL ADD THE PORK TO THE VEGGIES...
...AND TOP THE SALAD WITH A TASTY HOT SPRING EGG.

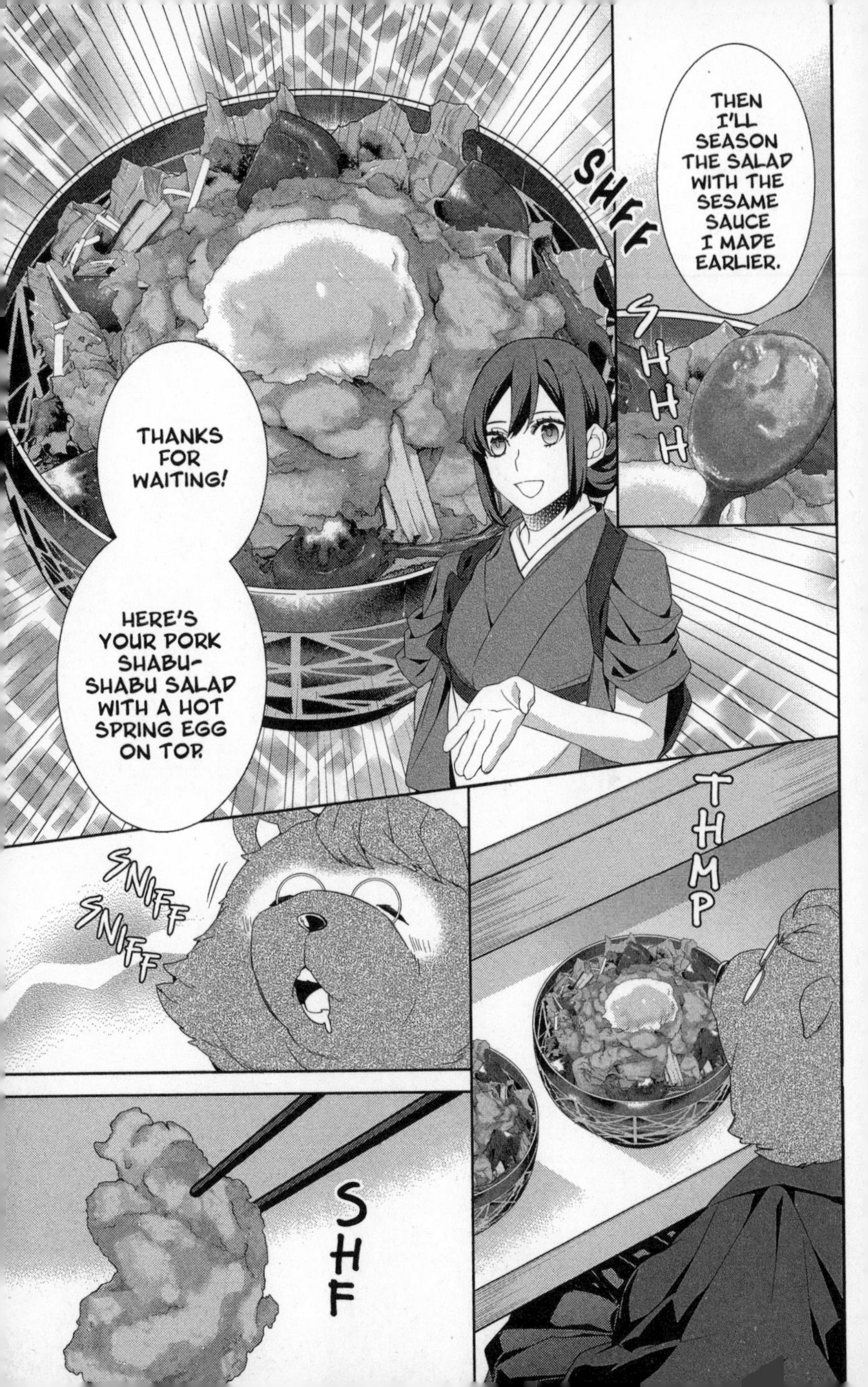
THEN I'LL SEASON THE SALAD WITH THE SESAME SAUCE I MADE EARLIER.
SHFF
SHHH
THANKS FOR WAITING!
HERE'S YOUR PORK SHABU-SHABU SALAD WITH A HOT SPRING EGG ON TOP.
THMP
SNIFF SNIFF
SHF

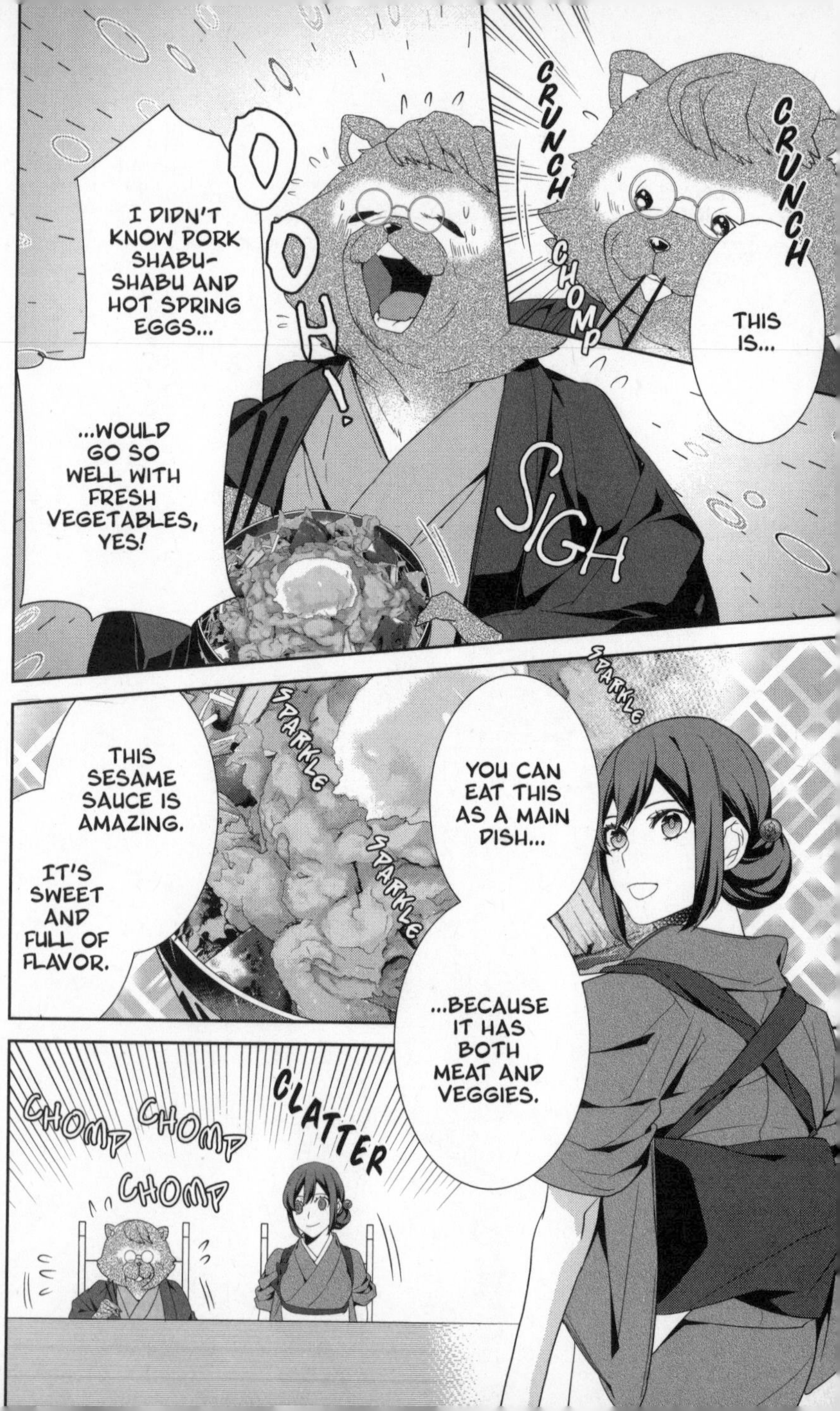
CRUNCH
CRUNCH
CHOMP
THIS IS...
OH!
I DIDN'T KNOW PORK SHABU-SHABU AND HOT SPRING EGGS...
...WOULD GO SO WELL WITH FRESH VEGETABLES, YES!
SIGH
SPARKLE
YOU CAN EAT THIS AS A MAIN DISH...
...BECAUSE IT HAS BOTH MEAT AND VEGGIES.
SPARKLE
SPARKLE
THIS SESAME SAUCE IS AMAZING.
IT'S SWEET AND FULL OF FLAVOR.
CLATTER
CHOMP CHOMP
CHOMP

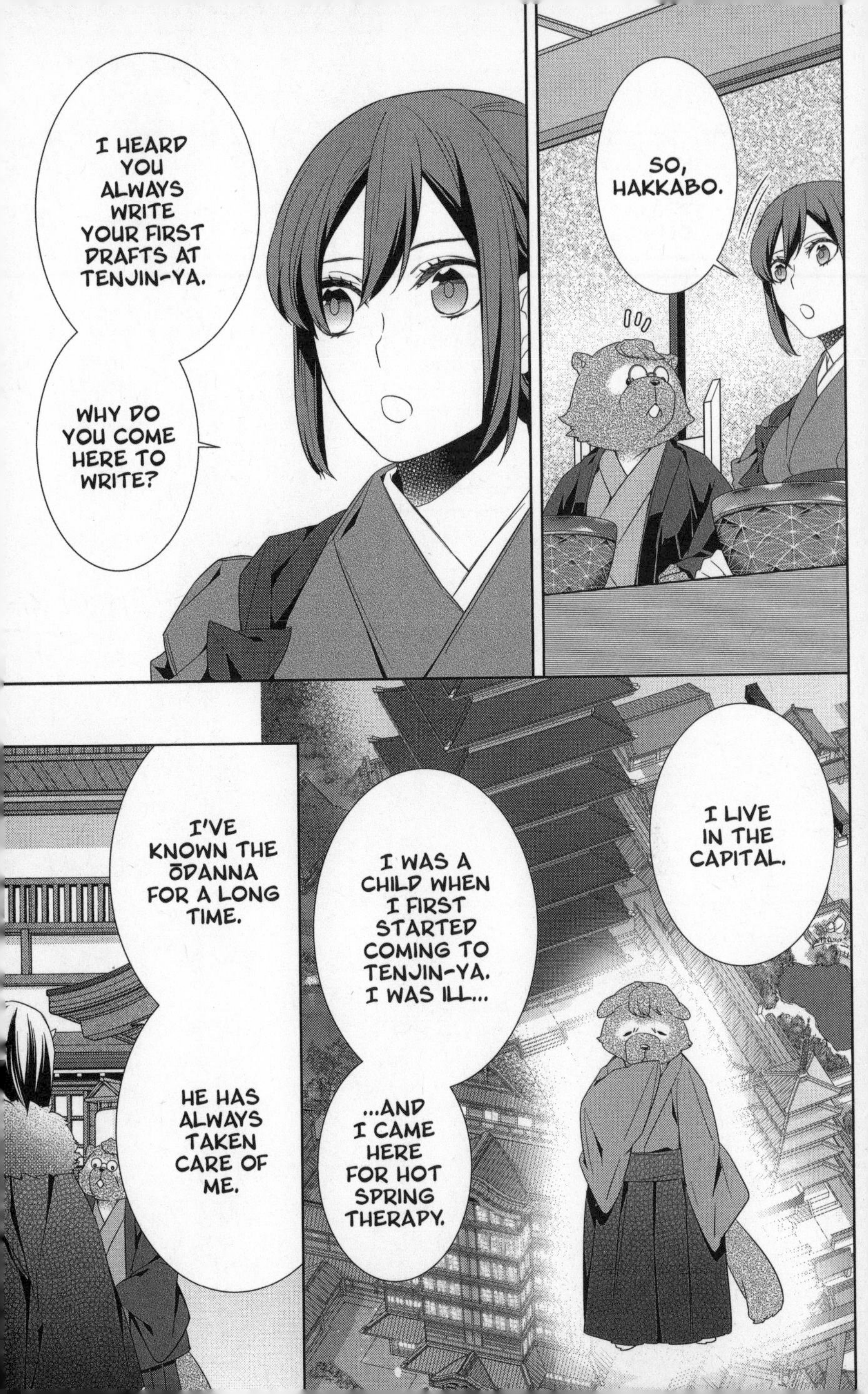
SO, HAKKABO.
I HEARD YOU ALWAYS WRITE YOUR FIRST DRAFTS AT TENJIN-YA.
WHY DO YOU COME HERE TO WRITE?
I LIVE IN THE CAPITAL.
I WAS A CHILD WHEN I FIRST STARTED COMING TO TENJIN-YA. I WAS ILL...
...AND I CAME HERE FOR HOT SPRING THERAPY.
I'VE KNOWN THE ŌDANNA FOR A LONG TIME.
HE HAS ALWAYS TAKEN CARE OF ME.

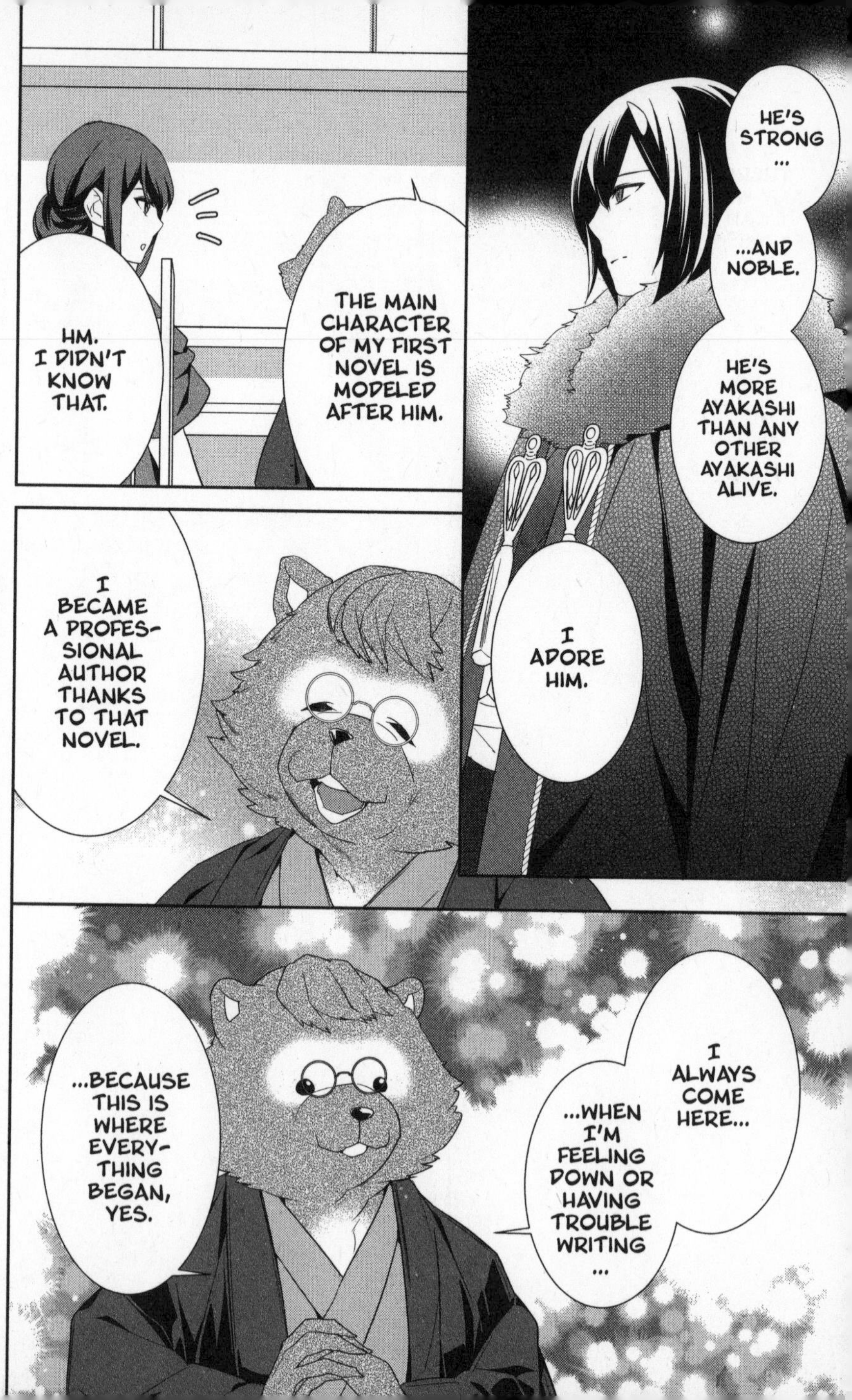
HE'S STRONG...
...AND NOBLE.
HE'S MORE AYAKASHI THAN ANY OTHER AYAKASHI ALIVE.
I ADORE HIM.
THE MAIN CHARACTER OF MY FIRST NOVEL IS MODELED AFTER HIM.
HM. I DIDN'T KNOW THAT.
I BECAME A PROFES-SIONAL AUTHOR THANKS TO THAT NOVEL.
I ALWAYS COME HERE...
...WHEN I'M FEELING DOWN OR HAVING TROUBLE WRITING...
...BECAUSE THIS IS WHERE EVERY-THING BEGAN, YES.

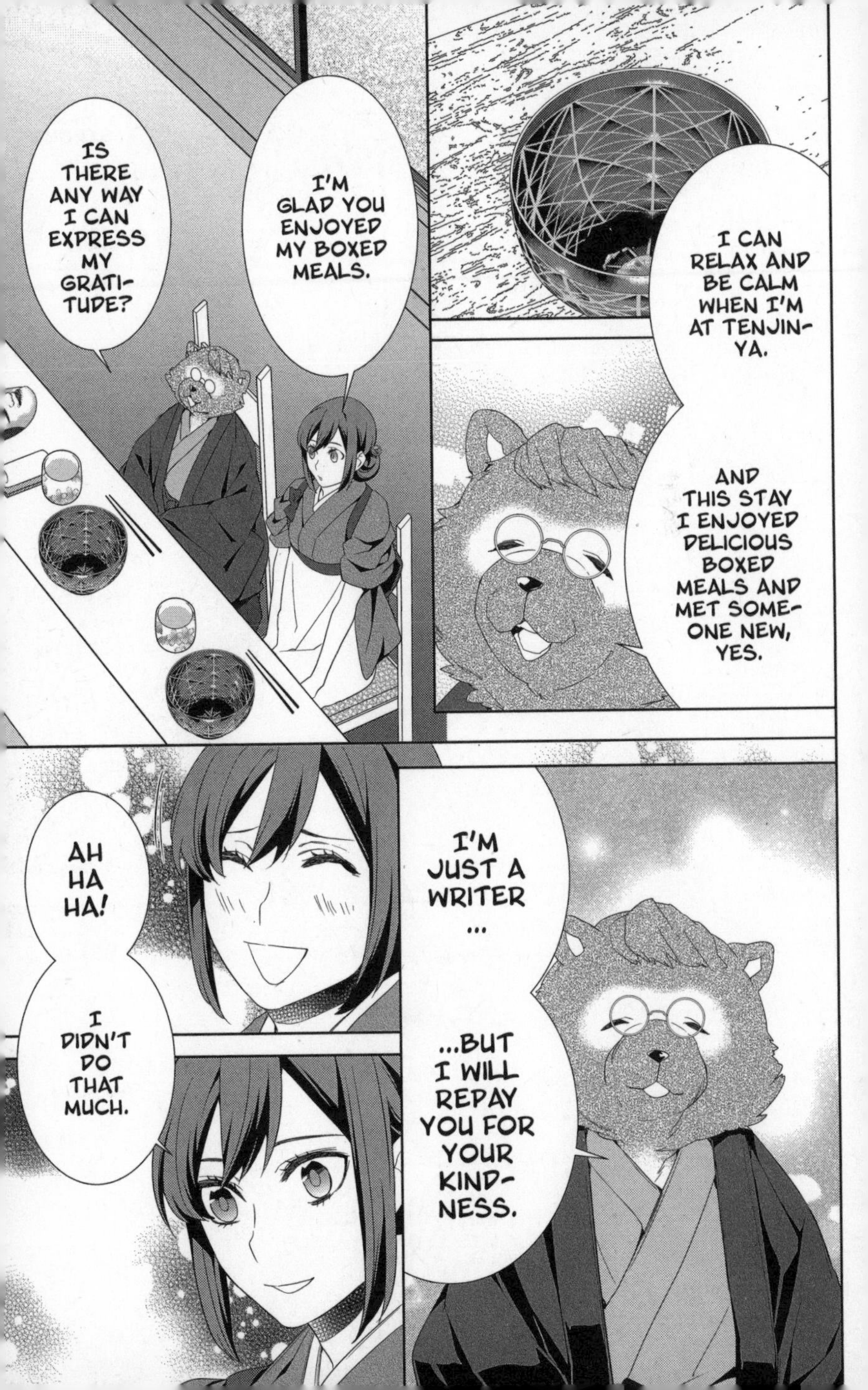
I CAN RELAX AND BE CALM WHEN I'M AT TENJIN-YA.
AND THIS STAY I ENJOYED DELICIOUS BOXED MEALS AND MET SOME-ONE NEW, YES.
I'M GLAD YOU ENJOYED MY BOXED MEALS.
IS THERE ANY WAY I CAN EXPRESS MY GRATI-TUDE?
I'M JUST A WRITER ...
...BUT I WILL REPAY YOU FOR YOUR KIND-NESS.
AH HA HA!
I DIDN'T DO THAT MUCH.

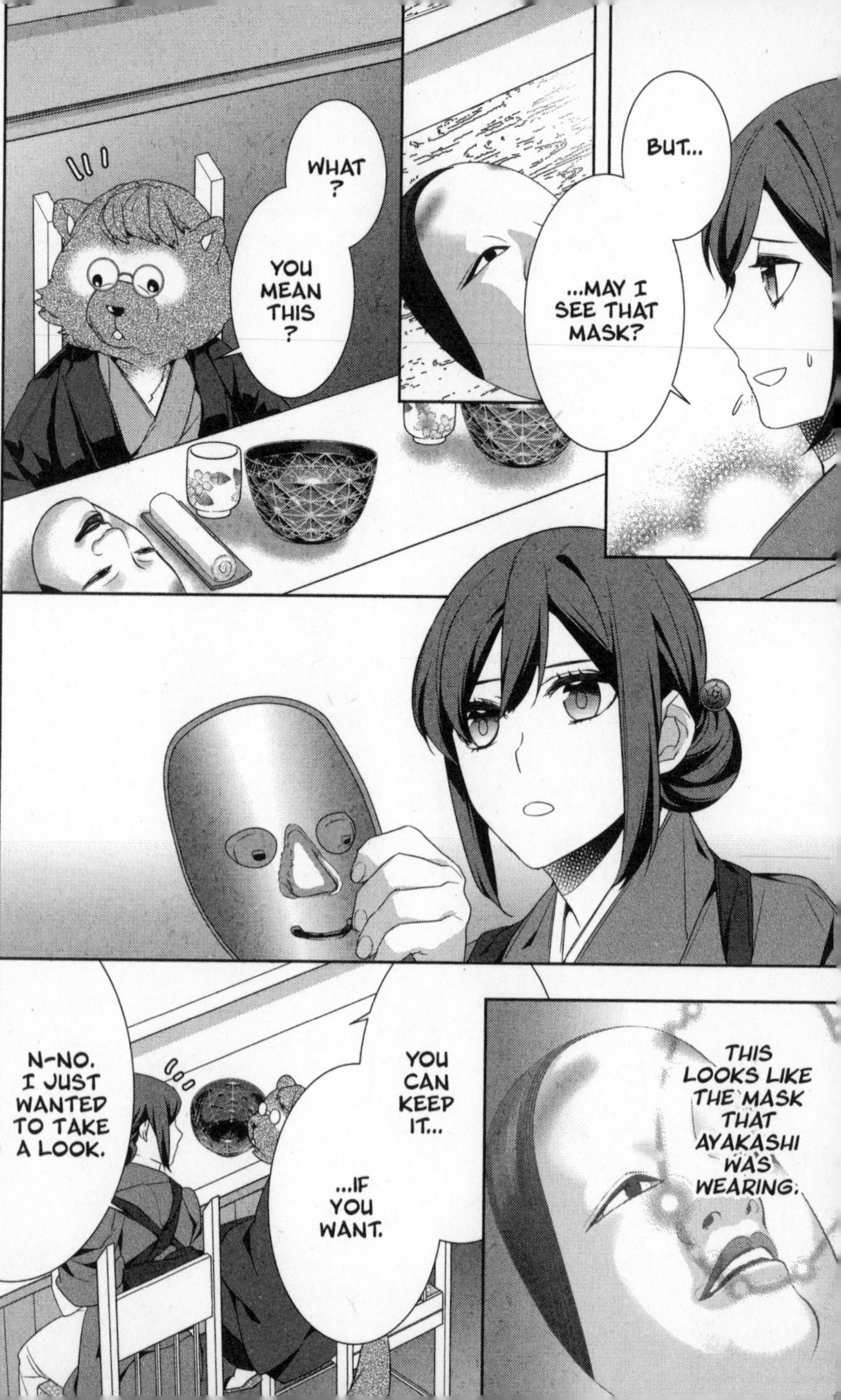
BUT...
...MAY I SEE THAT MASK?
WHAT?
YOU MEAN THIS?
THIS LOOKS LIKE THE MASK THAT AYAKASHI WAS WEARING.
YOU CAN KEEP IT...
...IF YOU WANT.
N-NO. I JUST WANTED TO TAKE A LOOK.

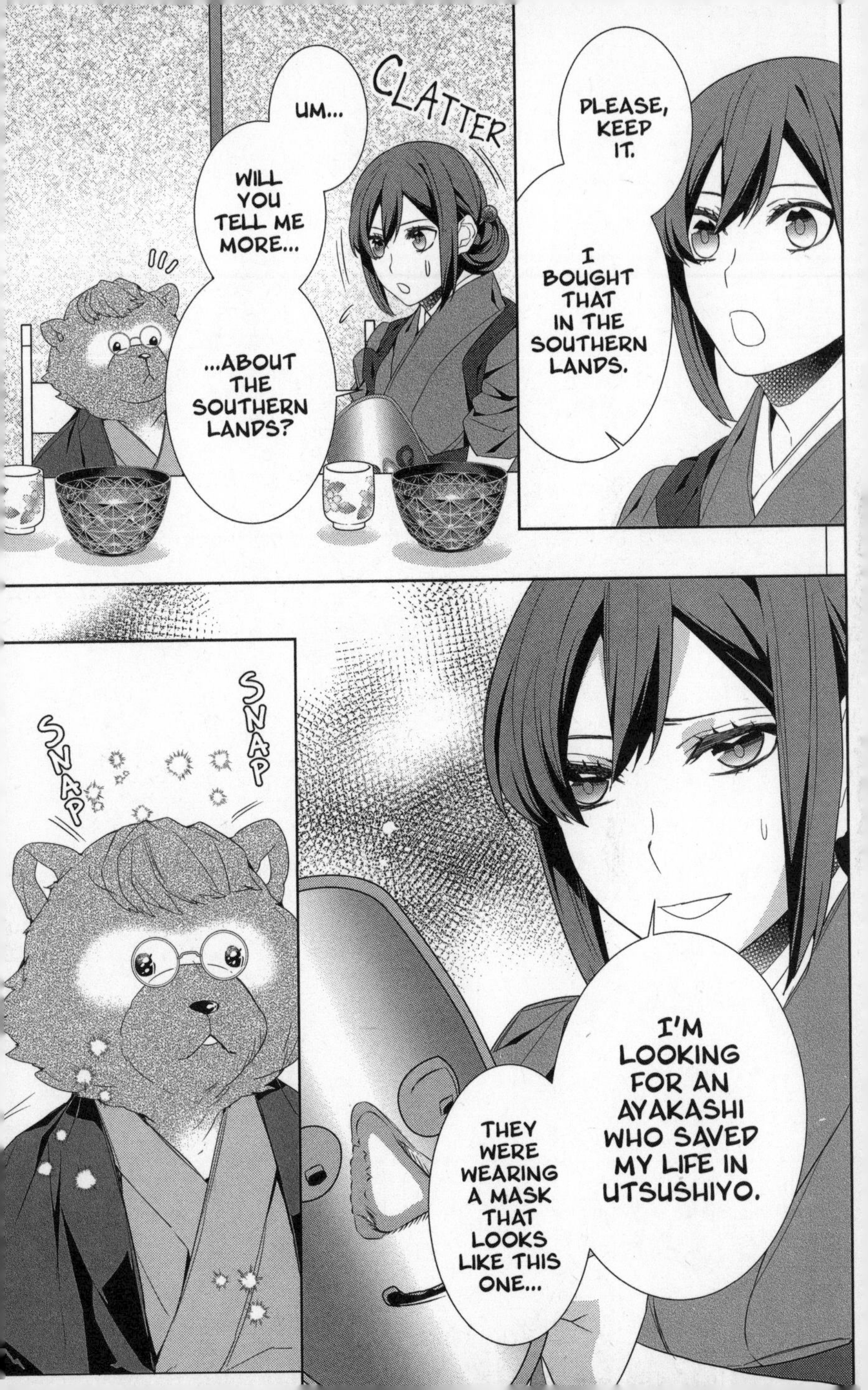
PLEASE, KEEP IT.
I BOUGHT THAT IN THE SOUTHERN LANDS.
CLATTER
UM...
WILL YOU TELL ME MORE...
...ABOUT THE SOUTHERN LANDS?
I'M LOOKING FOR AN AYAKASHI WHO SAVED MY LIFE IN UTSUSHIYO.
THEY WERE WEARING A MASK THAT LOOKS LIKE THIS ONE...
SNAP
SNAP

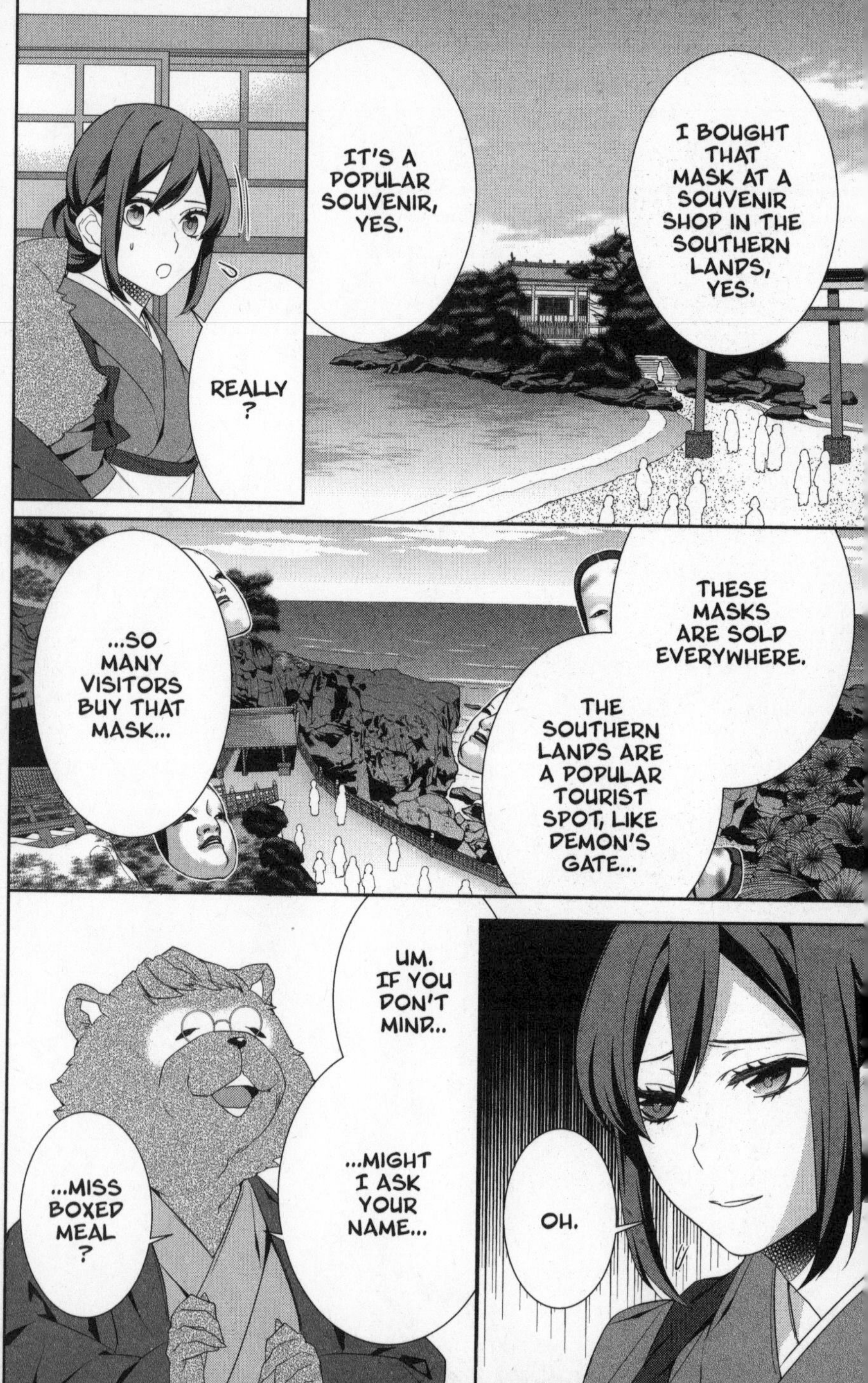
I BOUGHT THAT MASK AT A SOUVENIR SHOP IN THE SOUTHERN LANDS, YES.
IT'S A POPULAR SOUVENIR, YES.
REALLY?
THESE MASKS ARE SOLD EVERYWHERE.
THE SOUTHERN LANDS ARE A POPULAR TOURIST SPOT, LIKE DEMON'S GATE...
...SO MANY VISITORS BUY THAT MASK...
OH.
UM. IF YOU DON'T MIND...
...MIGHT I ASK YOUR NAME...
...MISS BOXED MEAL?

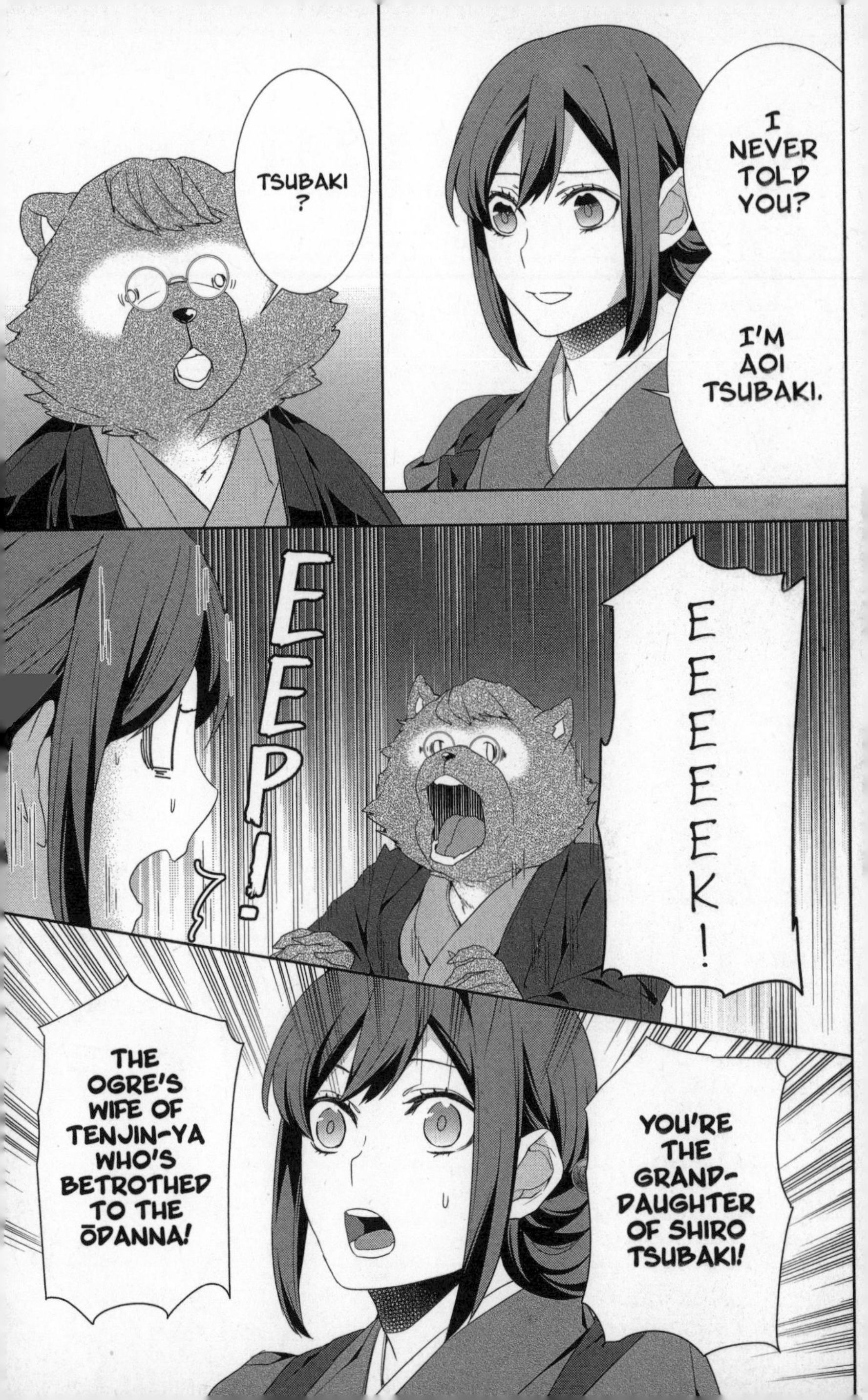
I NEVER TOLD YOU?
I'M AOI TSUBAKI.
TSUBAKI?
EEEEEEK!
EEP!
YOU'RE THE GRAND-DAUGHTER OF SHIRO TSUBAKI!
THE OGRE'S WIFE OF TENJIN-YA WHO'S BETROTHED TO THE ŌDANNA!

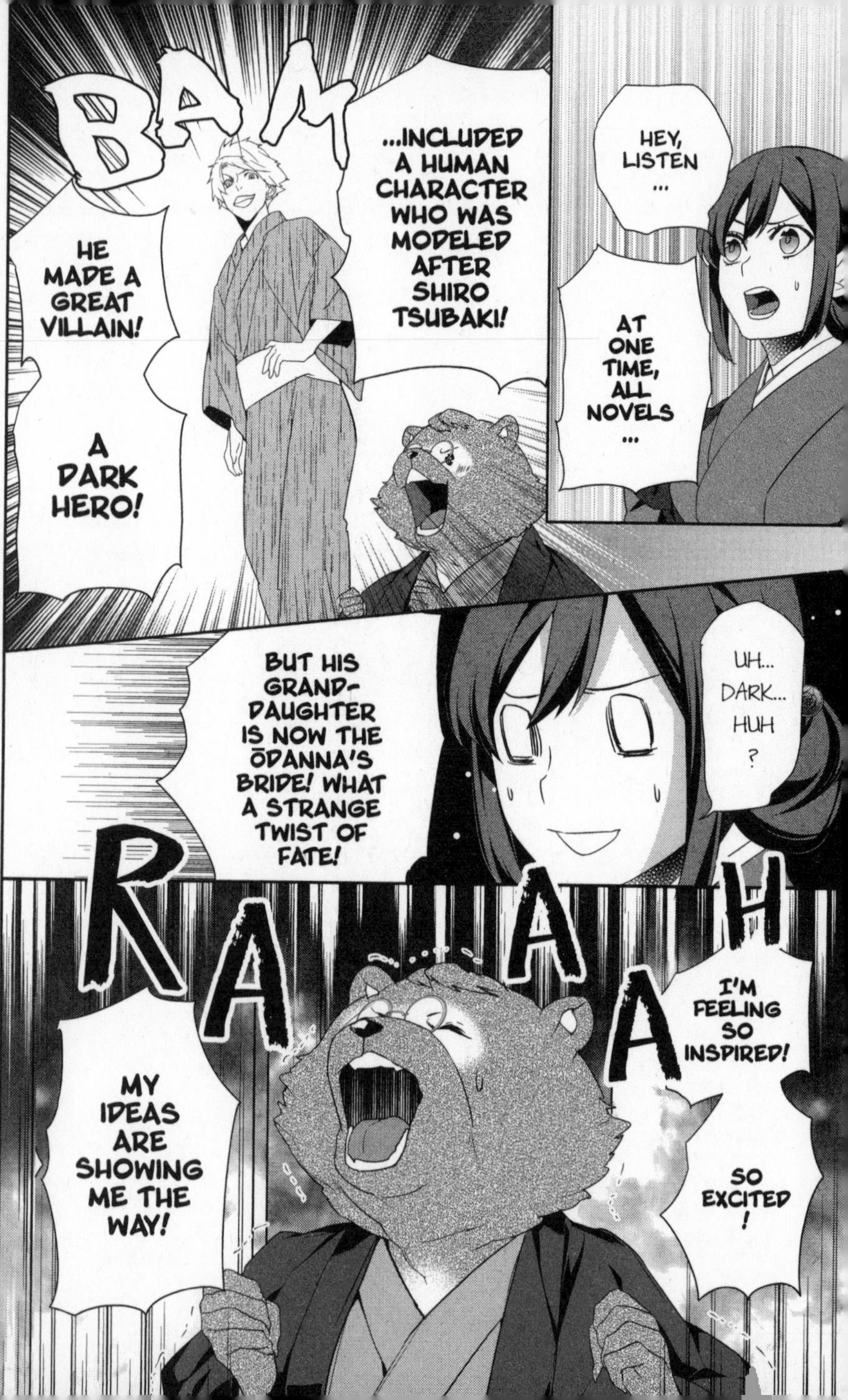
HEY, LISTEN ...
AT ONE TIME, ALL NOVELS ...
BAM
...INCLUDED A HUMAN CHARACTER WHO WAS MODELED AFTER SHIRO TSUBAKI!
HE MADE A GREAT VILLAIN!
A DARK HERO!
UH... DARK... HUH ?
BUT HIS GRAND-DAUGHTER IS NOW THE ŌDANNA'S BRIDE! WHAT A STRANGE TWIST OF FATE!
RAAAH
I'M FEELING SO INSPIRED!
SO EXCITED !
MY IDEAS ARE SHOWING ME THE WAY!

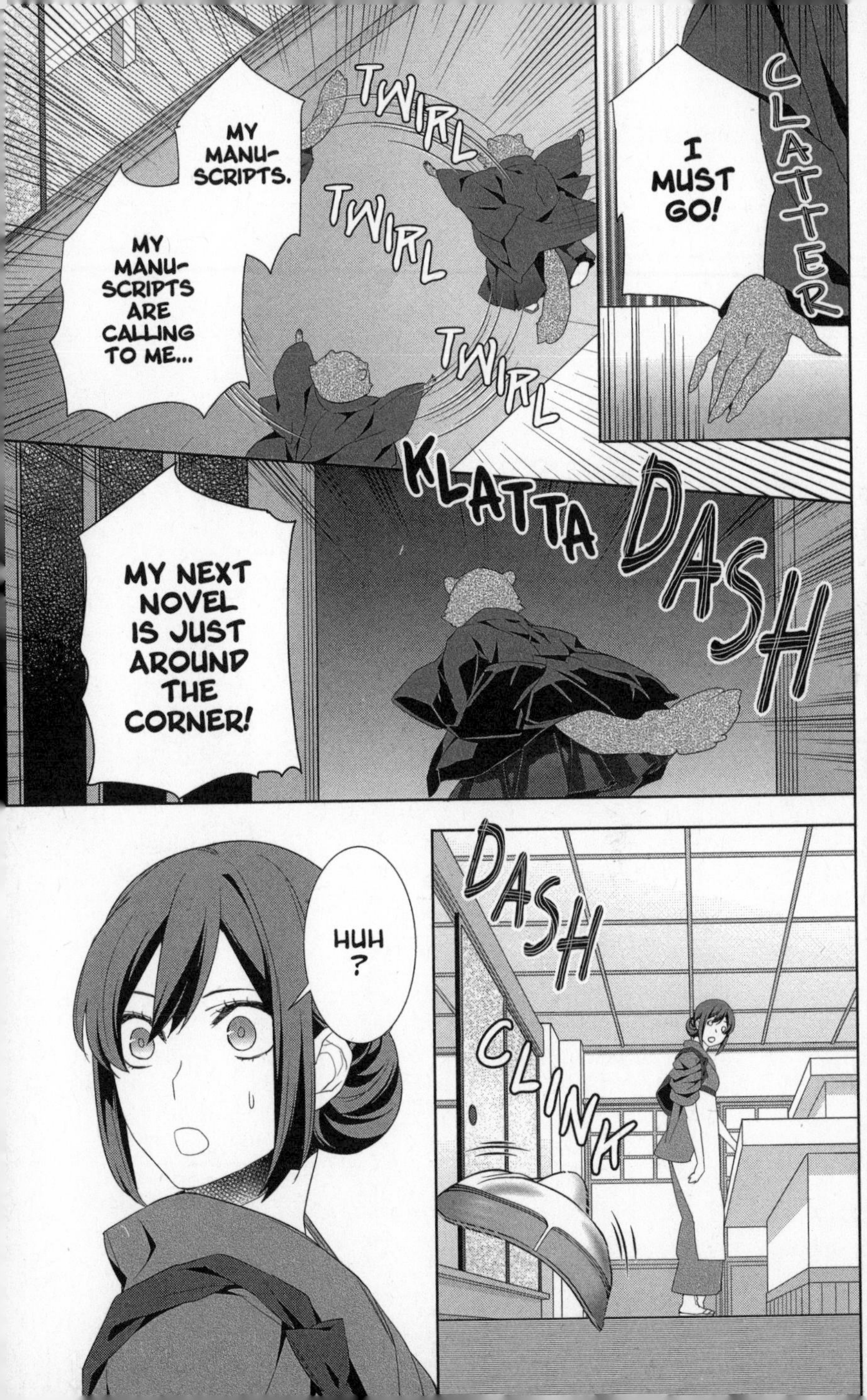
CLATTER
I MUST GO!
TWIRL
MY MANU-SCRIPTS.
TWIRL
MY MANU-SCRIPTS ARE CALLING TO ME...
TWIRL
DASH
KLATTA
MY NEXT NOVEL IS JUST AROUND THE CORNER!
DASH
CLINK
HUH?

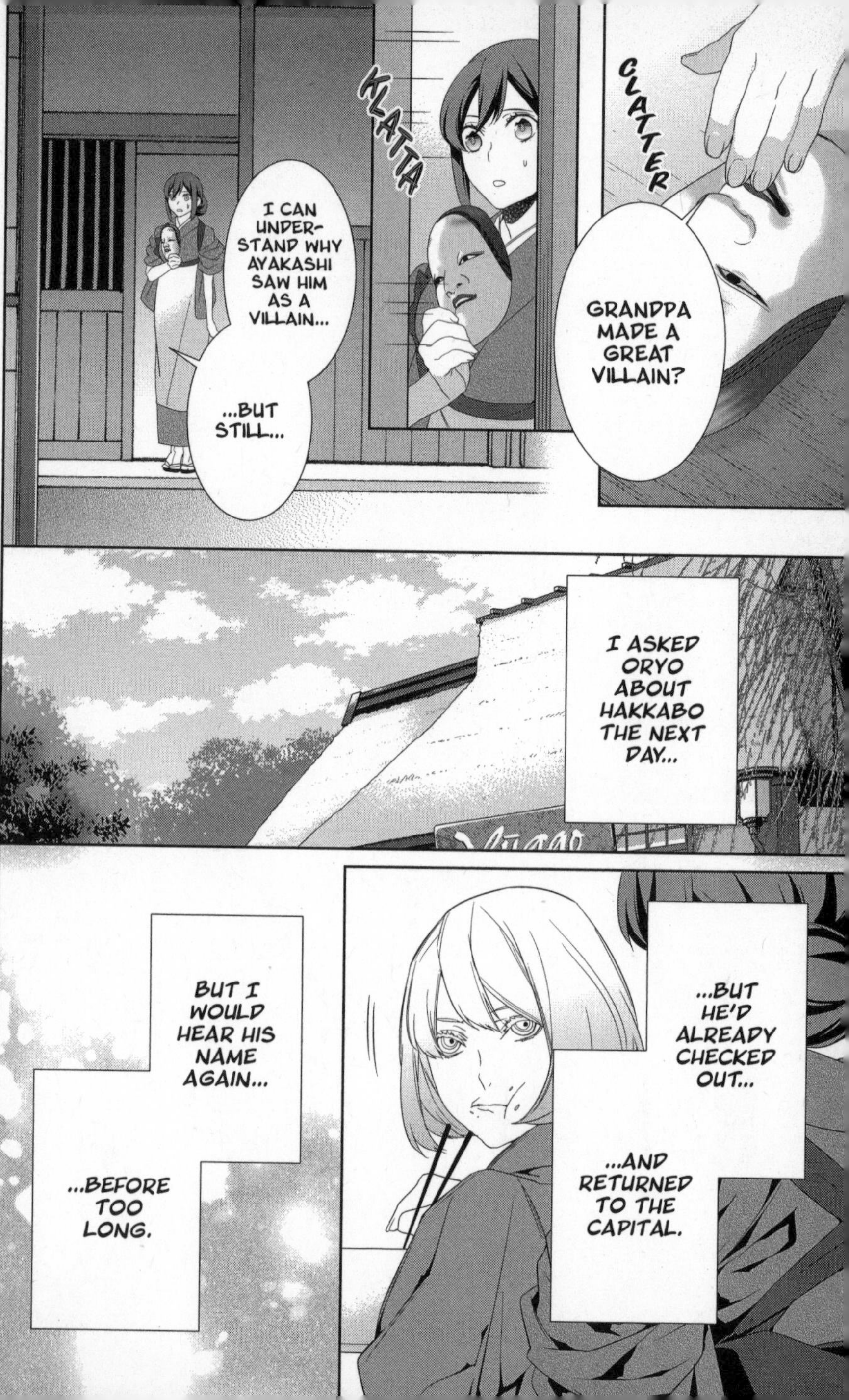
CLATTER
GRANDPA MADE A GREAT VILLAIN?
KLATTA
I CAN UNDER-STAND WHY AYAKASHI SAW HIM AS A VILLAIN...
...BUT STILL...
I ASKED ORYO ABOUT HAKKABO THE NEXT DAY...
...BUT HE'D ALREADY CHECKED OUT...
...AND RETURNED TO THE CAPITAL.
BUT I WOULD HEAR HIS NAME AGAIN...
...BEFORE TOO LONG.

Kakuriyo
Bed & Breakfast for Spirits

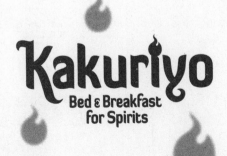

Kakuriyo
Bed & Breakfast for Spirits

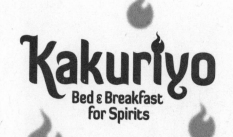

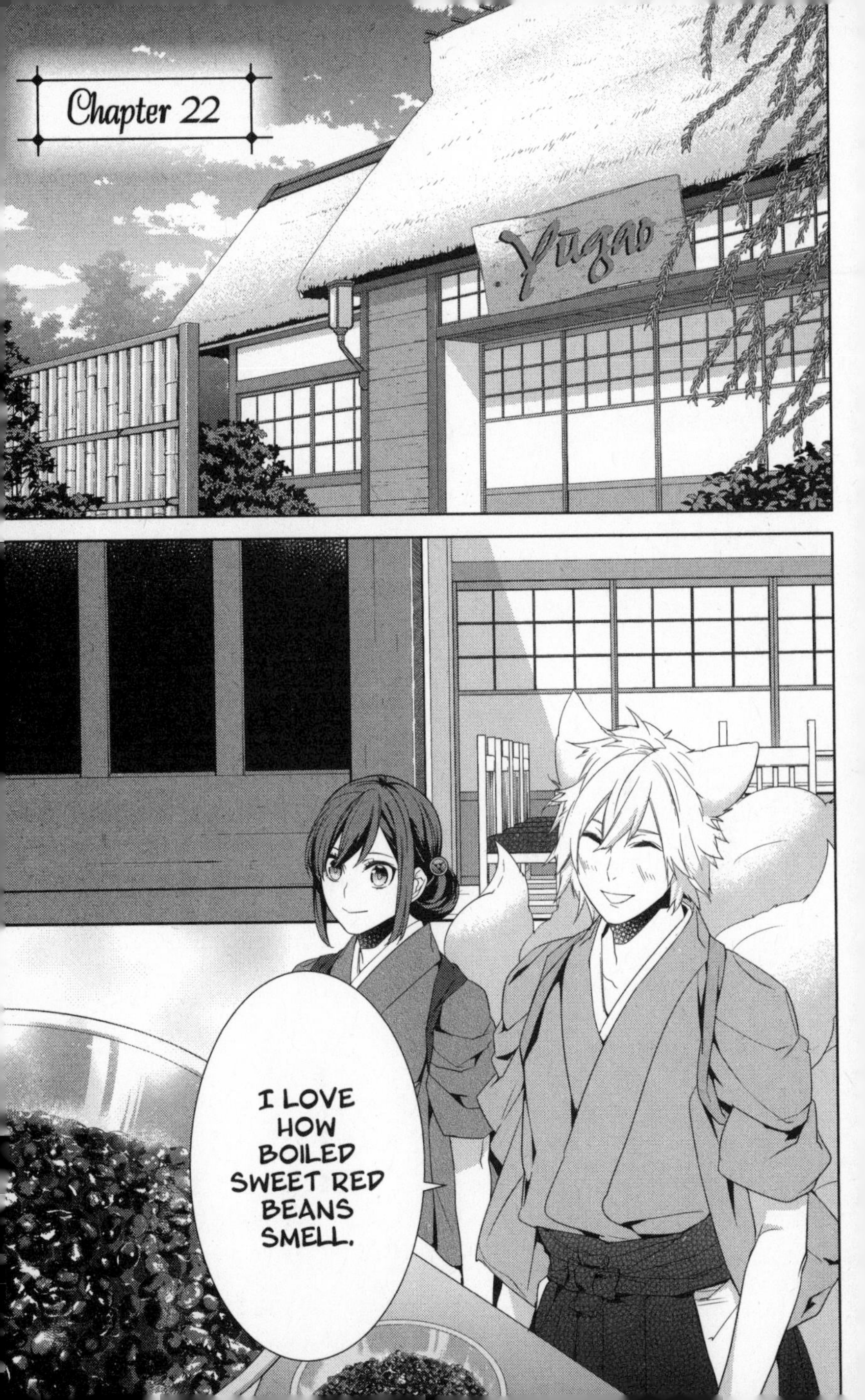
Chapter 22
Yugao
I LOVE HOW BOILED SWEET RED BEANS SMELL.

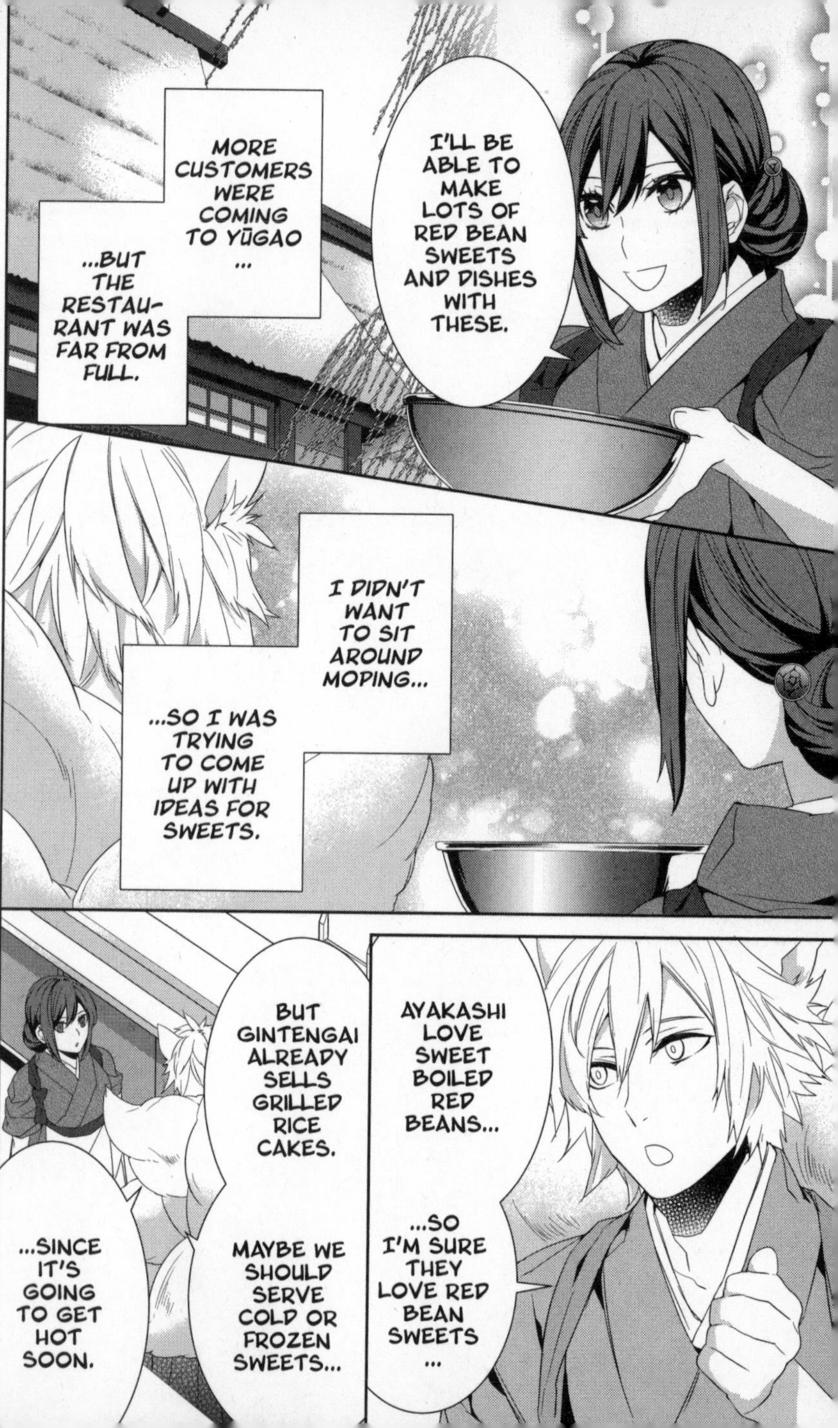
I'LL BE ABLE TO MAKE LOTS OF RED BEAN SWEETS AND DISHES WITH THESE.
MORE CUSTOMERS WERE COMING TO YŪGAO ...
...BUT THE RESTAU-RANT WAS FAR FROM FULL.
I DIDN'T WANT TO SIT AROUND MOPING...
...SO I WAS TRYING TO COME UP WITH IDEAS FOR SWEETS.
AYAKASHI LOVE SWEET BOILED RED BEANS...
...SO I'M SURE THEY LOVE RED BEAN SWEETS ...
BUT GINTENGAI ALREADY SELLS GRILLED RICE CAKES.
MAYBE WE SHOULD SERVE COLD OR FROZEN SWEETS...
...SINCE IT'S GOING TO GET HOT SOON.

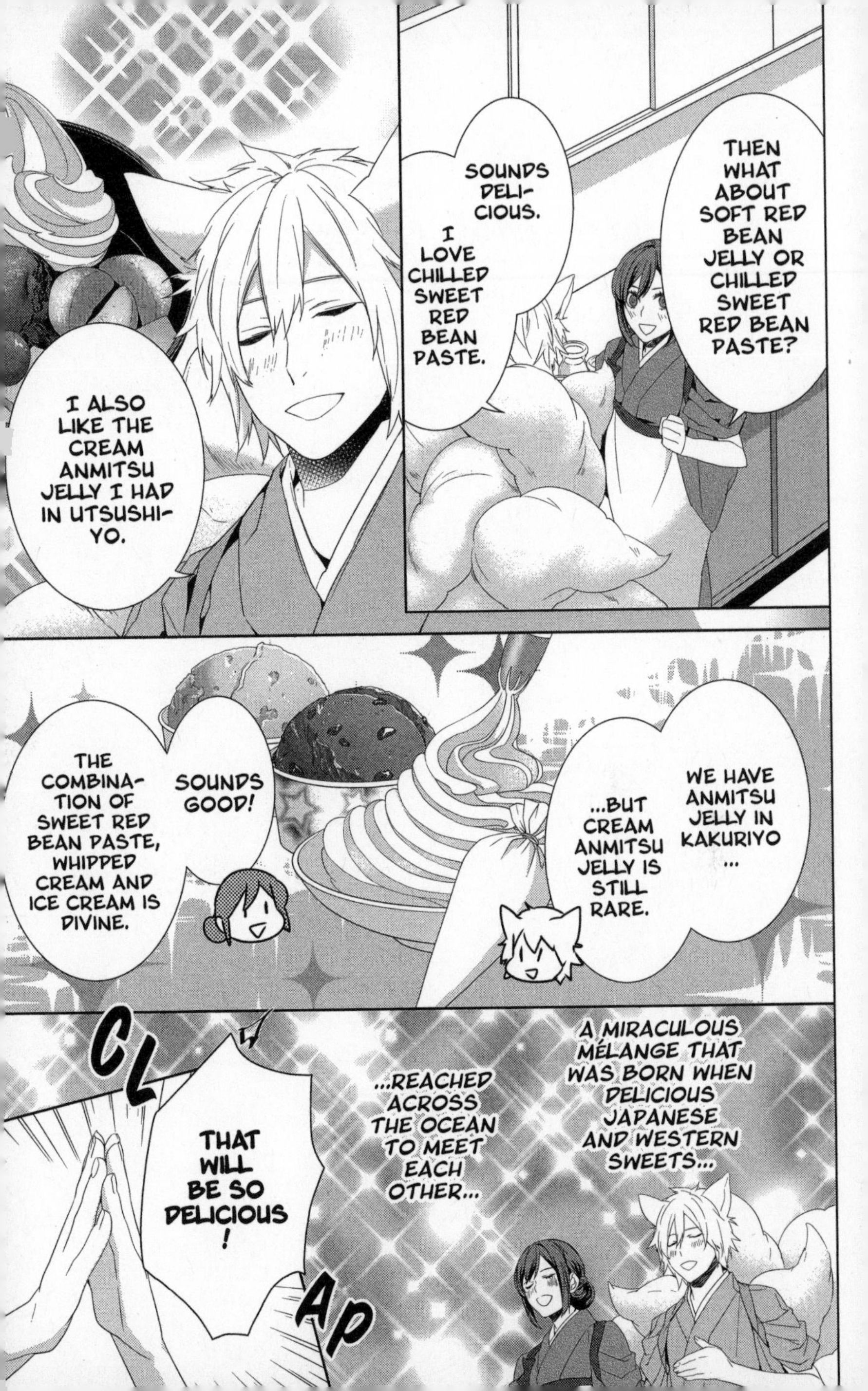
THEN WHAT ABOUT SOFT RED BEAN JELLY OR CHILLED SWEET RED BEAN PASTE?
SOUNDS DELICIOUS. I LOVE CHILLED SWEET RED BEAN PASTE.
I ALSO LIKE THE CREAM ANMITSU JELLY I HAD IN UTSUSHI-YO.
WE HAVE ANMITSU JELLY IN KAKURIYO ...
...BUT CREAM ANMITSU JELLY IS STILL RARE.
SOUNDS GOOD!
THE COMBINATION OF SWEET RED BEAN PASTE, WHIPPED CREAM AND ICE CREAM IS DIVINE.
A MIRACULOUS MÉLANGE THAT WAS BORN WHEN DELICIOUS JAPANESE AND WESTERN SWEETS...
...REACHED ACROSS THE OCEAN TO MEET EACH OTHER...
CL
AP
THAT WILL BE SO DELICIOUS!

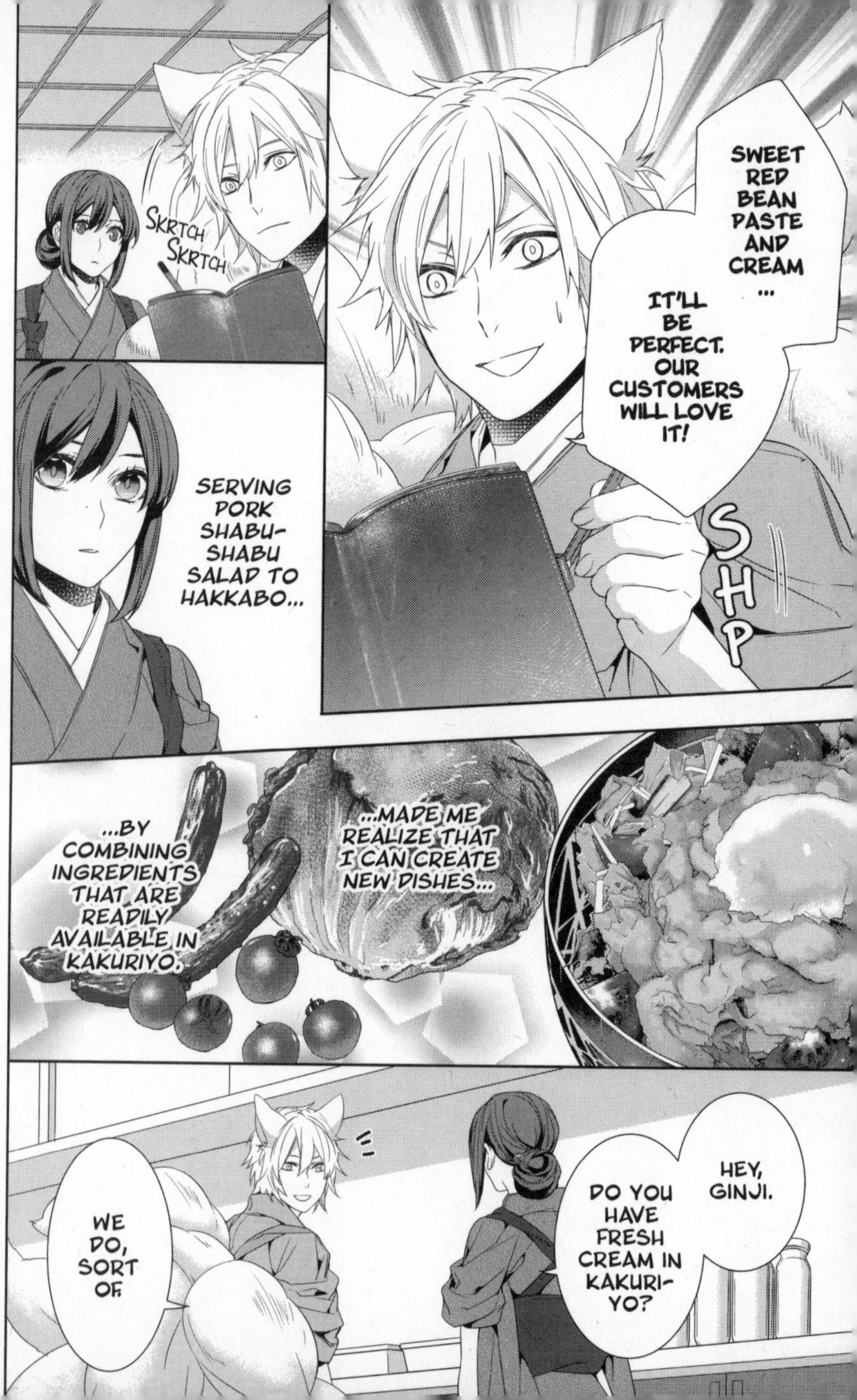
SWEET RED BEAN PASTE AND CREAM...
IT'LL BE PERFECT. OUR CUSTOMERS WILL LOVE IT!
SHP
SKRTCH SKRTCH
SERVING PORK SHABU-SHABU SALAD TO HAKKABO...
...MADE ME REALIZE THAT I CAN CREATE NEW DISHES...
...BY COMBINING INGREDIENTS THAT ARE READILY AVAILABLE IN KAKURIYO.
HEY, GINJI.
DO YOU HAVE FRESH CREAM IN KAKURI-YO?
WE DO, SORT OF.

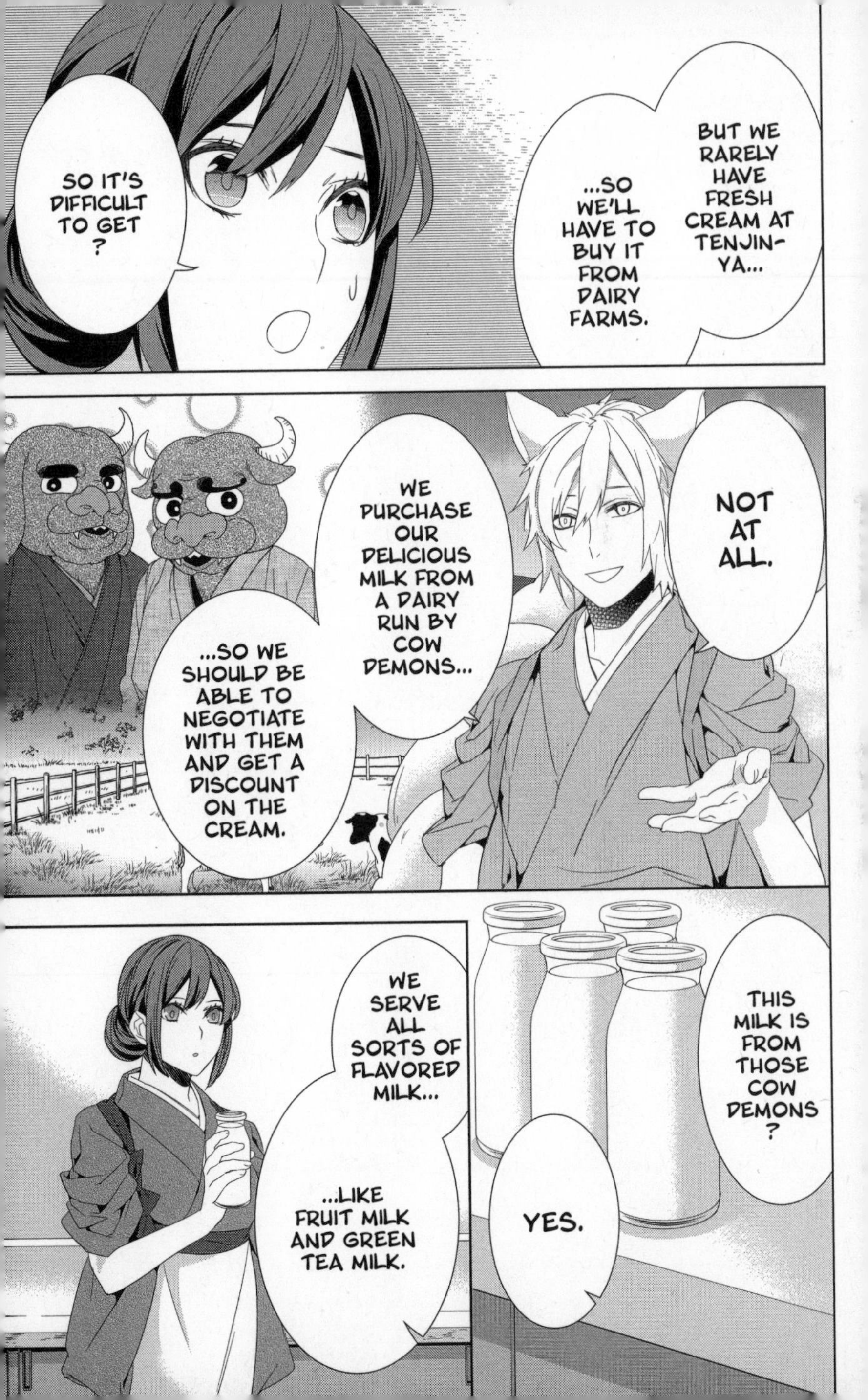
BUT WE RARELY HAVE FRESH CREAM AT TENJIN-YA...
...SO WE'LL HAVE TO BUY IT FROM DAIRY FARMS.
SO IT'S DIFFICULT TO GET?
NOT AT ALL.
WE PURCHASE OUR DELICIOUS MILK FROM A DAIRY RUN BY COW DEMONS...
...SO WE SHOULD BE ABLE TO NEGOTIATE WITH THEM AND GET A DISCOUNT ON THE CREAM.
THIS MILK IS FROM THOSE COW DEMONS?
YES.
WE SERVE ALL SORTS OF FLAVORED MILK...
...LIKE FRUIT MILK AND GREEN TEA MILK.

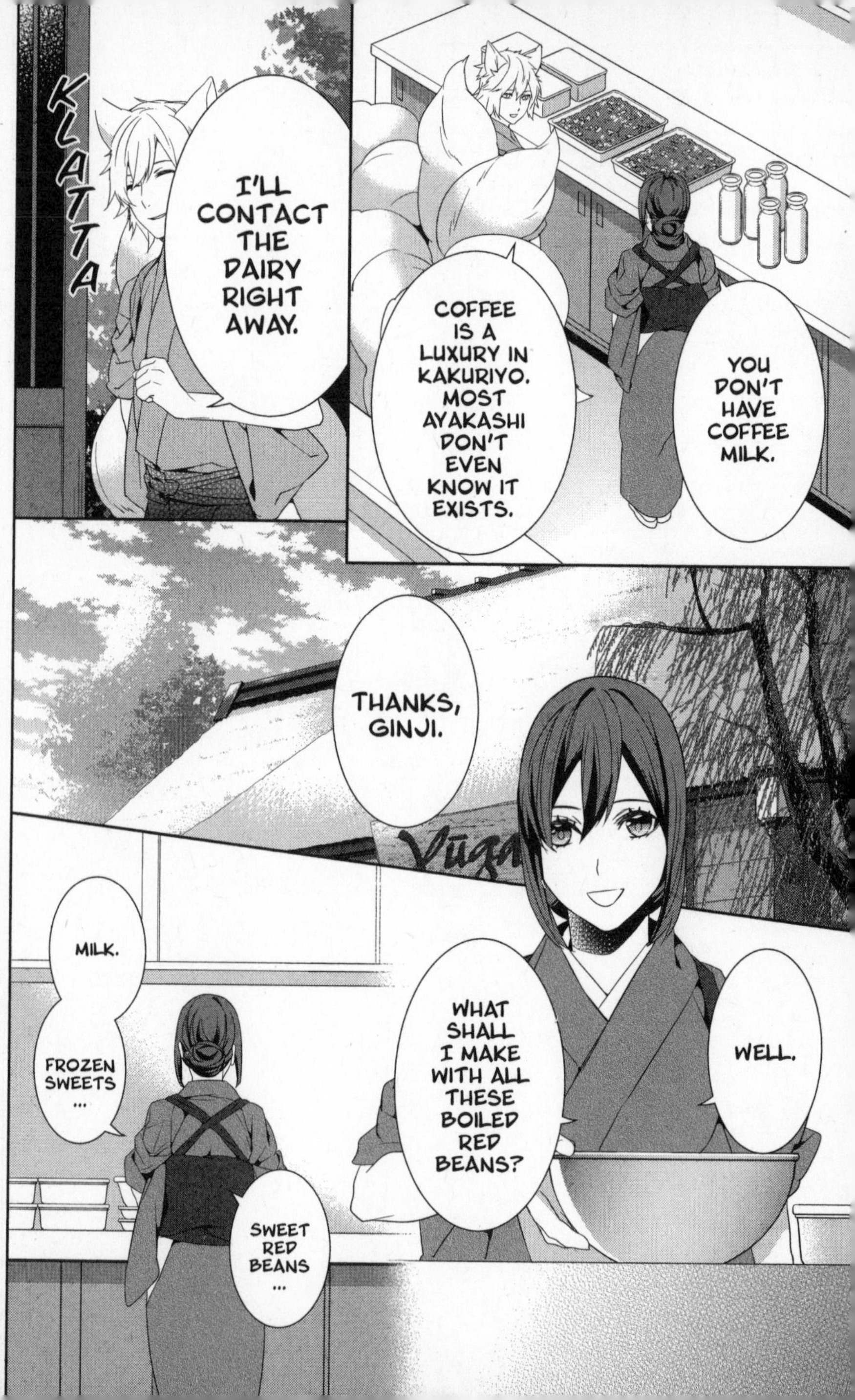
YOU DON'T HAVE COFFEE MILK.
COFFEE IS A LUXURY IN KAKURIYO. MOST AYAKASHI DON'T EVEN KNOW IT EXISTS.
KLATTA
I'LL CONTACT THE DAIRY RIGHT AWAY.
THANKS, GINJI.
WELL.
WHAT SHALL I MAKE WITH ALL THESE BOILED RED BEANS?
MILK.
FROZEN SWEETS...
SWEET RED BEANS...

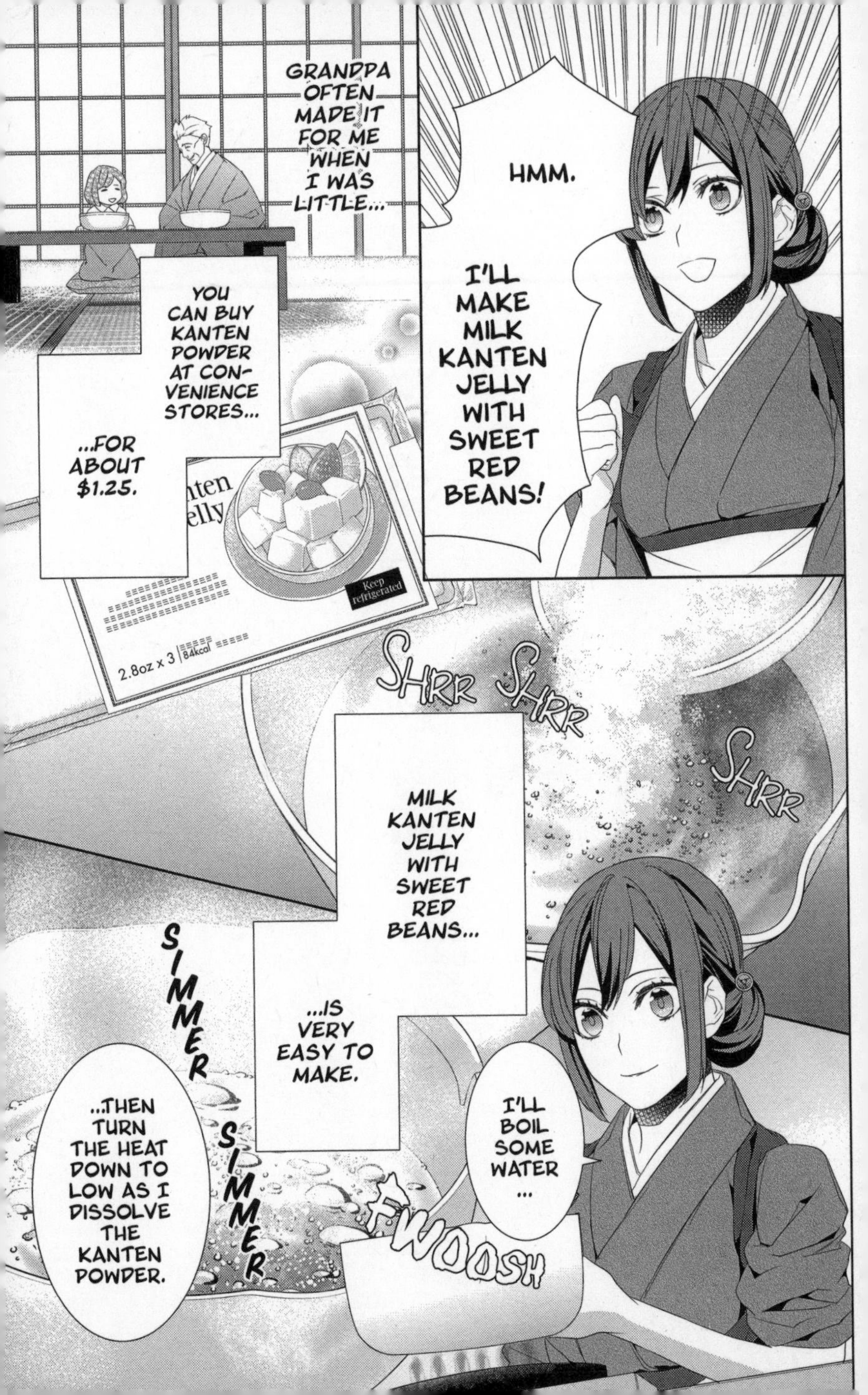
HMM.
I'LL MAKE MILK KANTEN JELLY WITH SWEET RED BEANS!
GRANDPA OFTEN MADE IT FOR ME WHEN I WAS LITTLE...
YOU CAN BUY KANTEN POWDER AT CONVENIENCE STORES...
...FOR ABOUT $1.25.
Keep refrigerated
2.8oz x 3 | 84kcal
SHRR SHRR
SHRR
MILK KANTEN JELLY WITH SWEET RED BEANS...
...IS VERY EASY TO MAKE.
I'LL BOIL SOME WATER...
FWOOSH
SIMMER
SIMMER
...THEN TURN THE HEAT DOWN TO LOW AS I DISSOLVE THE KANTEN POWDER.

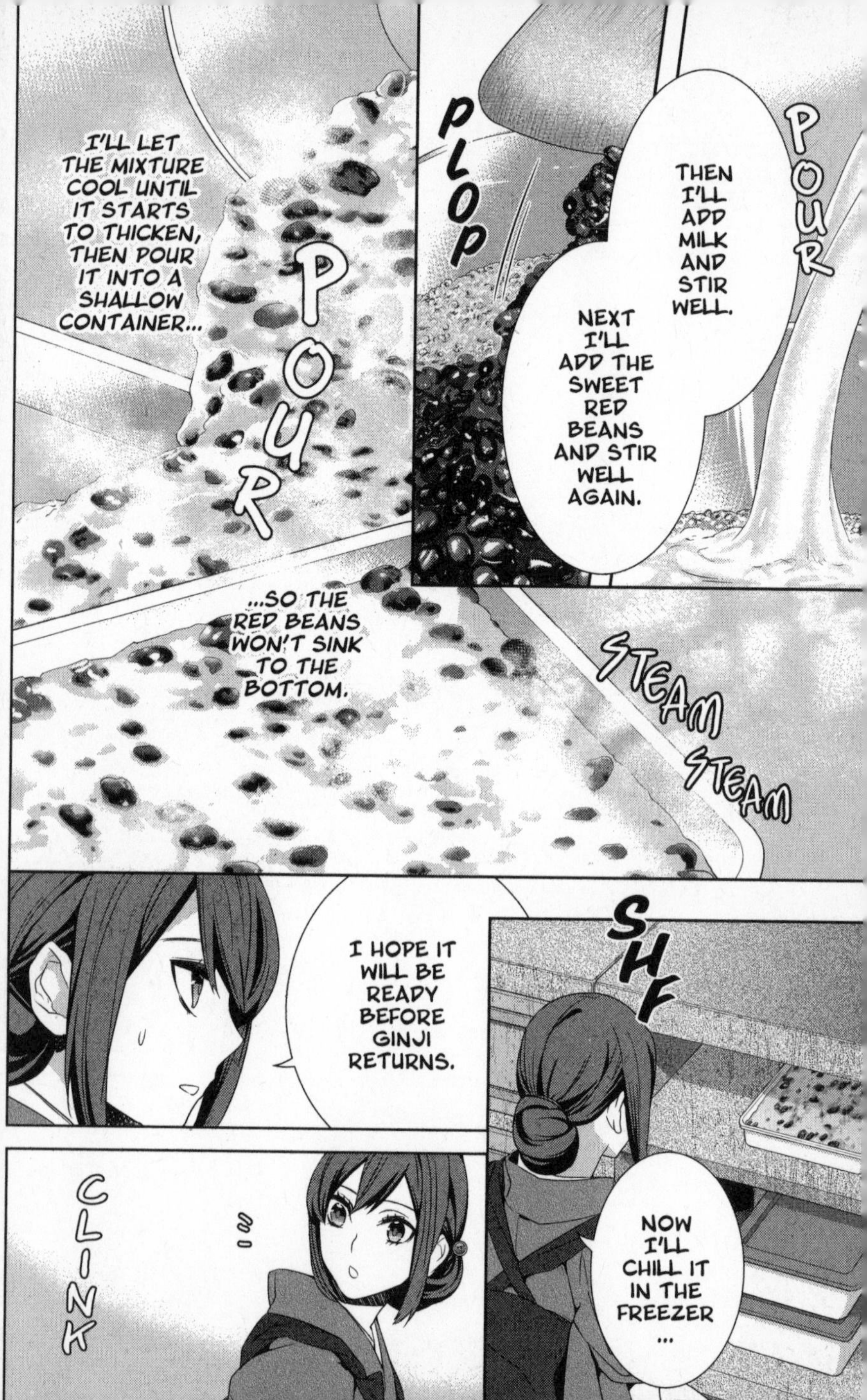
POUR
THEN I'LL ADD MILK AND STIR WELL.
PLOP
NEXT I'LL ADD THE SWEET RED BEANS AND STIR WELL AGAIN.
I'LL LET THE MIXTURE COOL UNTIL IT STARTS TO THICKEN, THEN POUR IT INTO A SHALLOW CONTAINER...
POUR
...SO THE RED BEANS WON'T SINK TO THE BOTTOM.
STEAM STEAM
SHF
NOW I'LL CHILL IT IN THE FREEZER...
I HOPE IT WILL BE READY BEFORE GINJI RETURNS.
!!
CLINK

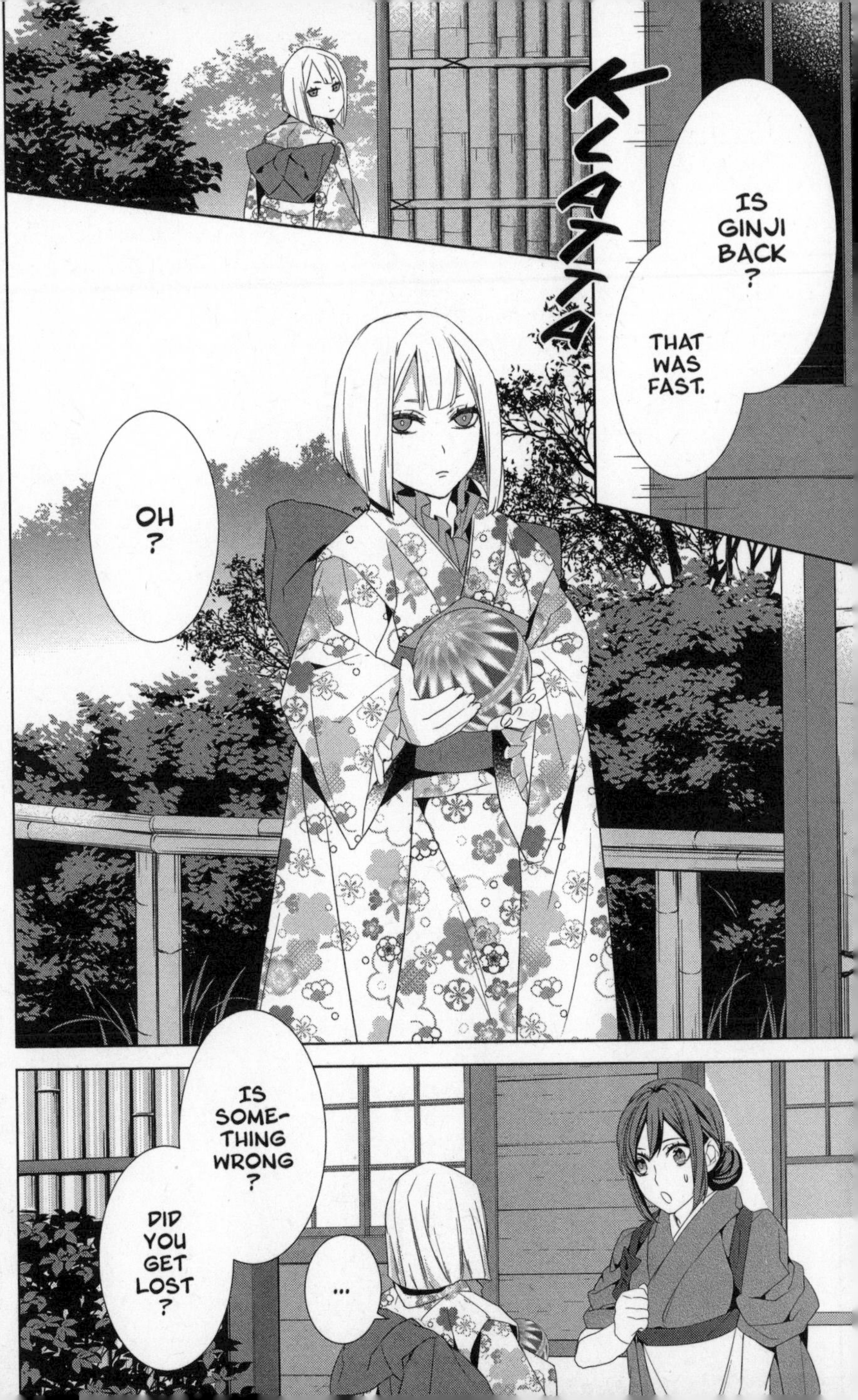
KLATTA
IS GINJI BACK?
THAT WAS FAST.
OH?
IS SOMETHING WRONG?
DID YOU GET LOST?
...

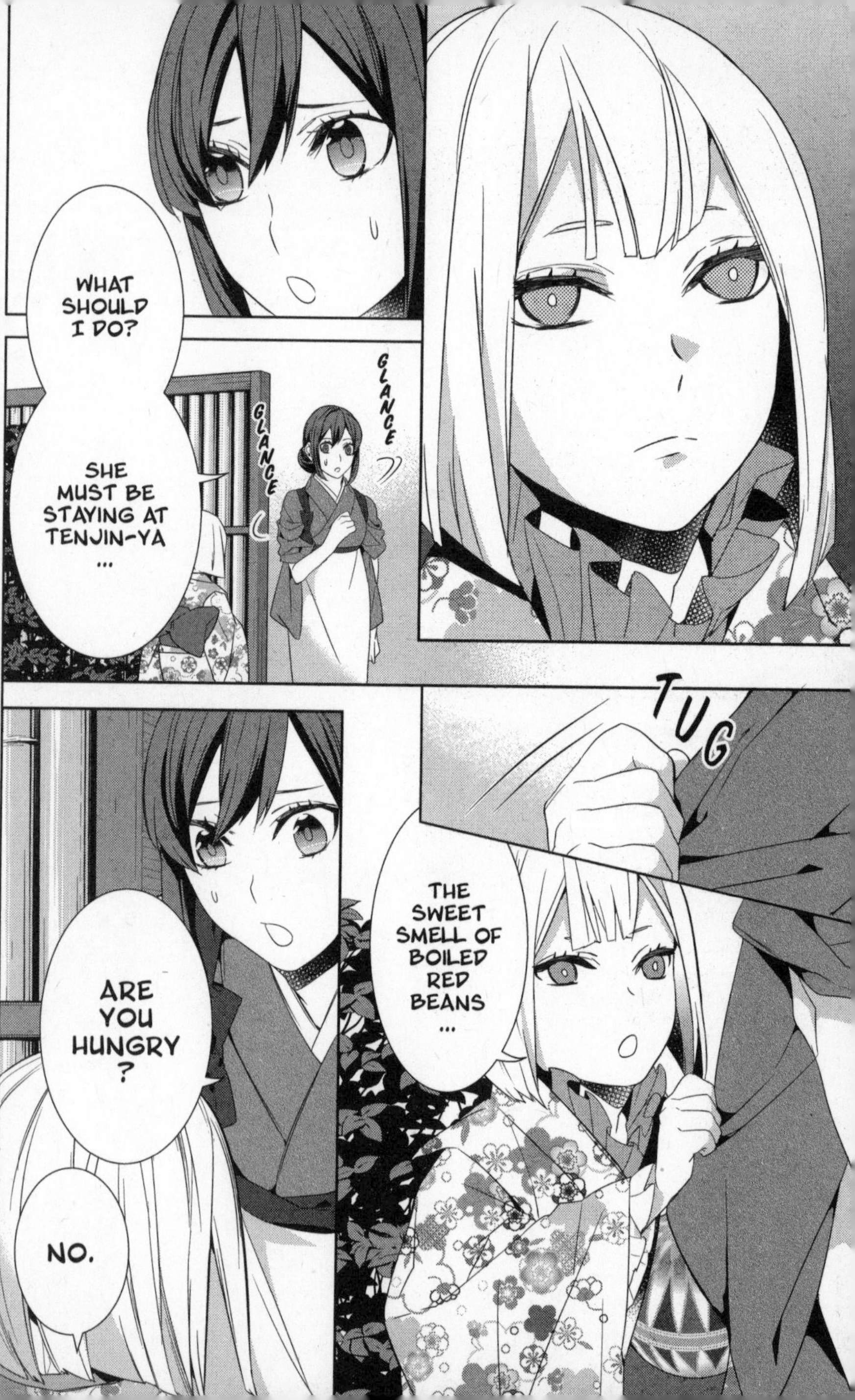
WHAT SHOULD I DO?
GLANCE
GLANCE
SHE MUST BE STAYING AT TENJIN-YA ...
TUG
THE SWEET SMELL OF BOILED RED BEANS ...
ARE YOU HUNGRY ?
NO.

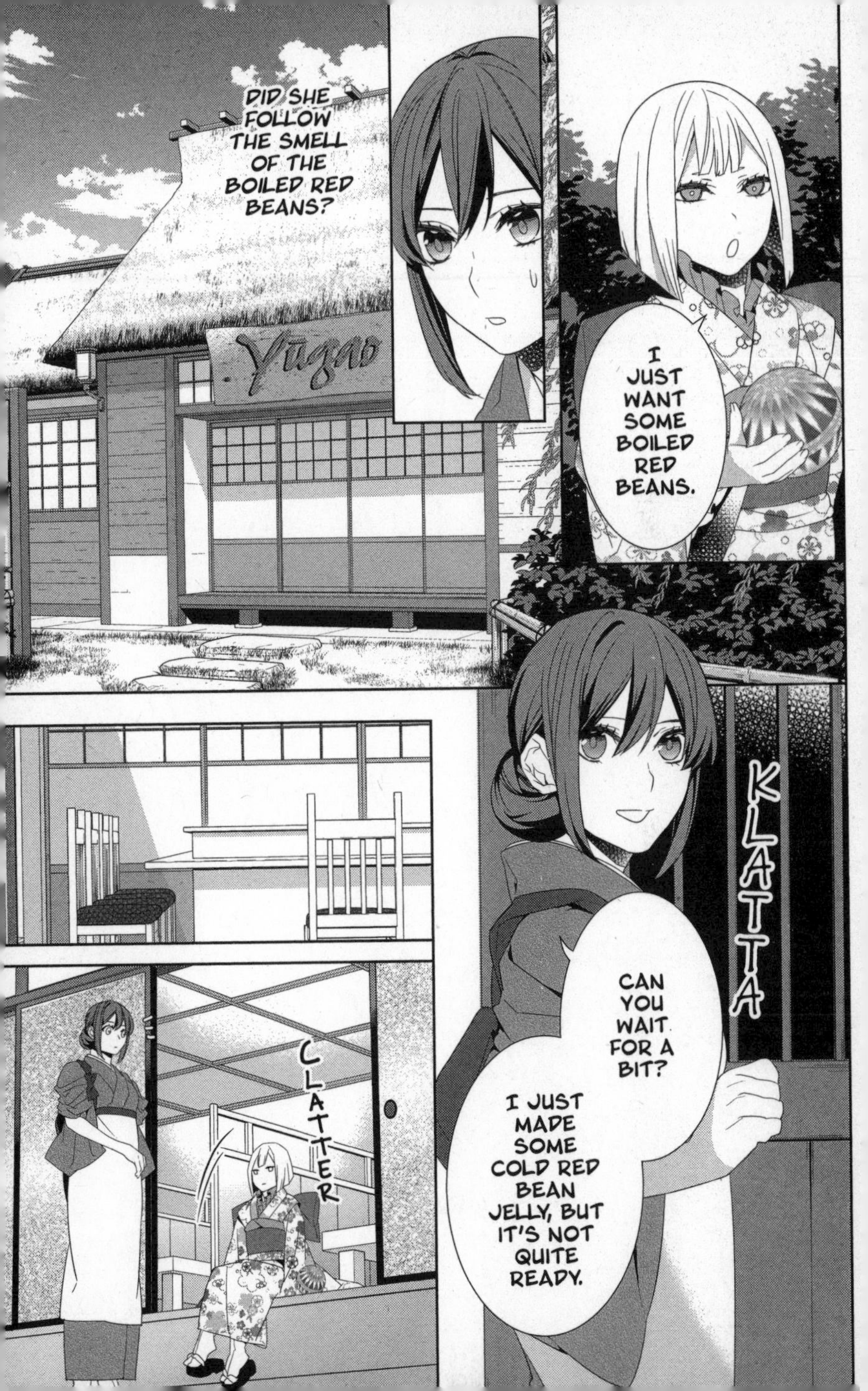
I JUST WANT SOME BOILED RED BEANS.
DID SHE FOLLOW THE SMELL OF THE BOILED RED BEANS?
Yugao
KLATTA
CAN YOU WAIT FOR A BIT?
I JUST MADE SOME COLD RED BEAN JELLY, BUT IT'S NOT QUITE READY.
CLATTER

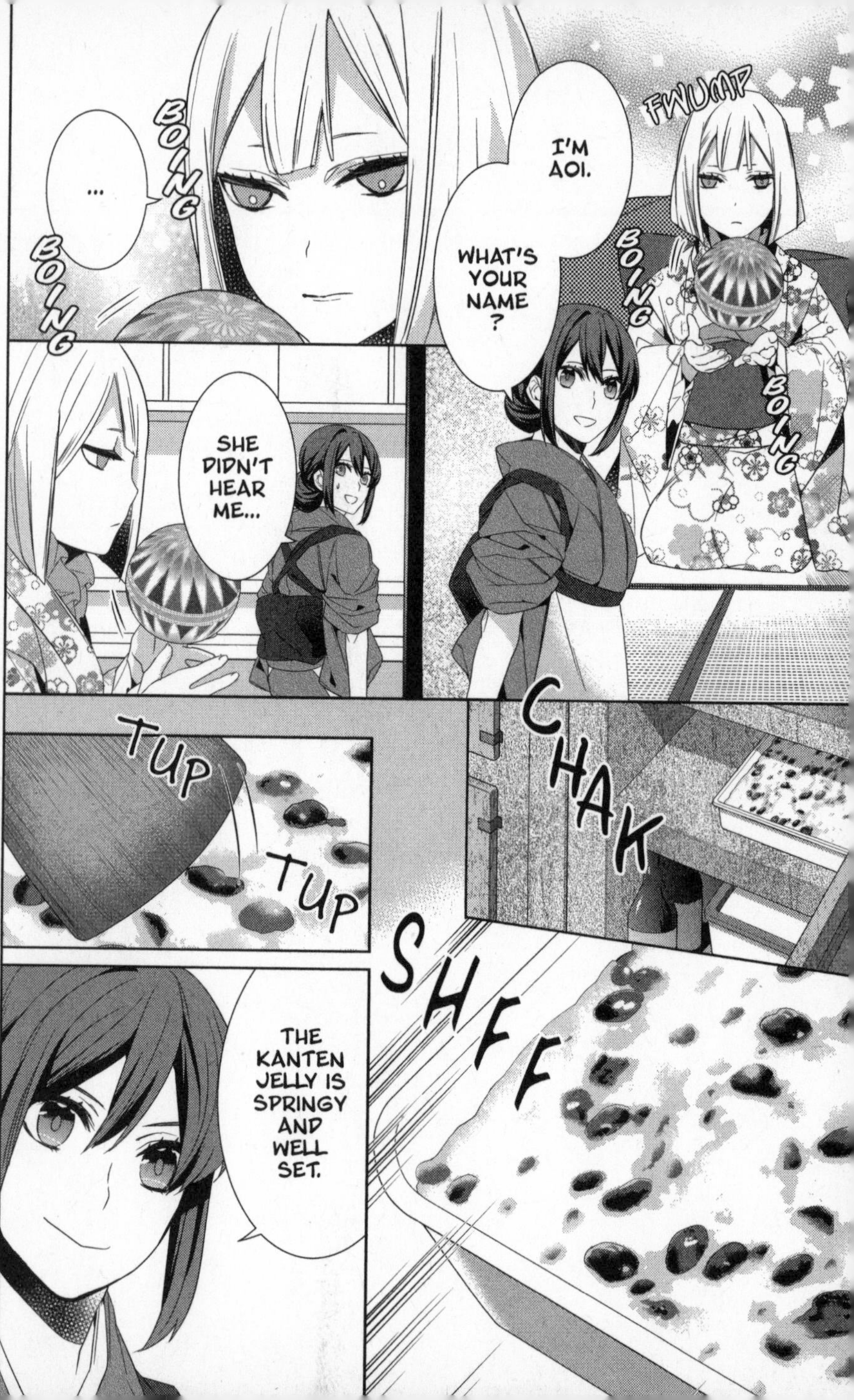
FWUMP
I'M AOI.
WHAT'S YOUR NAME?
BOING
BOING
...
BOING
BOING
SHE DIDN'T HEAR ME...
CHAK
TUP
TUP
SHFF
THE KANTEN JELLY IS SPRINGY AND WELL SET.

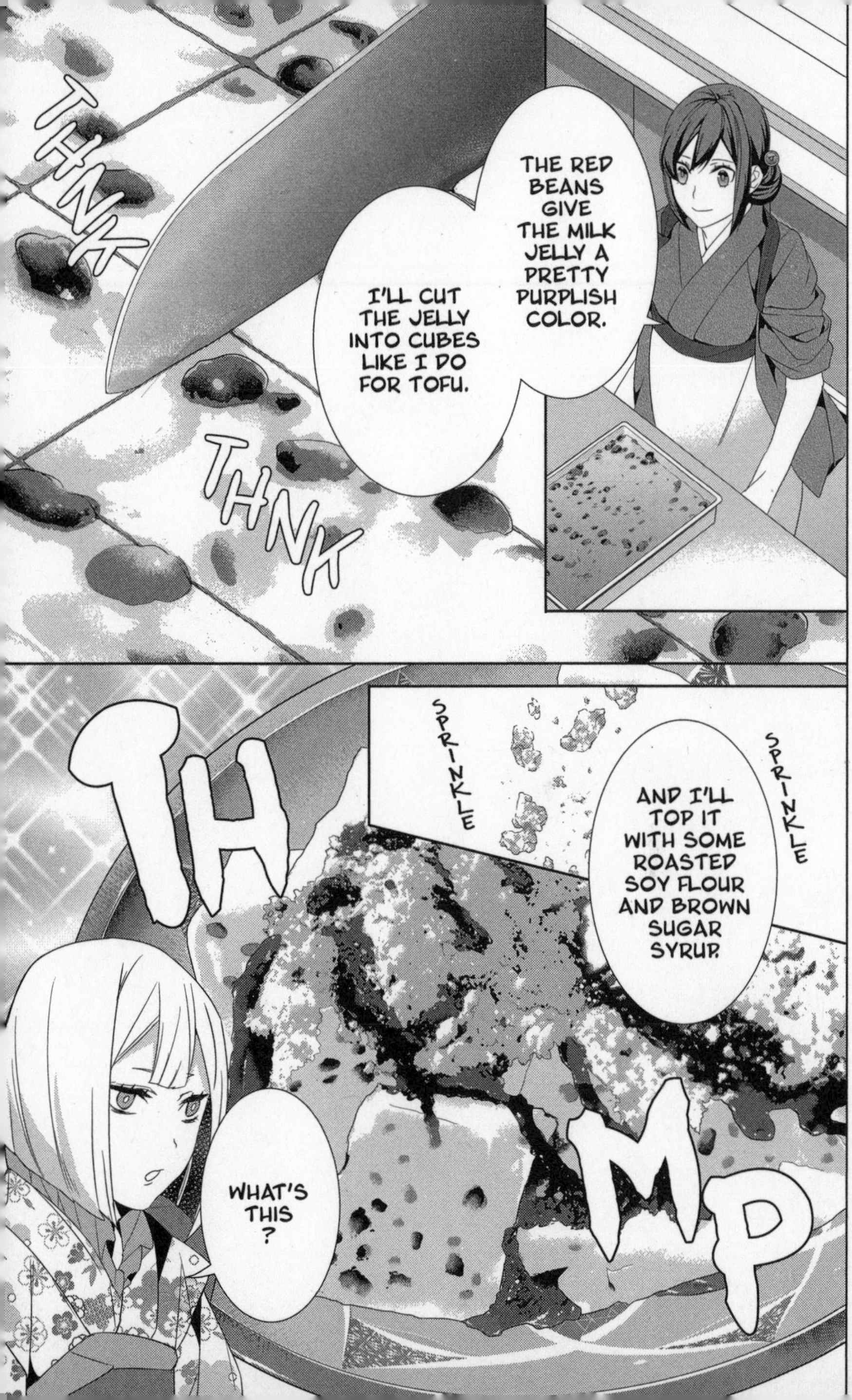
THE RED BEANS GIVE THE MILK JELLY A PRETTY PURPLISH COLOR.
I'LL CUT THE JELLY INTO CUBES LIKE I DO FOR TOFU.
THNK
THNK
SPRINKLE
AND I'LL TOP IT WITH SOME ROASTED SOY FLOUR AND BROWN SUGAR SYRUP.
SPRINKLE
THMP
WHAT'S THIS?

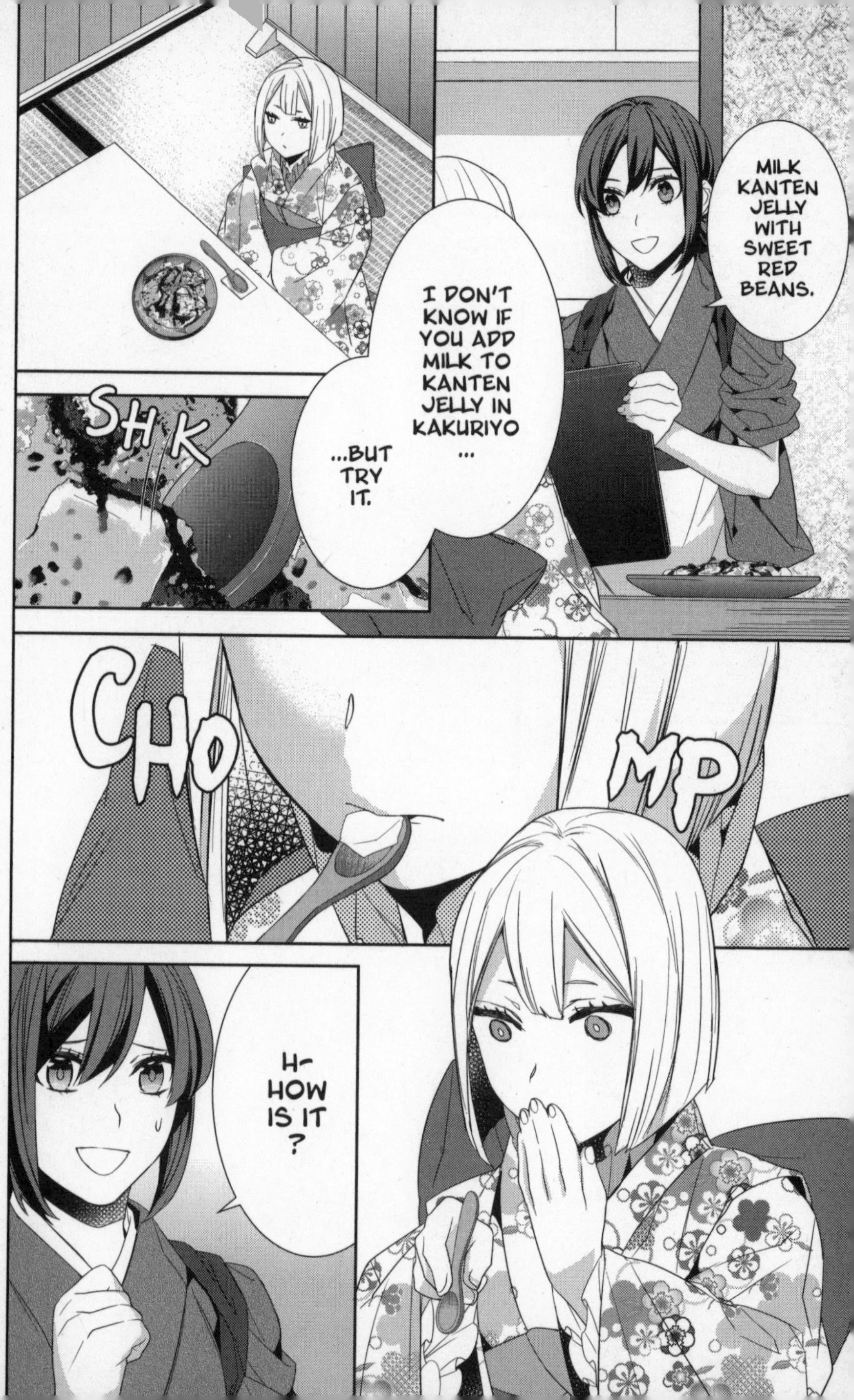
MILK KANTEN JELLY WITH SWEET RED BEANS.
I DON'T KNOW IF YOU ADD MILK TO KANTEN JELLY IN KAKURIYO ...
...BUT TRY IT.
SHK
CHOMP
H-HOW IS IT?

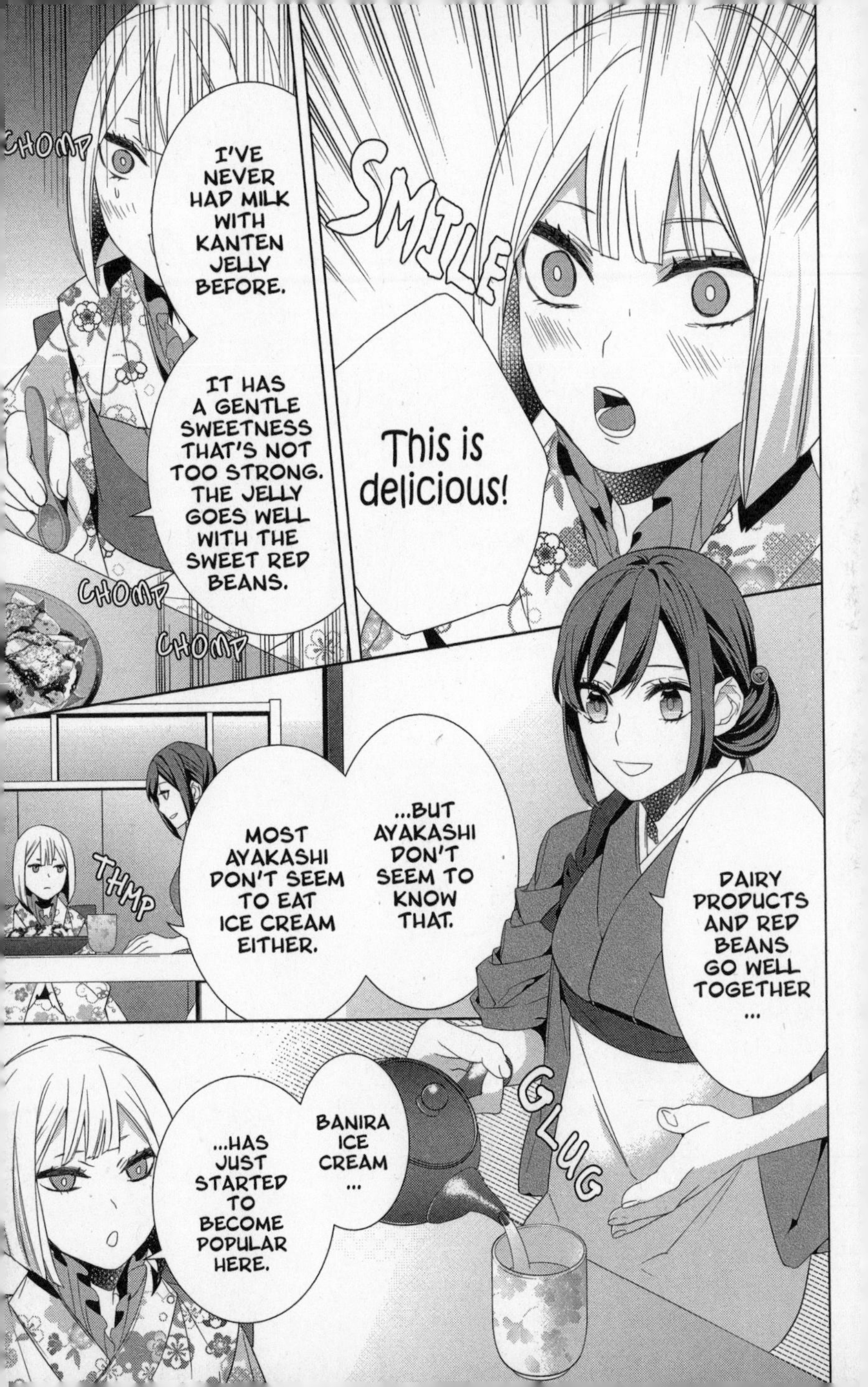
SMILE
This is delicious!
CHOMP
I'VE NEVER HAD MILK WITH KANTEN JELLY BEFORE.
IT HAS A GENTLE SWEETNESS THAT'S NOT TOO STRONG. THE JELLY GOES WELL WITH THE SWEET RED BEANS.
CHOMP
CHOMP
DAIRY PRODUCTS AND RED BEANS GO WELL TOGETHER...
...BUT AYAKASHI DON'T SEEM TO KNOW THAT.
MOST AYAKASHI DON'T SEEM TO EAT ICE CREAM EITHER.
THMP
GLUG
BANIRA ICE CREAM...
...HAS JUST STARTED TO BECOME POPULAR HERE.

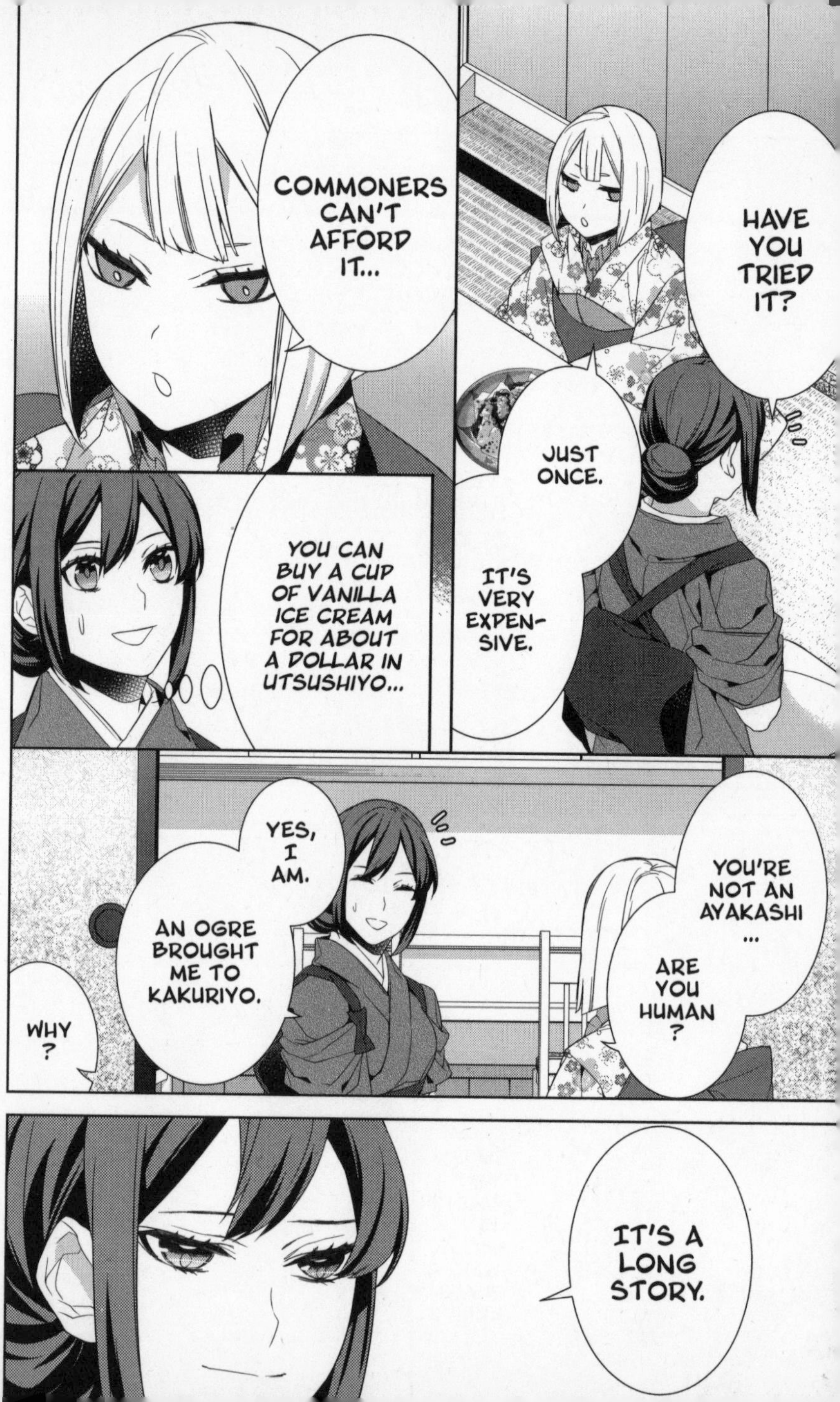
HAVE YOU TRIED IT?
JUST ONCE.
IT'S VERY EXPEN-SIVE.
COMMONERS CAN'T AFFORD IT...
YOU CAN BUY A CUP OF VANILLA ICE CREAM FOR ABOUT A DOLLAR IN UTSUSHIYO...
YOU'RE NOT AN AYAKASHI...
ARE YOU HUMAN?
YES, I AM.
AN OGRE BROUGHT ME TO KAKURIYO.
WHY?
IT'S A LONG STORY.

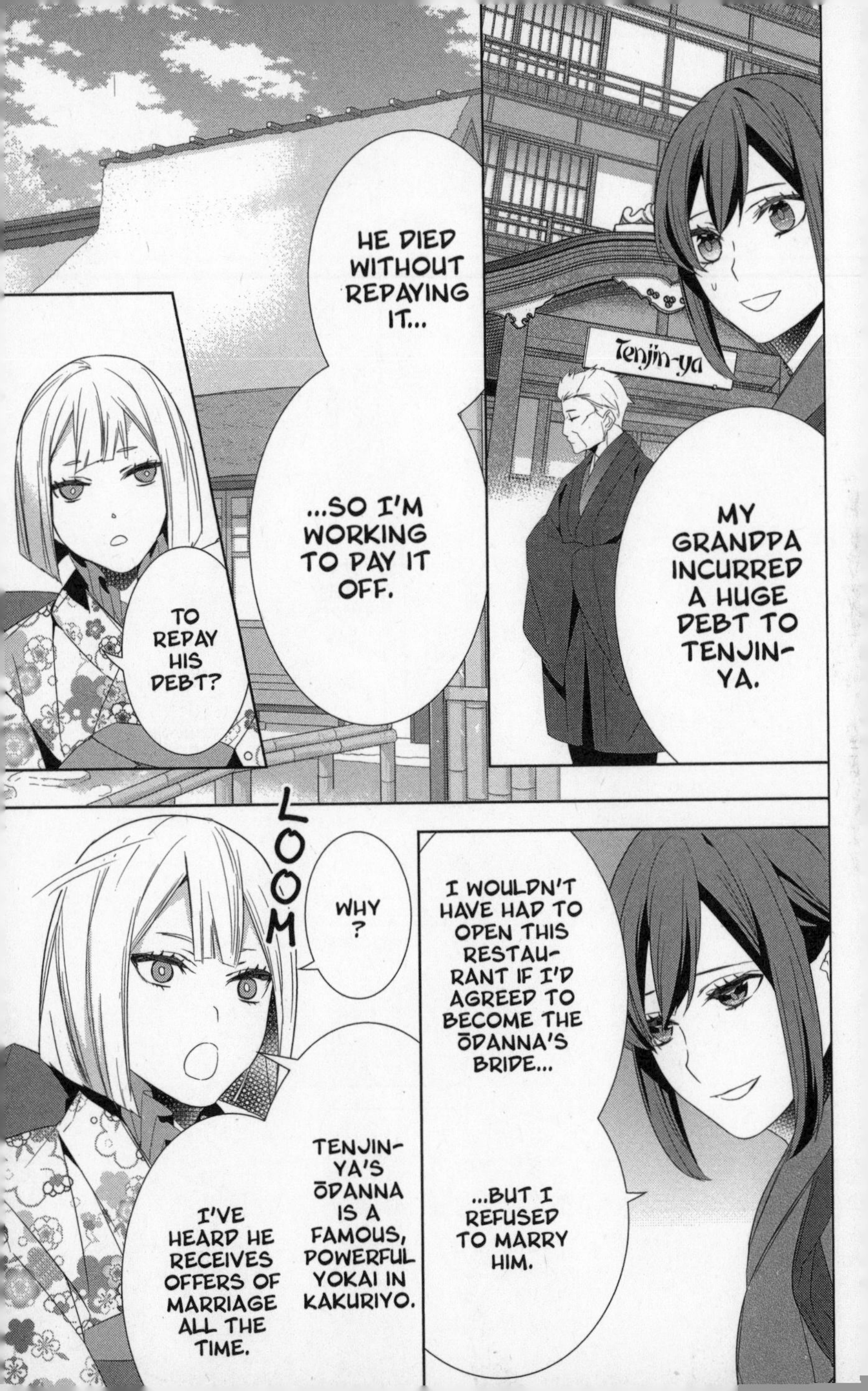
Tenjin-ya
MY GRANDPA INCURRED A HUGE DEBT TO TENJIN-YA.
HE DIED WITHOUT REPAYING IT...
...SO I'M WORKING TO PAY IT OFF.
TO REPAY HIS DEBT?
I WOULDN'T HAVE HAD TO OPEN THIS RESTAURANT IF I'D AGREED TO BECOME THE ŌDANNA'S BRIDE...
...BUT I REFUSED TO MARRY HIM.
LOOM
WHY?
TENJIN-YA'S ŌDANNA IS A FAMOUS, POWERFUL YOKAI IN KAKURIYO.
I'VE HEARD HE RECEIVES OFFERS OF MARRIAGE ALL THE TIME.

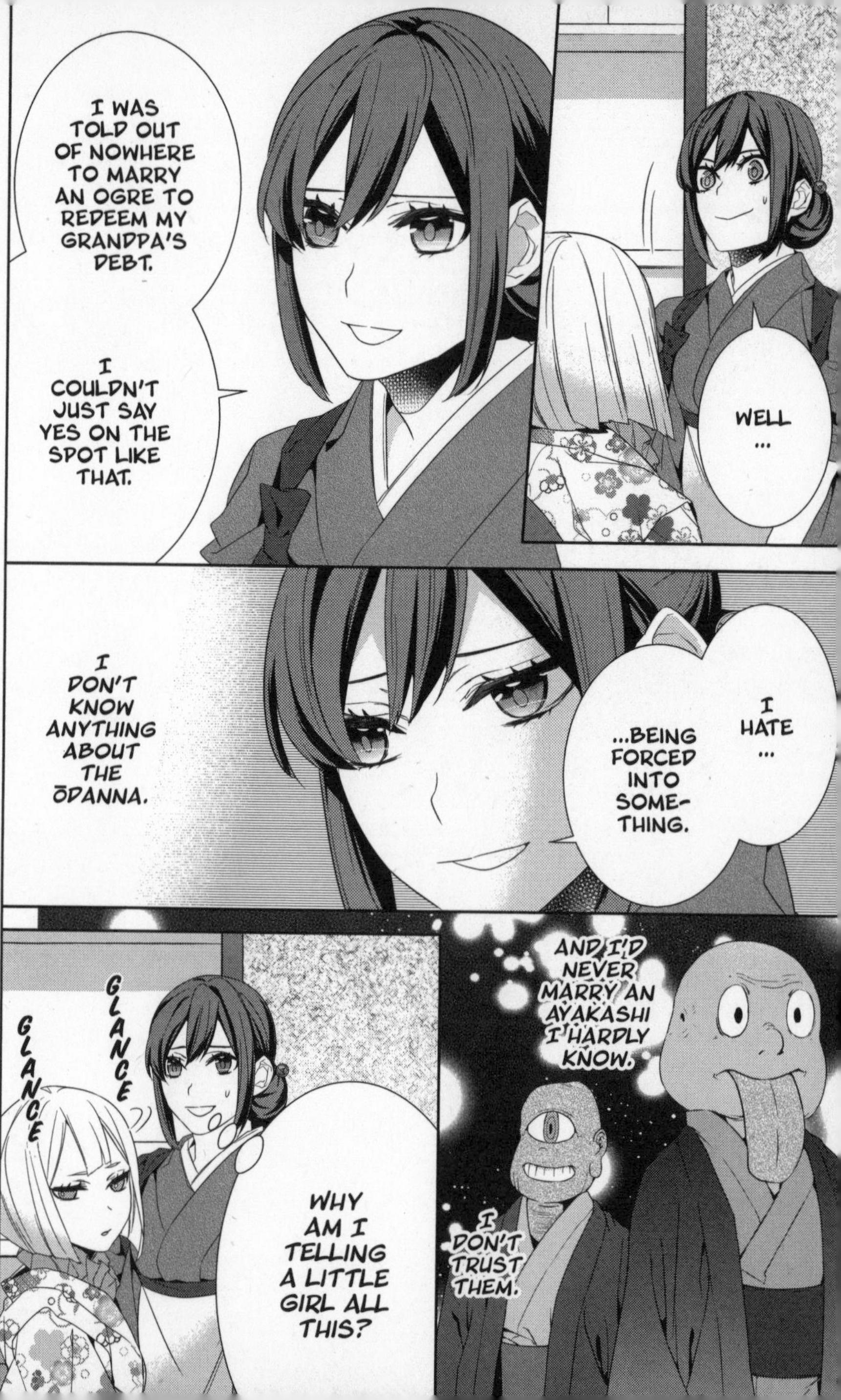
WELL...
I WAS TOLD OUT OF NOWHERE TO MARRY AN OGRE TO REDEEM MY GRANDPA'S DEBT.
I COULDN'T JUST SAY YES ON THE SPOT LIKE THAT.
I HATE...
...BEING FORCED INTO SOME-THING.
I DON'T KNOW ANYTHING ABOUT THE ŌDANNA.
AND I'D NEVER MARRY AN AYAKASHI I HARDLY KNOW.
I DON'T TRUST THEM.
GLANCE
GLANCE
WHY AM I TELLING A LITTLE GIRL ALL THIS?

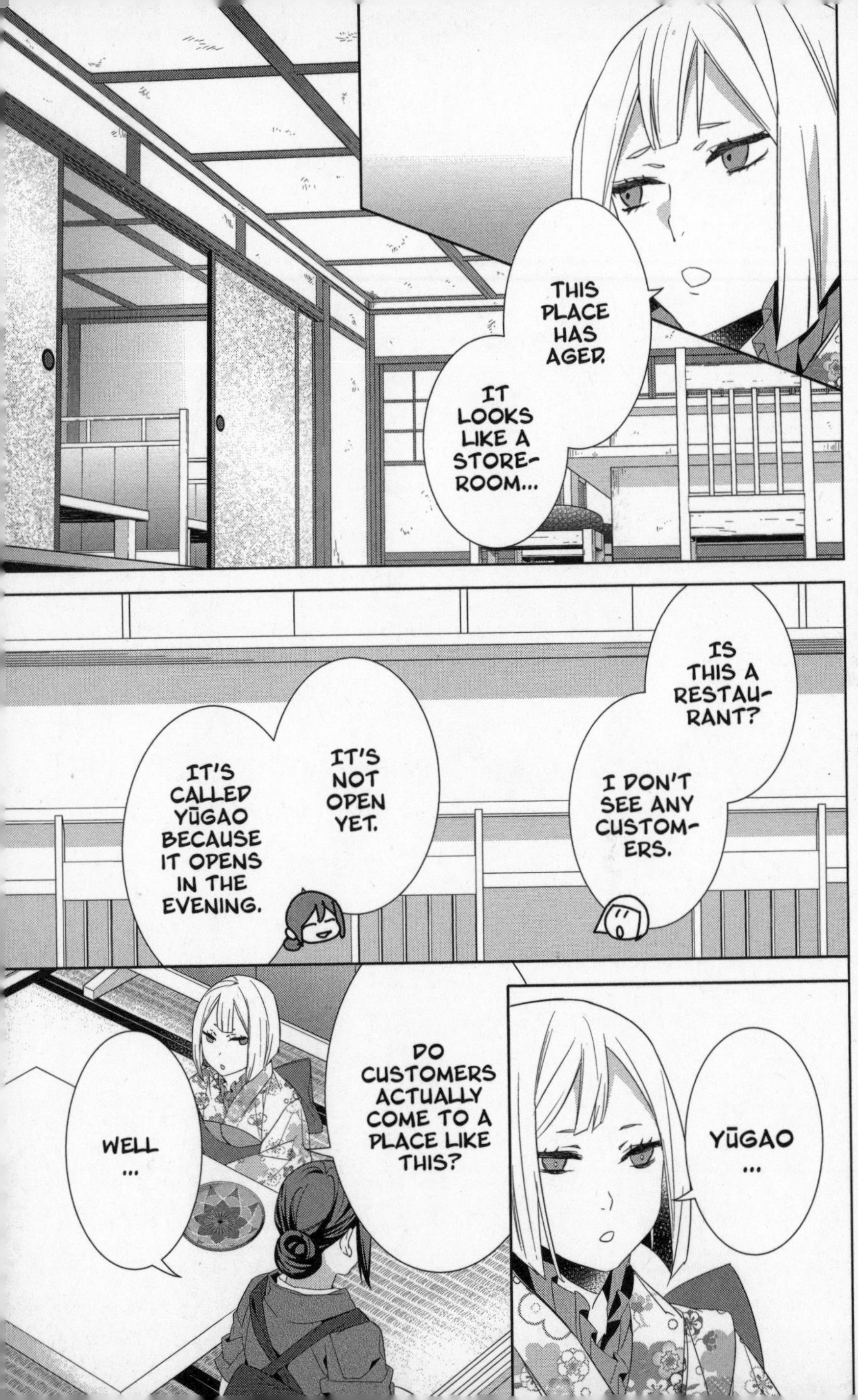
THIS PLACE HAS AGED.
IT LOOKS LIKE A STORE-ROOM...
IS THIS A RESTAU-RANT?
I DON'T SEE ANY CUSTOM-ERS.
IT'S NOT OPEN YET.
IT'S CALLED YŪGAO BECAUSE IT OPENS IN THE EVENING.
YŪGAO ...
DO CUSTOMERS ACTUALLY COME TO A PLACE LIKE THIS?
WELL ...

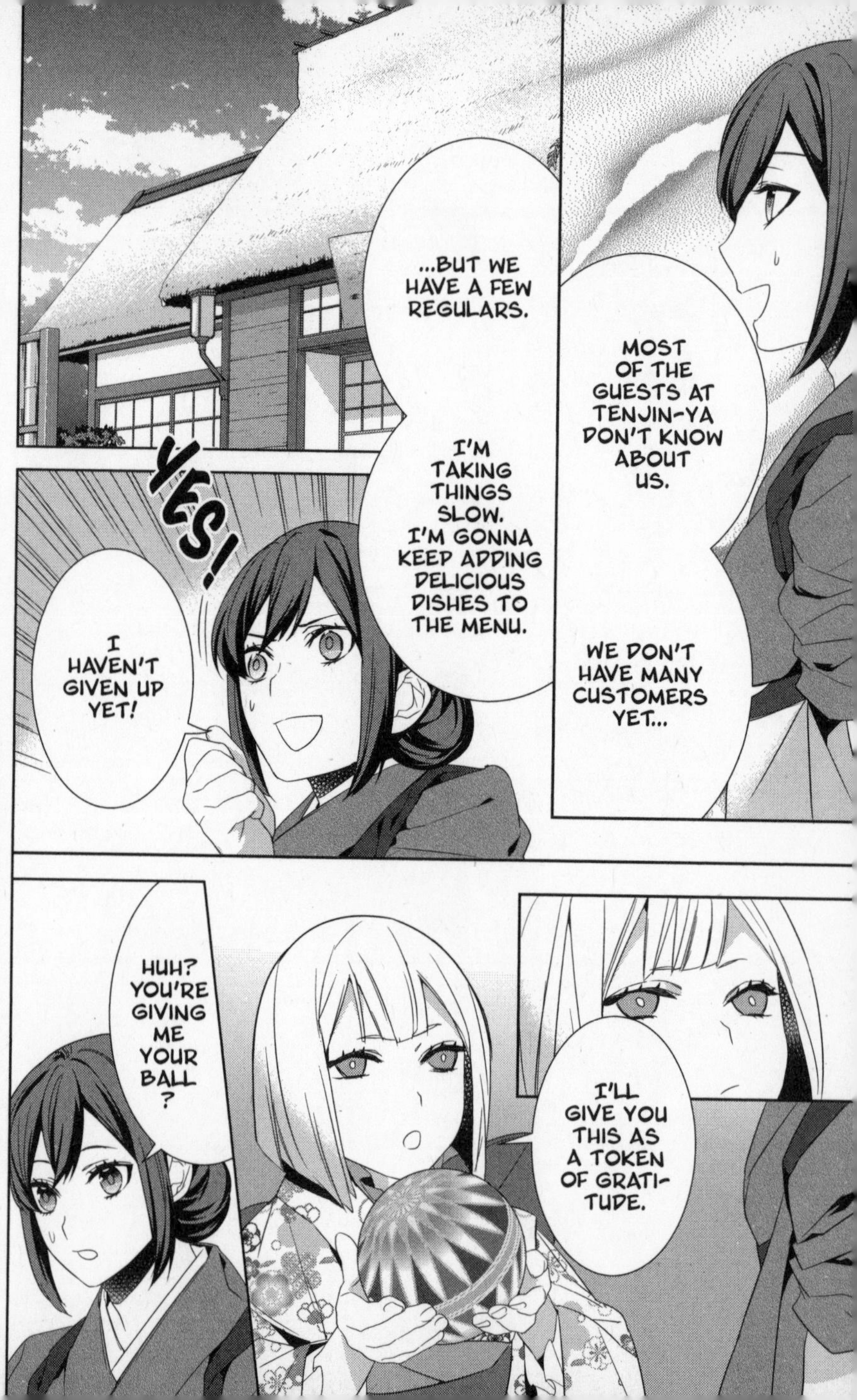
MOST OF THE GUESTS AT TENJIN-YA DON'T KNOW ABOUT US.
WE DON'T HAVE MANY CUSTOMERS YET...
...BUT WE HAVE A FEW REGULARS.
I'M TAKING THINGS SLOW. I'M GONNA KEEP ADDING DELICIOUS DISHES TO THE MENU.
YES!
I HAVEN'T GIVEN UP YET!
I'LL GIVE YOU THIS AS A TOKEN OF GRATI-TUDE.
HUH? YOU'RE GIVING ME YOUR BALL?

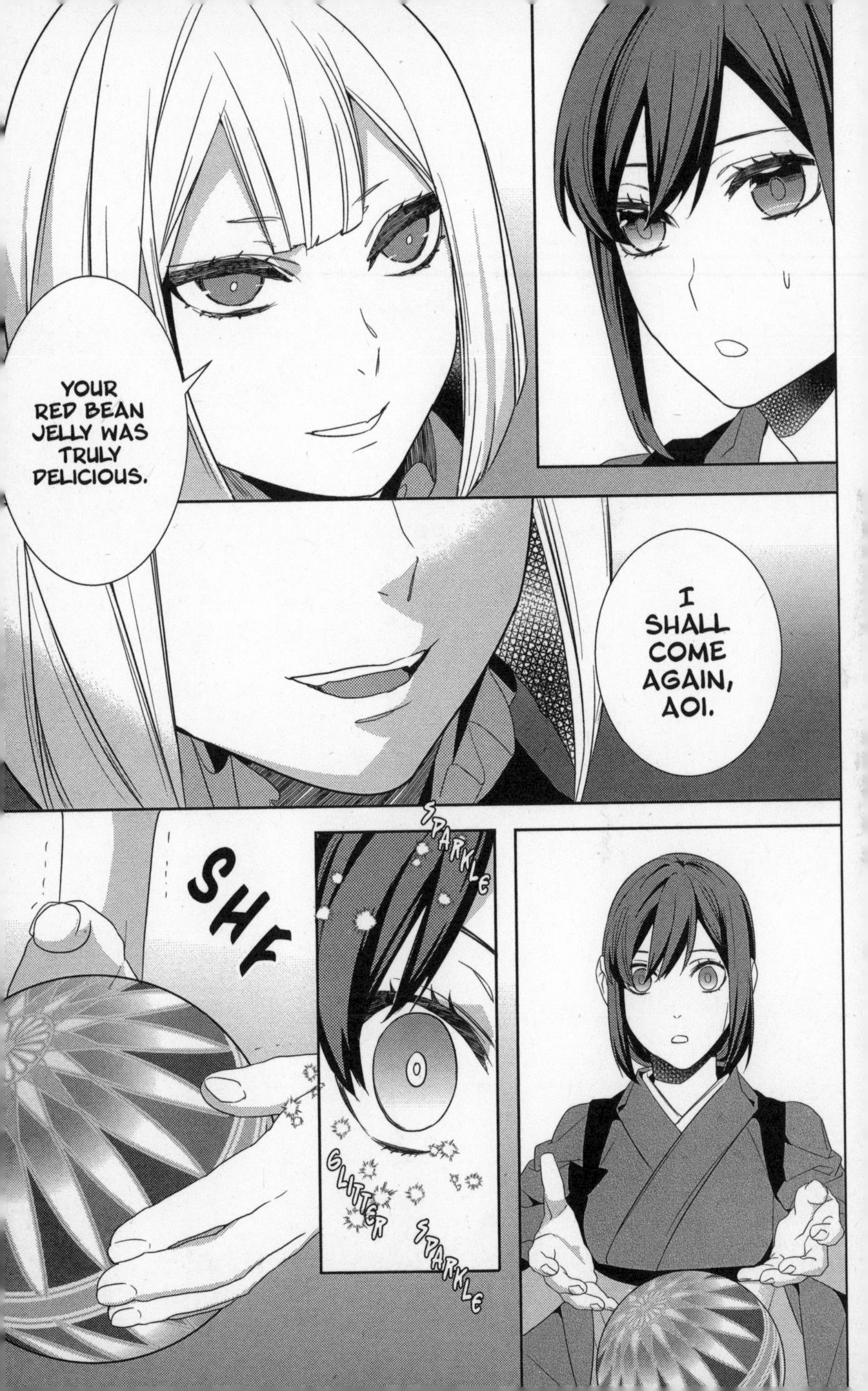
YOUR RED BEAN JELLY WAS TRULY DELICIOUS.
I SHALL COME AGAIN, AOI.
SPARKLE
GLITTER
SPARKLE
SHF

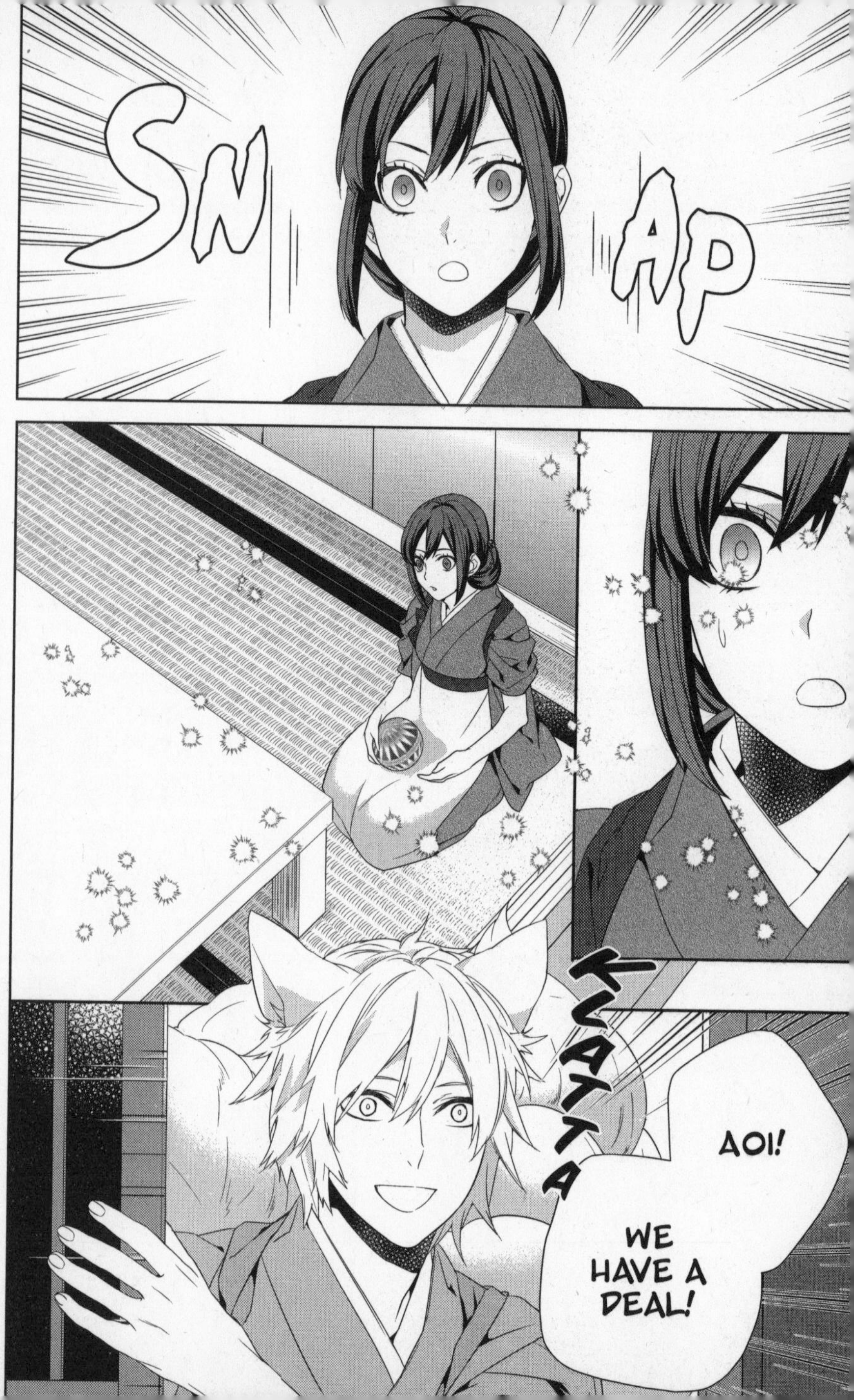
SNAP
KLATTA
AOI!
WE HAVE A DEAL!

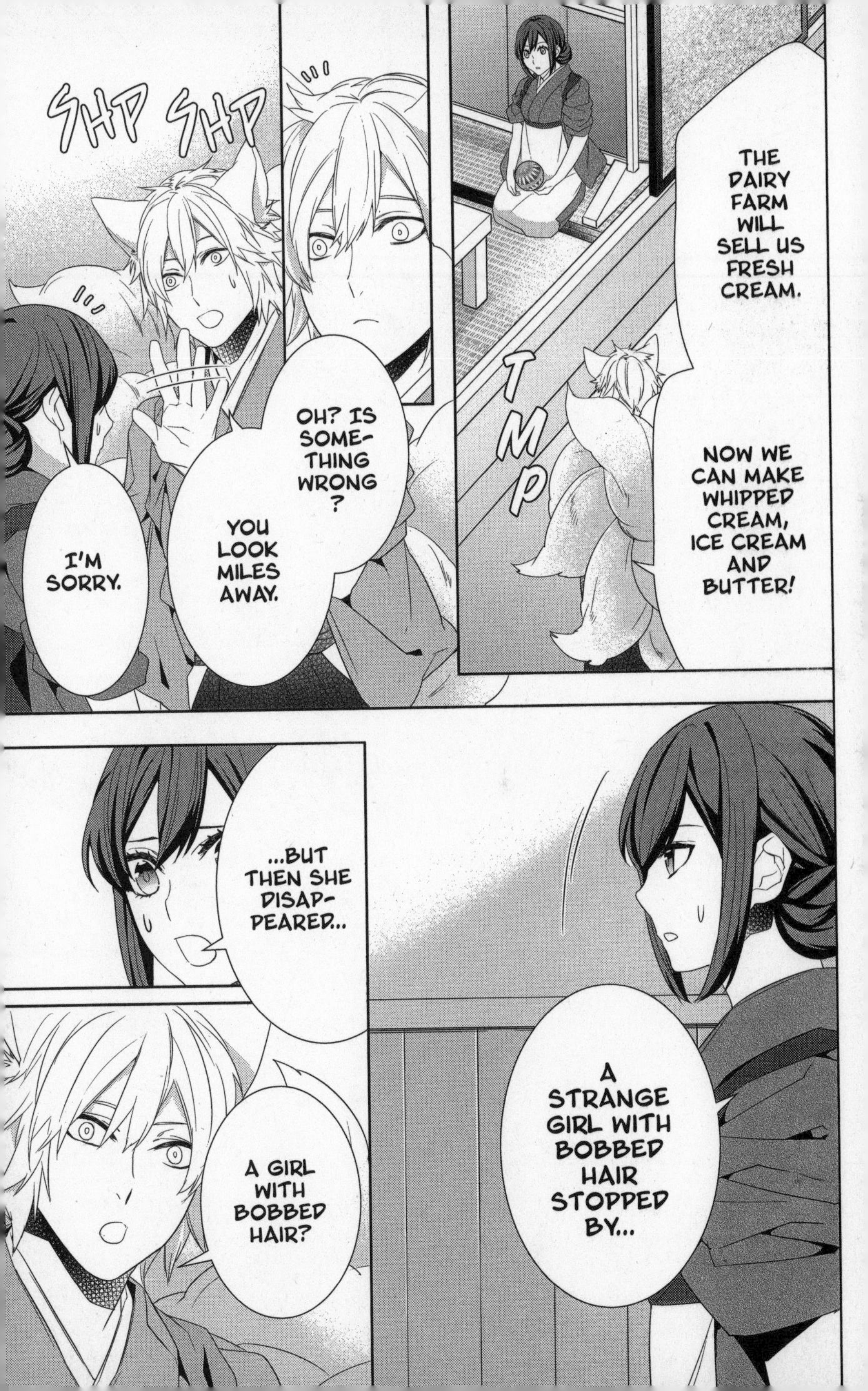
THE DAIRY FARM WILL SELL US FRESH CREAM.
TMP
NOW WE CAN MAKE WHIPPED CREAM, ICE CREAM AND BUTTER!
SHP SHP
OH? IS SOME-THING WRONG?
YOU LOOK MILES AWAY.
I'M SORRY.
A STRANGE GIRL WITH BOBBED HAIR STOPPED BY...
...BUT THEN SHE DISAP-PEARED...
A GIRL WITH BOBBED HAIR?

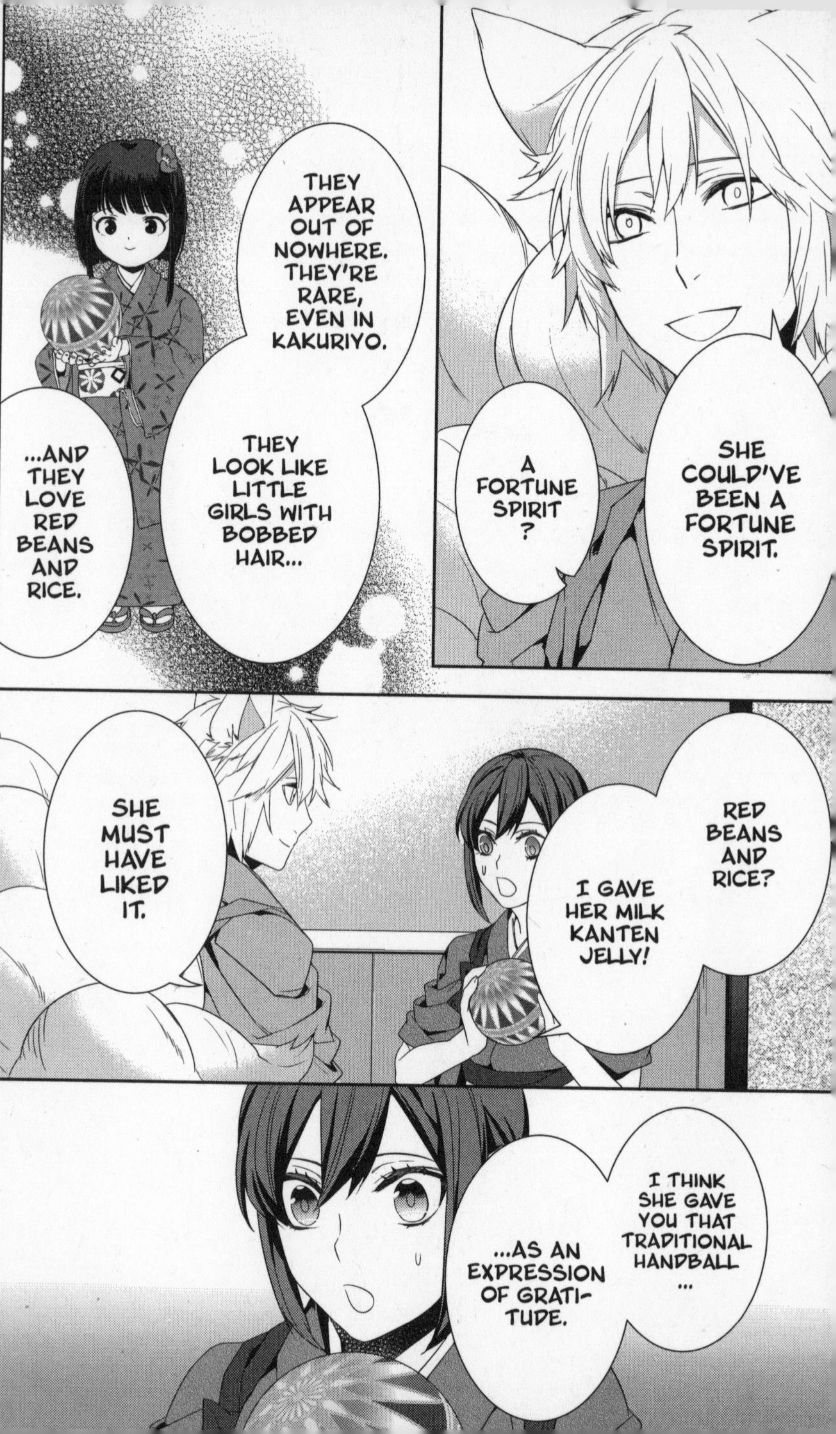
SHE COULD'VE BEEN A FORTUNE SPIRIT.
A FORTUNE SPIRIT?
THEY APPEAR OUT OF NOWHERE. THEY'RE RARE, EVEN IN KAKURIYO.
THEY LOOK LIKE LITTLE GIRLS WITH BOBBED HAIR...
...AND THEY LOVE RED BEANS AND RICE.
RED BEANS AND RICE?
I GAVE HER MILK KANTEN JELLY!
SHE MUST HAVE LIKED IT.
I THINK SHE GAVE YOU THAT TRADITIONAL HANDBALL...
...AS AN EXPRESSION OF GRATI-TUDE.

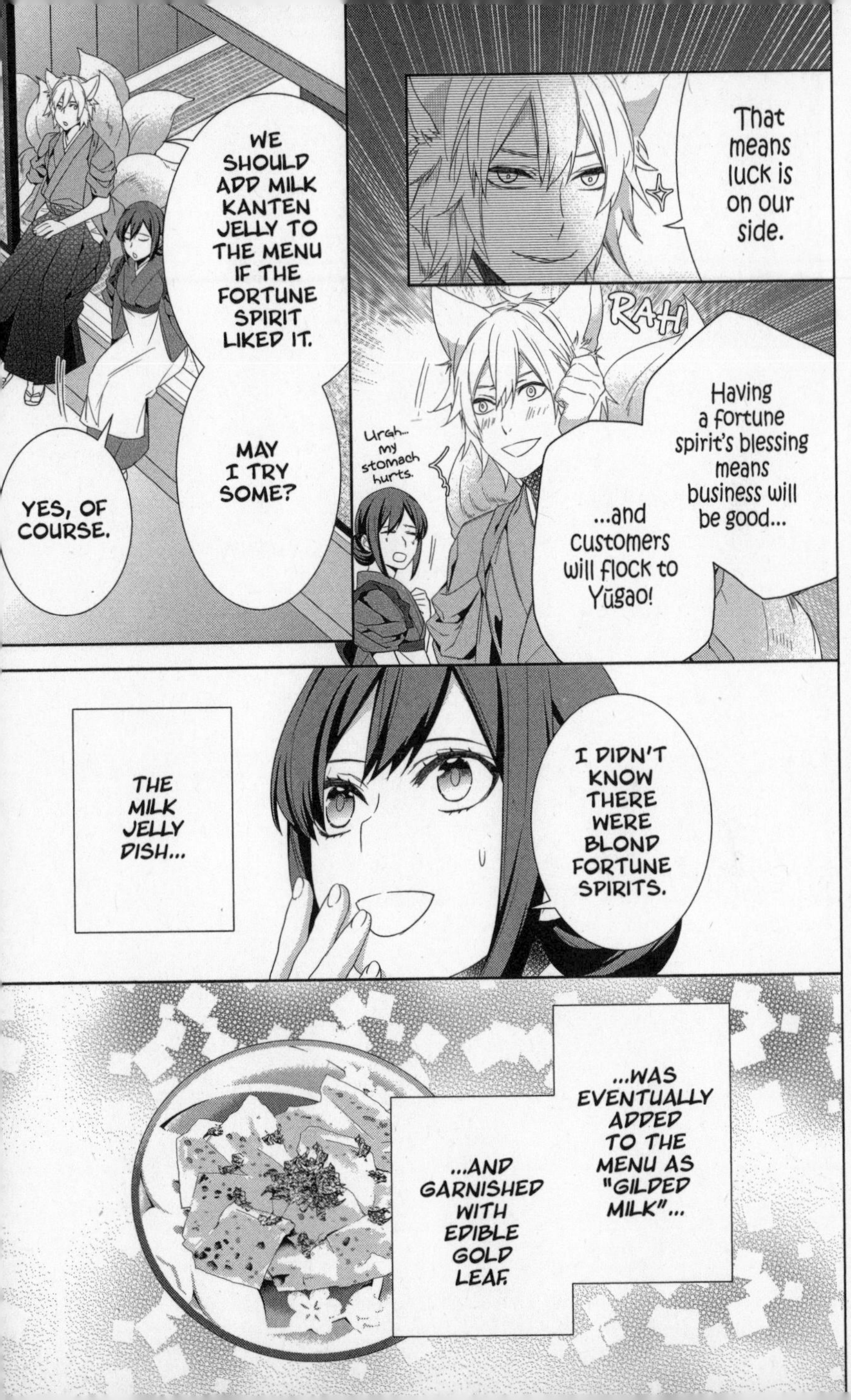
That means luck is on our side.
RAH
Having a fortune spirit's blessing means business will be good...
...and customers will flock to Yūgao!
Urgh... my stomach hurts.
WE SHOULD ADD MILK KANTEN JELLY TO THE MENU IF THE FORTUNE SPIRIT LIKED IT.
MAY I TRY SOME?
YES, OF COURSE.
I DIDN'T KNOW THERE WERE BLOND FORTUNE SPIRITS.
THE MILK JELLY DISH...
...WAS EVENTUALLY ADDED TO THE MENU AS "GILDED MILK"...
...AND GARNISHED WITH EDIBLE GOLD LEAF.

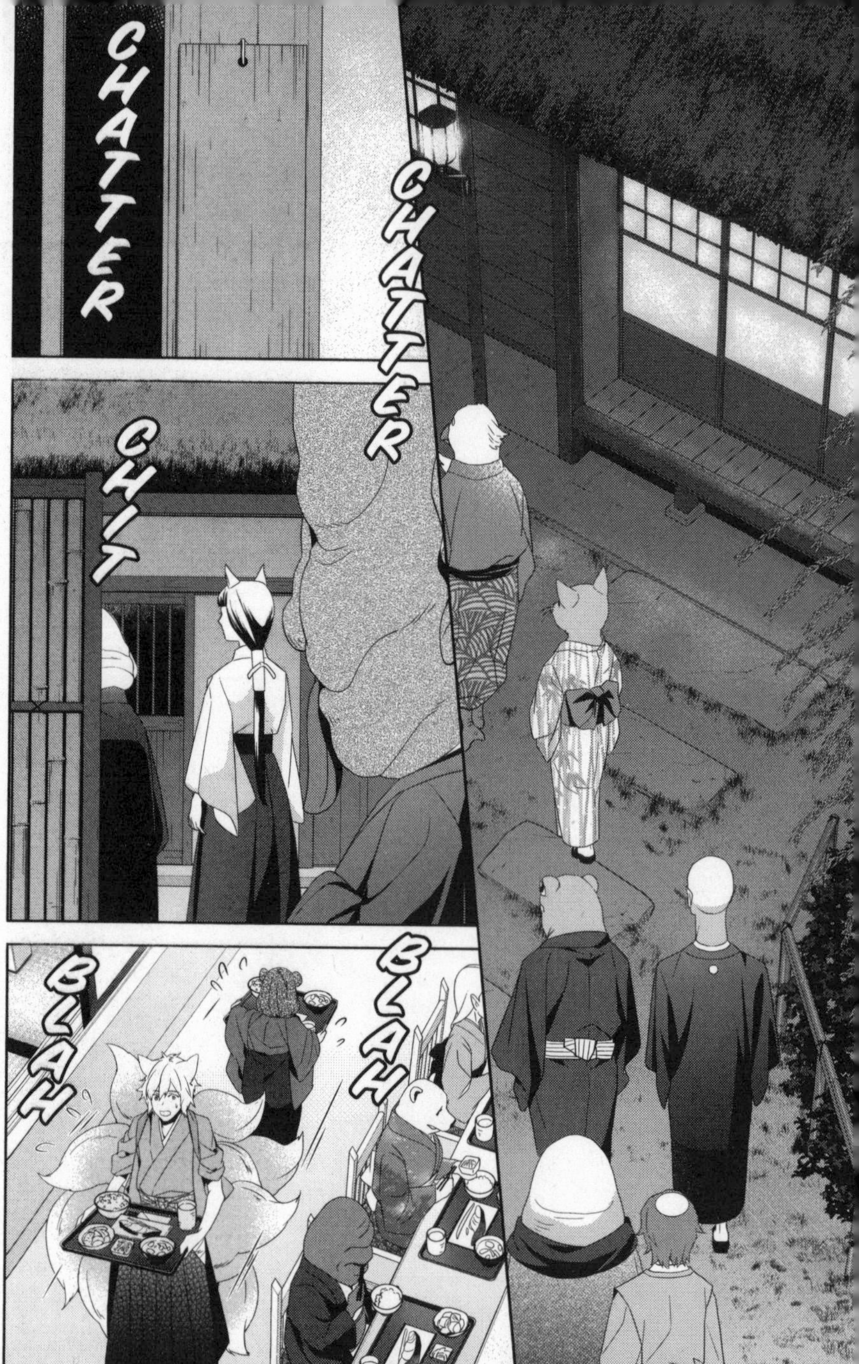
CHATTER
CHATTER
CHIT
BLAH
BLAH

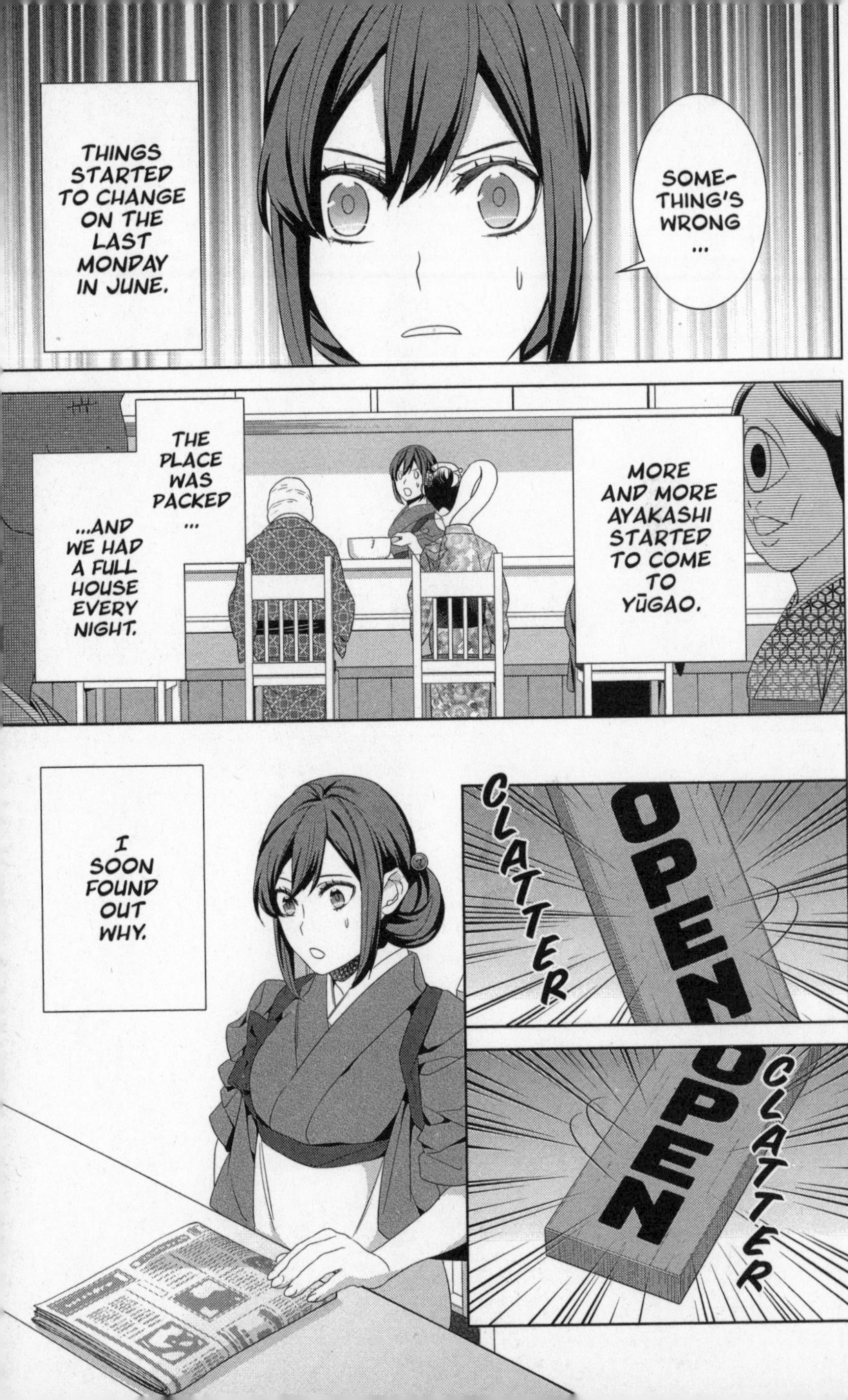
SOME-THING'S WRONG ...
THINGS STARTED TO CHANGE ON THE LAST MONDAY IN JUNE.
MORE AND MORE AYAKASHI STARTED TO COME TO YŪGAO.
THE PLACE WAS PACKED ...
...AND WE HAD A FULL HOUSE EVERY NIGHT.
OPEN
CLATTER
OPEN
CLATTER
I SOON FOUND OUT WHY.

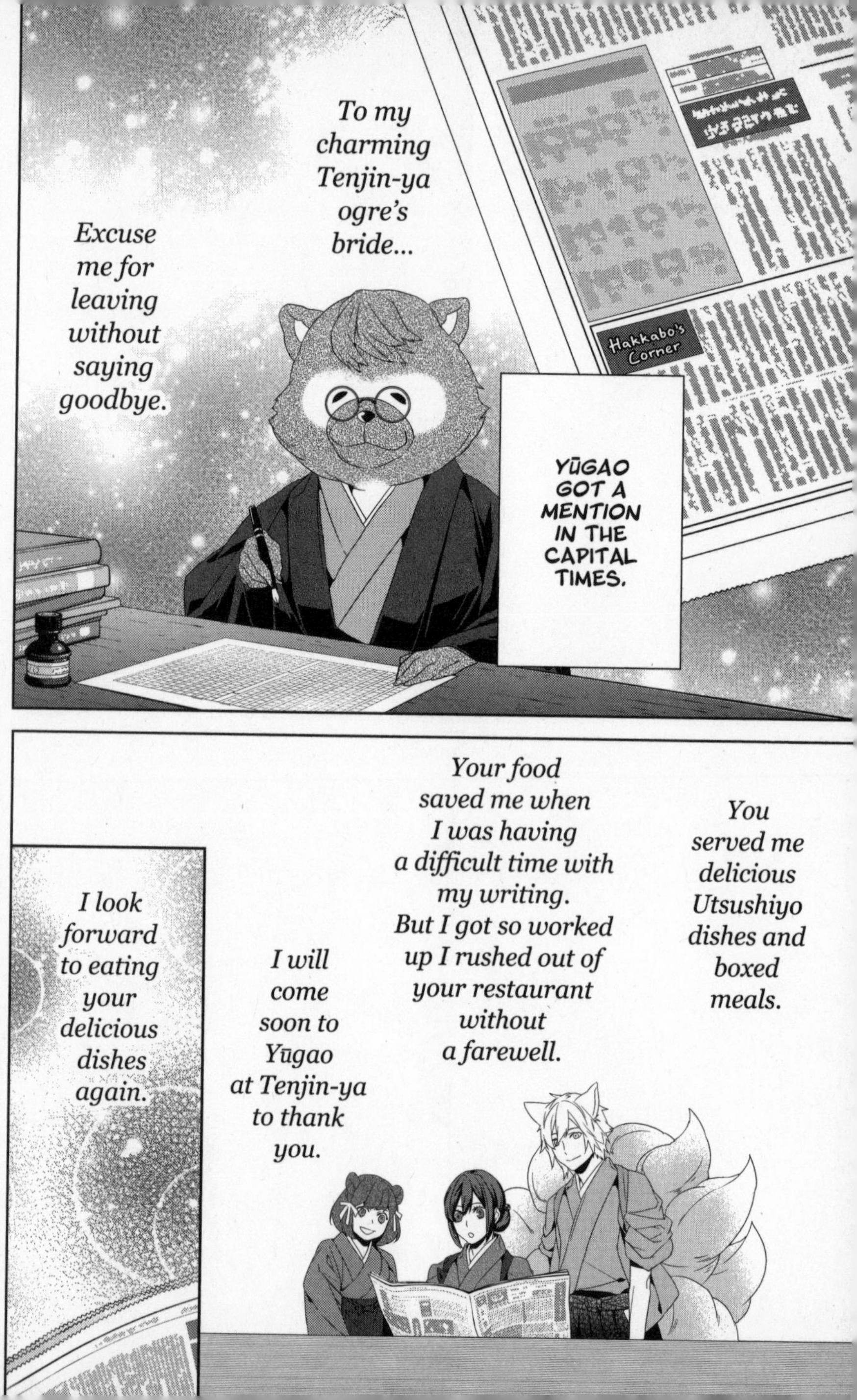

Hakkabo's Corner
YŪGAO GOT A MENTION IN THE CAPITAL TIMES.
To my charming Tenjin-ya ogre's bride...
Excuse me for leaving without saying goodbye.
You served me delicious Utsushiyo dishes and boxed meals.
Your food saved me when I was having a difficult time with my writing. But I got so worked up I rushed out of your restaurant without a farewell.
I will come soon to Yūgao at Tenjin-ya to thank you.
I look forward to eating your delicious dishes again.

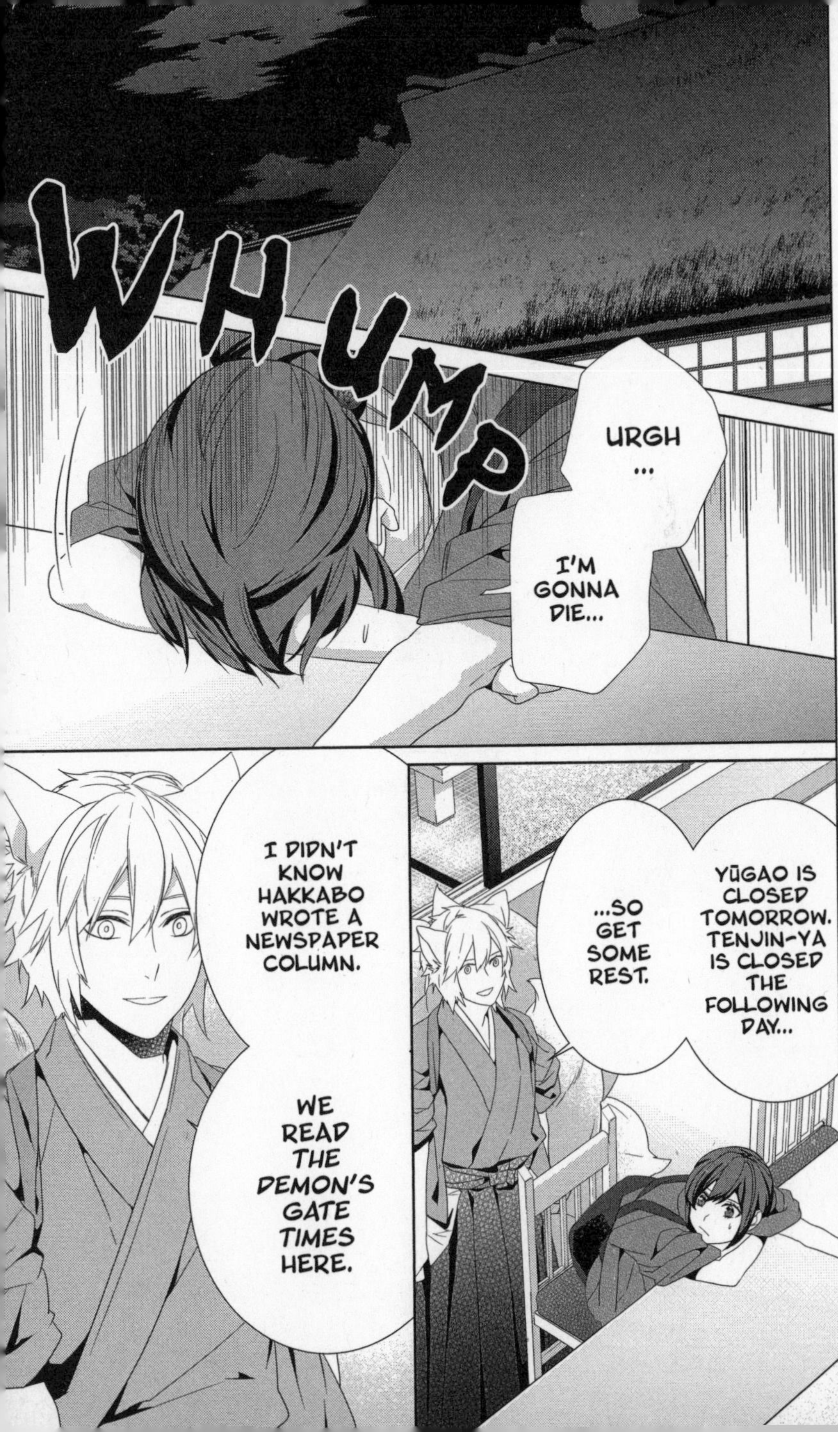
WHUMP
URGH ...
I'M GONNA DIE...
YŪGAO IS CLOSED TOMORROW. TENJIN-YA IS CLOSED THE FOLLOWING DAY...
...SO GET SOME REST.
I DIDN'T KNOW HAKKABO WROTE A NEWSPAPER COLUMN.
WE READ THE DEMON'S GATE TIMES HERE.

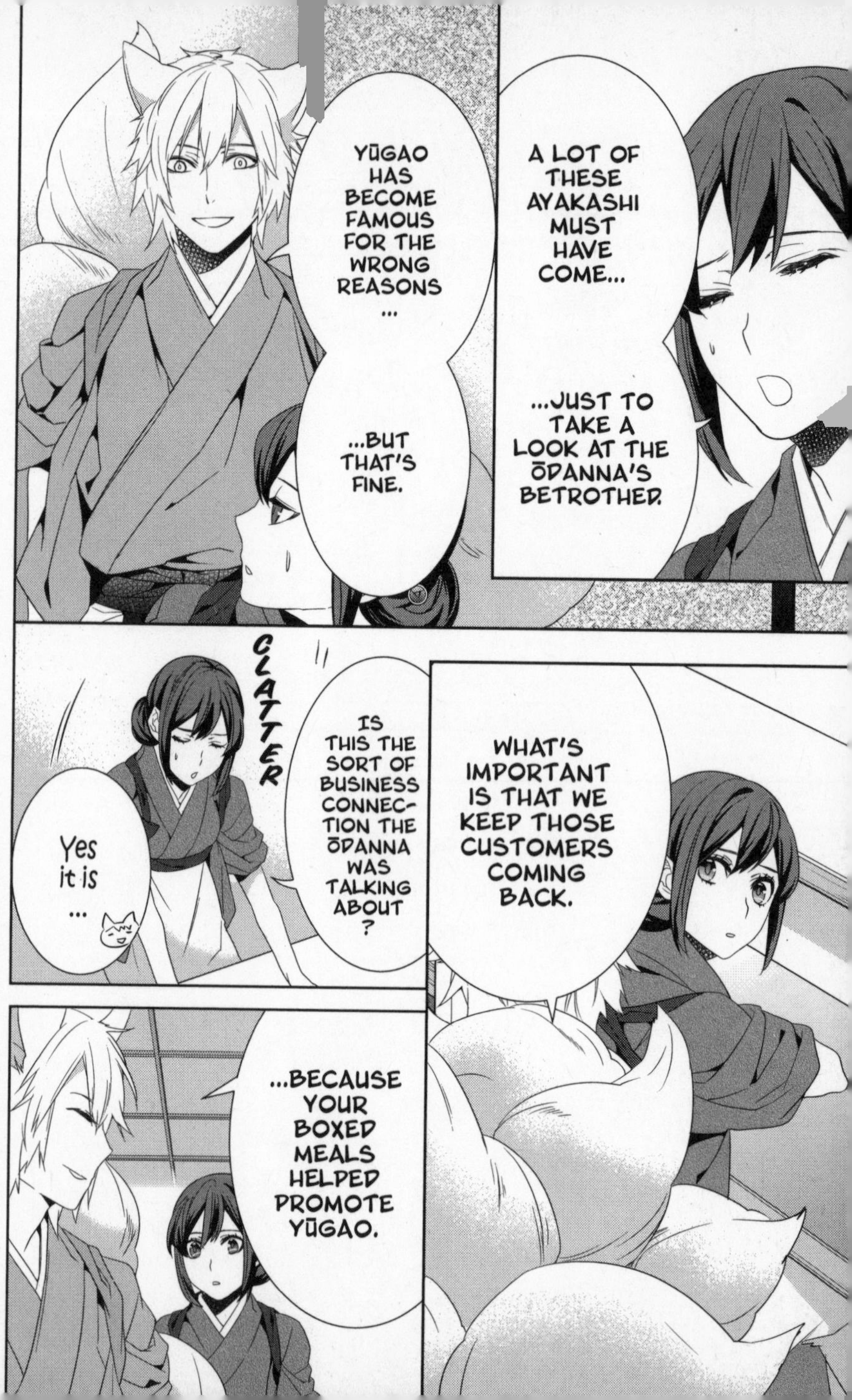
A LOT OF THESE AYAKASHI MUST HAVE COME...
...JUST TO TAKE A LOOK AT THE ŌDANNA'S BETROTHED.
YŪGAO HAS BECOME FAMOUS FOR THE WRONG REASONS...
...BUT THAT'S FINE.
WHAT'S IMPORTANT IS THAT WE KEEP THOSE CUSTOMERS COMING BACK.
CLATTER
IS THIS THE SORT OF BUSINESS CONNECTION THE ŌDANNA WAS TALKING ABOUT?
Yes it is...
...BECAUSE YOUR BOXED MEALS HELPED PROMOTE YŪGAO.

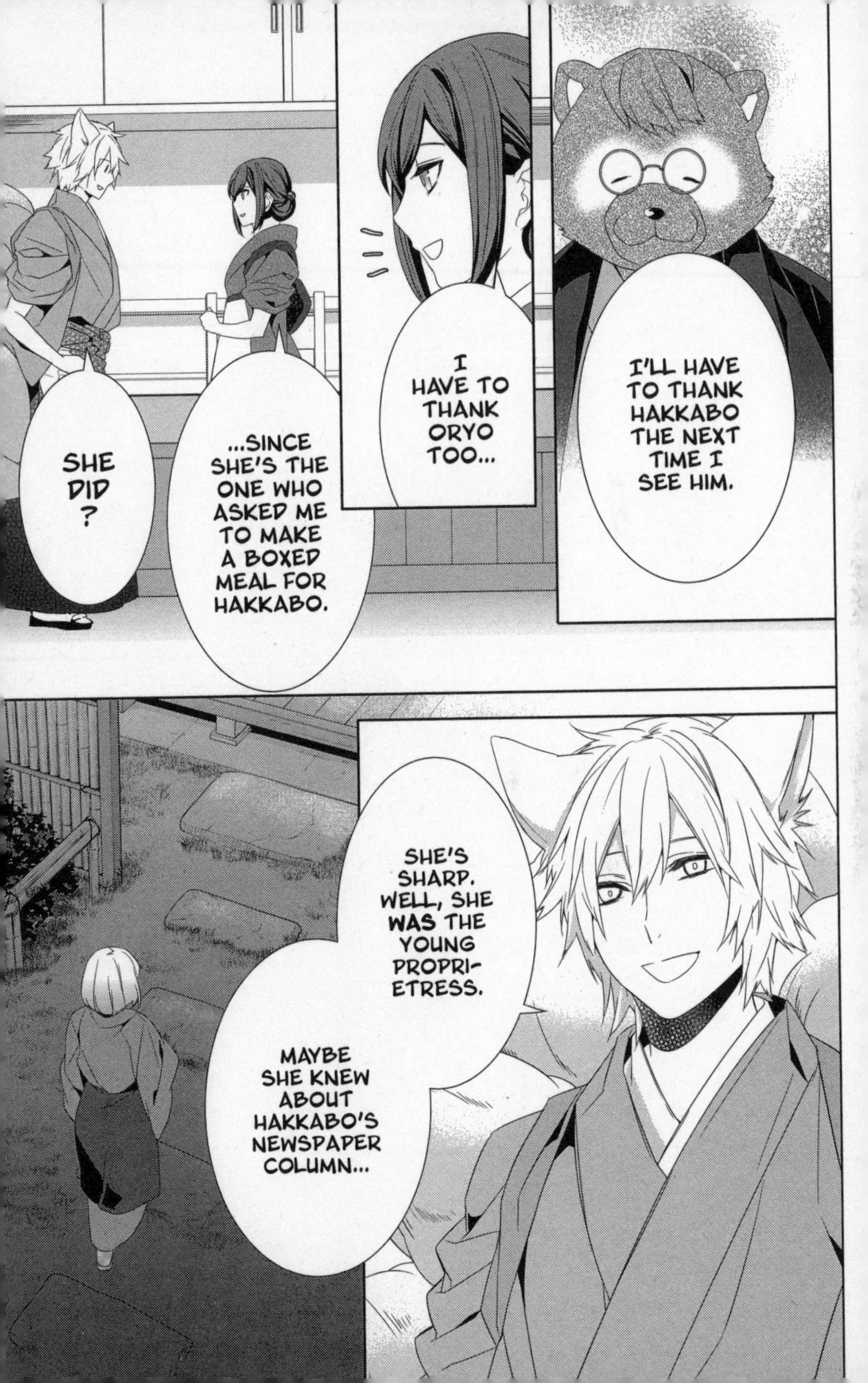
I'LL HAVE TO THANK HAKKABO THE NEXT TIME I SEE HIM.
I HAVE TO THANK ORYO TOO...
...SINCE SHE'S THE ONE WHO ASKED ME TO MAKE A BOXED MEAL FOR HAKKABO.
SHE DID?
SHE'S SHARP. WELL, SHE WAS THE YOUNG PROPRI-ETRESS.
MAYBE SHE KNEW ABOUT HAKKABO'S NEWSPAPER COLUMN...

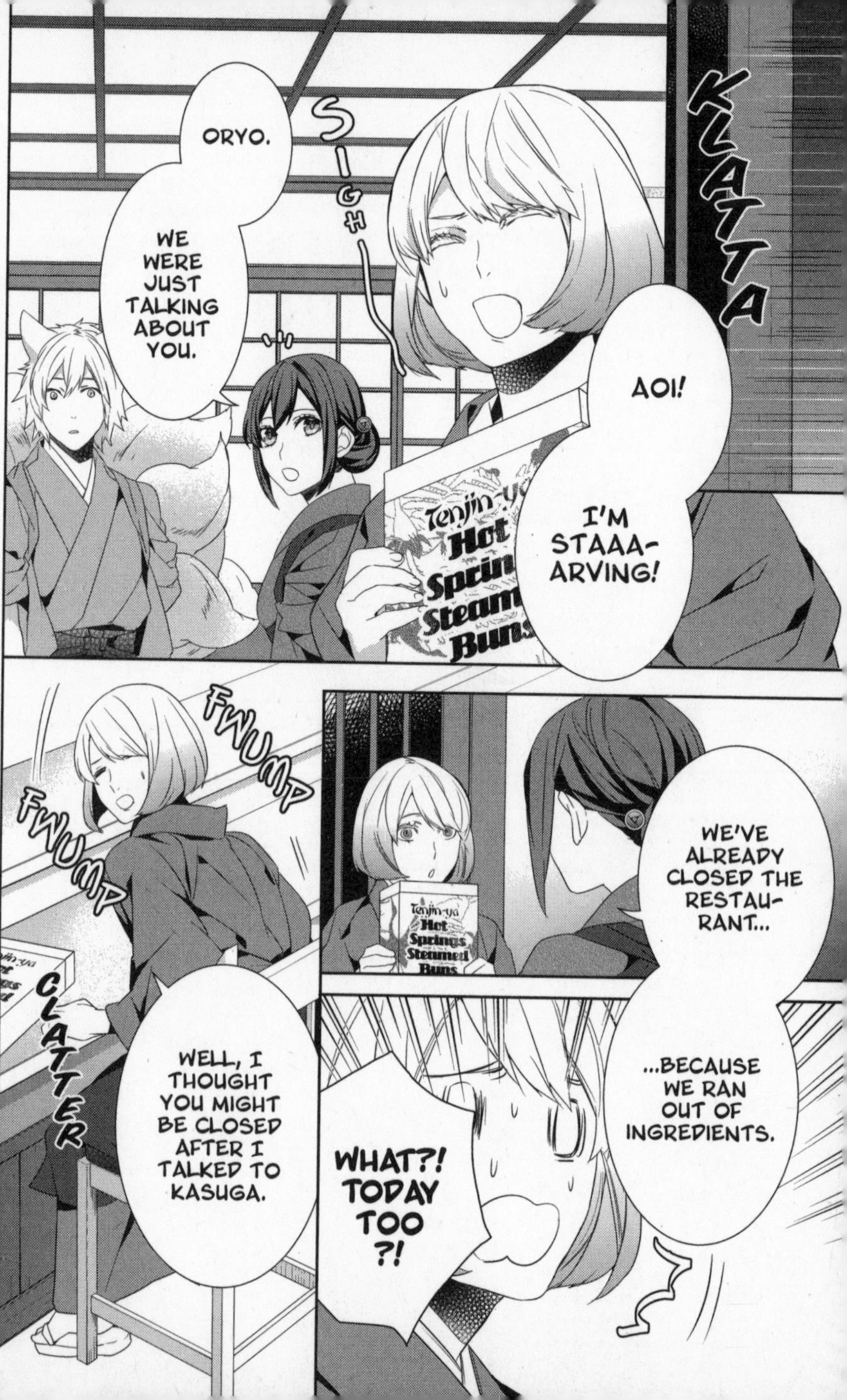
KLATTA
AOI!
I'M STAAAA-ARVING!
Tenjin-ya Hot Springs Steamed Buns
SIGH
ORYO.
WE WERE JUST TALKING ABOUT YOU.
WE'VE ALREADY CLOSED THE RESTAU-RANT...
Tenjin-ya Hot Springs Steamed Buns
...BECAUSE WE RAN OUT OF INGREDIENTS.
WHAT?! TODAY TOO?!
FWUMP
FWUMP
CLATTER
WELL, I THOUGHT YOU MIGHT BE CLOSED AFTER I TALKED TO KASUGA.

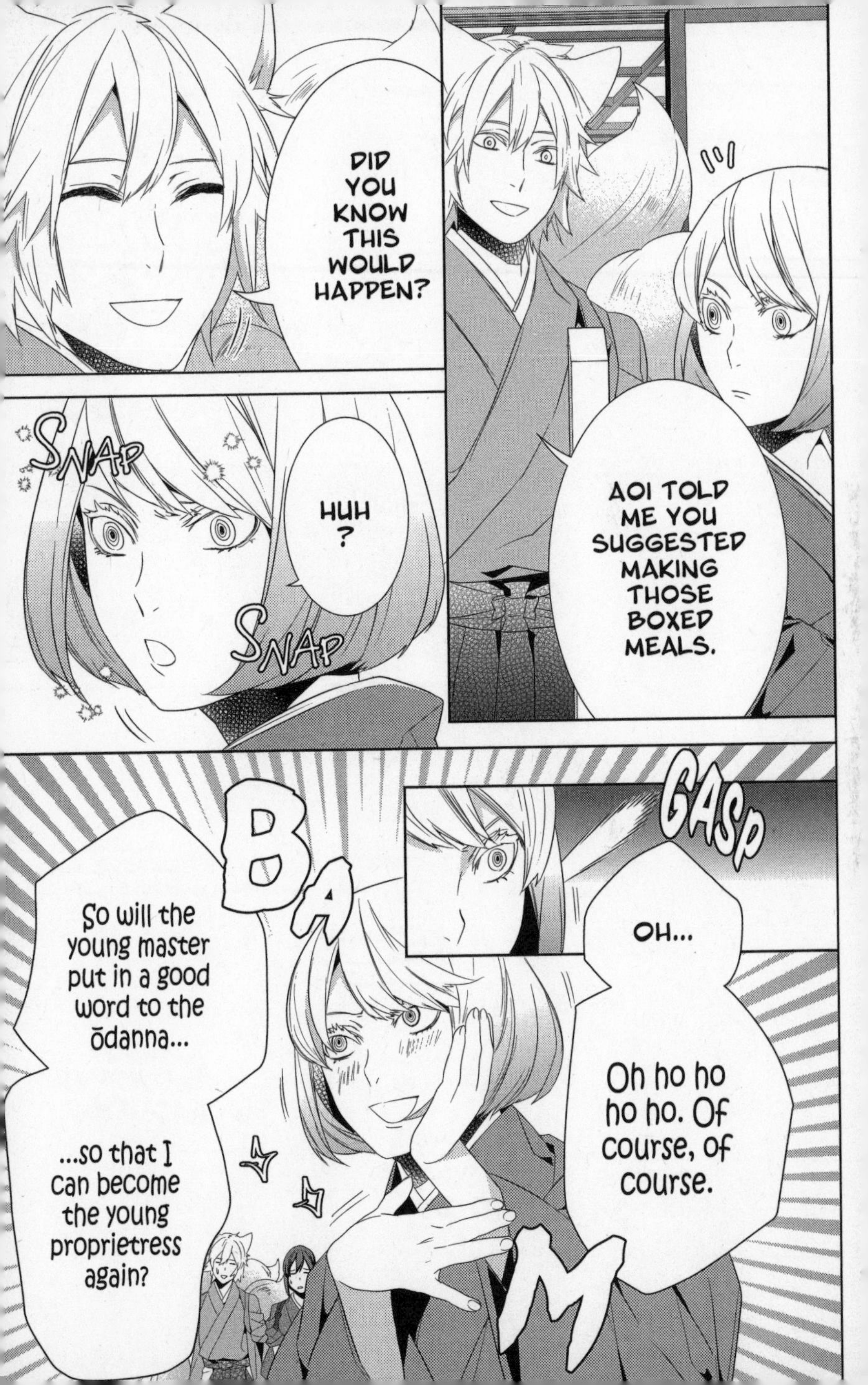
AOI TOLD ME YOU SUGGESTED MAKING THOSE BOXED MEALS.
DID YOU KNOW THIS WOULD HAPPEN?
SNAP
HUH?
SNAP
GASP
OH...
Oh ho ho ho ho. Of course, of course.
BAM
So will the young master put in a good word to the ōdanna...
...so that I can become the young proprietress again?

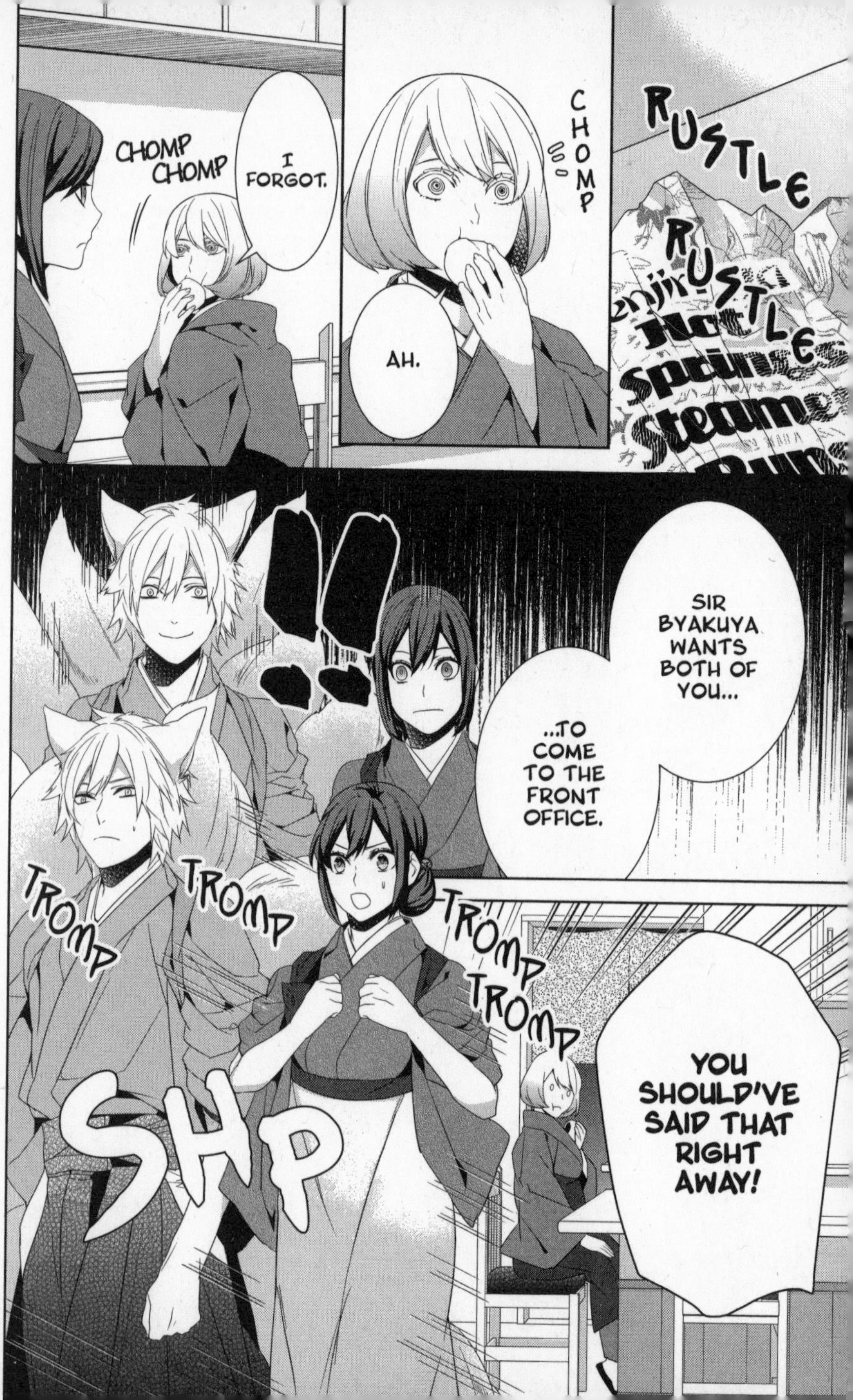
RUSTLE
RUSTLE
CHOMP CHOMP
AH.
CHOMP CHOMP
I FORGOT.
SIR BYAKUYA WANTS BOTH OF YOU...
...TO COME TO THE FRONT OFFICE.
!!
TROMP TROMP
TROMP TROMP
YOU SHOULD'VE SAID THAT RIGHT AWAY!
TROMP
TROMP
SHP

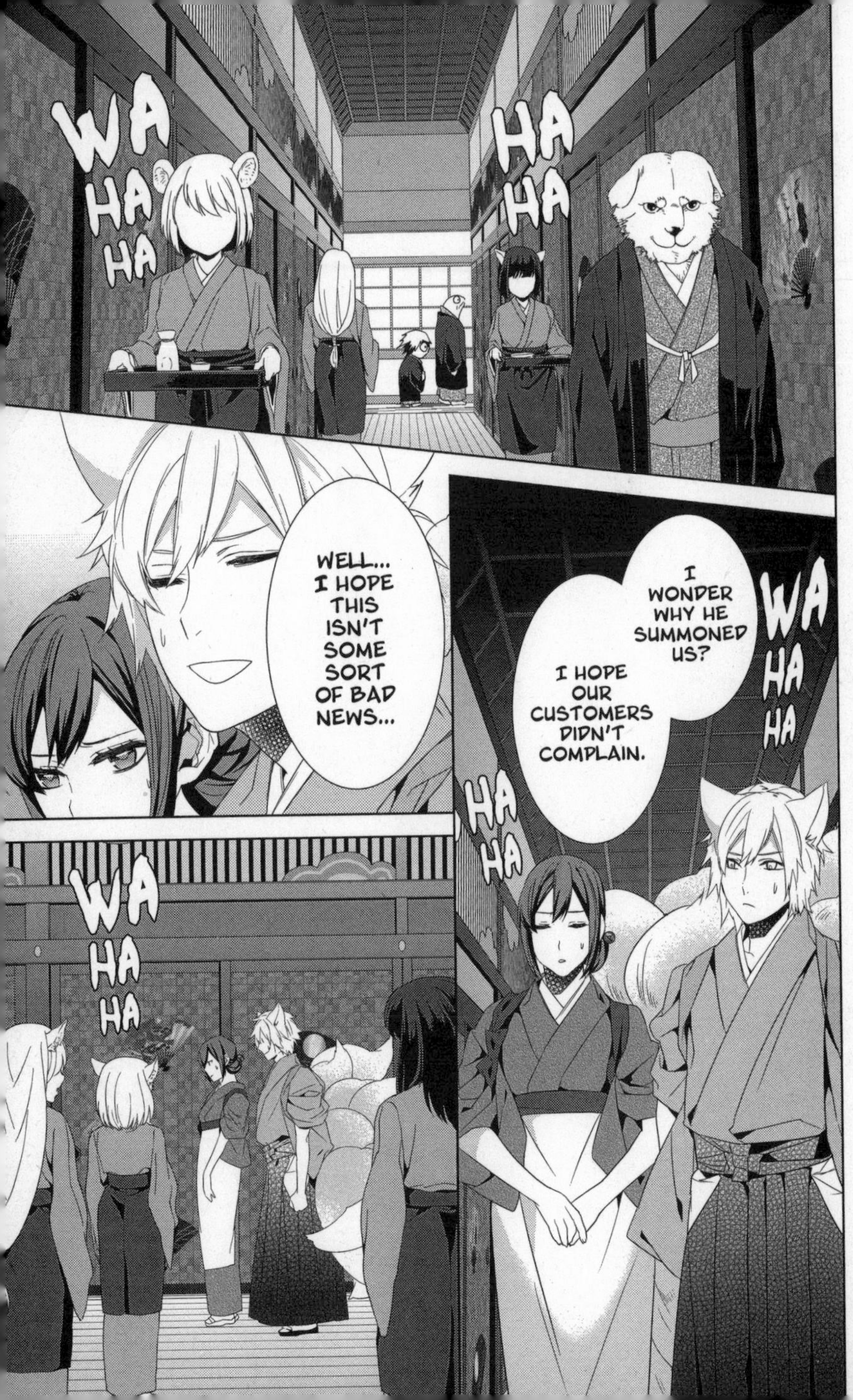
HA HA
WA HA HA
WA HA HA
I WONDER WHY HE SUMMONED US?
I HOPE OUR CUSTOMERS DIDN'T COMPLAIN.
HA HA
WELL... I HOPE THIS ISN'T SOME SORT OF BAD NEWS...
WA HA HA

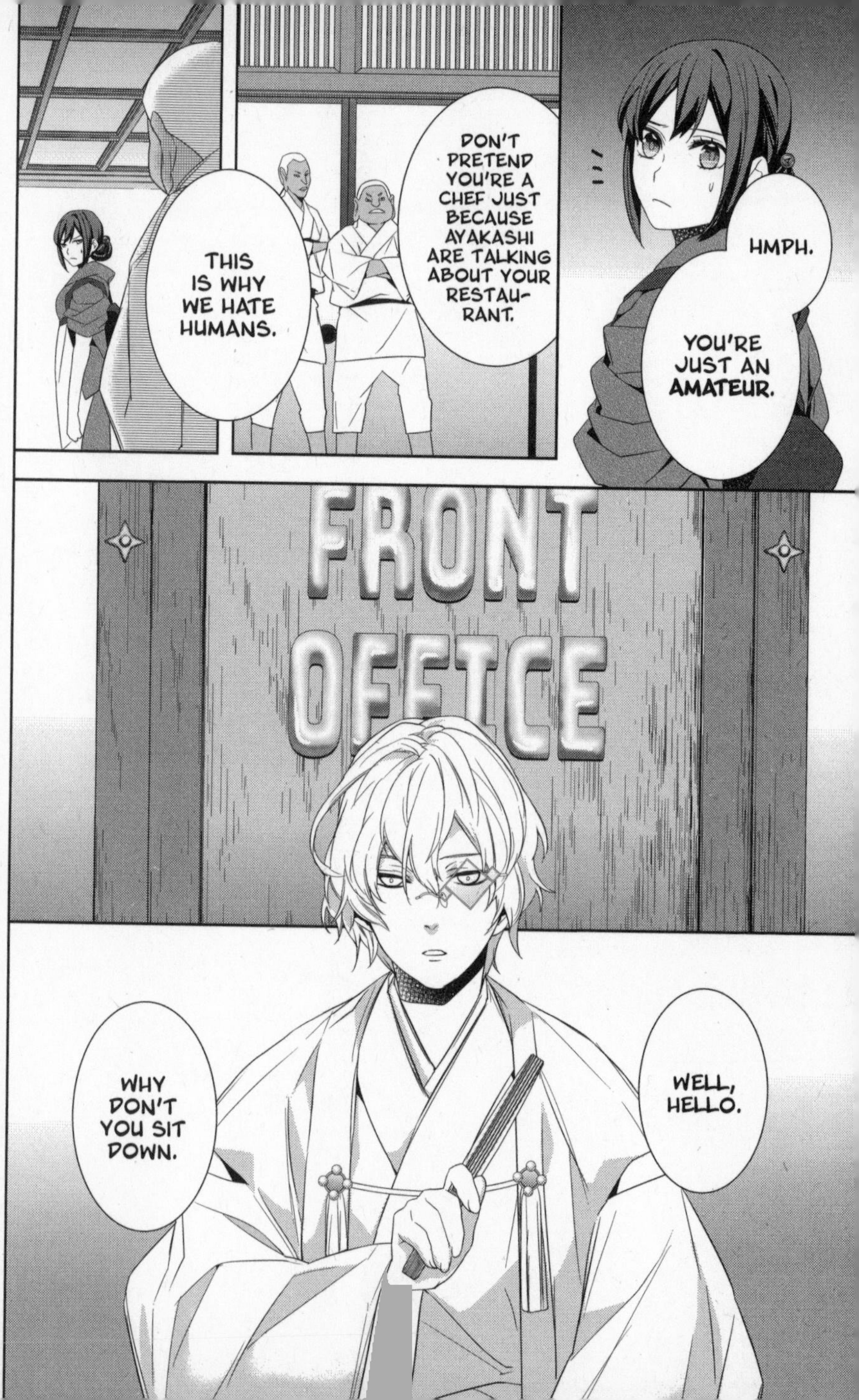
HMPH.
YOU'RE JUST AN AMATEUR.
DON'T PRETEND YOU'RE A CHEF JUST BECAUSE AYAKASHI ARE TALKING ABOUT YOUR RESTAU-RANT.
THIS IS WHY WE HATE HUMANS.
FRONT OFFICE
WELL, HELLO.
WHY DON'T YOU SIT DOWN.

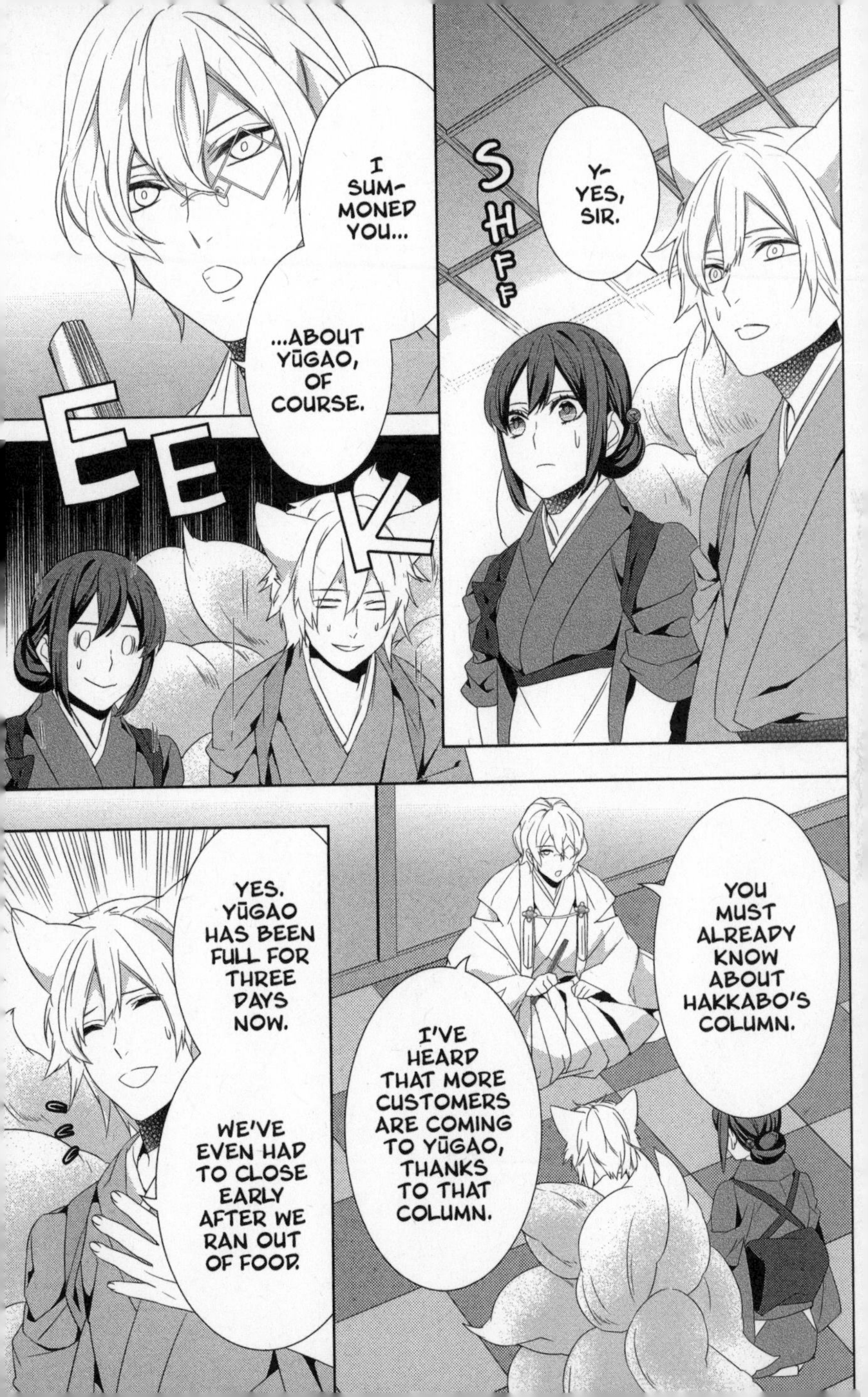
SHFF
Y-YES, SIR.
I SUMMONED YOU...
...ABOUT YŪGAO, OF COURSE.
EEK
YOU MUST ALREADY KNOW ABOUT HAKKABO'S COLUMN.
I'VE HEARD THAT MORE CUSTOMERS ARE COMING TO YŪGAO, THANKS TO THAT COLUMN.
YES. YŪGAO HAS BEEN FULL FOR THREE DAYS NOW.
WE'VE EVEN HAD TO CLOSE EARLY AFTER WE RAN OUT OF FOOD.

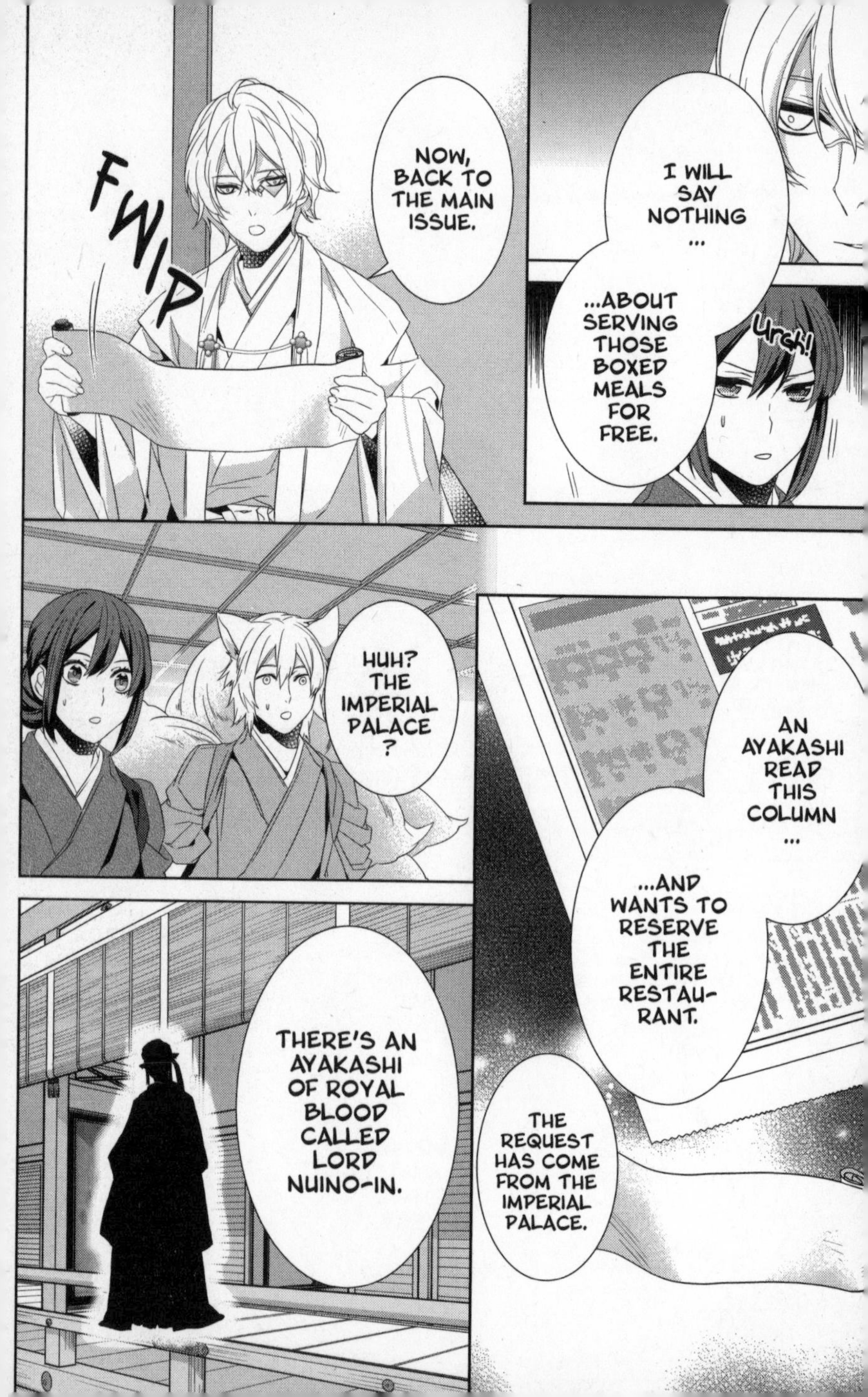
I WILL SAY NOTHING ...
...ABOUT SERVING THOSE BOXED MEALS FOR FREE.
Urgh!
NOW, BACK TO THE MAIN ISSUE.
FWIP
AN AYAKASHI READ THIS COLUMN ...
...AND WANTS TO RESERVE THE ENTIRE RESTAU-RANT.
THE REQUEST HAS COME FROM THE IMPERIAL PALACE.
HUH? THE IMPERIAL PALACE?
THERE'S AN AYAKASHI OF ROYAL BLOOD CALLED LORD NUINO-IN.

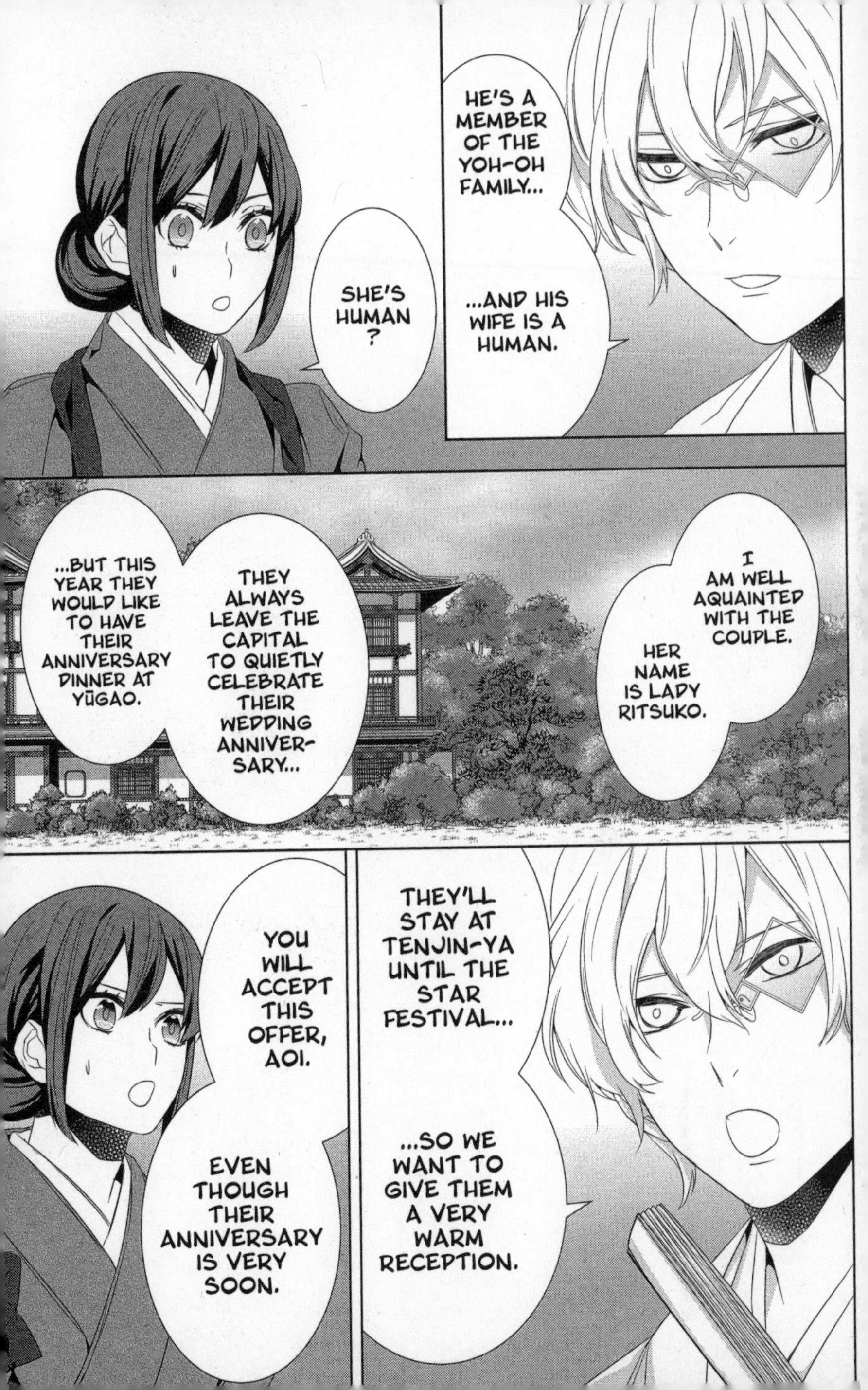
HE'S A MEMBER OF THE YOH-OH FAMILY...
...AND HIS WIFE IS A HUMAN.
SHE'S HUMAN?
I AM WELL AQUAINTED WITH THE COUPLE.
HER NAME IS LADY RITSUKO.
THEY ALWAYS LEAVE THE CAPITAL TO QUIETLY CELEBRATE THEIR WEDDING ANNIVER-SARY...
...BUT THIS YEAR THEY WOULD LIKE TO HAVE THEIR ANNIVERSARY DINNER AT YŪGAO.
THEY'LL STAY AT TENJIN-YA UNTIL THE STAR FESTIVAL...
...SO WE WANT TO GIVE THEM A VERY WARM RECEPTION.
YOU WILL ACCEPT THIS OFFER, AOI.
EVEN THOUGH THEIR ANNIVERSARY IS VERY SOON.

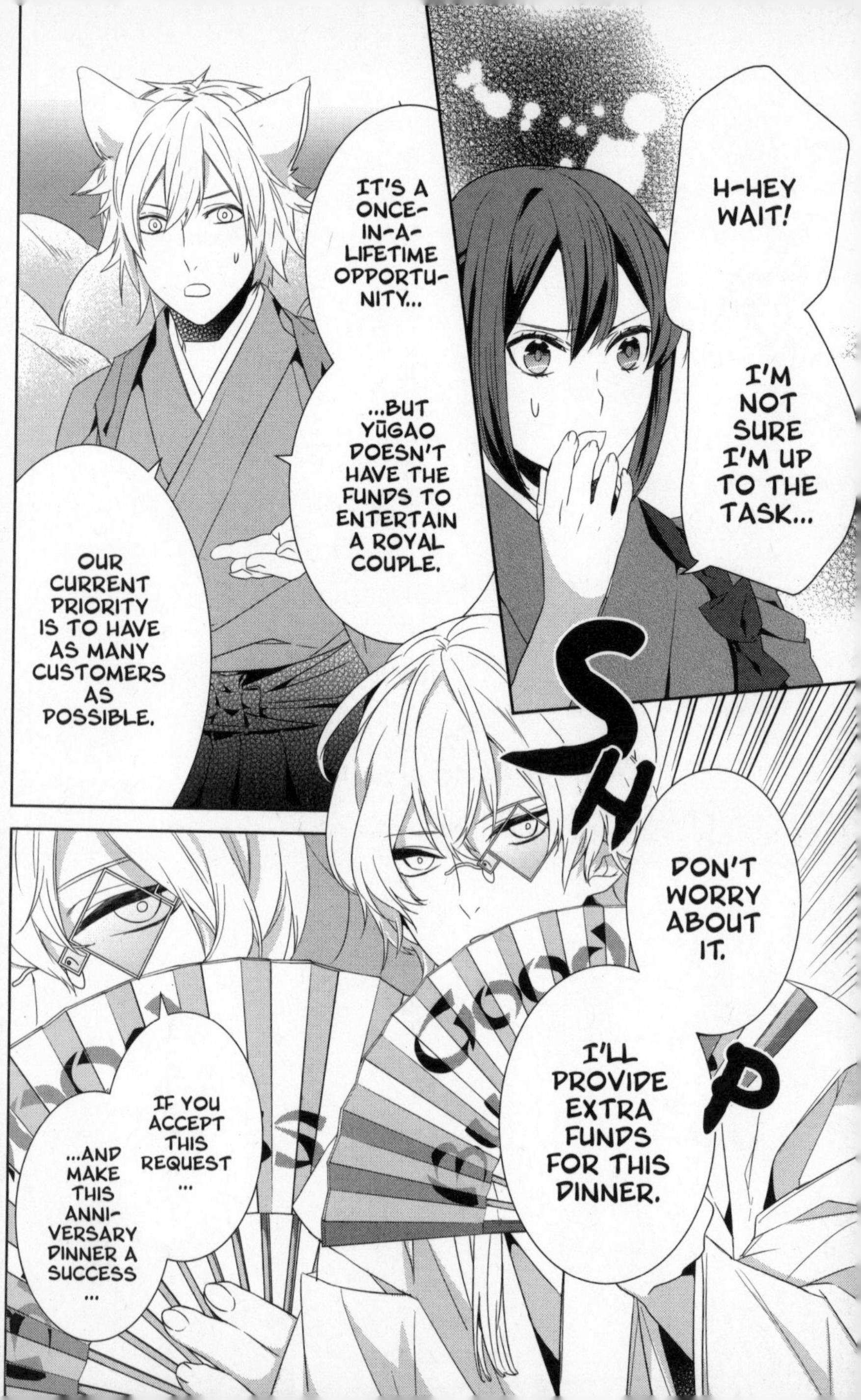
H-HEY WAIT!
I'M NOT SURE I'M UP TO THE TASK...
IT'S A ONCE-IN-A-LIFETIME OPPORTUNITY...
...BUT YŪGAO DOESN'T HAVE THE FUNDS TO ENTERTAIN A ROYAL COUPLE.
OUR CURRENT PRIORITY IS TO HAVE AS MANY CUSTOMERS AS POSSIBLE.
SHP
DON'T WORRY ABOUT IT.
I'LL PROVIDE EXTRA FUNDS FOR THIS DINNER.
IF YOU ACCEPT THIS REQUEST...
...AND MAKE THIS ANNIVERSARY DINNER A SUCCESS...

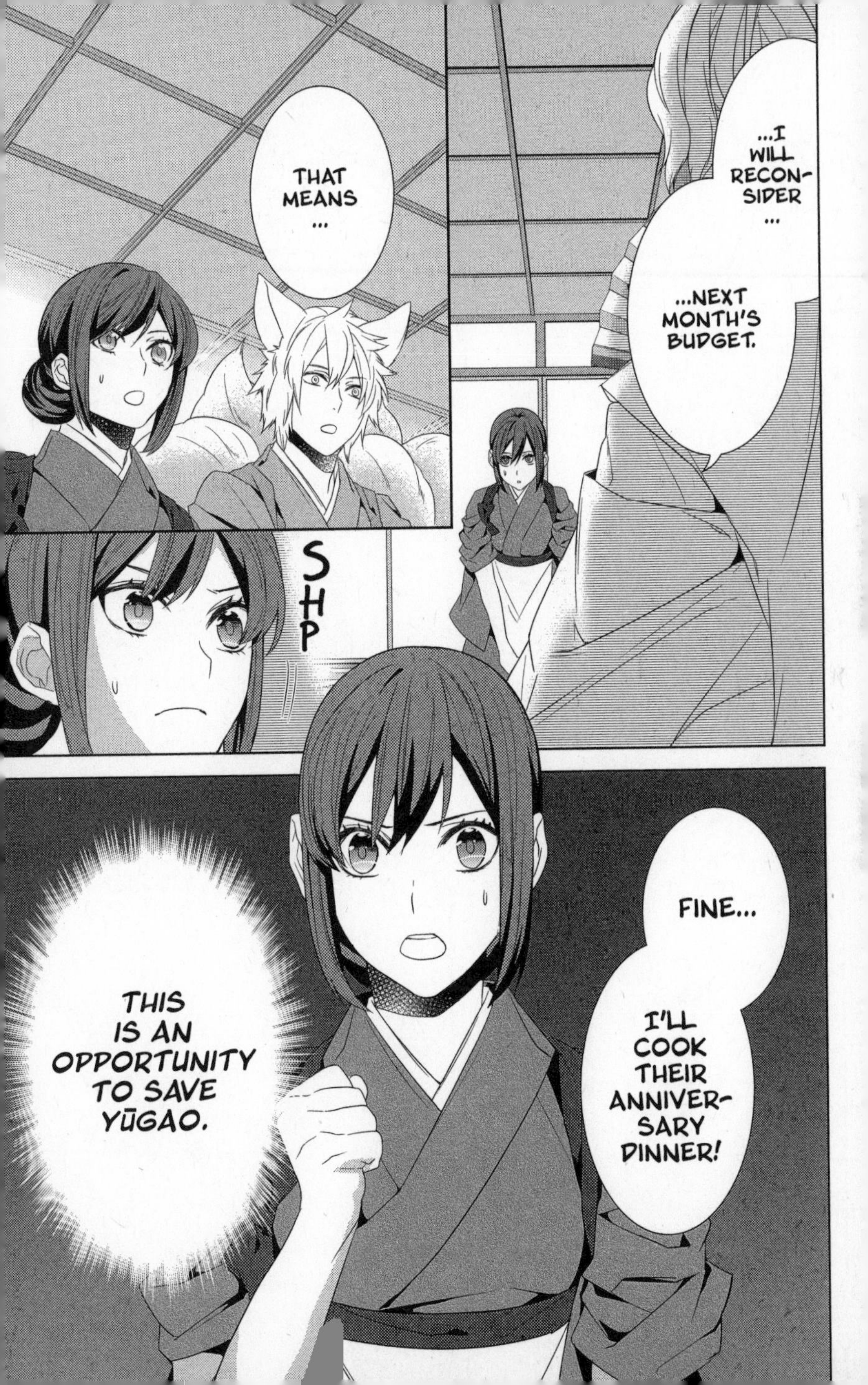
...I WILL RECONSIDER...
...NEXT MONTH'S BUDGET.
THAT MEANS...
SHP
FINE...
I'LL COOK THEIR ANNIVERSARY DINNER!
THIS IS AN OPPORTUNITY TO SAVE YŪGAO.

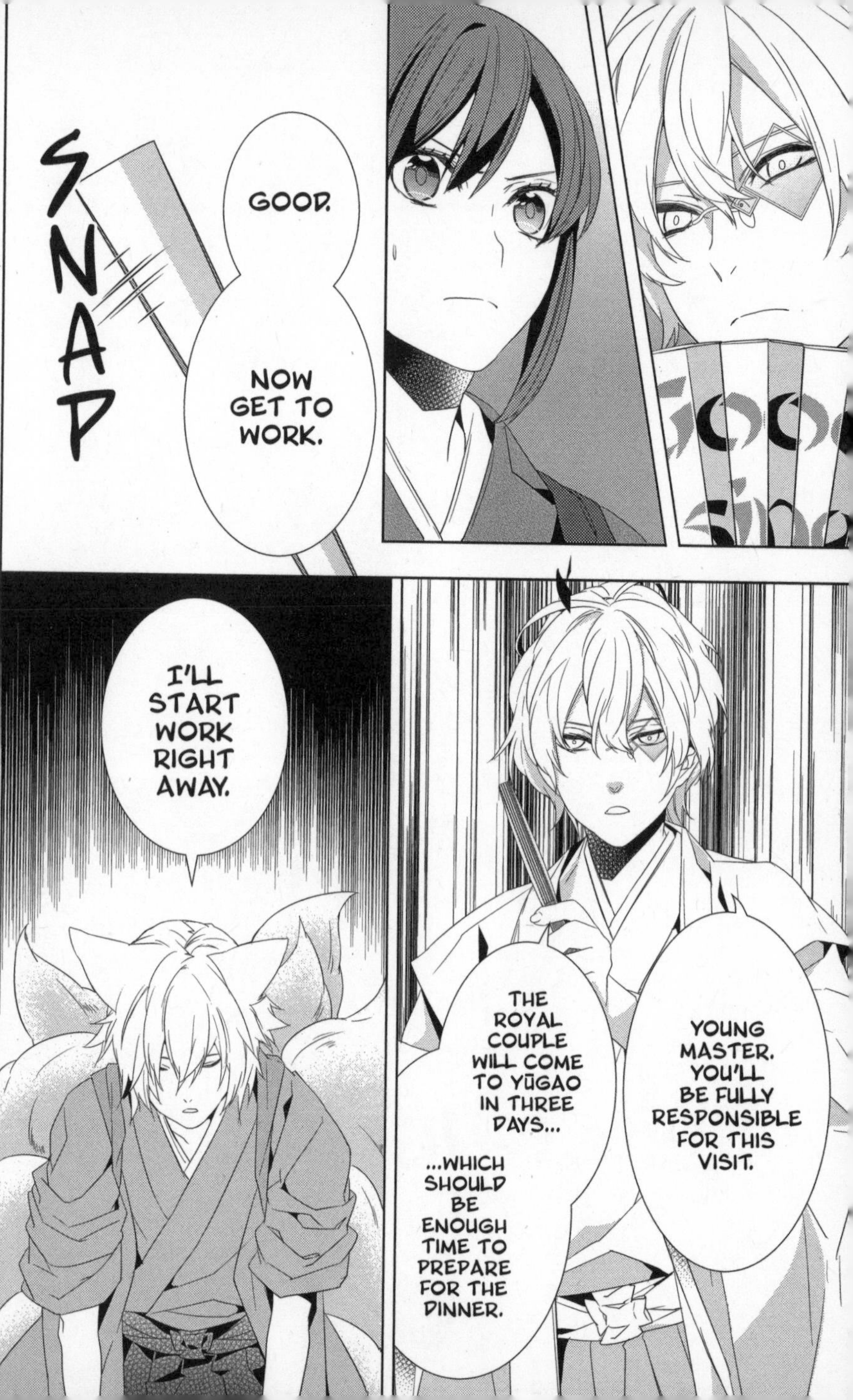
GOOD.
NOW GET TO WORK.
SNAP
YOUNG MASTER. YOU'LL BE FULLY RESPONSIBLE FOR THIS VISIT.
THE ROYAL COUPLE WILL COME TO YŪGAO IN THREE DAYS...
...WHICH SHOULD BE ENOUGH TIME TO PREPARE FOR THE DINNER.
I'LL START WORK RIGHT AWAY.

Kakuriyo
Bed & Breakfast
for Spirits

Kakuriyo
Bed & Breakfast for Spirits

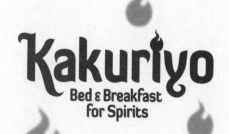

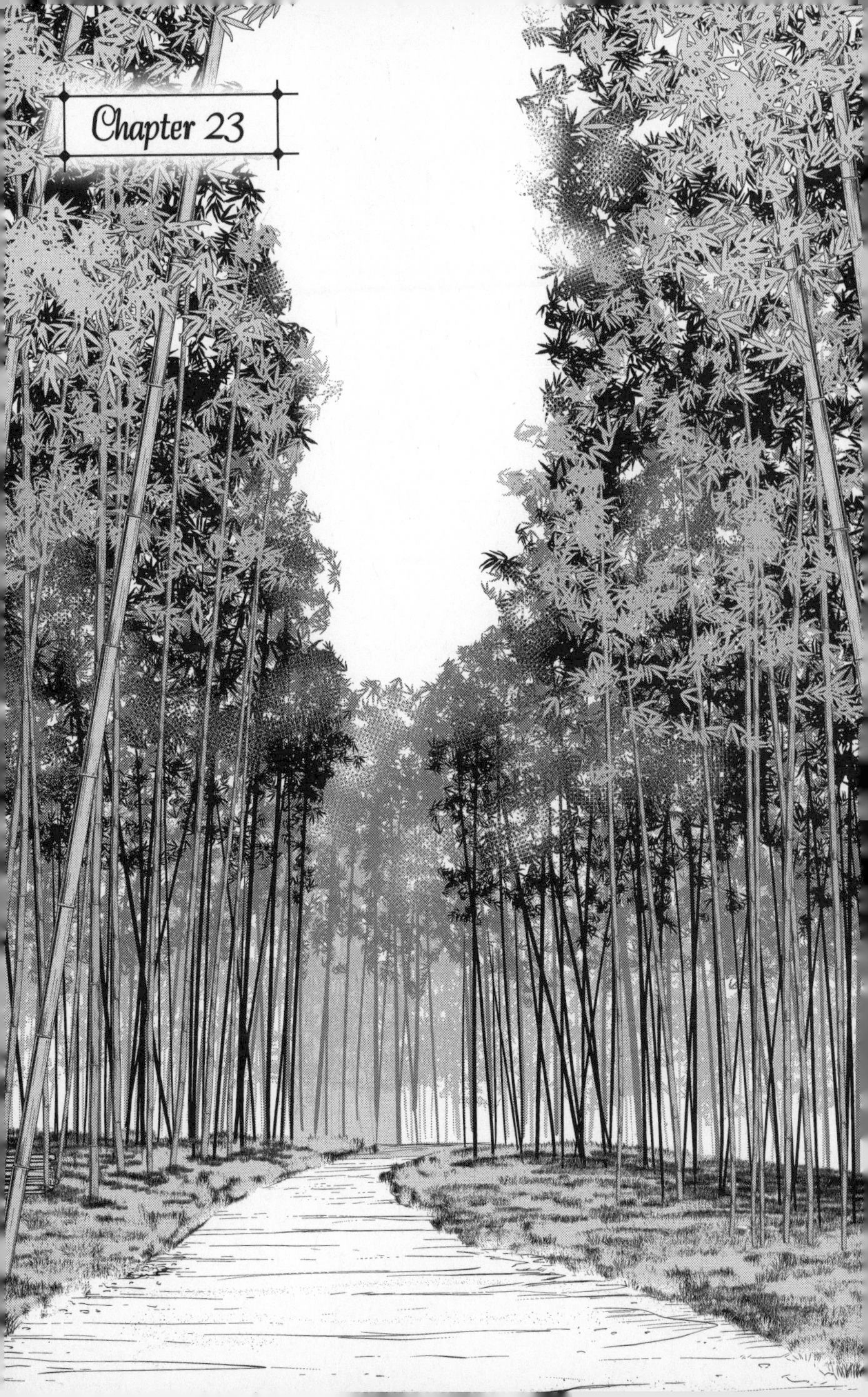
Chapter 23

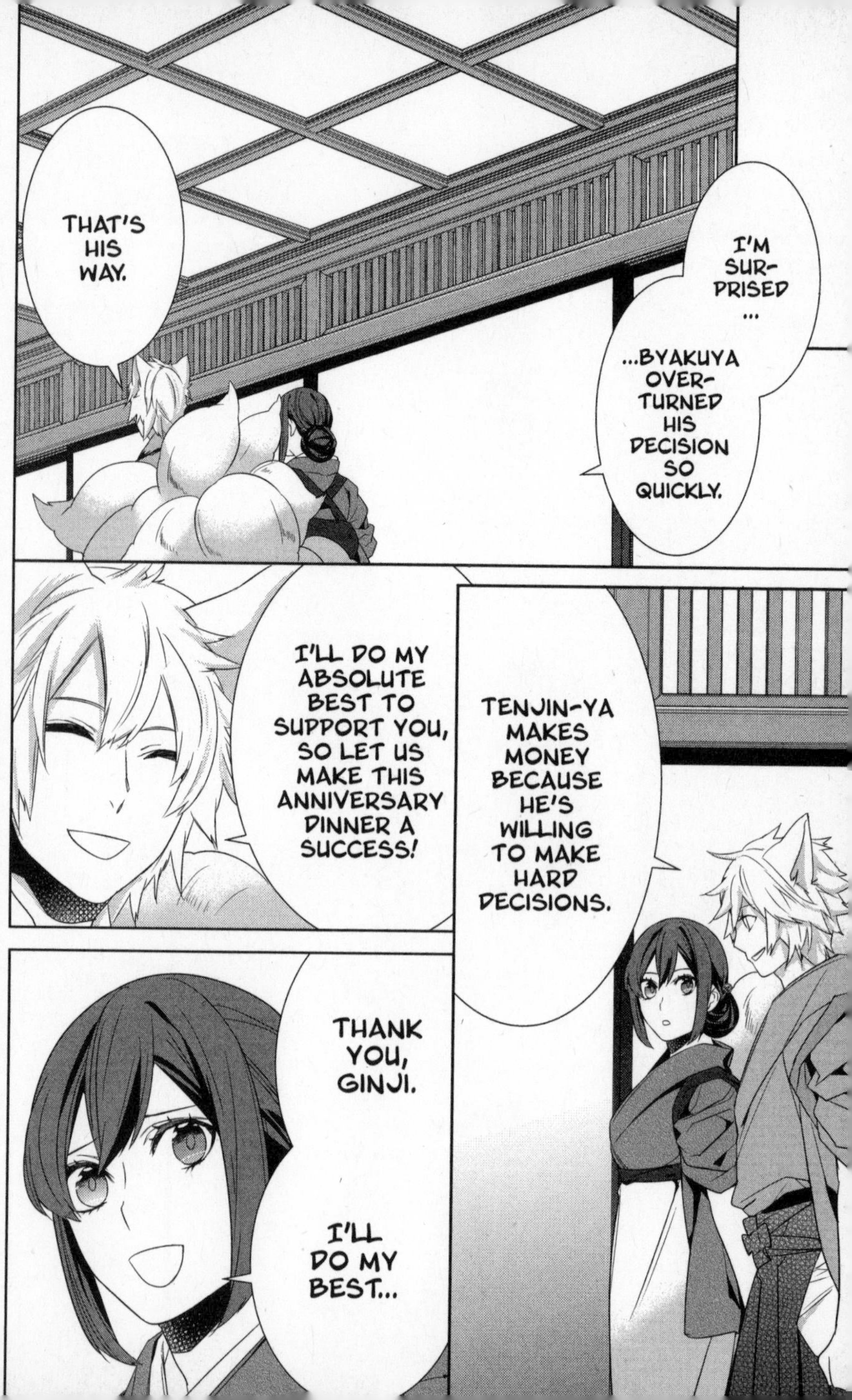
I'M SUR-PRISED...
...BYAKUYA OVER-TURNED HIS DECISION SO QUICKLY.
THAT'S HIS WAY.
TENJIN-YA MAKES MONEY BECAUSE HE'S WILLING TO MAKE HARD DECISIONS.
I'LL DO MY ABSOLUTE BEST TO SUPPORT YOU, SO LET US MAKE THIS ANNIVERSARY DINNER A SUCCESS!
THANK YOU, GINJI.
I'LL DO MY BEST...

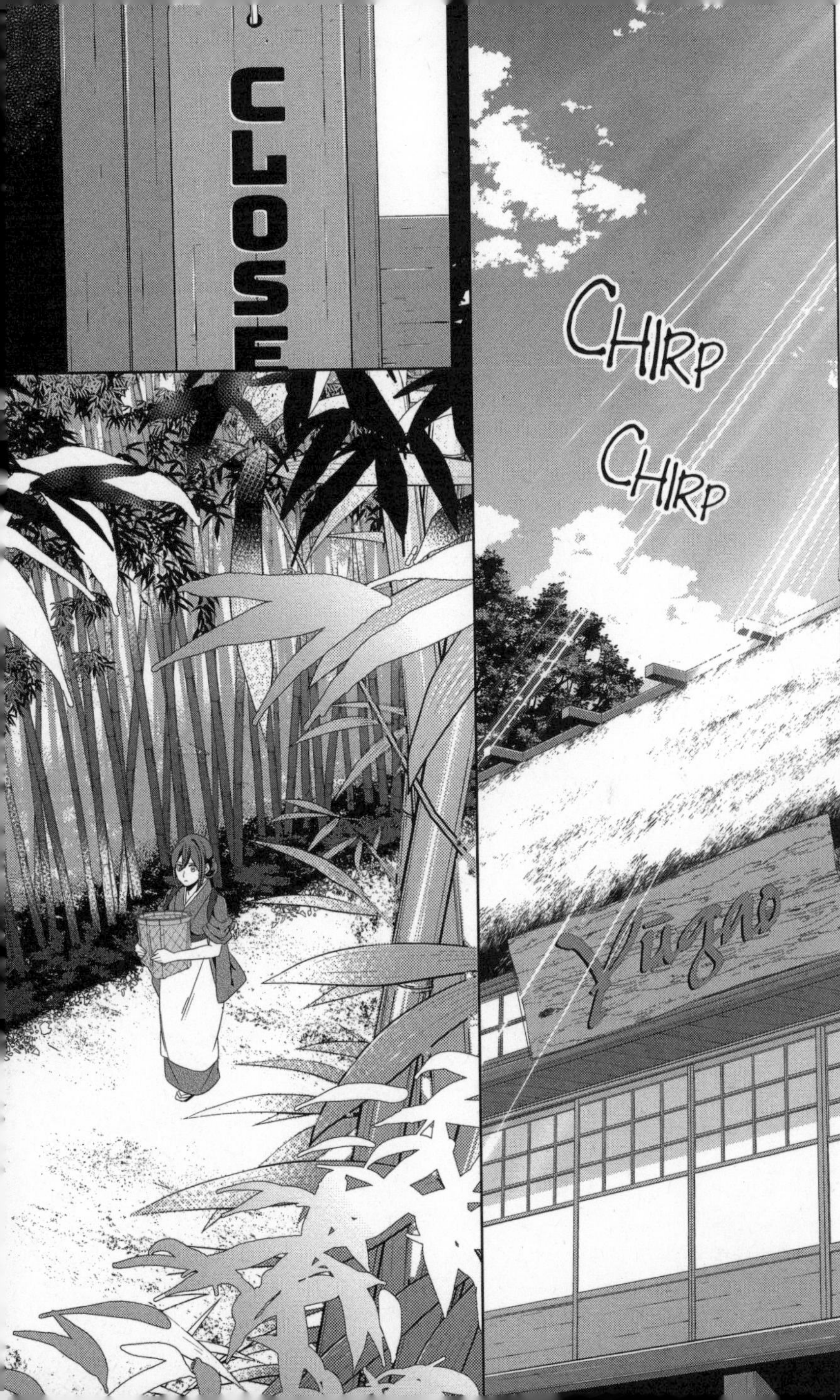
CHIRP
CHIRP
Yugao
CLOSE

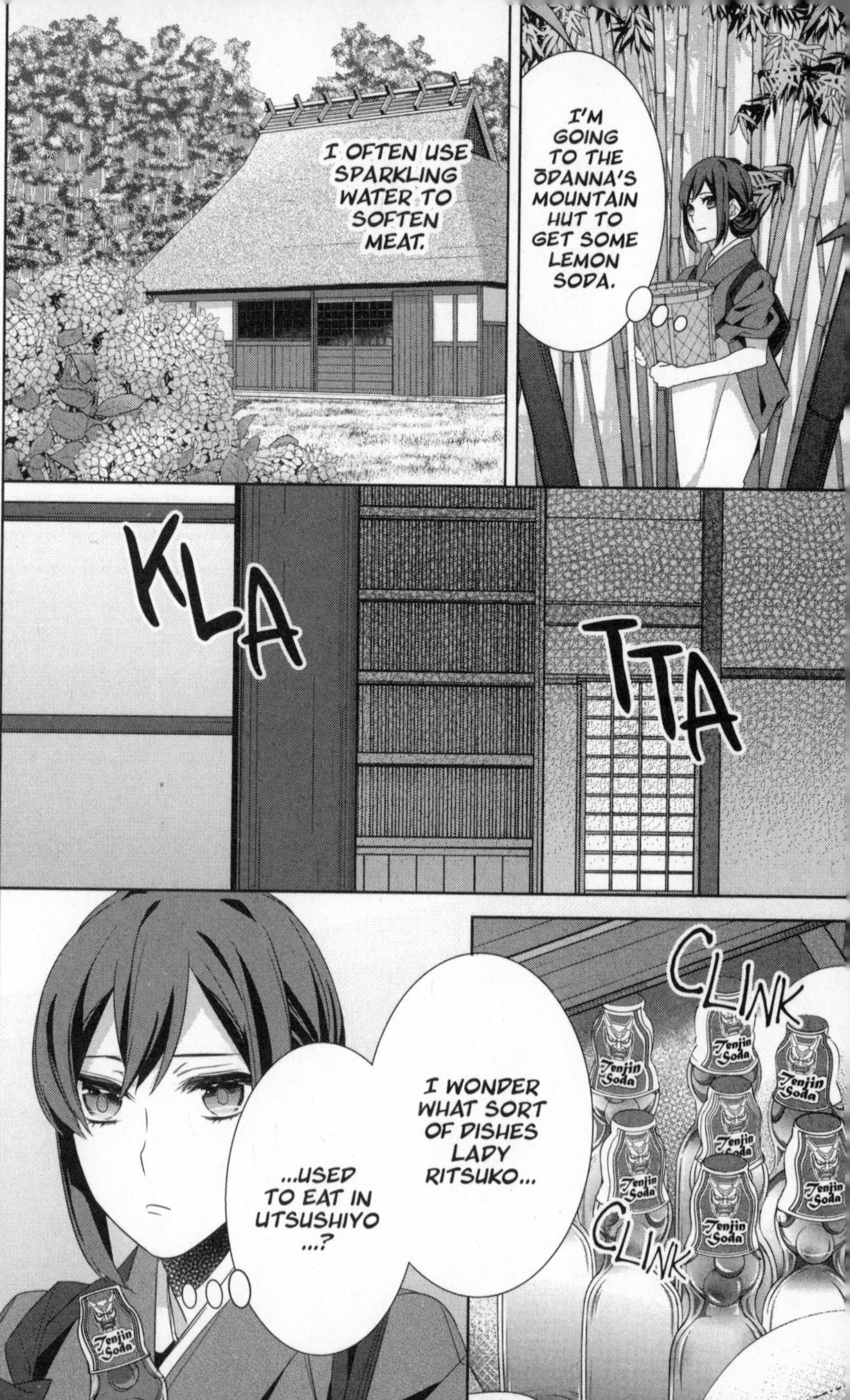
I'M GOING TO THE ŌDANNA'S MOUNTAIN HUT TO GET SOME LEMON SODA.
I OFTEN USE SPARKLING WATER TO SOFTEN MEAT.
KLA TTA
CLINK
CLINK
Tenjin Soda
I WONDER WHAT SORT OF DISHES LADY RITSUKO...
...USED TO EAT IN UTSUSHIYO ...?

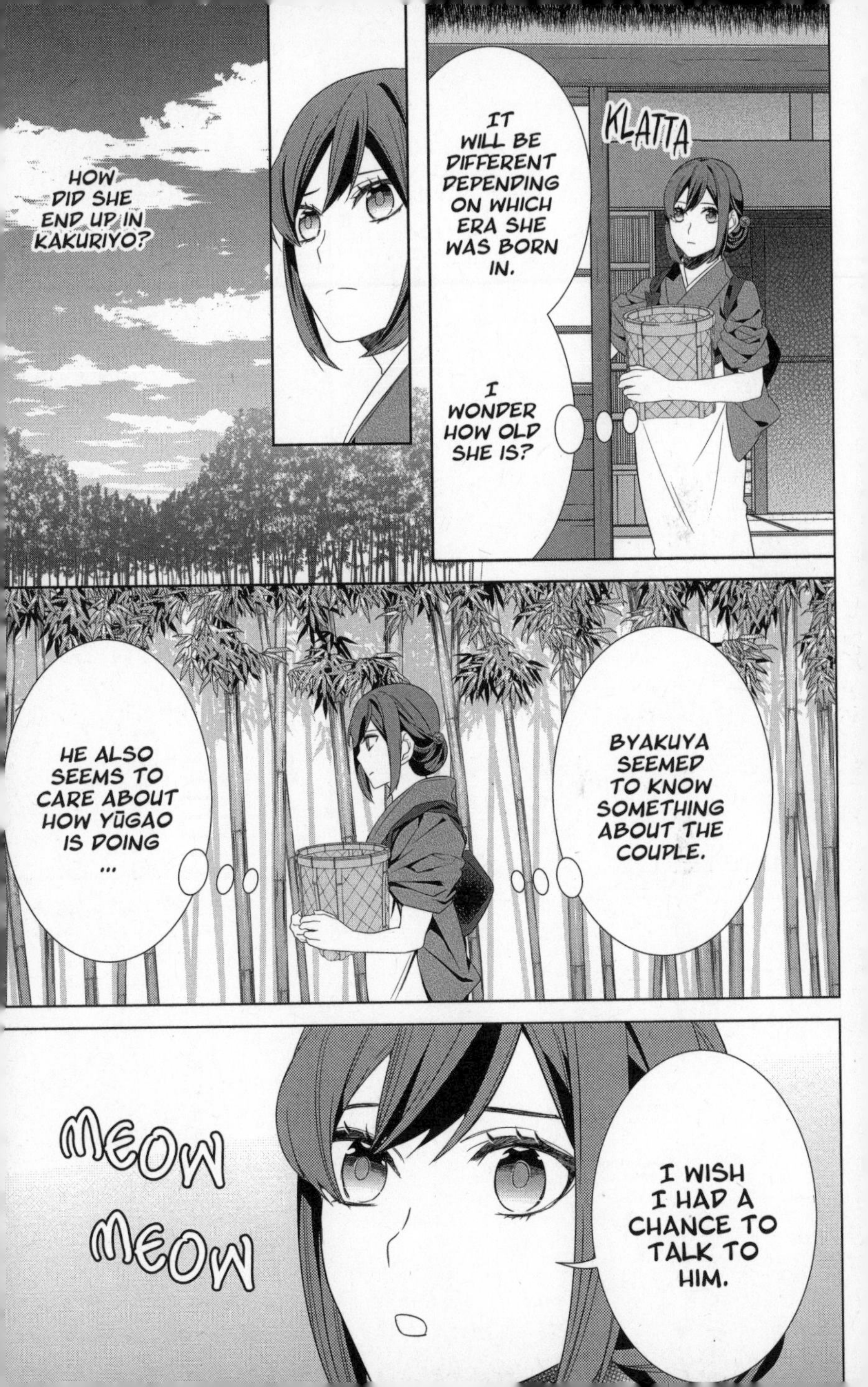
KLATTA
I WONDER HOW OLD SHE IS?
IT WILL BE DIFFERENT DEPENDING ON WHICH ERA SHE WAS BORN IN.
HOW DID SHE END UP IN KAKURIYO?
BYAKUYA SEEMED TO KNOW SOMETHING ABOUT THE COUPLE.
HE ALSO SEEMS TO CARE ABOUT HOW YŪGAO IS DOING ...
I WISH I HAD A CHANCE TO TALK TO HIM.
MEOW
MEOW

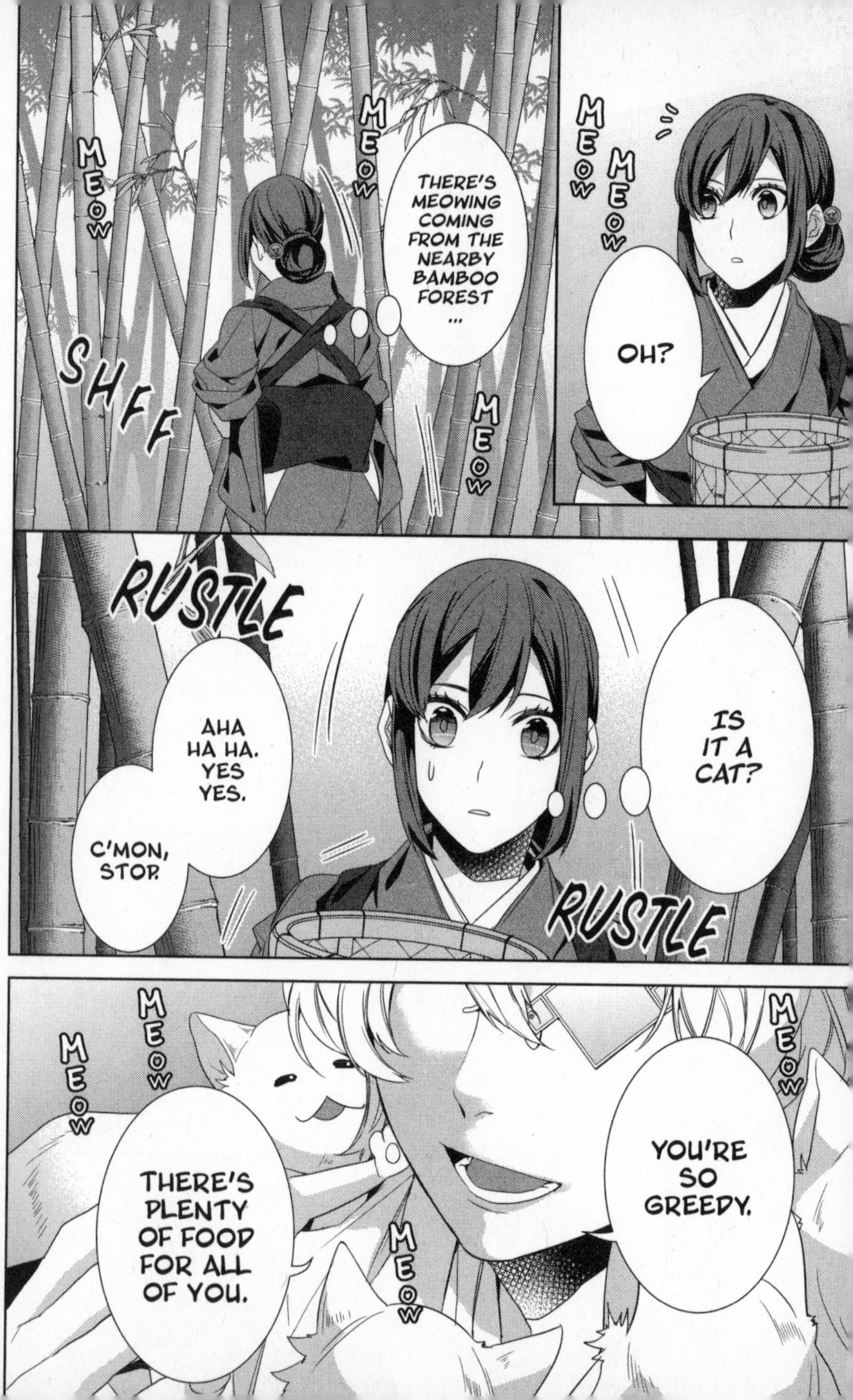
MEOW
MEOW
OH?
MEOW
THERE'S MEOWING COMING FROM THE NEARBY BAMBOO FOREST ...
MEOW
SHFF
MEOW
IS IT A CAT?
RUSTLE
AHA HA HA. YES YES.
C'MON, STOP.
RUSTLE
MEOW
YOU'RE SO GREEDY.
MEOW
MEOW
THERE'S PLENTY OF FOOD FOR ALL OF YOU.
MEOW

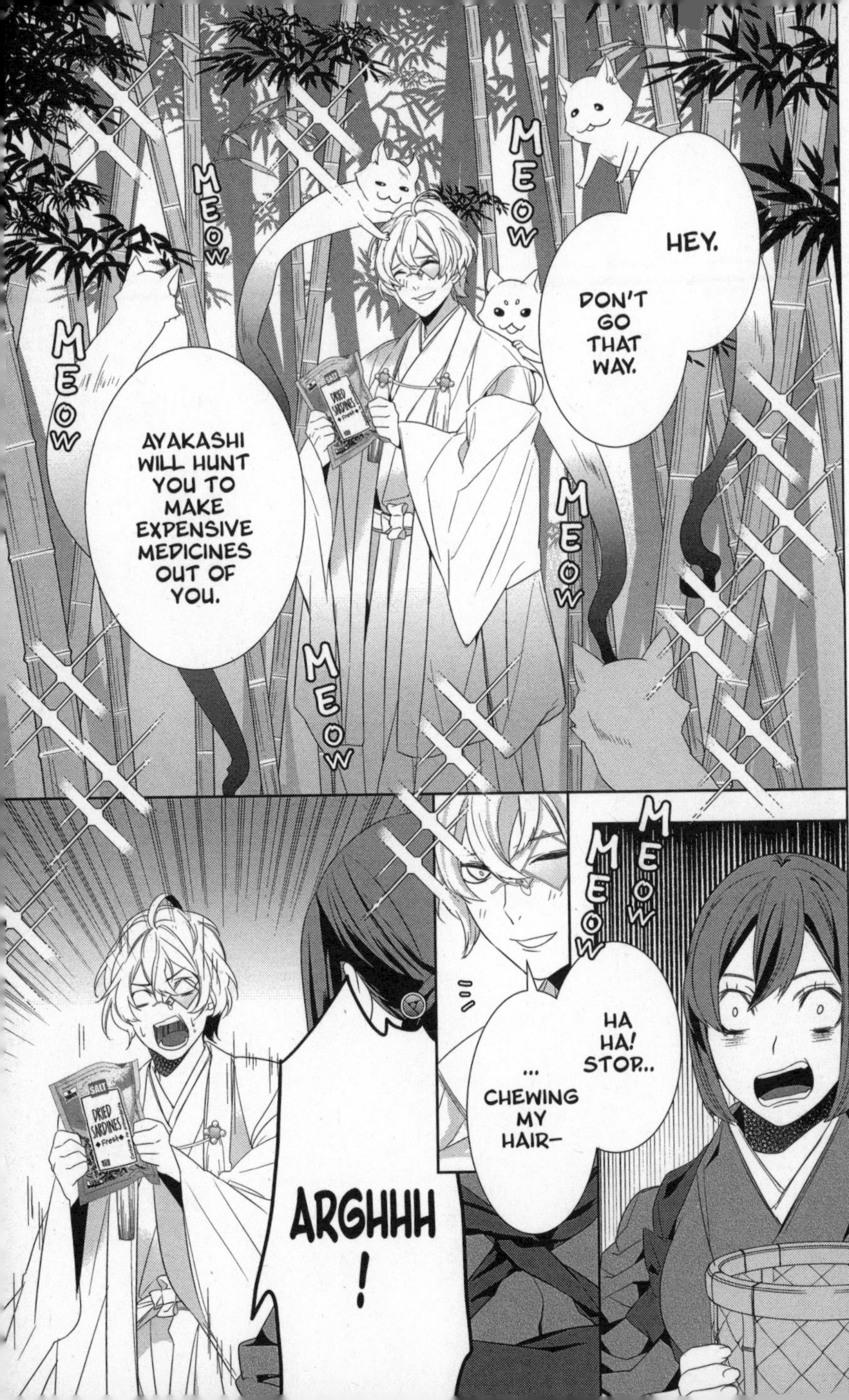
MEOW
HEY.
DON'T GO THAT WAY.
MEOW
MEOW
AYAKASHI WILL HUNT YOU TO MAKE EXPENSIVE MEDICINES OUT OF YOU.
MEOW
MEOW
SALT
DRIED SARDINES
Fresh
MEOW
MEOW
HA HA! STOP..
... CHEWING MY HAIR-
ARGHHH !
SALT
DRIED SARDINES
Fresh

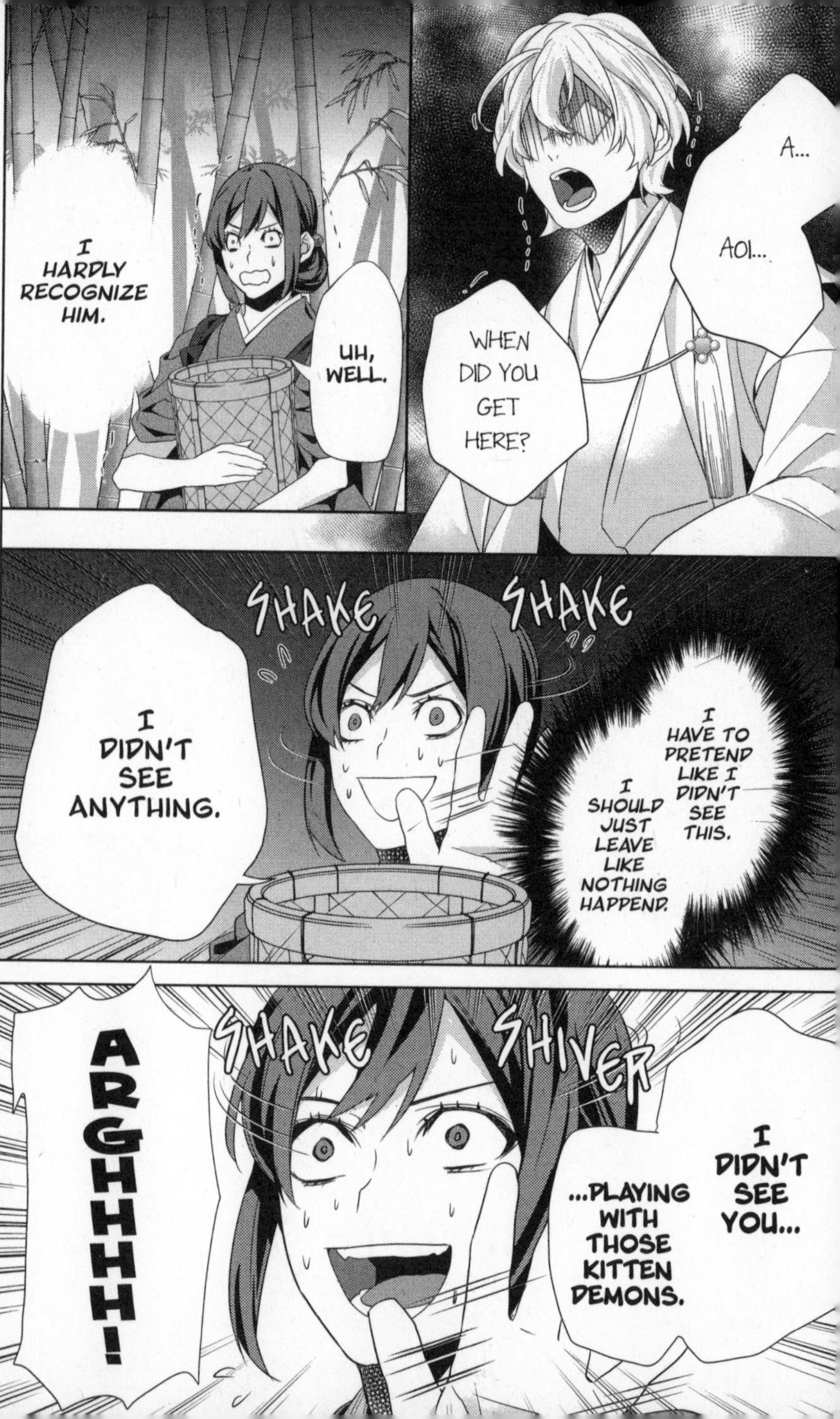
A...
AOI...
WHEN DID YOU GET HERE?
UH, WELL.
I HARDLY RECOGNIZE HIM.
SHAKE SHAKE
I HAVE TO PRETEND LIKE I DIDN'T SEE THIS.
I SHOULD JUST LEAVE LIKE NOTHING HAPPEND.
I DIDN'T SEE ANYTHING.
SHAKE SHIVER
I DIDN'T SEE YOU...
...PLAYING WITH THOSE KITTEN DEMONS.
ARGHHHH!

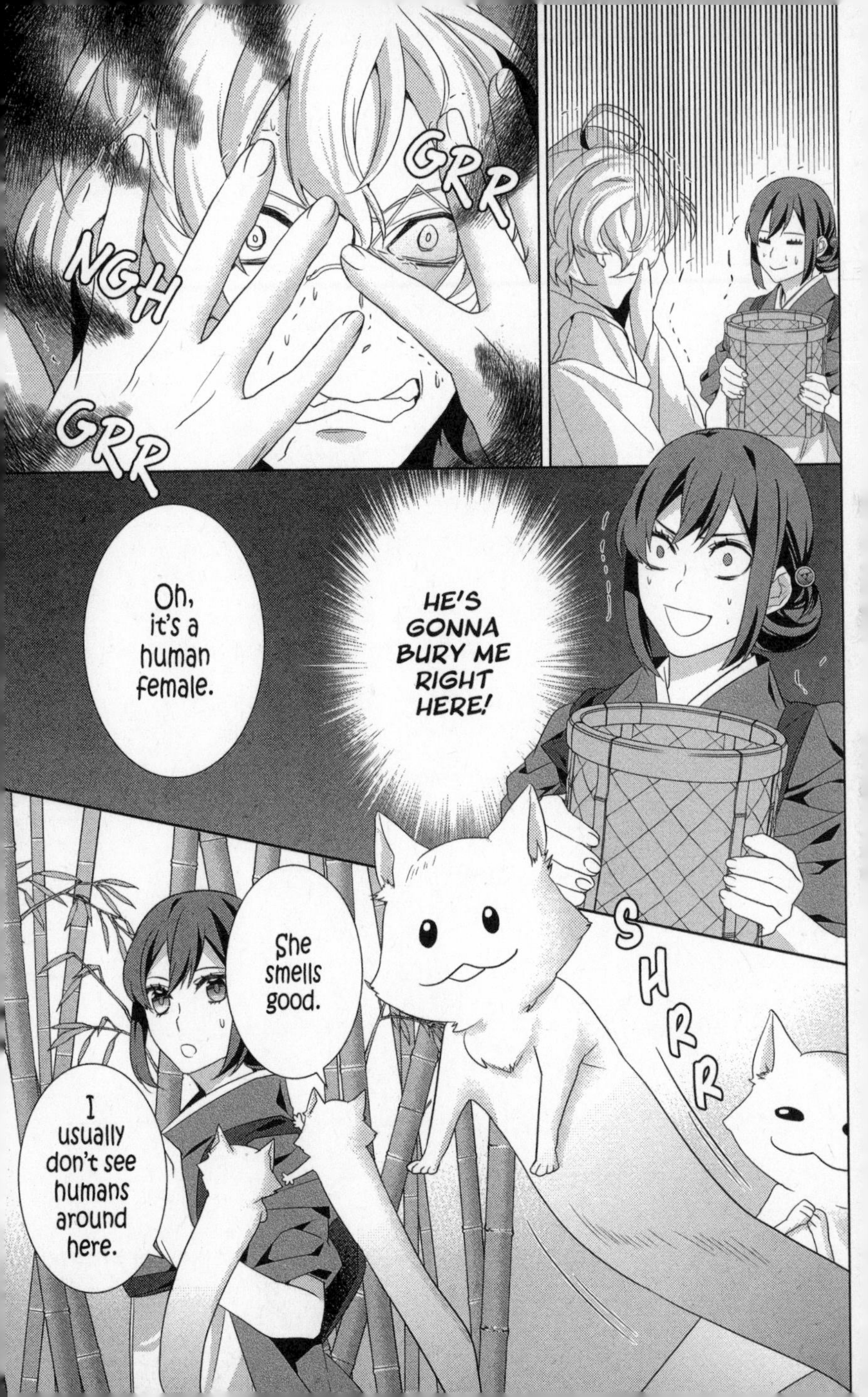
GRR
NGH
GRR
HE'S GONNA BURY ME RIGHT HERE!
Oh, it's a human female.
SHRR
She smells good.
I usually don't see humans around here.

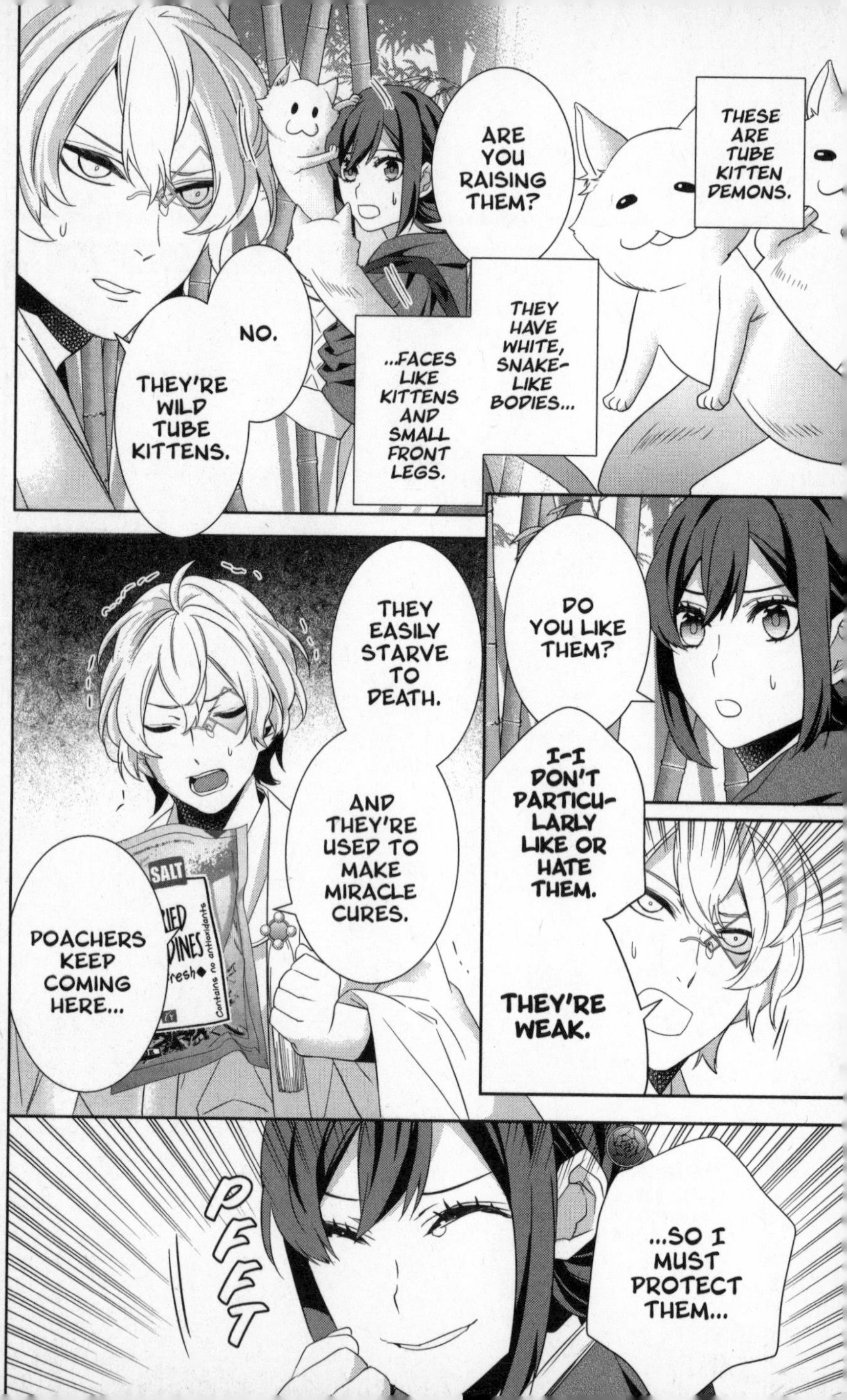
THESE ARE TUBE KITTEN DEMONS.
THEY HAVE WHITE, SNAKE-LIKE BODIES...
...FACES LIKE KITTENS AND SMALL FRONT LEGS.
ARE YOU RAISING THEM?
NO.
THEY'RE WILD TUBE KITTENS.
DO YOU LIKE THEM?
I-I DON'T PARTICU-LARLY LIKE OR HATE THEM.
THEY'RE WEAK.
THEY EASILY STARVE TO DEATH.
AND THEY'RE USED TO MAKE MIRACLE CURES.
POACHERS KEEP COMING HERE...
SALT
Contains no antioxidants
...SO I MUST PROTECT THEM...
PFFT

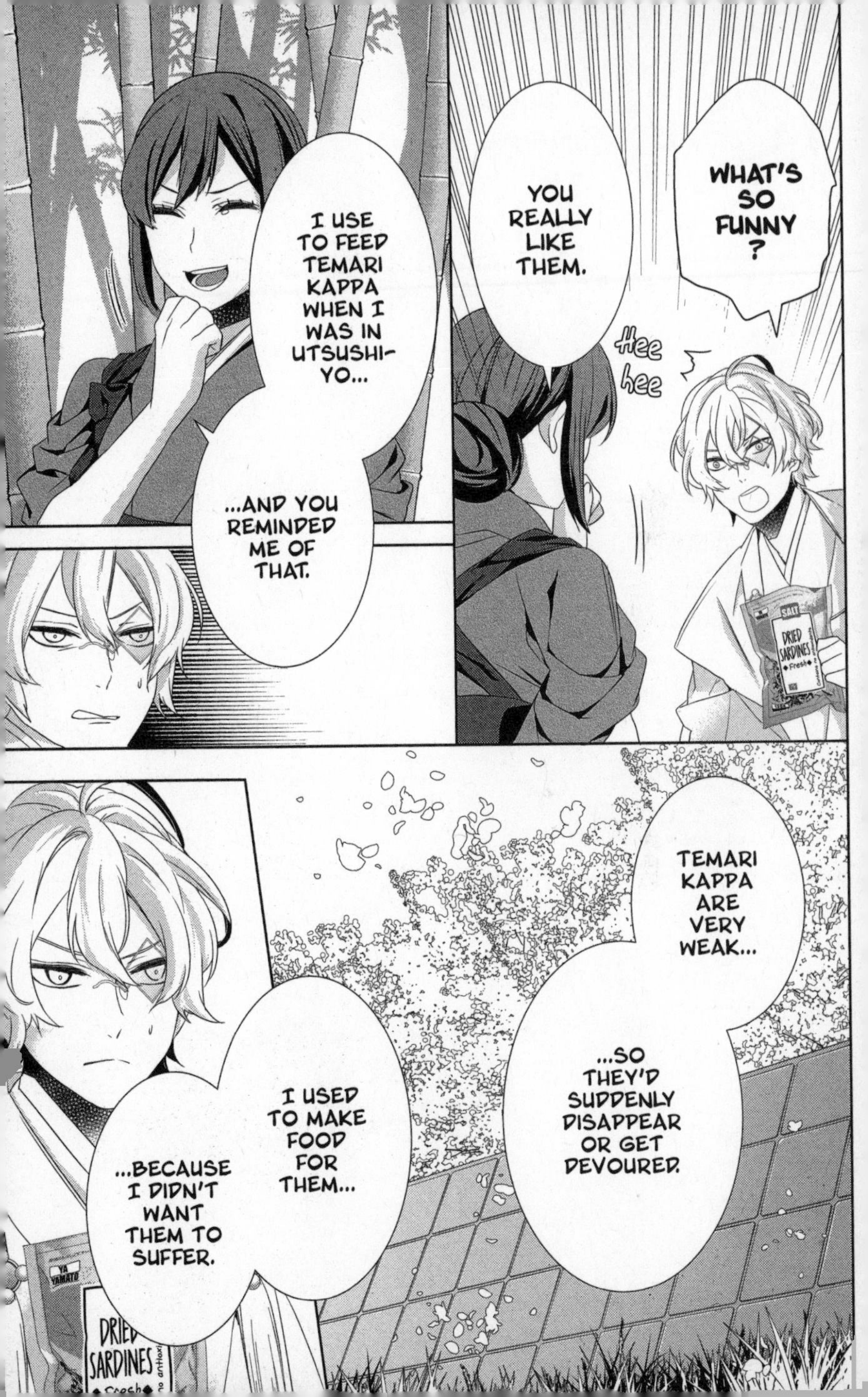
WHAT'S SO FUNNY?
YOU REALLY LIKE THEM.
Hee hee
SALT
DRIED SARDINES
Fresh
I USE TO FEED TEMARI KAPPA WHEN I WAS IN UTSUSHI-YO...
...AND YOU REMINDED ME OF THAT.
TEMARI KAPPA ARE VERY WEAK...
...SO THEY'D SUDDENLY DISAPPEAR OR GET DEVOURED.
I USED TO MAKE FOOD FOR THEM...
...BECAUSE I DIDN'T WANT THEM TO SUFFER.
YA YAMATO
DRIED SARDINES

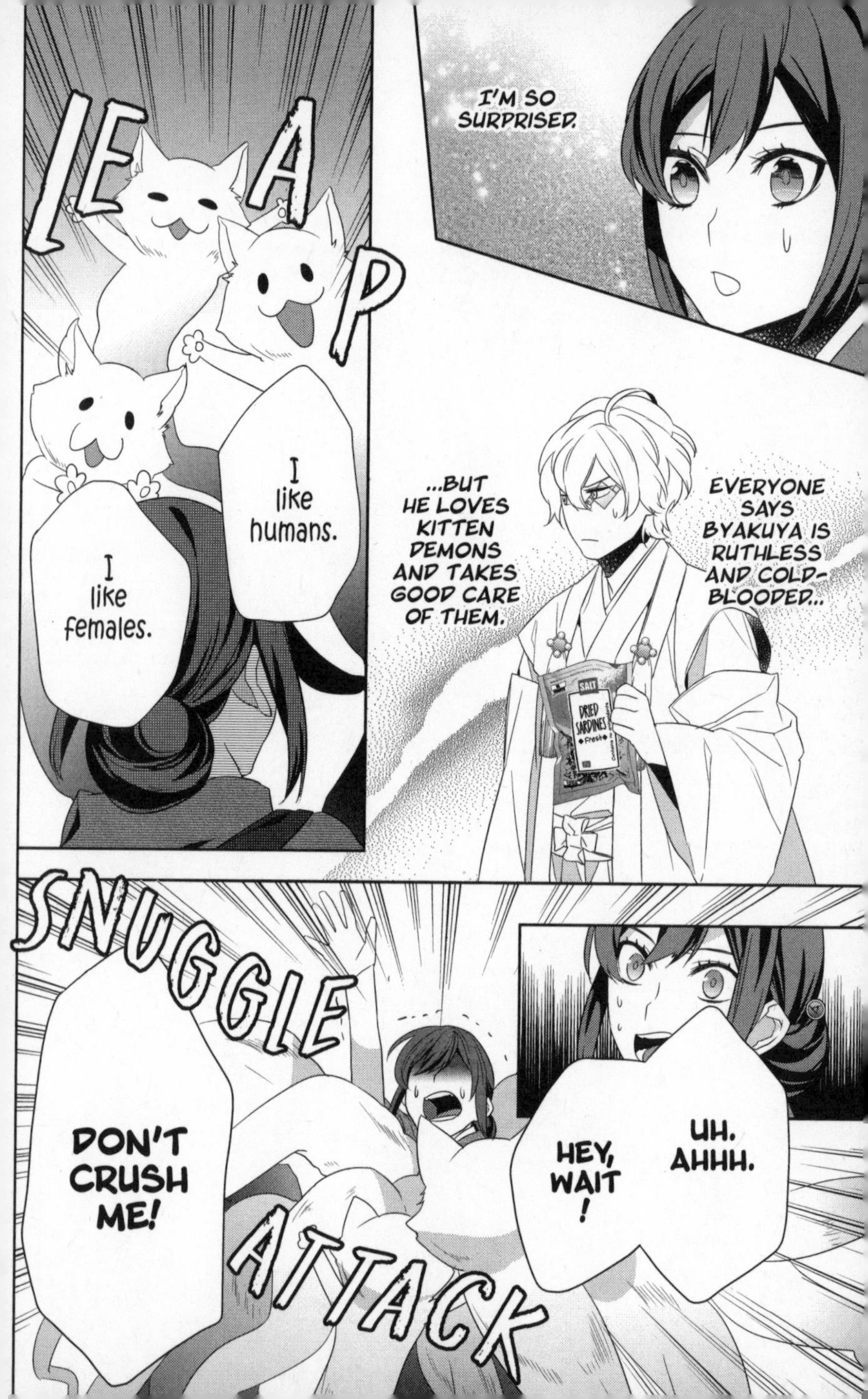
I'M SO SURPRISED.
EVERYONE SAYS BYAKUYA IS RUTHLESS AND COLD-BLOODED...
...BUT HE LOVES KITTEN DEMONS AND TAKES GOOD CARE OF THEM.
DRIED SARDINES
LEAP
I like humans.
I like females.
UH. AHHH.
HEY, WAIT!
SNUGGLE
ATTACK
DON'T CRUSH ME!

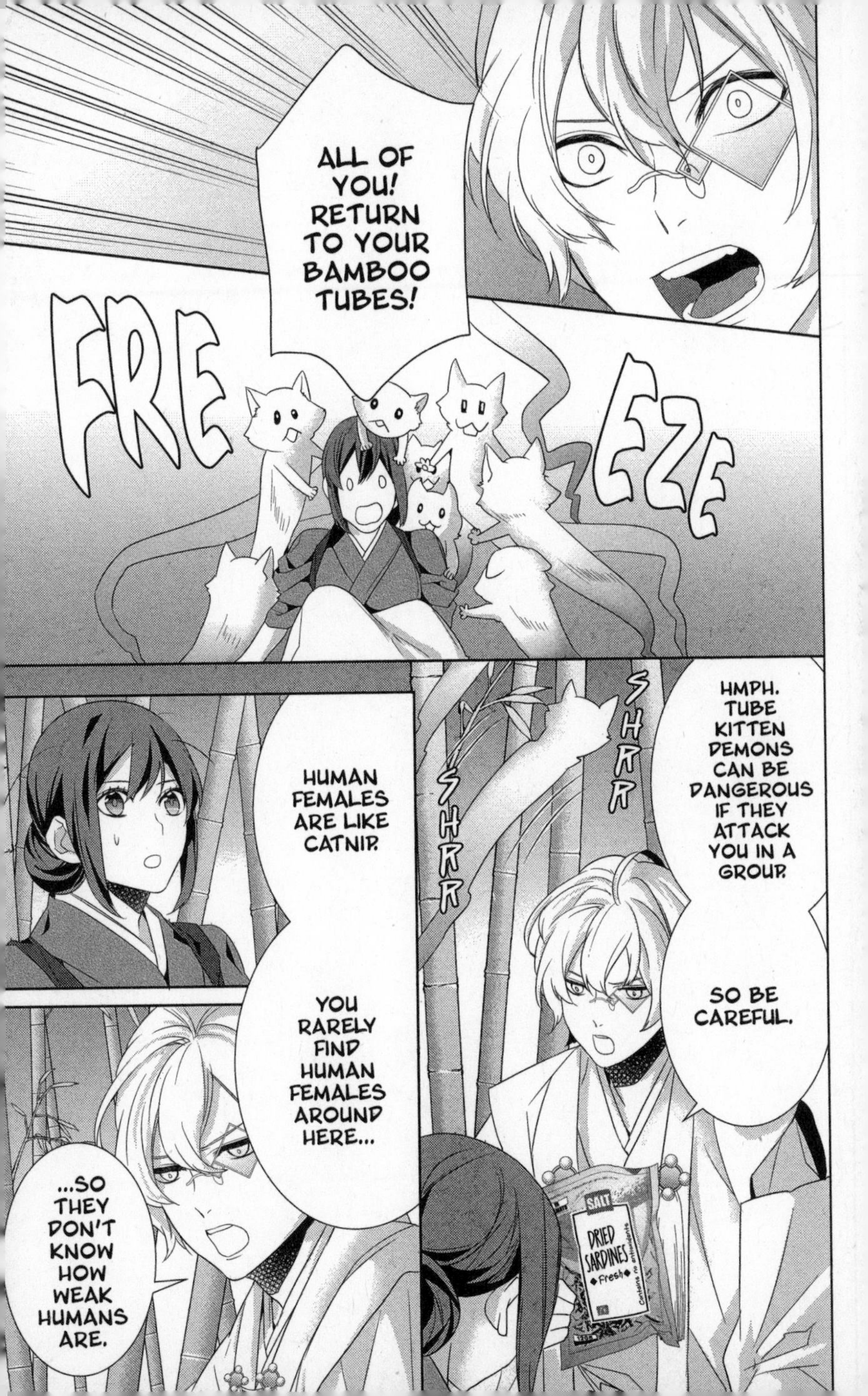

ALL OF YOU! RETURN TO YOUR BAMBOO TUBES!
FREEZE
HMPH. TUBE KITTEN DEMONS CAN BE DANGEROUS IF THEY ATTACK YOU IN A GROUP.
SHRR
SHRR
SO BE CAREFUL.
HUMAN FEMALES ARE LIKE CATNIP.
YOU RARELY FIND HUMAN FEMALES AROUND HERE...
...SO THEY DON'T KNOW HOW WEAK HUMANS ARE.
SALT
DRIED SARDINES
Fresh

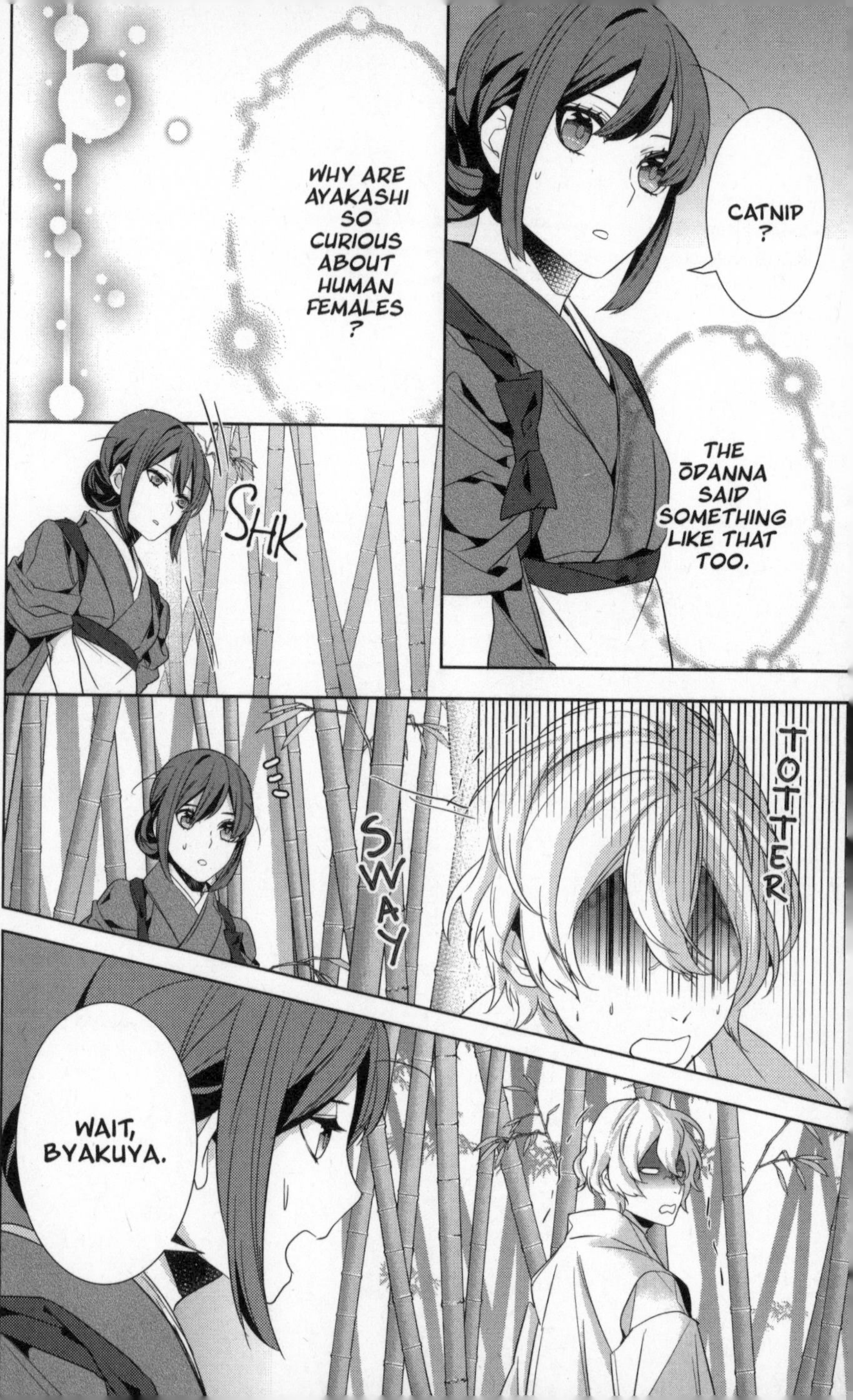
CATNIP?
THE ŌDANNA SAID SOMETHING LIKE THAT TOO.
WHY ARE AYAKASHI SO CURIOUS ABOUT HUMAN FEMALES?
SHK
TOTTER
SWAY
WAIT, BYAKUYA.

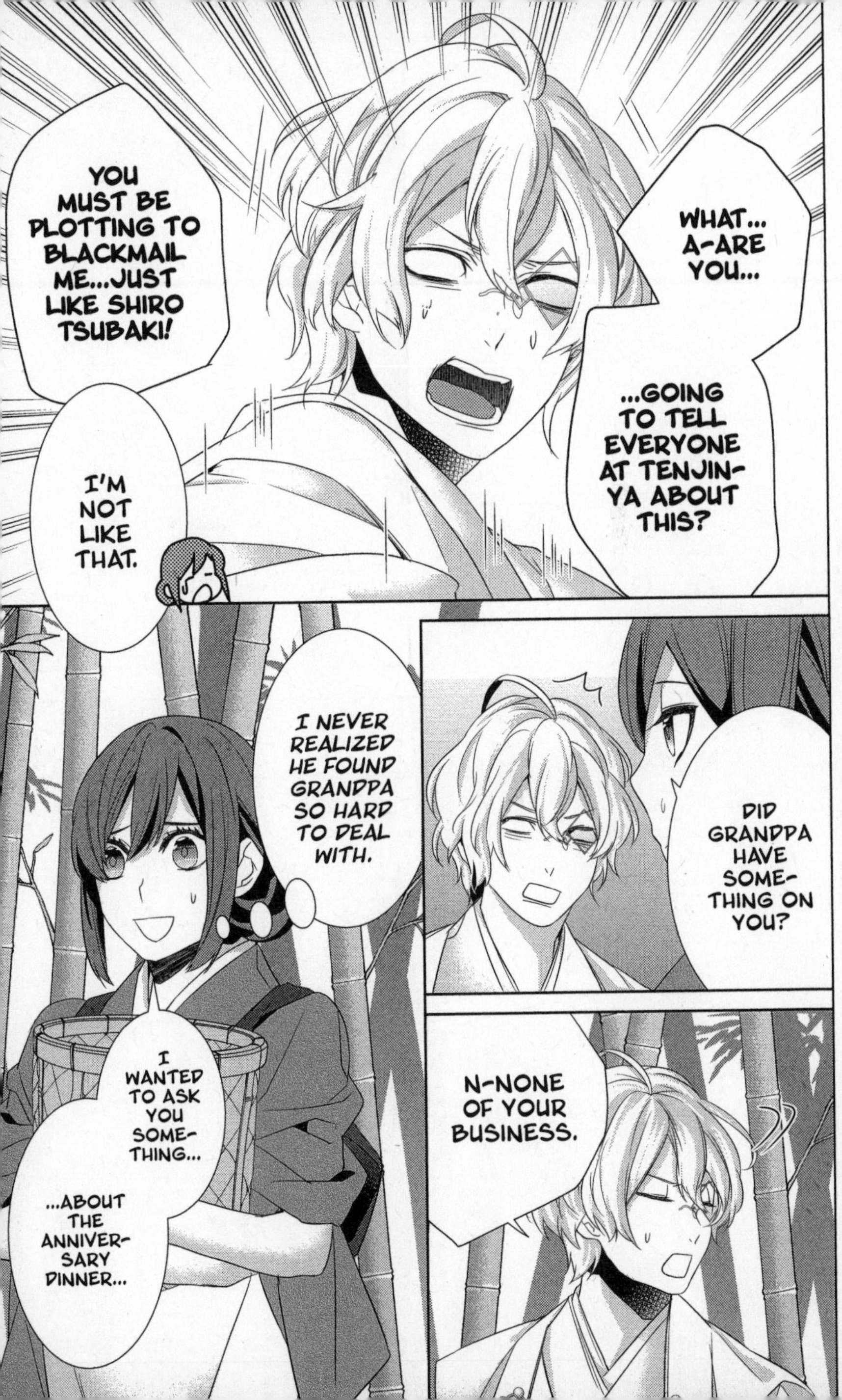
WHAT... A-ARE YOU...
...GOING TO TELL EVERYONE AT TENJIN-YA ABOUT THIS?
YOU MUST BE PLOTTING TO BLACKMAIL ME...JUST LIKE SHIRO TSUBAKI!
I'M NOT LIKE THAT.
DID GRANDPA HAVE SOME-THING ON YOU?
N-NONE OF YOUR BUSINESS.
I NEVER REALIZED HE FOUND GRANDPA SO HARD TO DEAL WITH.
I WANTED TO ASK YOU SOME-THING...
...ABOUT THE ANNIVER-SARY DINNER...

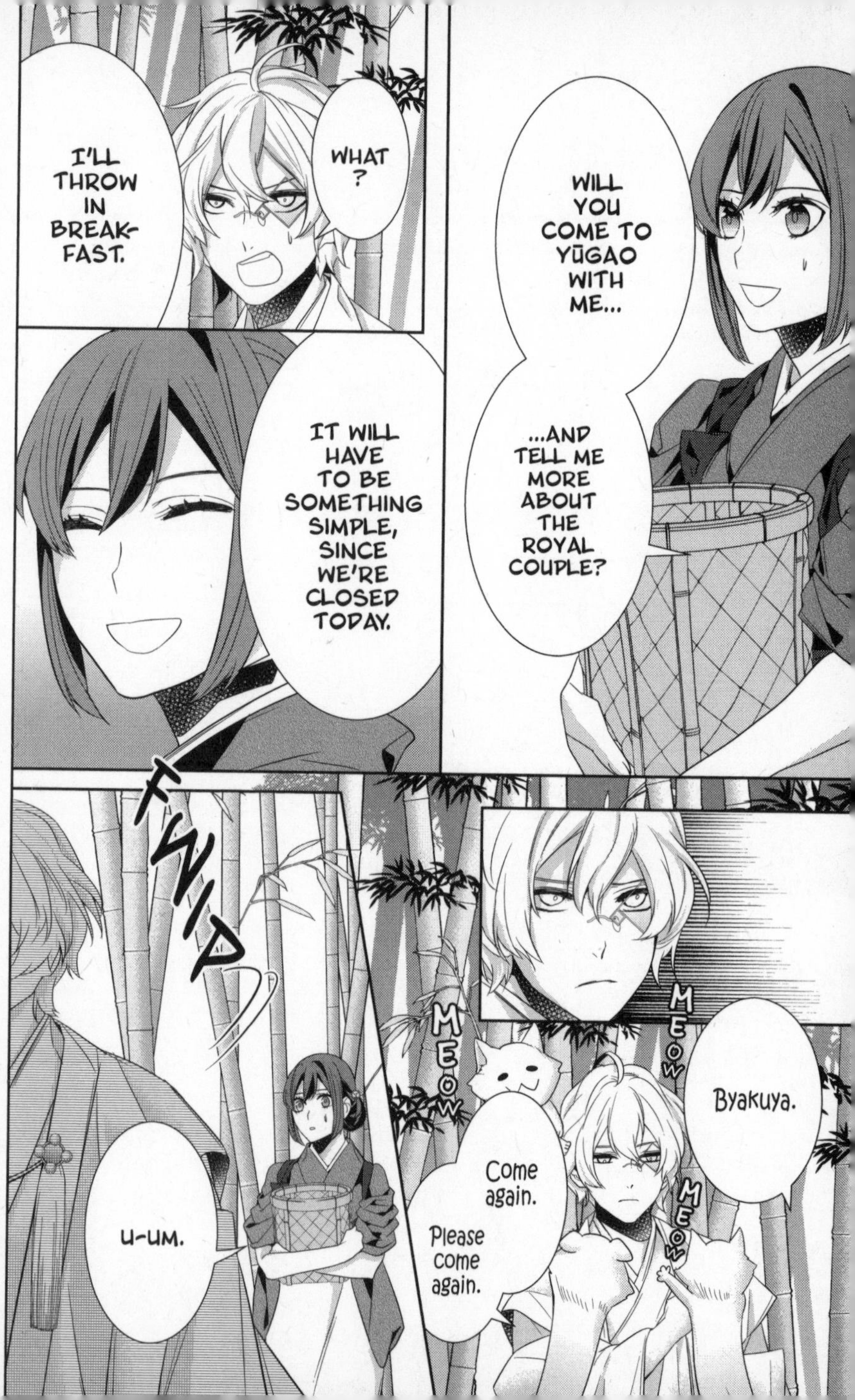
WILL YOU COME TO YŪGAO WITH ME...
...AND TELL ME MORE ABOUT THE ROYAL COUPLE?
WHAT?
I'LL THROW IN BREAK-FAST.
IT WILL HAVE TO BE SOMETHING SIMPLE, SINCE WE'RE CLOSED TODAY.
MEOW
Byakuya.
MEOW
MEOW
Come again.
Please come again.
FWIP
U-UM.

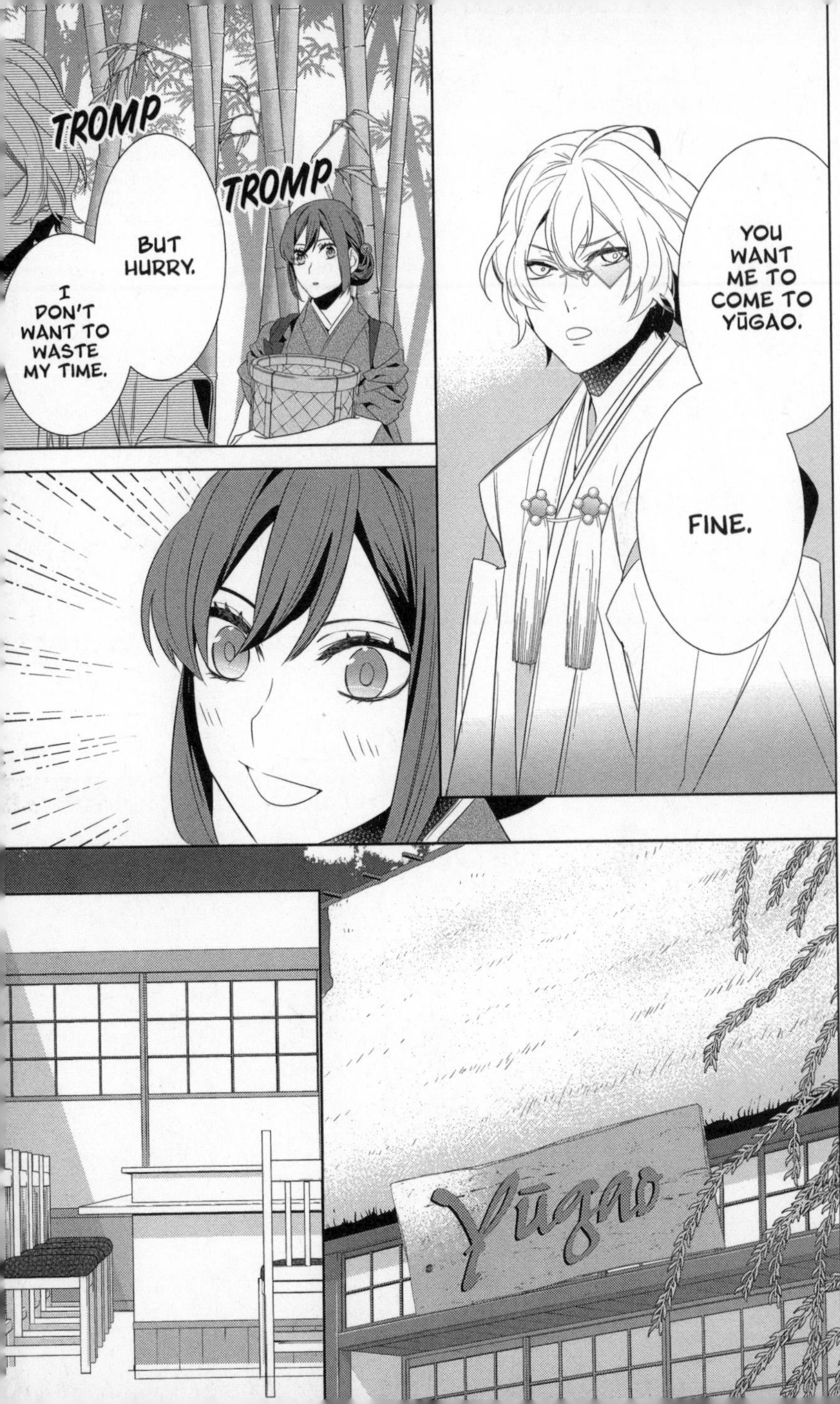
YOU WANT ME TO COME TO YŪGAO.
FINE.
TROMP
TROMP
BUT HURRY.
I DON'T WANT TO WASTE MY TIME.
Yūgao

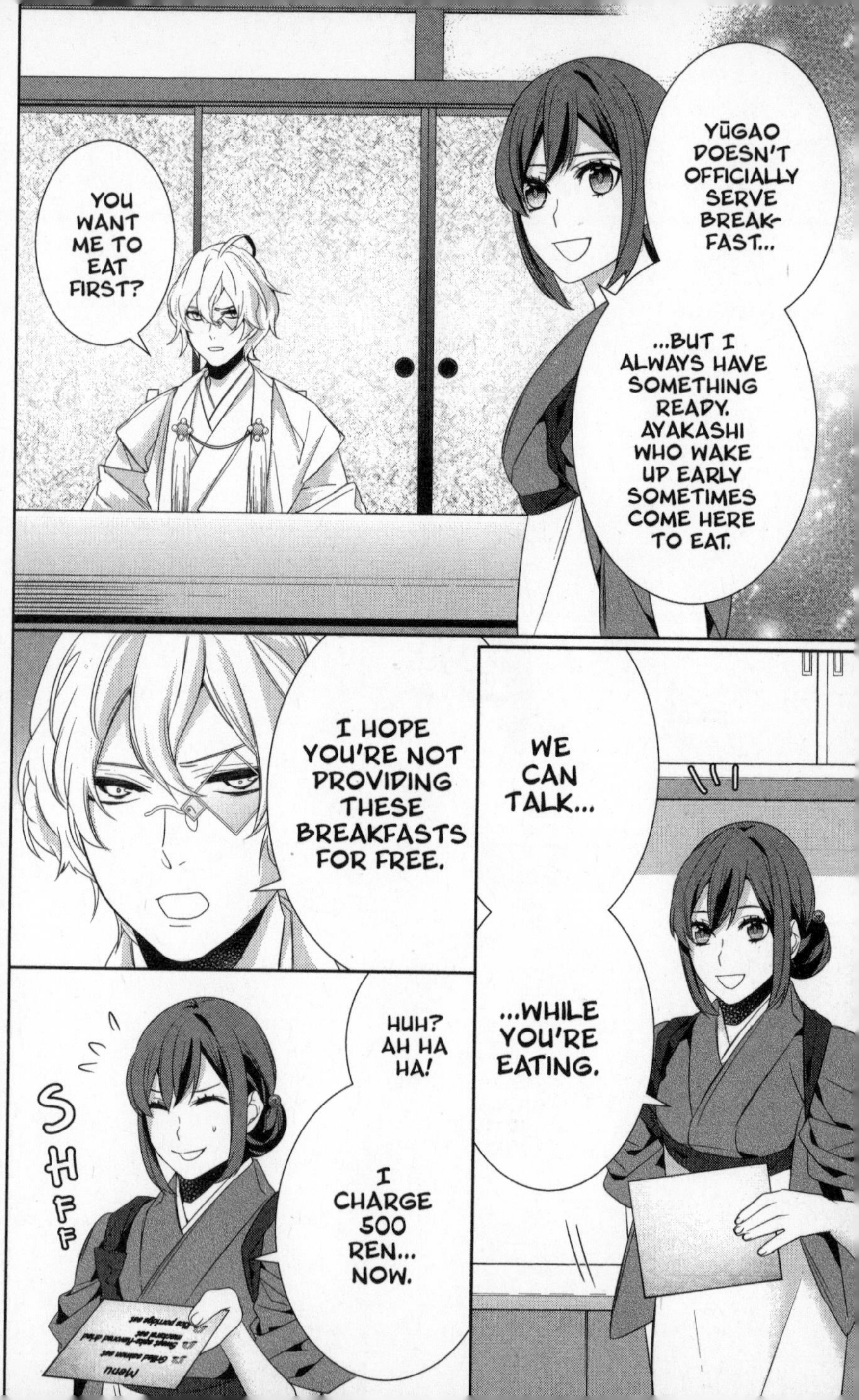
YŪGAO DOESN'T OFFICIALLY SERVE BREAK-FAST...
...BUT I ALWAYS HAVE SOMETHING READY. AYAKASHI WHO WAKE UP EARLY SOMETIMES COME HERE TO EAT.
YOU WANT ME TO EAT FIRST?
WE CAN TALK...
...WHILE YOU'RE EATING.
I HOPE YOU'RE NOT PROVIDING THESE BREAKFASTS FOR FREE.
HUH? AH HA HA!
I CHARGE 500 REN... NOW.
SHFF

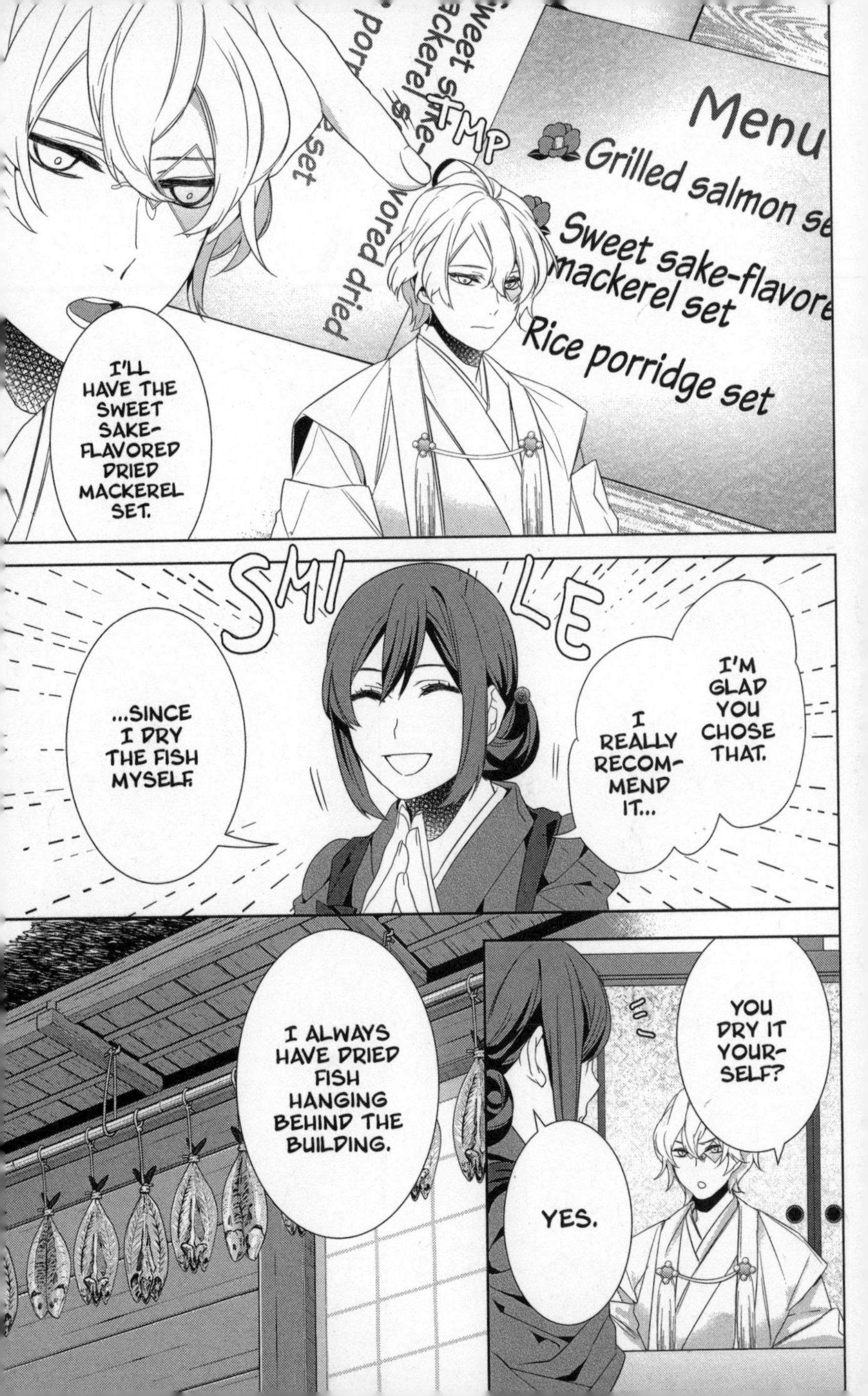
Menu
Grilled salmon set
Sweet sake-flavored mackerel set
Rice porridge set
STMP
I'LL HAVE THE SWEET SAKE-FLAVORED DRIED MACKEREL SET.
SMILE
I'M GLAD YOU CHOSE THAT.
I REALLY RECOMMEND IT...
...SINCE I DRY THE FISH MYSELF.
YOU DRY IT YOURSELF?
YES.
I ALWAYS HAVE DRIED FISH HANGING BEHIND THE BUILDING.

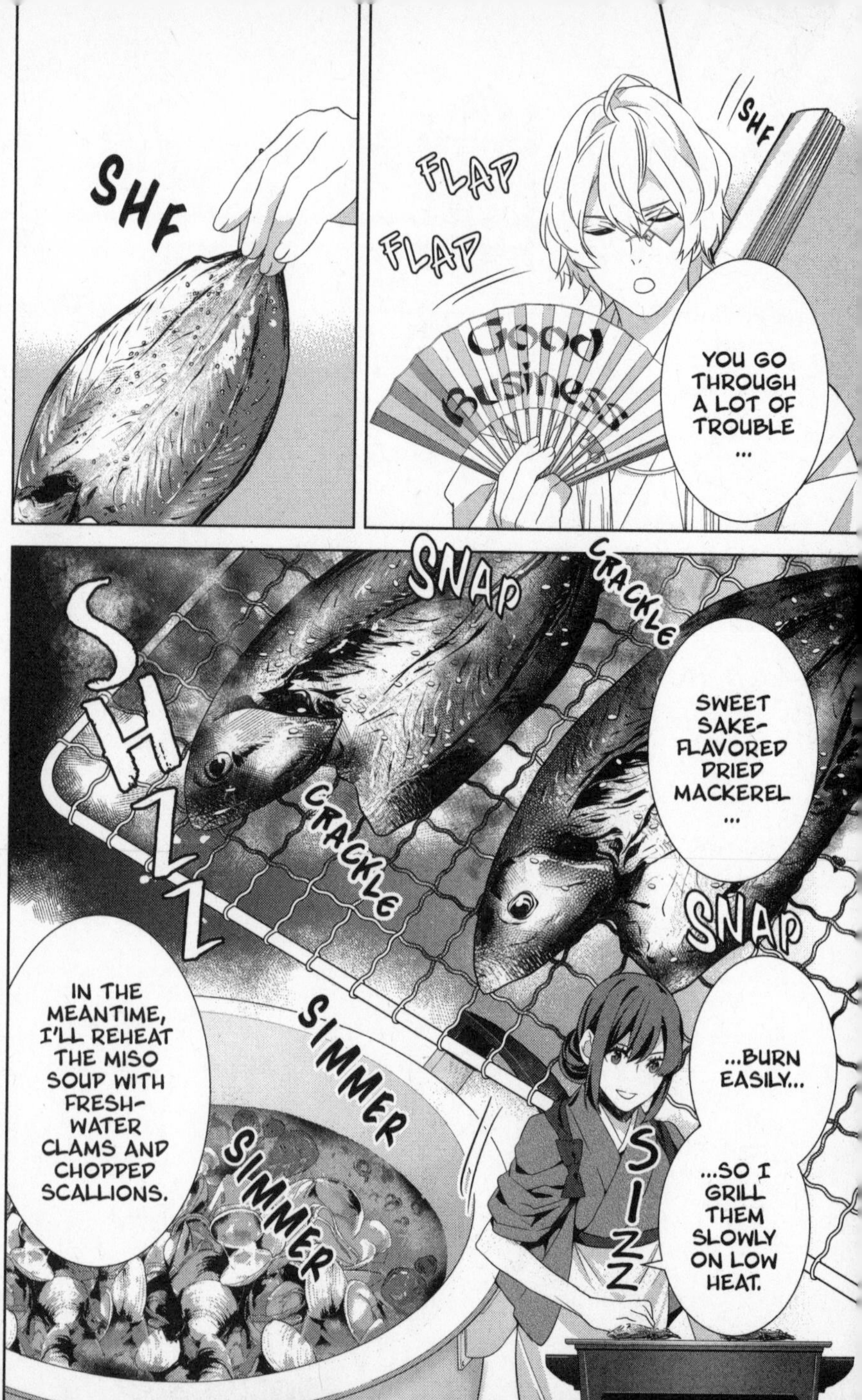
SHF
FLAP
FLAP
Good Business
YOU GO THROUGH A LOT OF TROUBLE ...
SHF
CRACKLE
SNAP
SHZZZ
SWEET SAKE-FLAVORED DRIED MACKEREL ...
SNAP
CRACKLE
...BURN EASILY...
...SO I GRILL THEM SLOWLY ON LOW HEAT.
SIZZ
SIMMER
SIMMER
IN THE MEANTIME, I'LL REHEAT THE MISO SOUP WITH FRESH-WATER CLAMS AND CHOPPED SCALLIONS.

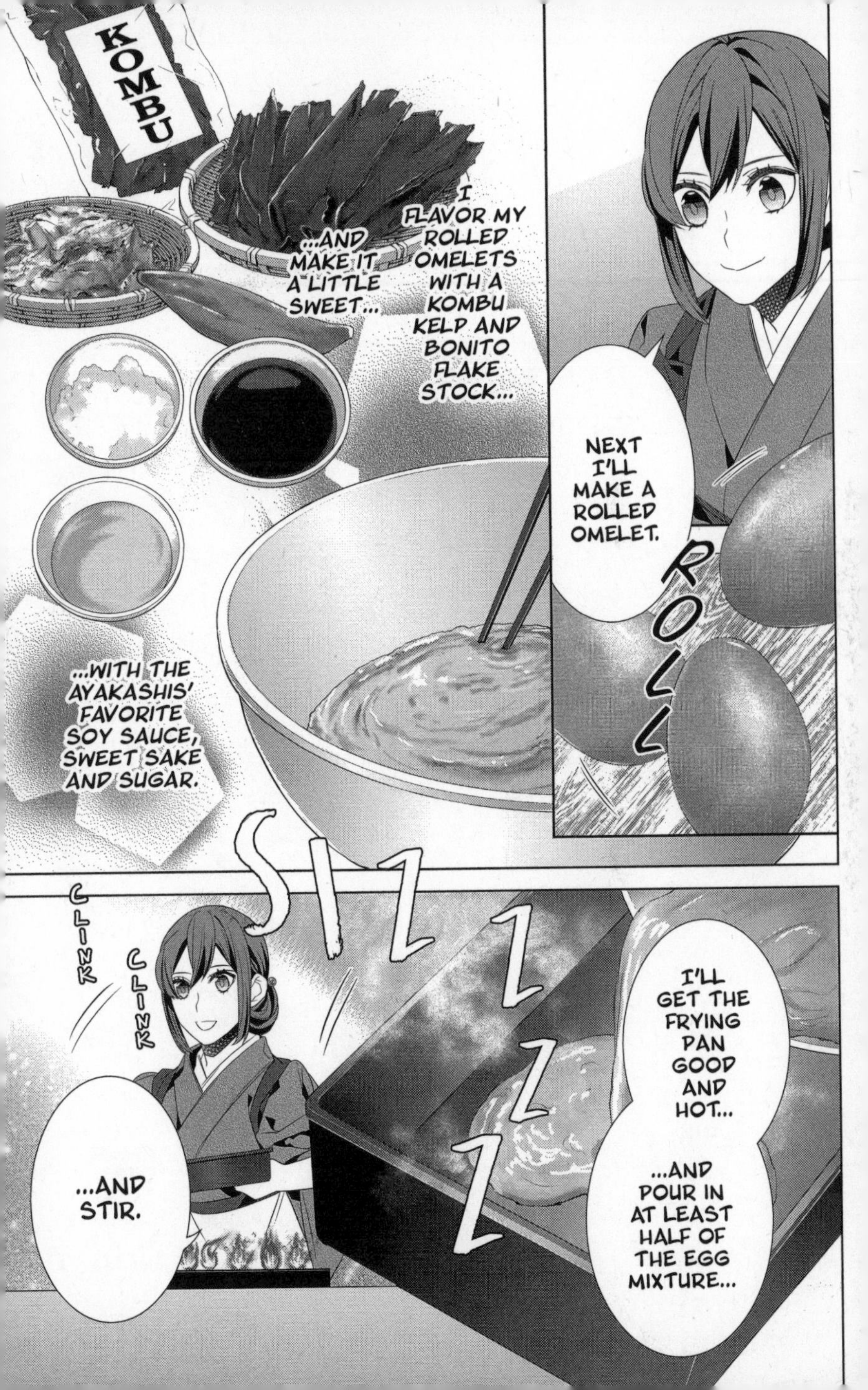
NEXT I'LL MAKE A ROLLED OMELET.
ROLL
KOMBU
I FLAVOR MY ROLLED OMELETS WITH A KOMBU KELP AND BONITO FLAKE STOCK...
...AND MAKE IT A LITTLE SWEET...
...WITH THE AYAKASHIS' FAVORITE SOY SAUCE, SWEET SAKE AND SUGAR.
SIZZZZ
I'LL GET THE FRYING PAN GOOD AND HOT...
...AND POUR IN AT LEAST HALF OF THE EGG MIXTURE...
CLINK
CLINK
...AND STIR.

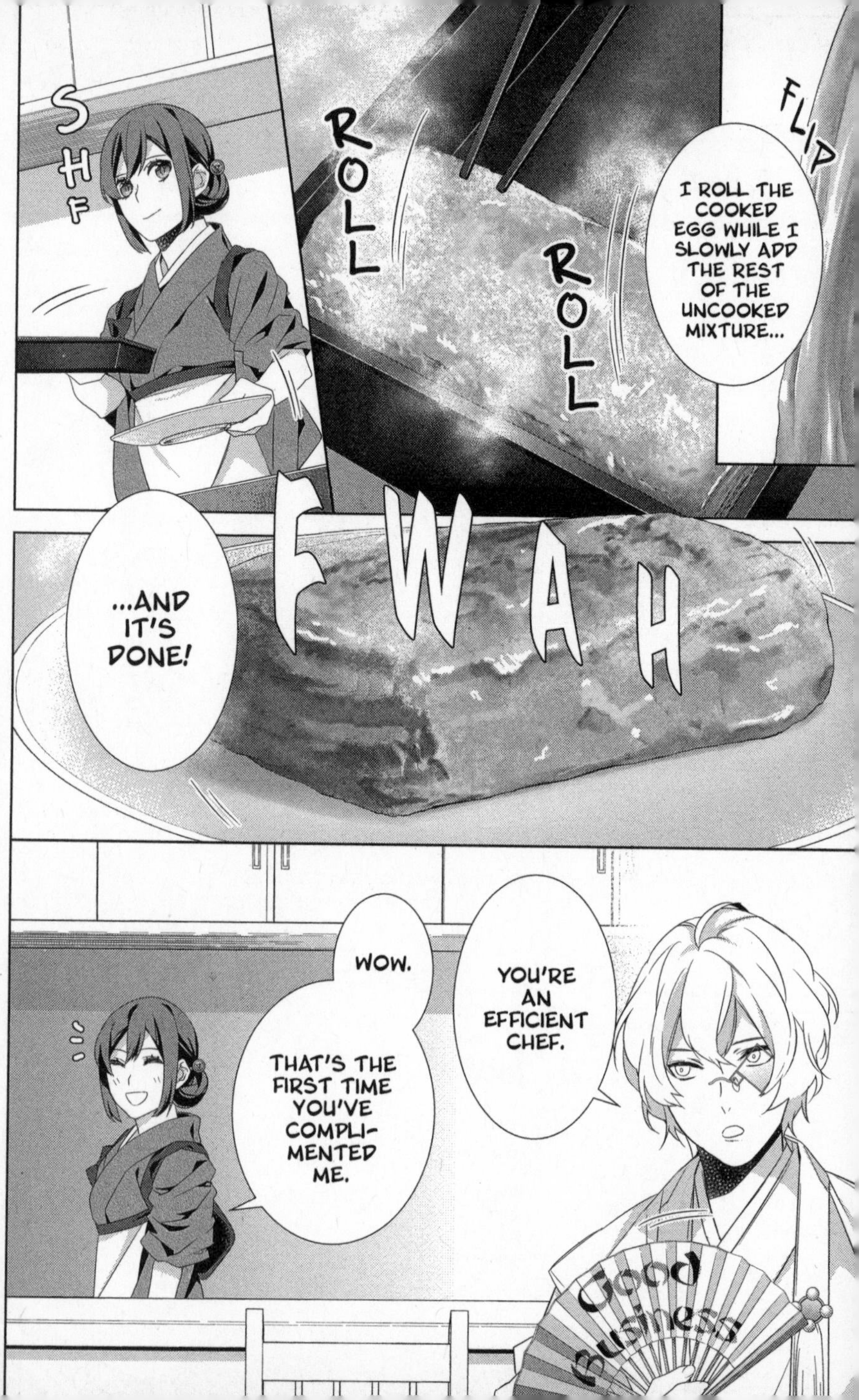
FLIP
I ROLL THE COOKED EGG WHILE I SLOWLY ADD THE REST OF THE UNCOOKED MIXTURE...
ROLL
ROLL
SHF
FWAH
...AND IT'S DONE!
YOU'RE AN EFFICIENT CHEF.
WOW.
THAT'S THE FIRST TIME YOU'VE COMPLIMENTED ME.
Good Business

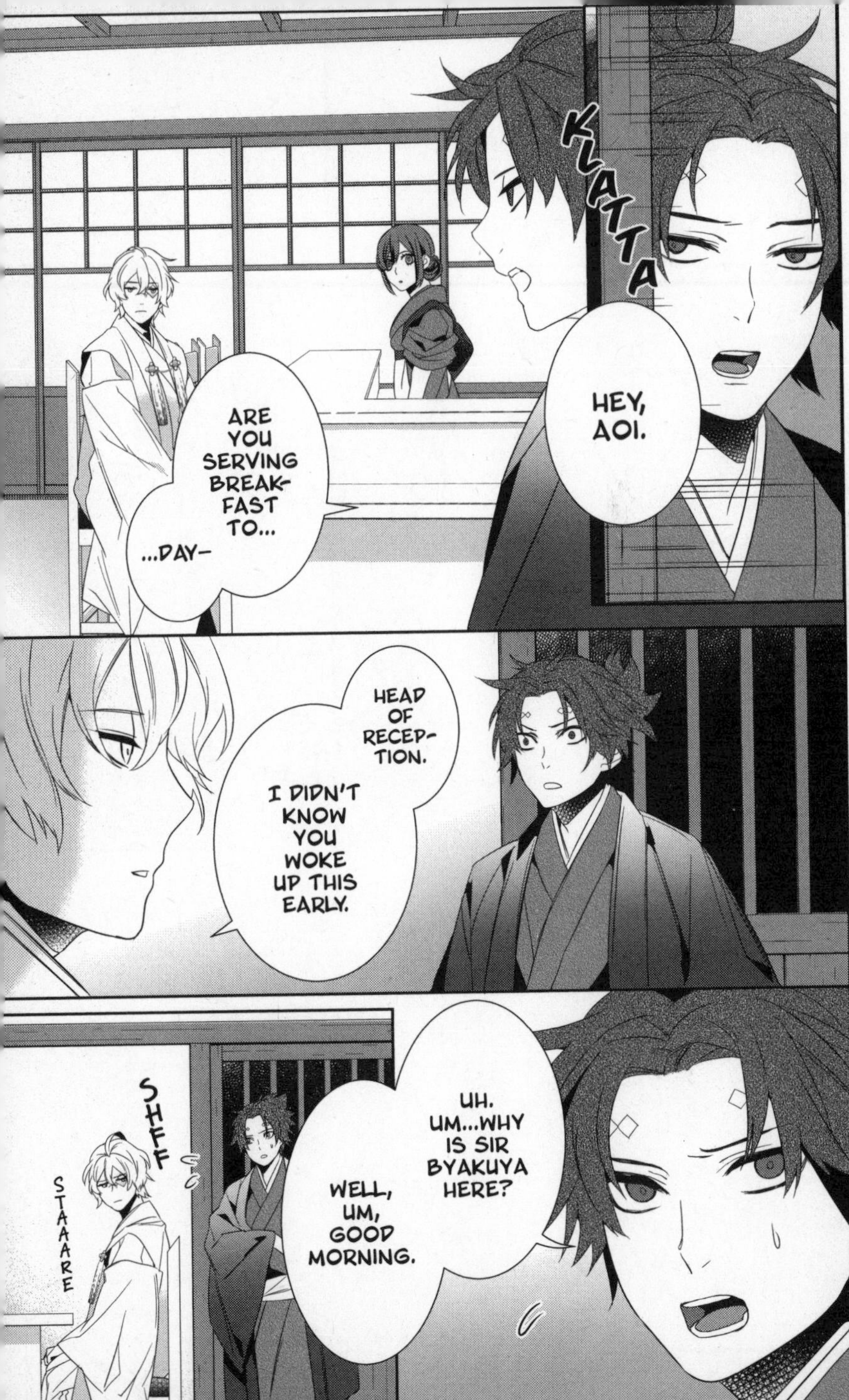
KLATTA
HEY, AOI.
ARE YOU SERVING BREAKFAST TO...
...DAY-
HEAD OF RECEPTION.
I DIDN'T KNOW YOU WOKE UP THIS EARLY.
UH. UM...WHY IS SIR BYAKUYA HERE?
WELL, UM, GOOD MORNING.
SHFF
STAAARE

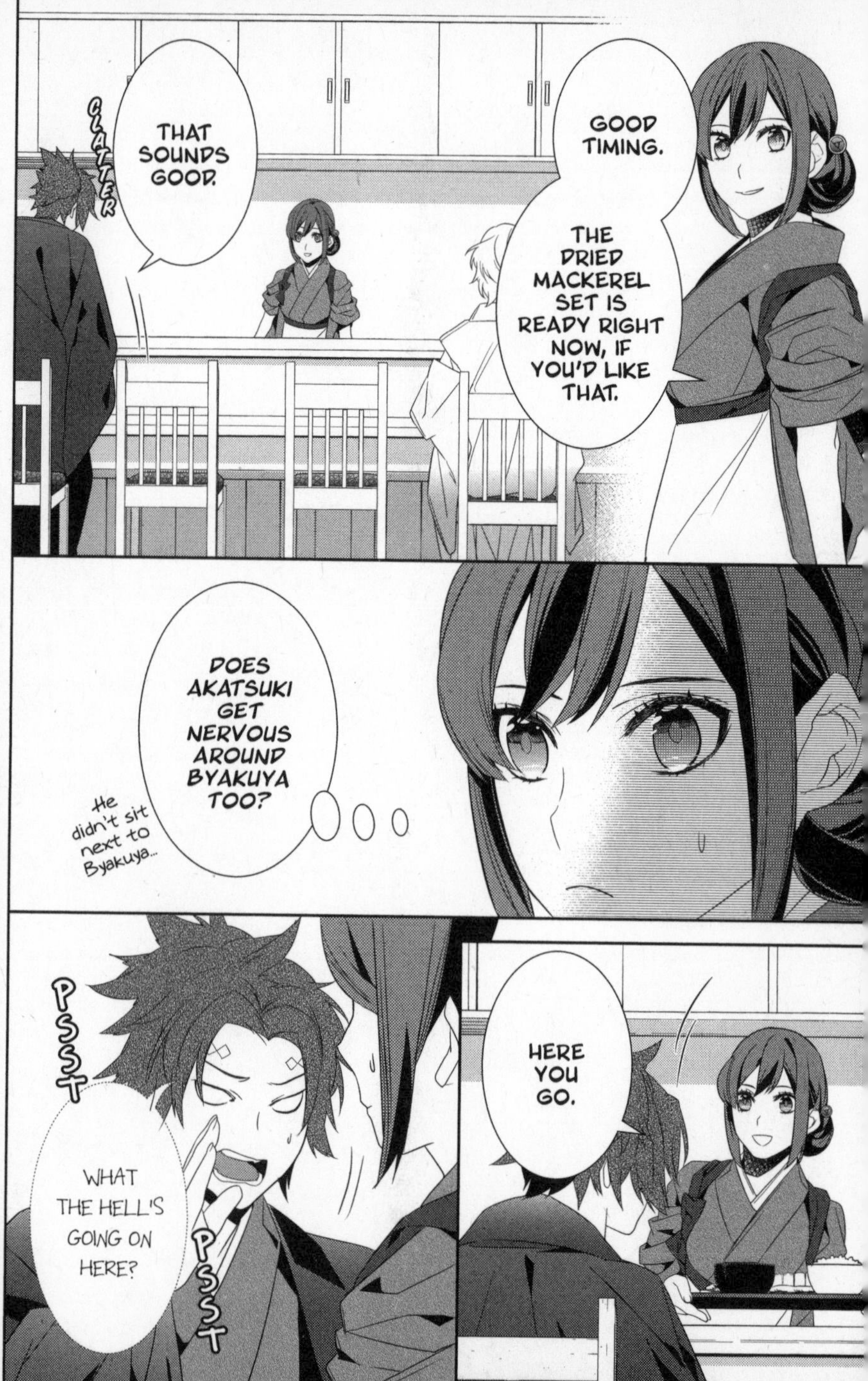
GOOD TIMING.
THE DRIED MACKEREL SET IS READY RIGHT NOW, IF YOU'D LIKE THAT.
THAT SOUNDS GOOD.
CLATTER
DOES AKATSUKI GET NERVOUS AROUND BYAKUYA TOO?
He didn't sit next to Byakuya...
HERE YOU GO.
PSST
WHAT THE HELL'S GOING ON HERE?
PSST

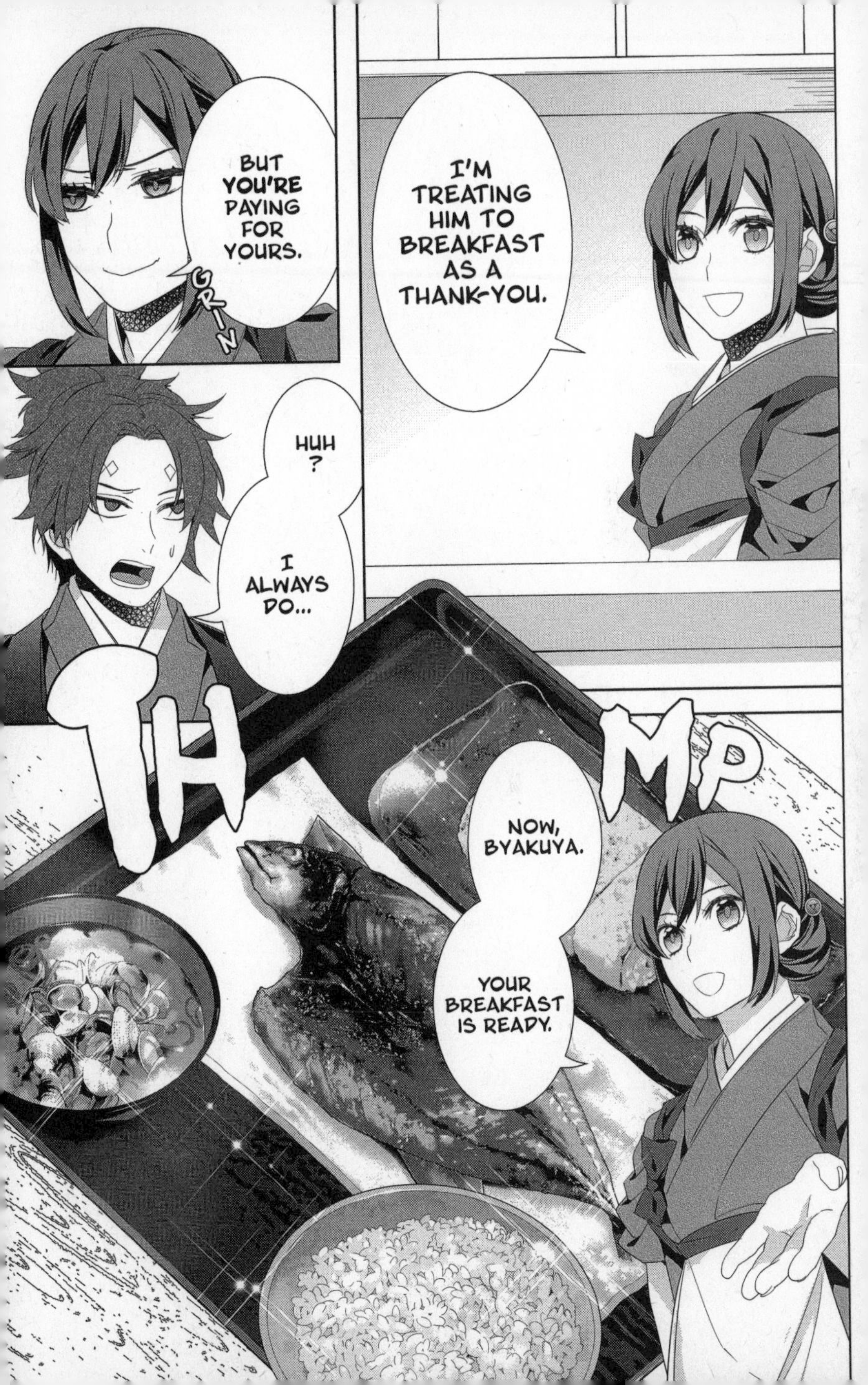
I'M TREATING HIM TO BREAKFAST AS A THANK-YOU.
BUT YOU'RE PAYING FOR YOURS.
GRIN
HUH?
I ALWAYS DO...
THMP
NOW, BYAKUYA.
YOUR BREAKFAST IS READY.

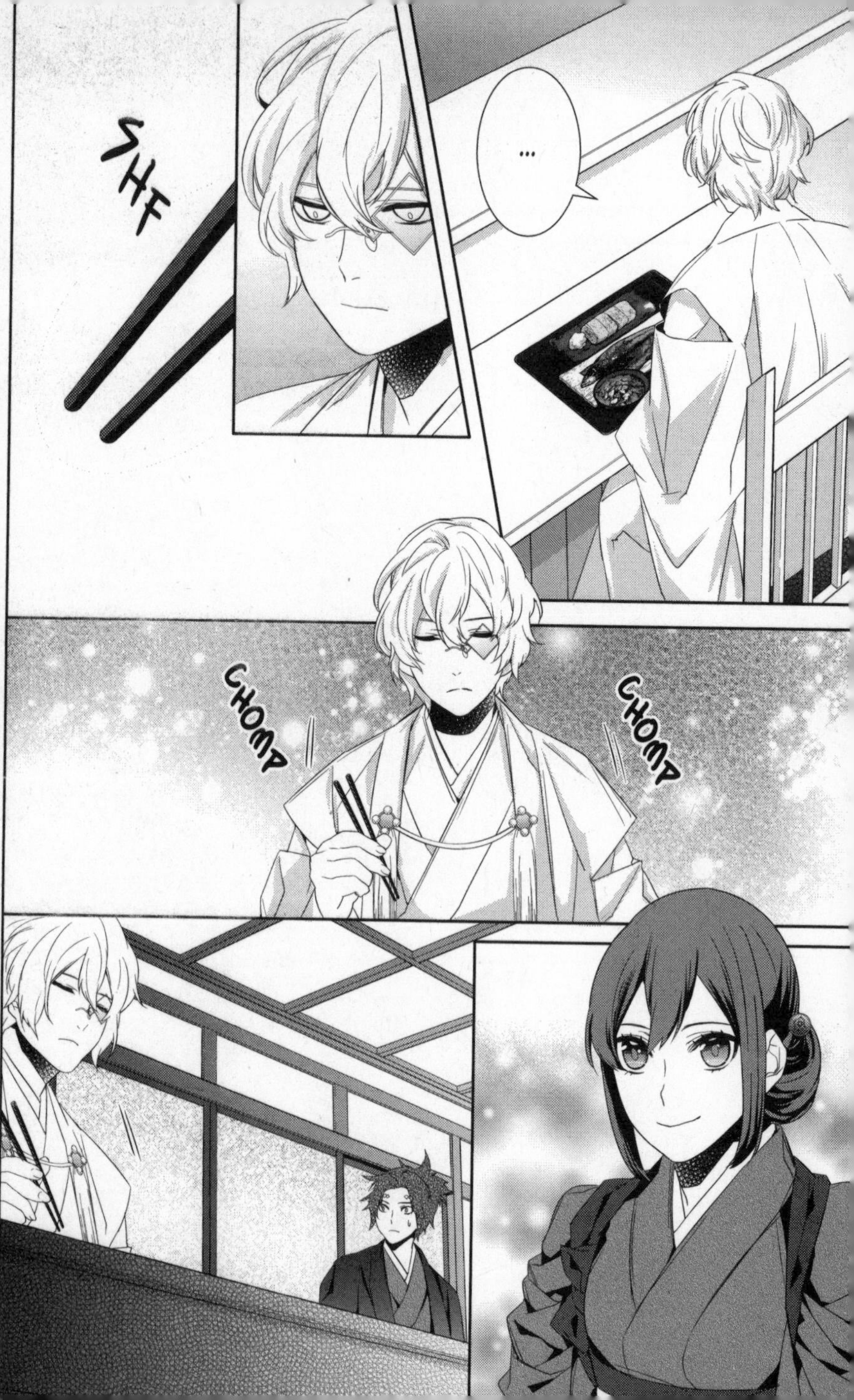
...
SHF
CHOMP
CHOMP

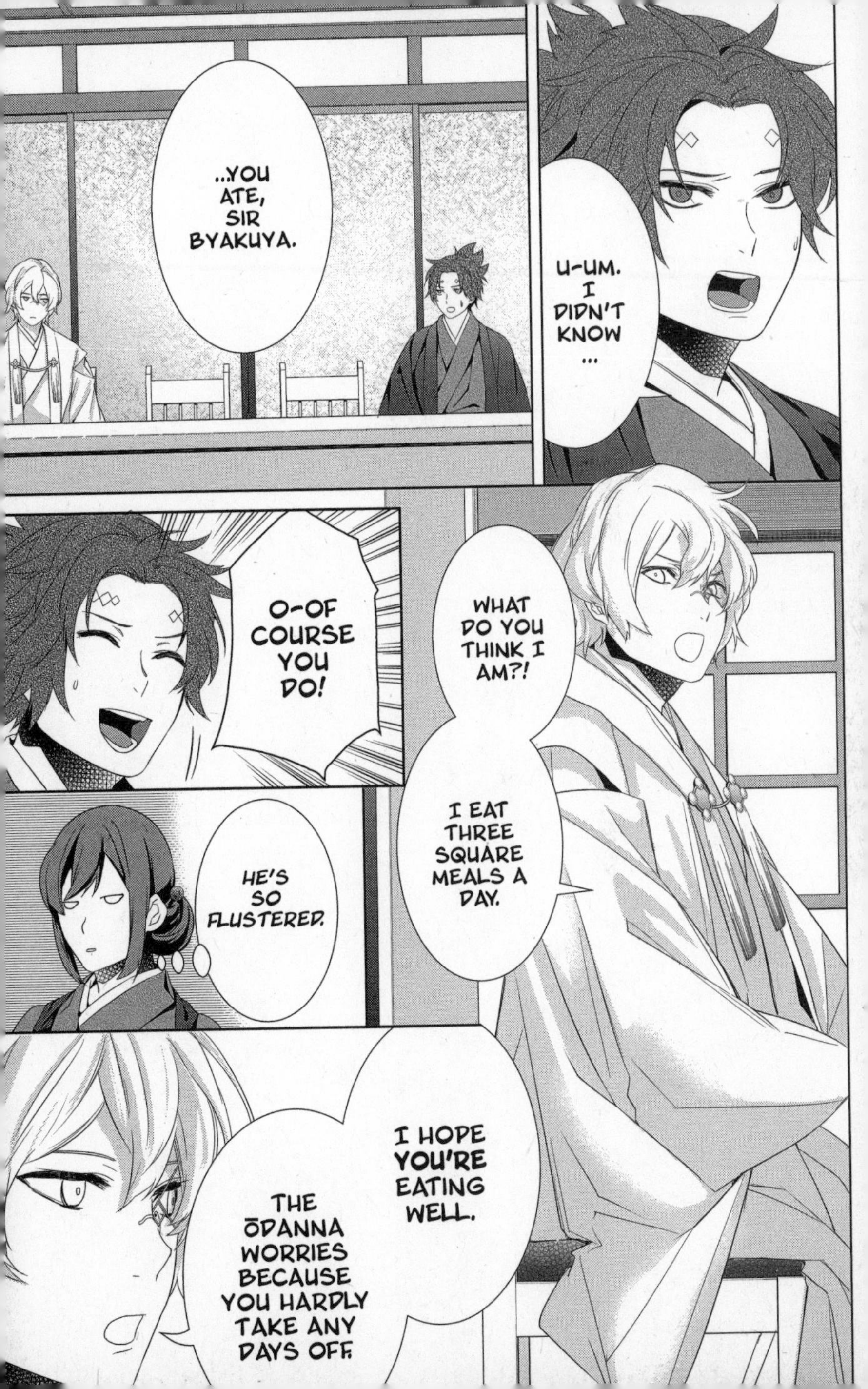
U-UM. I DIDN'T KNOW...
...YOU ATE, SIR BYAKUYA.
WHAT DO YOU THINK I AM?!
I EAT THREE SQUARE MEALS A DAY.
O-OF COURSE YOU DO!
HE'S SO FLUSTERED.
I HOPE YOU'RE EATING WELL.
THE ŌDANNA WORRIES BECAUSE YOU HARDLY TAKE ANY DAYS OFF.

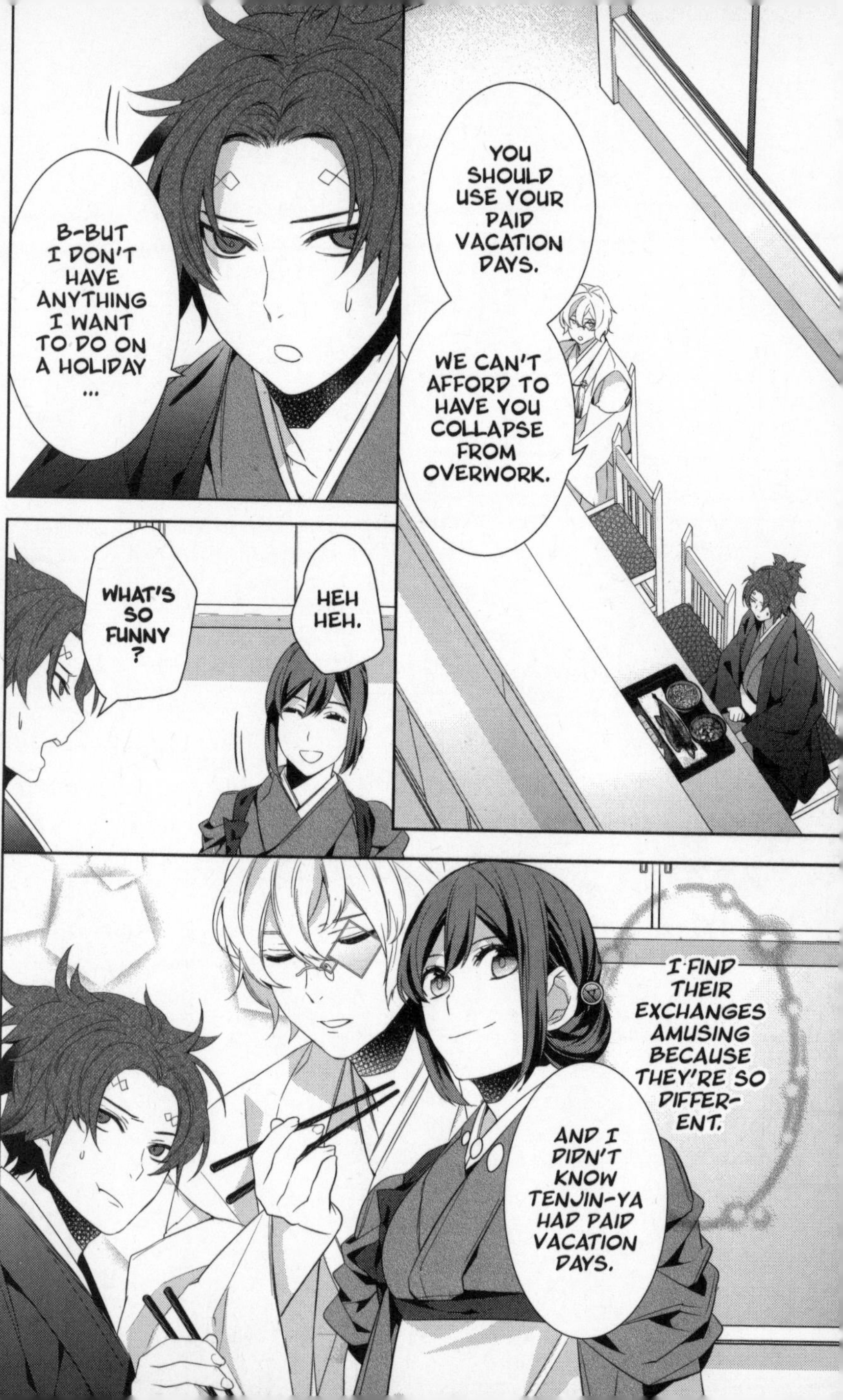
YOU SHOULD USE YOUR PAID VACATION DAYS.
WE CAN'T AFFORD TO HAVE YOU COLLAPSE FROM OVERWORK.
B-BUT I DON'T HAVE ANYTHING I WANT TO DO ON A HOLIDAY ...
HEH HEH.
WHAT'S SO FUNNY?
I FIND THEIR EXCHANGES AMUSING BECAUSE THEY'RE SO DIFFER-ENT.
AND I DIDN'T KNOW TENJIN-YA HAD PAID VACATION DAYS.

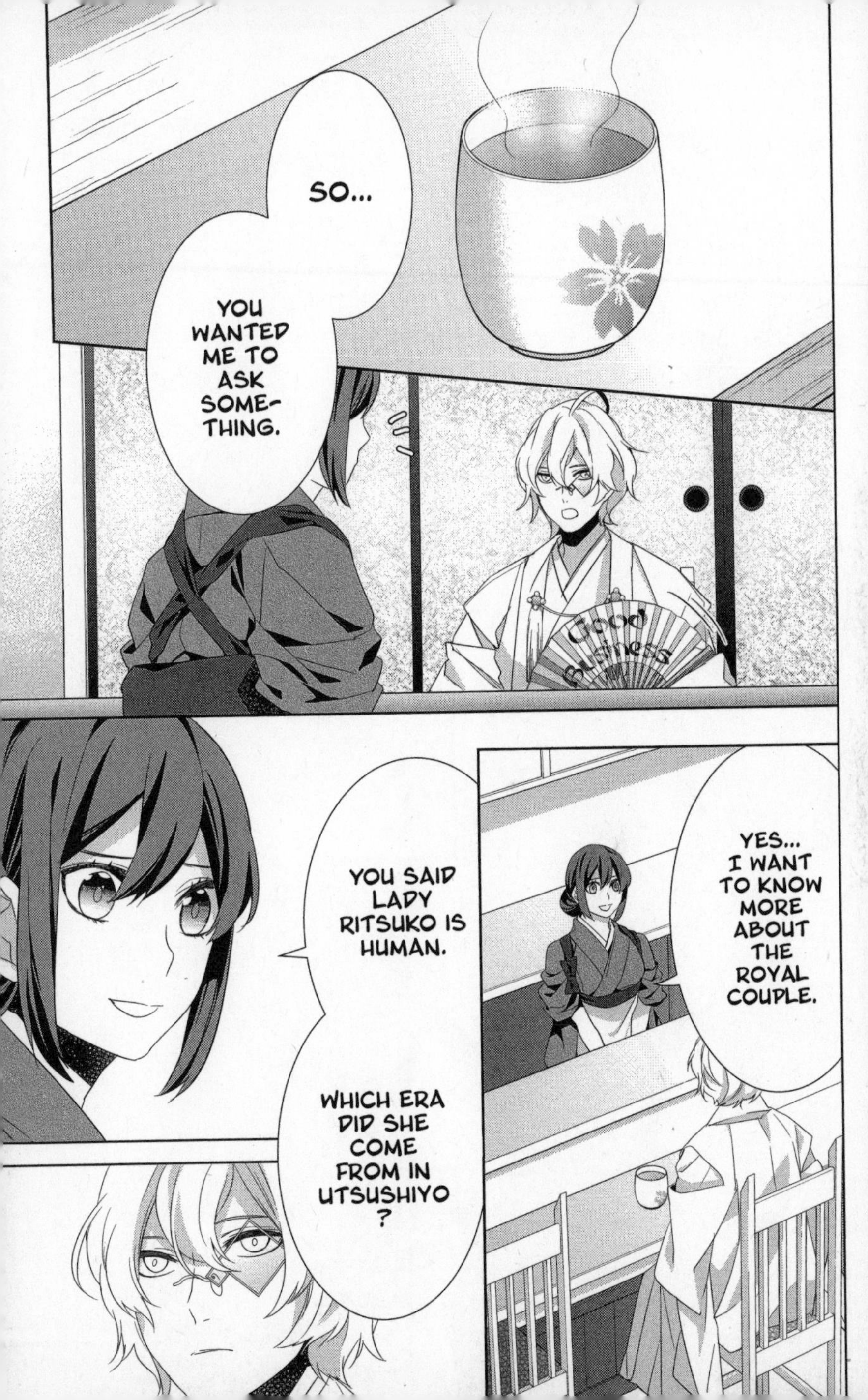
SO...
YOU WANTED ME TO ASK SOME-THING.
Good Business
YES... I WANT TO KNOW MORE ABOUT THE ROYAL COUPLE.
YOU SAID LADY RITSUKO IS HUMAN.
WHICH ERA DID SHE COME FROM IN UTSUSHIYO?

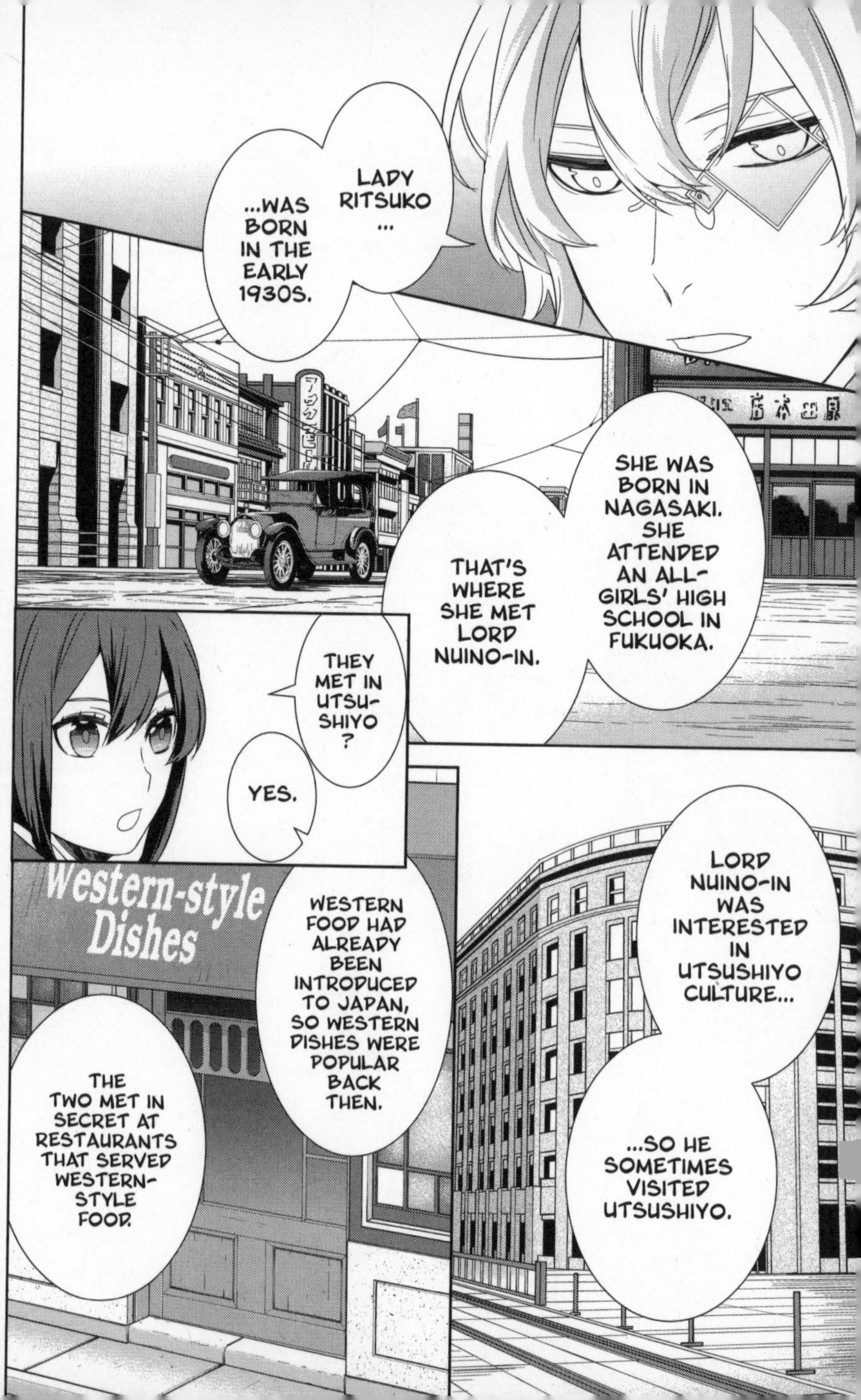

LADY RITSUKO ...
...WAS BORN IN THE EARLY 1930S.
SHE WAS BORN IN NAGASAKI. SHE ATTENDED AN ALL-GIRLS' HIGH SCHOOL IN FUKUOKA.
THAT'S WHERE SHE MET LORD NUINO-IN.
THEY MET IN UTSU-SHIYO?
YES.
LORD NUINO-IN WAS INTERESTED IN UTSUSHIYO CULTURE...
...SO HE SOMETIMES VISITED UTSUSHIYO.
Western-style Dishes
WESTERN FOOD HAD ALREADY BEEN INTRODUCED TO JAPAN, SO WESTERN DISHES WERE POPULAR BACK THEN.
THE TWO MET IN SECRET AT RESTAURANTS THAT SERVED WESTERN-STYLE FOOD.

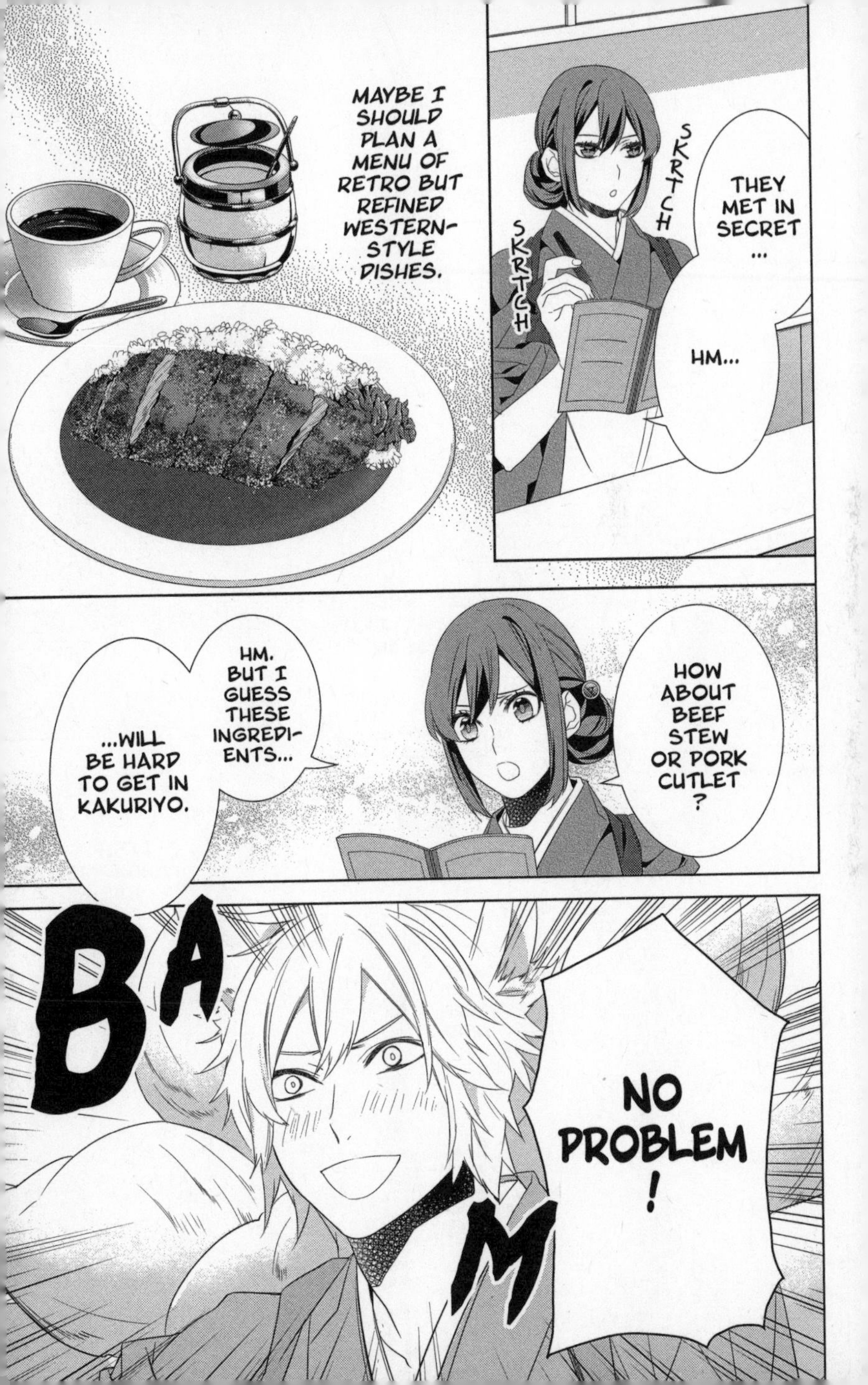
THEY MET IN SECRET...
SKRTCH
SKRTCH
HM...
MAYBE I SHOULD PLAN A MENU OF RETRO BUT REFINED WESTERN-STYLE DISHES.
HOW ABOUT BEEF STEW OR PORK CUTLET?
HM. BUT I GUESS THESE INGREDI-ENTS...
...WILL BE HARD TO GET IN KAKURIYO.
NO PROBLEM!
BAM

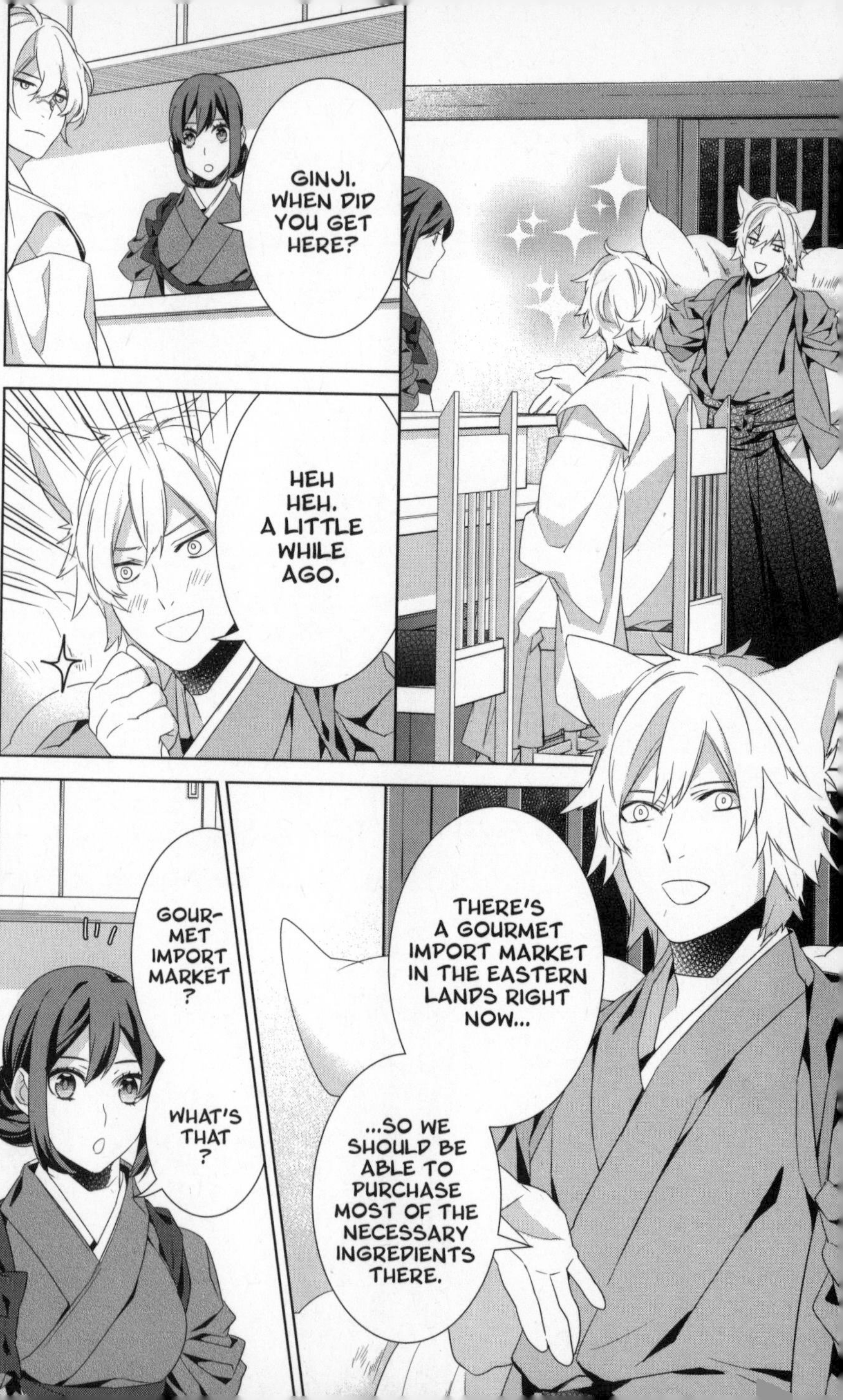
GINJI. WHEN DID YOU GET HERE?
HEH HEH. A LITTLE WHILE AGO.
THERE'S A GOURMET IMPORT MARKET IN THE EASTERN LANDS RIGHT NOW...
...SO WE SHOULD BE ABLE TO PURCHASE MOST OF THE NECESSARY INGREDIENTS THERE.
GOURMET IMPORT MARKET?
WHAT'S THAT?

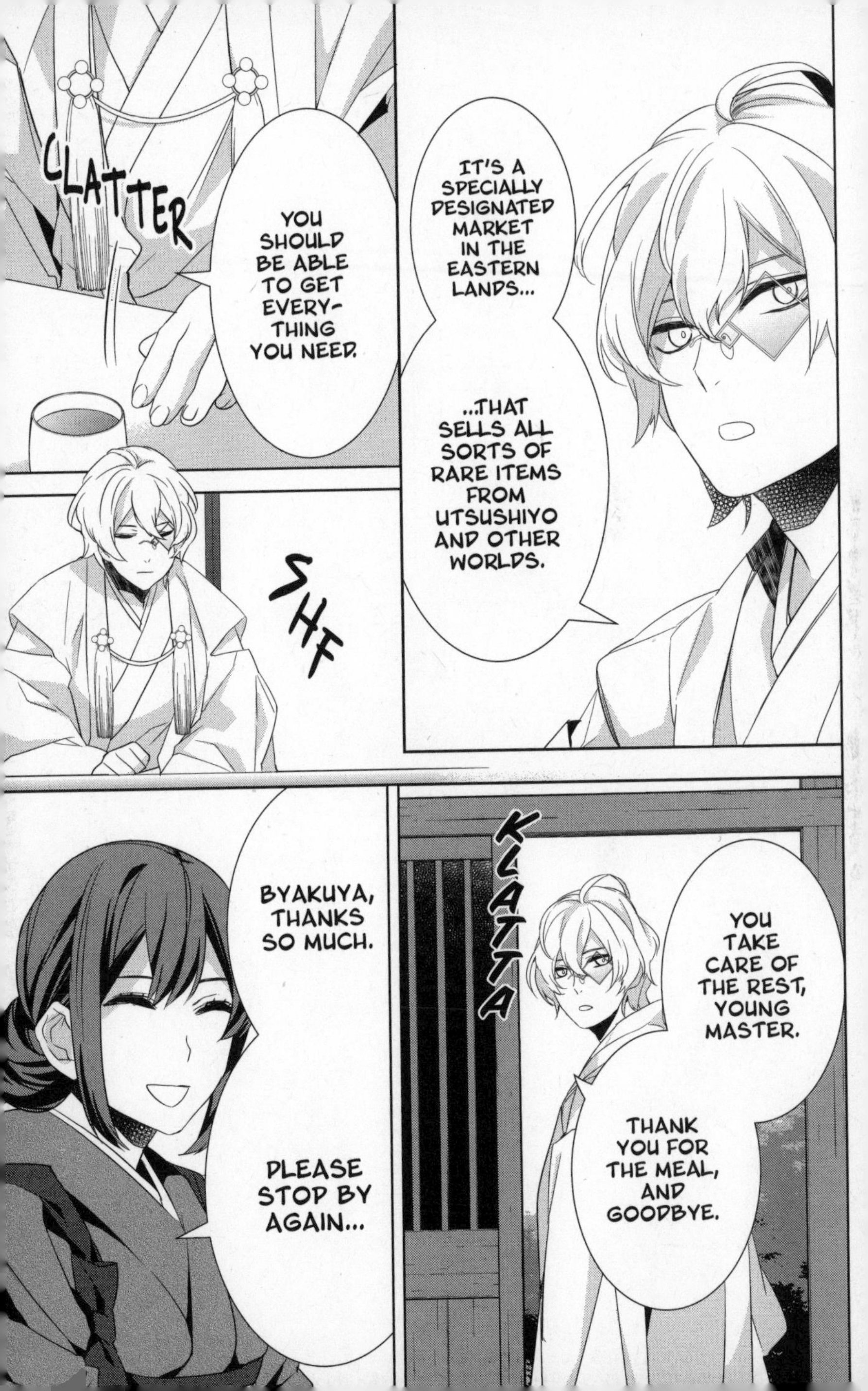
IT'S A SPECIALLY DESIGNATED MARKET IN THE EASTERN LANDS...
...THAT SELLS ALL SORTS OF RARE ITEMS FROM UTSUSHIYO AND OTHER WORLDS.
CLATTER
YOU SHOULD BE ABLE TO GET EVERY-THING YOU NEED.
SHF
KLATTA
YOU TAKE CARE OF THE REST, YOUNG MASTER.
THANK YOU FOR THE MEAL, AND GOODBYE.
BYAKUYA, THANKS SO MUCH.
PLEASE STOP BY AGAIN...

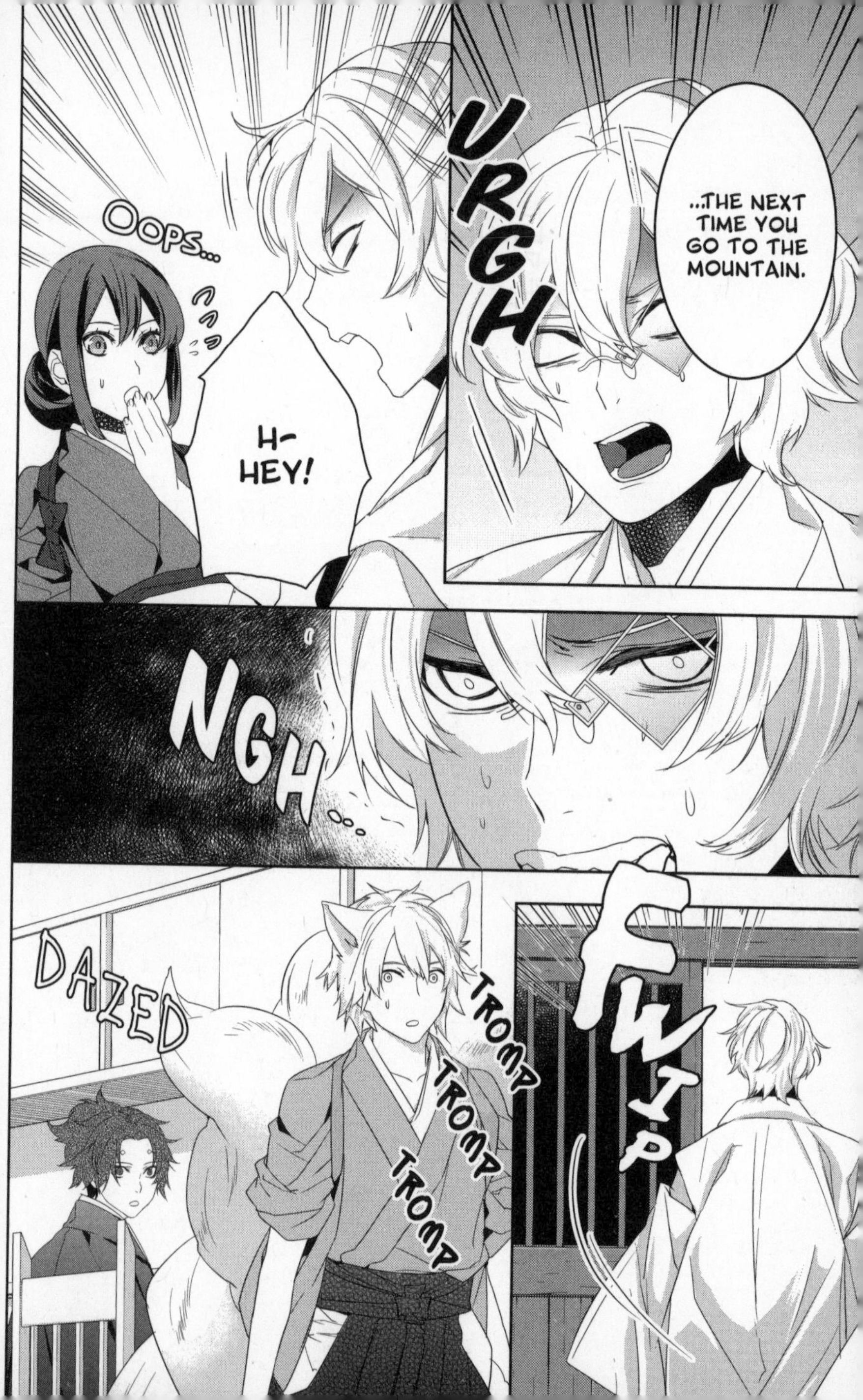
...THE NEXT TIME YOU GO TO THE MOUNTAIN.
URGH
OOPS...
H-HEY!
NGH...
FWIP
TROMP TROMP TROMP TROMP
DAZED

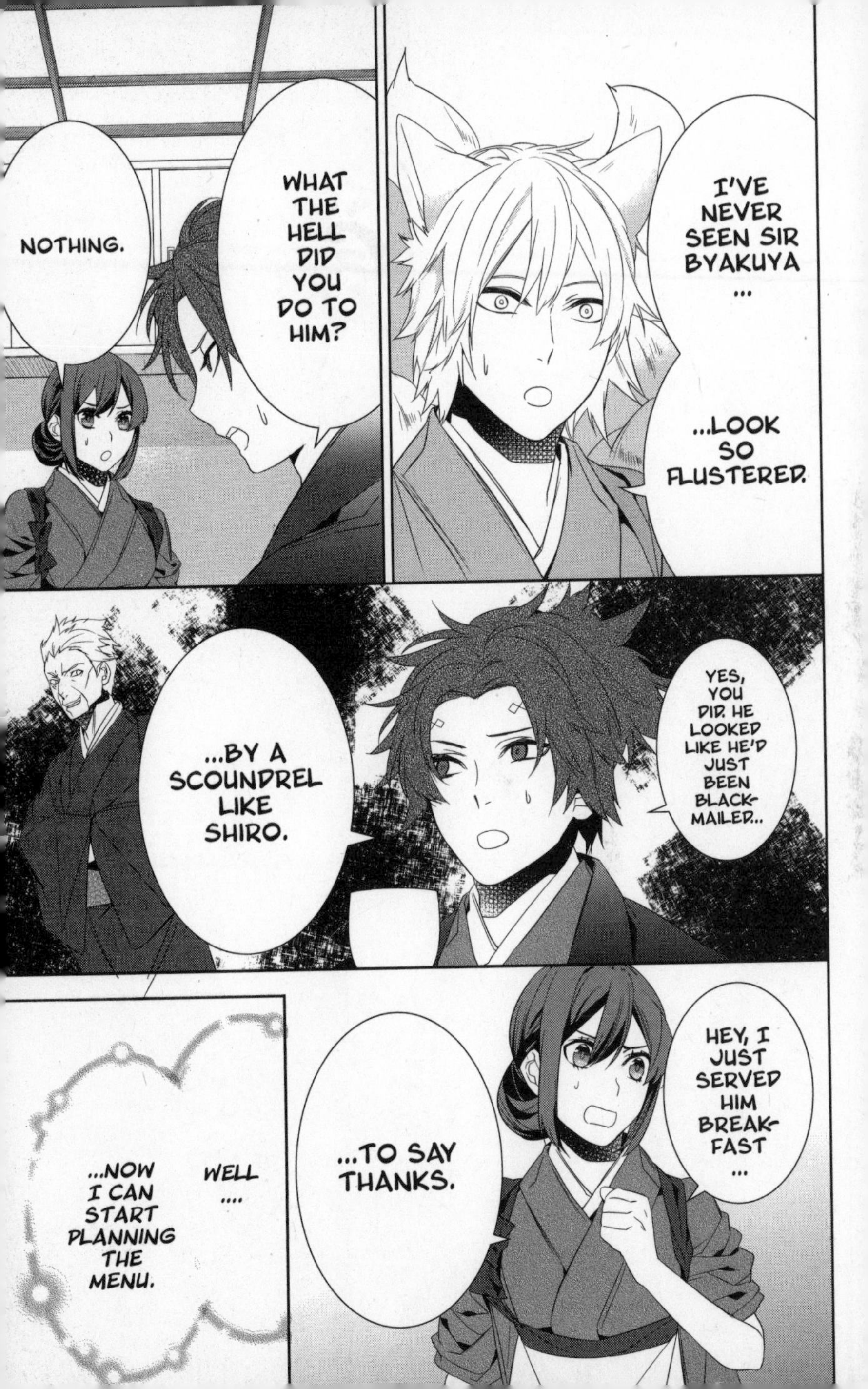
I'VE NEVER SEEN SIR BYAKUYA ...
...LOOK SO FLUSTERED.
WHAT THE HELL DID YOU DO TO HIM?
NOTHING.
YES, YOU DID. HE LOOKED LIKE HE'D JUST BEEN BLACK-MAILED...
...BY A SCOUNDREL LIKE SHIRO.
HEY, I JUST SERVED HIM BREAK-FAST ...
...TO SAY THANKS.
WELL ....
...NOW I CAN START PLANNING THE MENU.

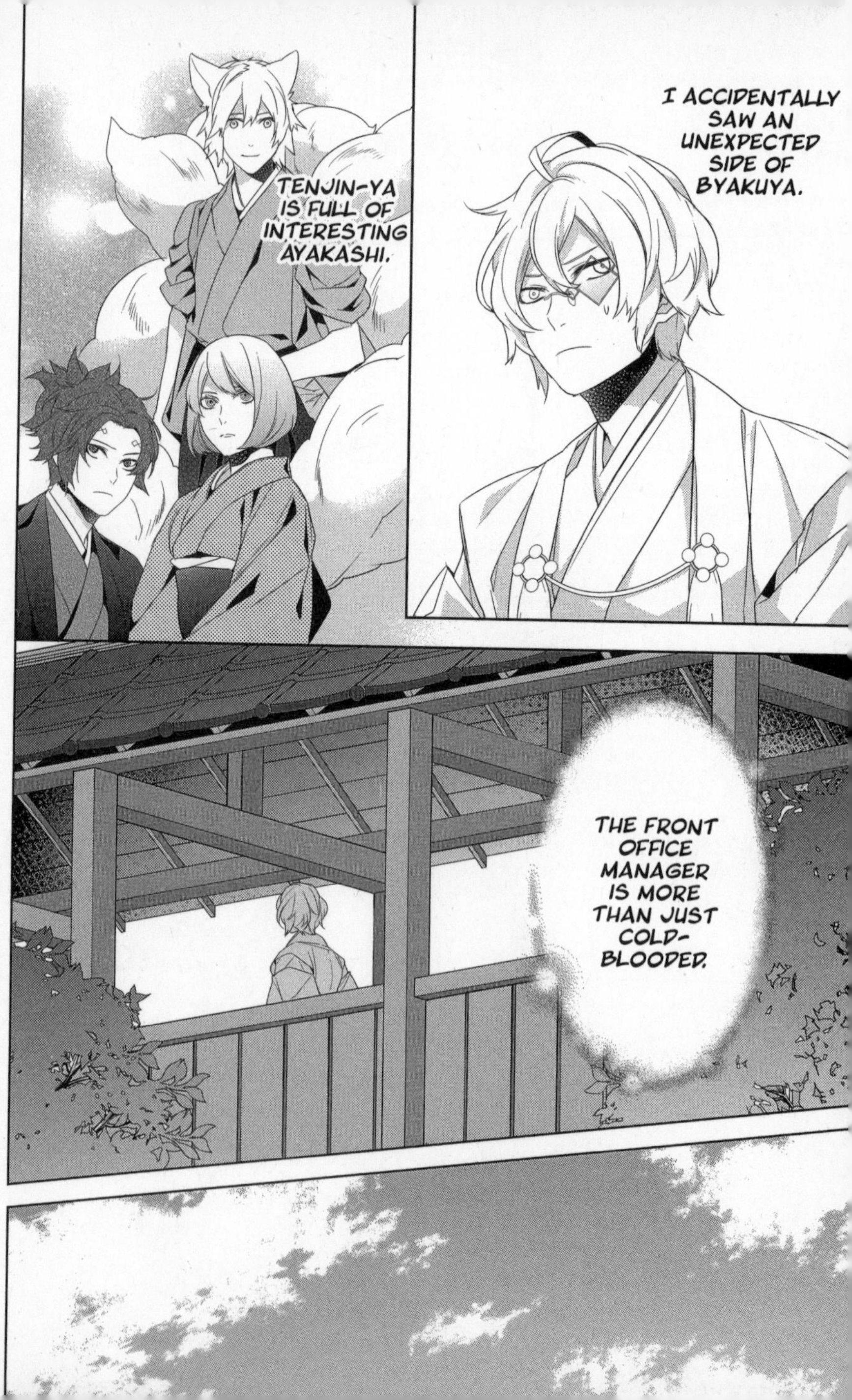
I ACCIDENTALLY SAW AN UNEXPECTED SIDE OF BYAKUYA.
TENJIN-YA IS FULL OF INTERESTING AYAKASHI.
THE FRONT OFFICE MANAGER IS MORE THAN JUST COLD-BLOODED.

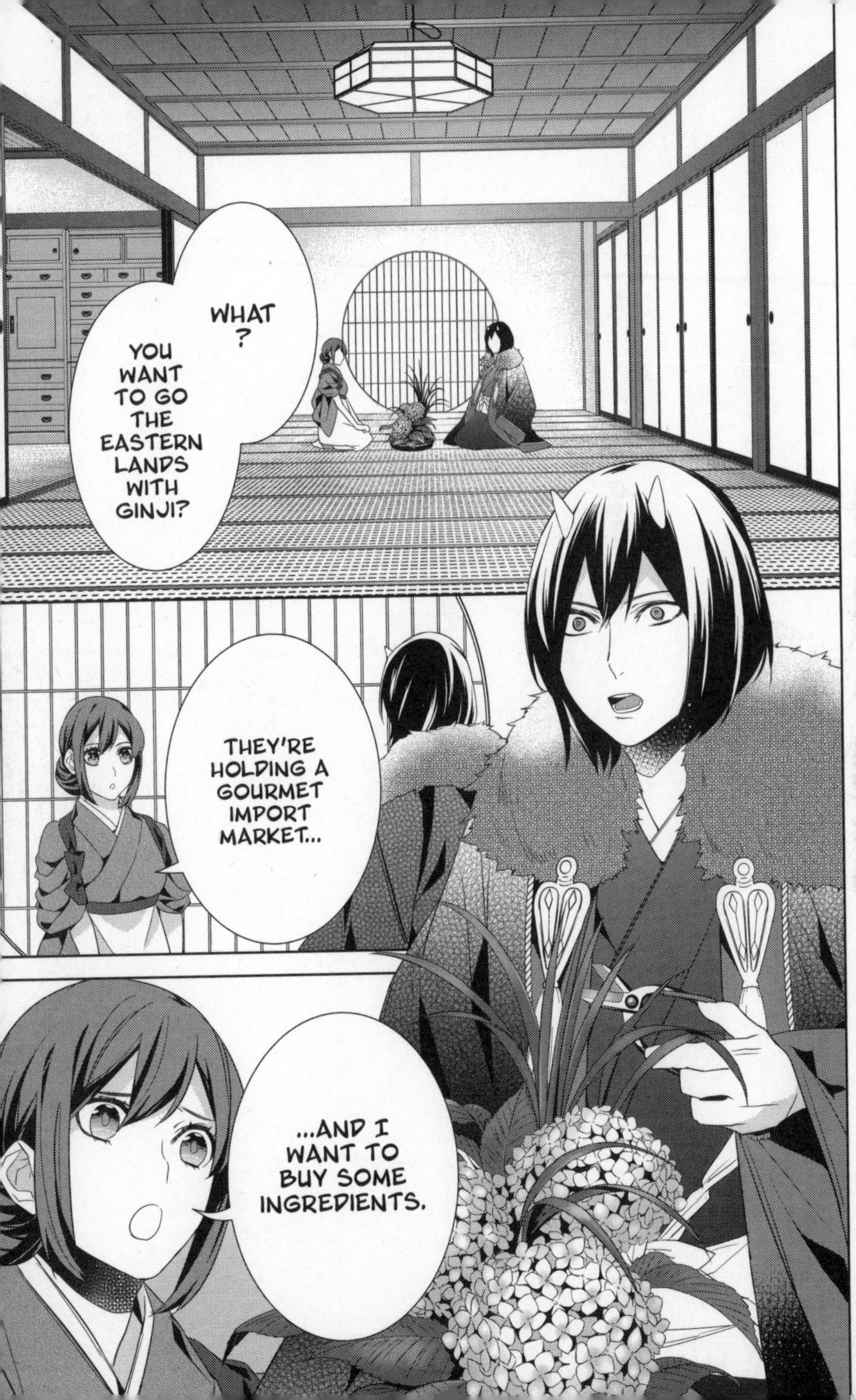
WHAT? YOU WANT TO GO THE EASTERN LANDS WITH GINJI?
THEY'RE HOLDING A GOURMET IMPORT MARKET...
...AND I WANT TO BUY SOME INGREDIENTS.

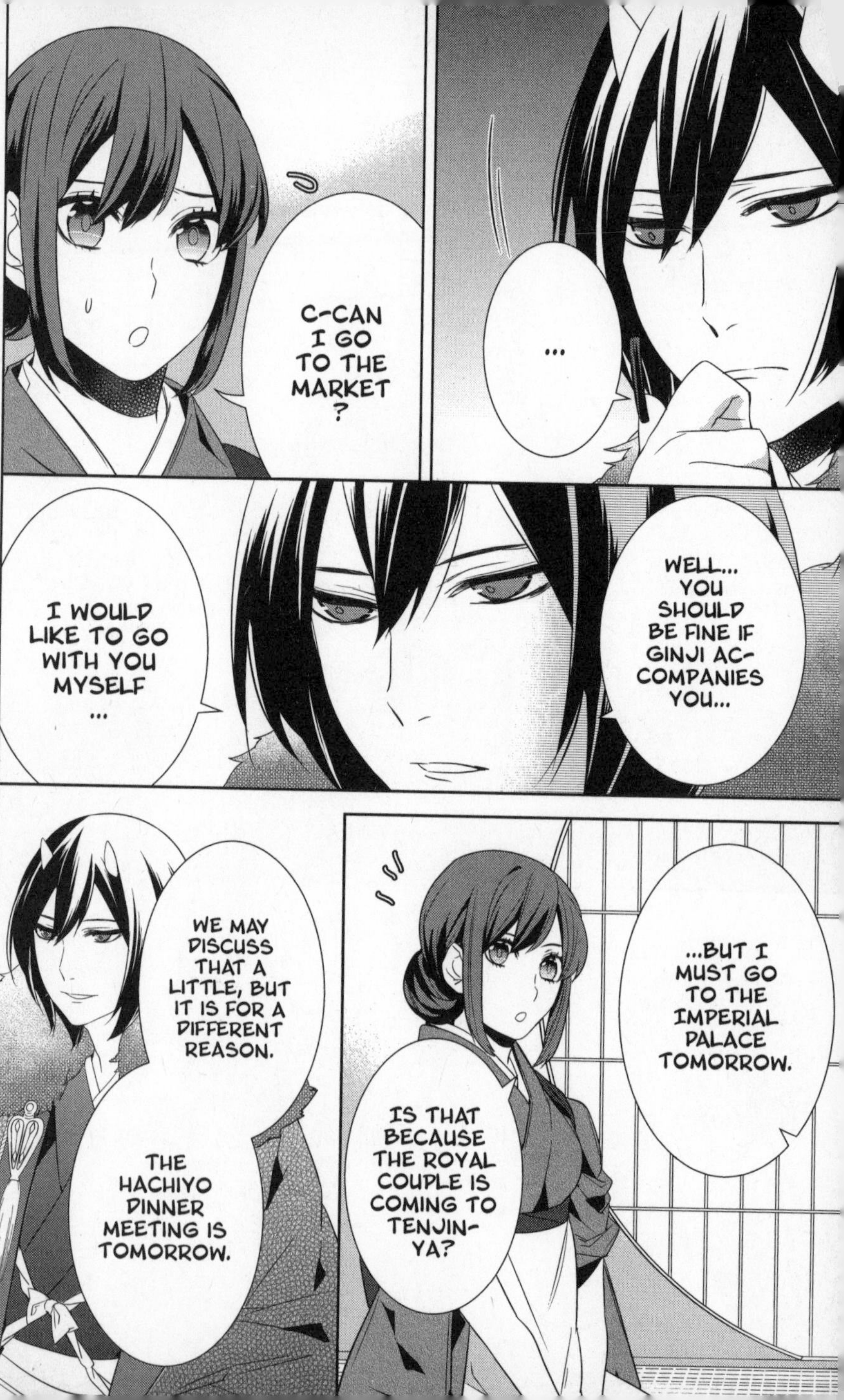
...
C-CAN I GO TO THE MARKET?
WELL... YOU SHOULD BE FINE IF GINJI AC-COMPANIES YOU...
I WOULD LIKE TO GO WITH YOU MYSELF...
...BUT I MUST GO TO THE IMPERIAL PALACE TOMORROW.
IS THAT BECAUSE THE ROYAL COUPLE IS COMING TO TENJIN-YA?
WE MAY DISCUSS THAT A LITTLE, BUT IT IS FOR A DIFFERENT REASON.
THE HACHIYO DINNER MEETING IS TOMORROW.

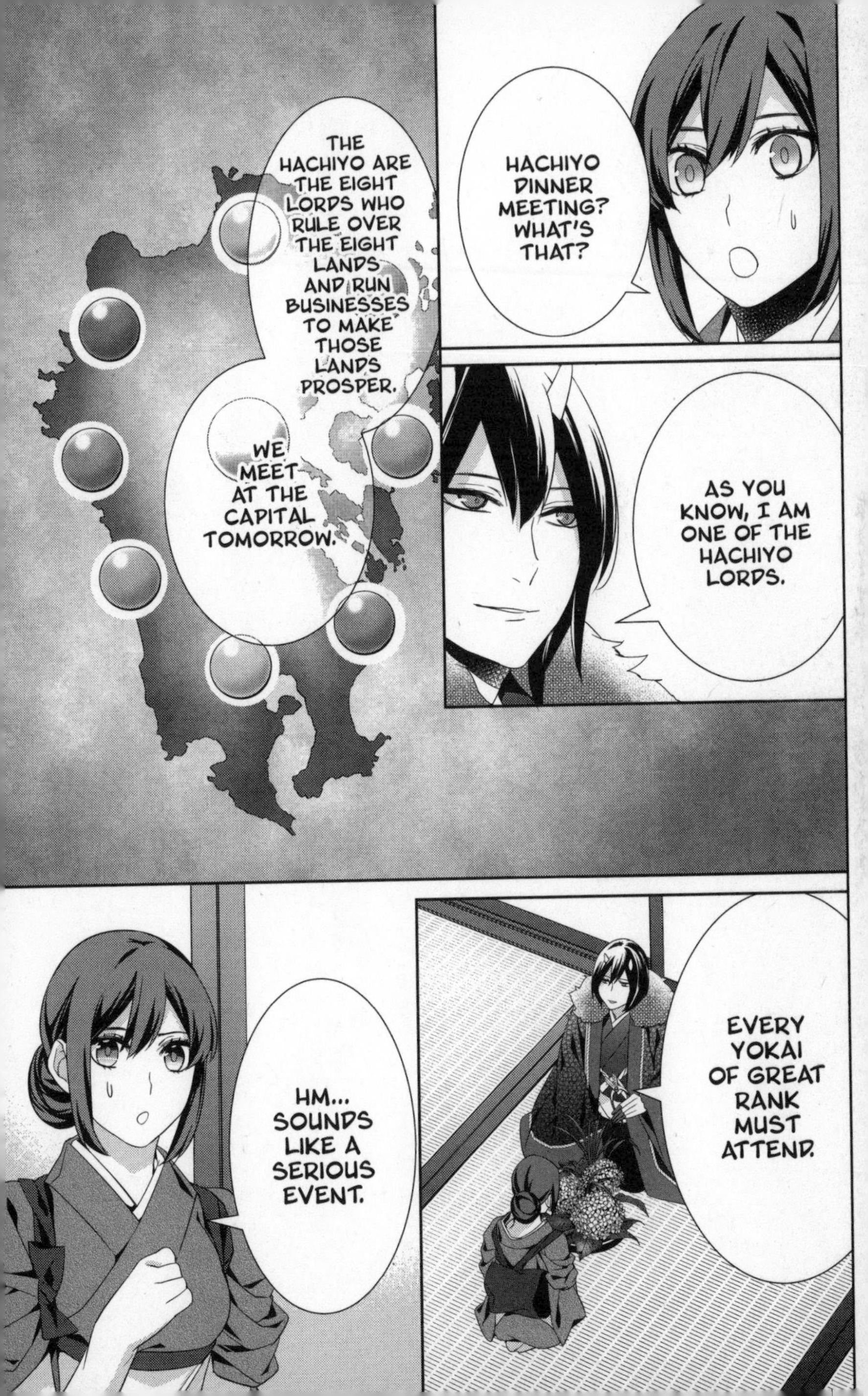
HACHIYO DINNER MEETING? WHAT'S THAT?
AS YOU KNOW, I AM ONE OF THE HACHIYO LORDS.
THE HACHIYO ARE THE EIGHT LORDS WHO RULE OVER THE EIGHT LANDS AND RUN BUSINESSES TO MAKE THOSE LANDS PROSPER.
WE MEET AT THE CAPITAL TOMORROW.
EVERY YOKAI OF GREAT RANK MUST ATTEND.
HM... SOUNDS LIKE A SERIOUS EVENT.

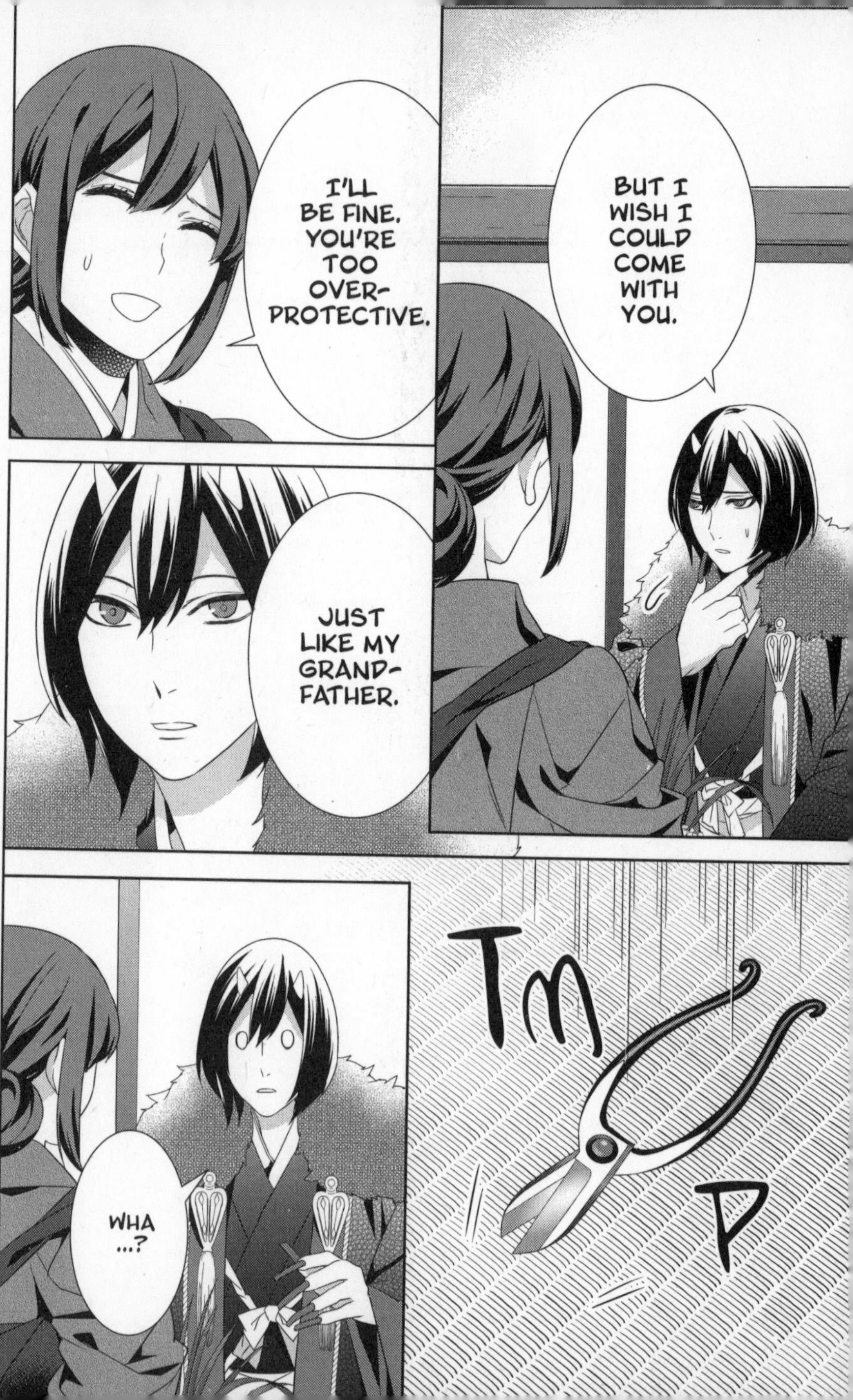
BUT I WISH I COULD COME WITH YOU.
I'LL BE FINE. YOU'RE TOO OVER-PROTECTIVE.
JUST LIKE MY GRAND-FATHER.
TMP
WHA ...?

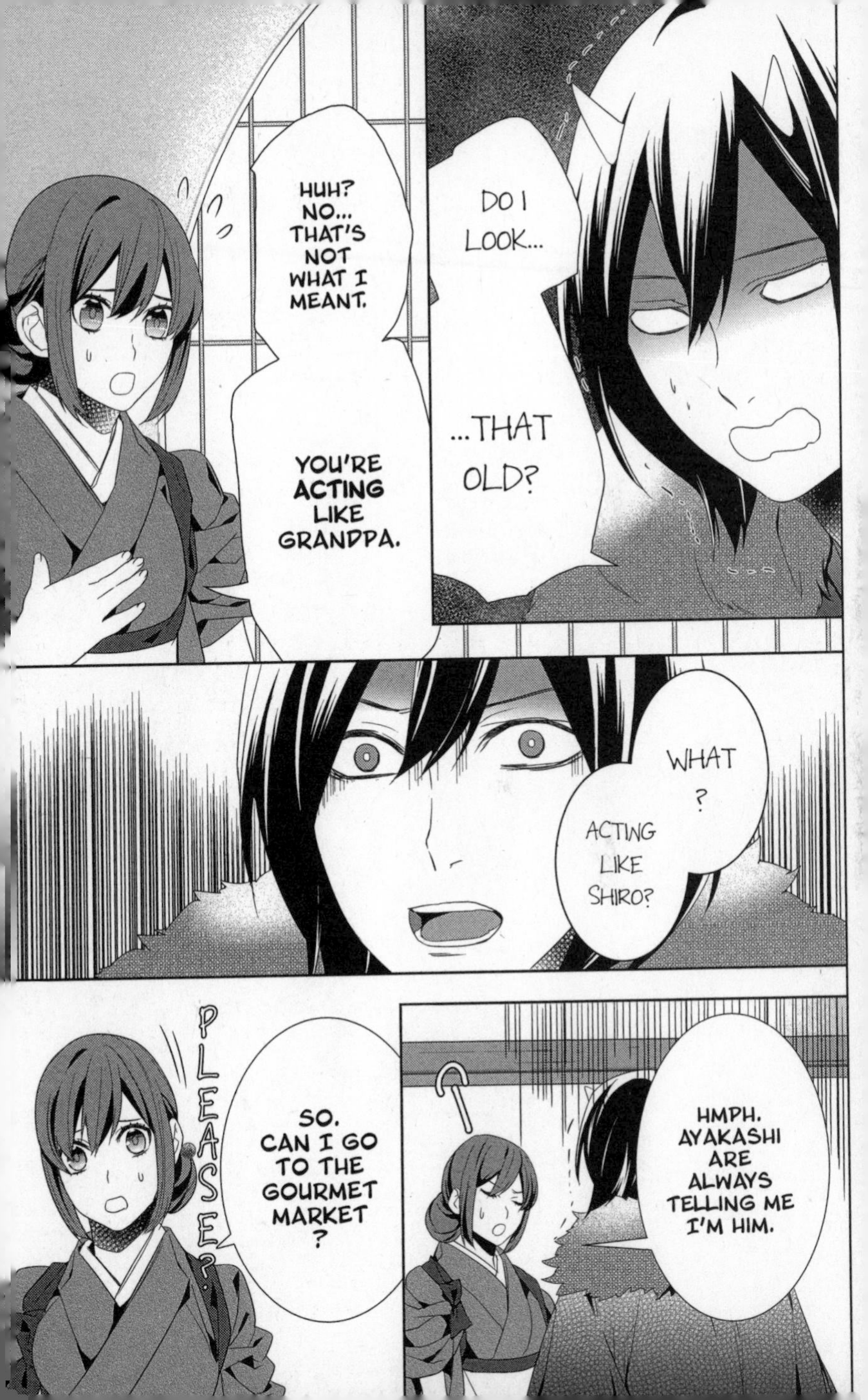
DO I LOOK...
...THAT OLD?
HUH? NO... THAT'S NOT WHAT I MEANT.
YOU'RE ACTING LIKE GRANDPA.
WHAT?
ACTING LIKE SHIRO?
HMPH. AYAKASHI ARE ALWAYS TELLING ME I'M HIM.
SO. CAN I GO TO THE GOURMET MARKET?
PLEASE?

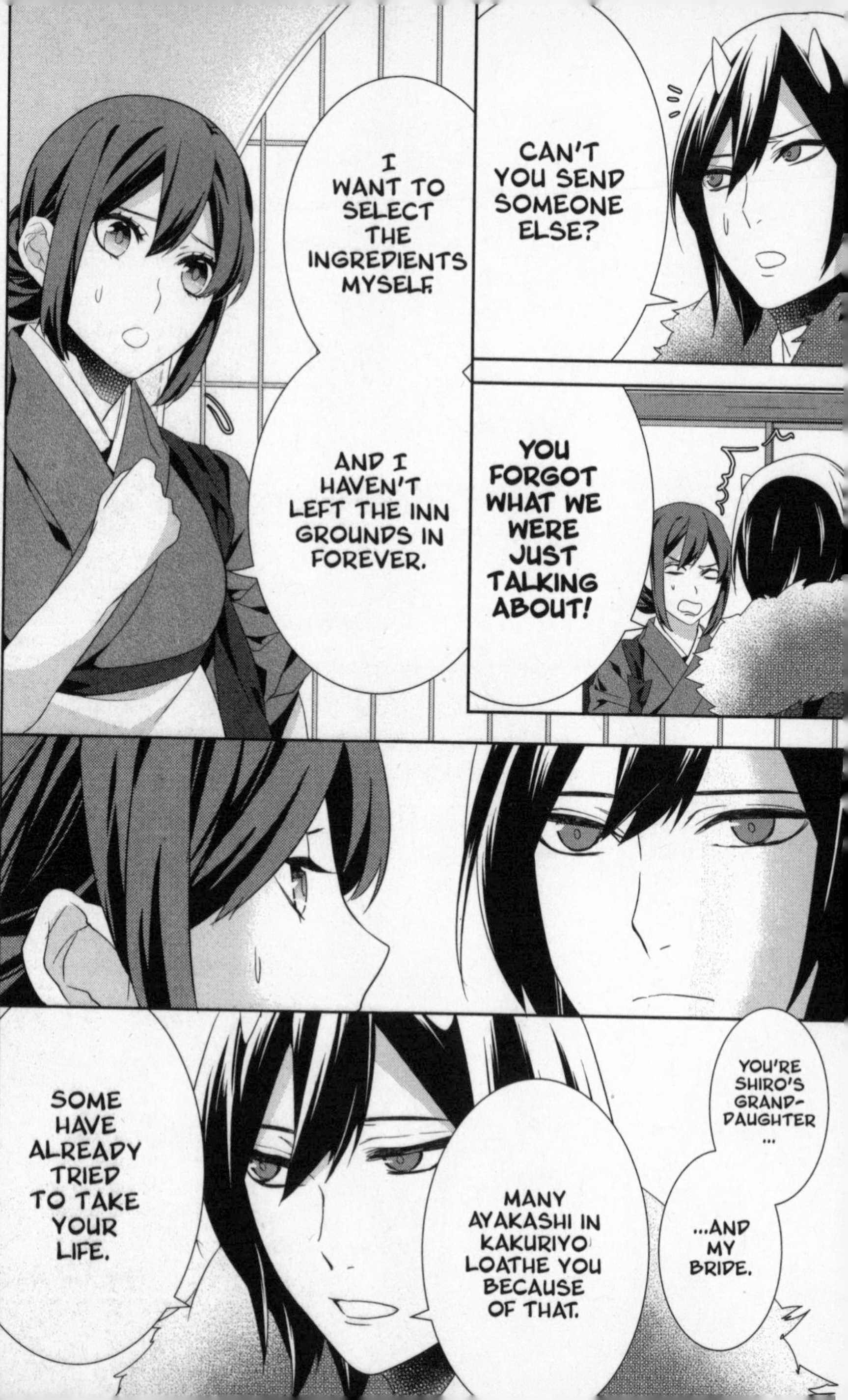
CAN'T YOU SEND SOMEONE ELSE?
YOU FORGOT WHAT WE WERE JUST TALKING ABOUT!
I WANT TO SELECT THE INGREDIENTS MYSELF.
AND I HAVEN'T LEFT THE INN GROUNDS IN FOREVER.
YOU'RE SHIRO'S GRAND-DAUGHTER...
...AND MY BRIDE.
MANY AYAKASHI IN KAKURIYO LOATHE YOU BECAUSE OF THAT.
SOME HAVE ALREADY TRIED TO TAKE YOUR LIFE.

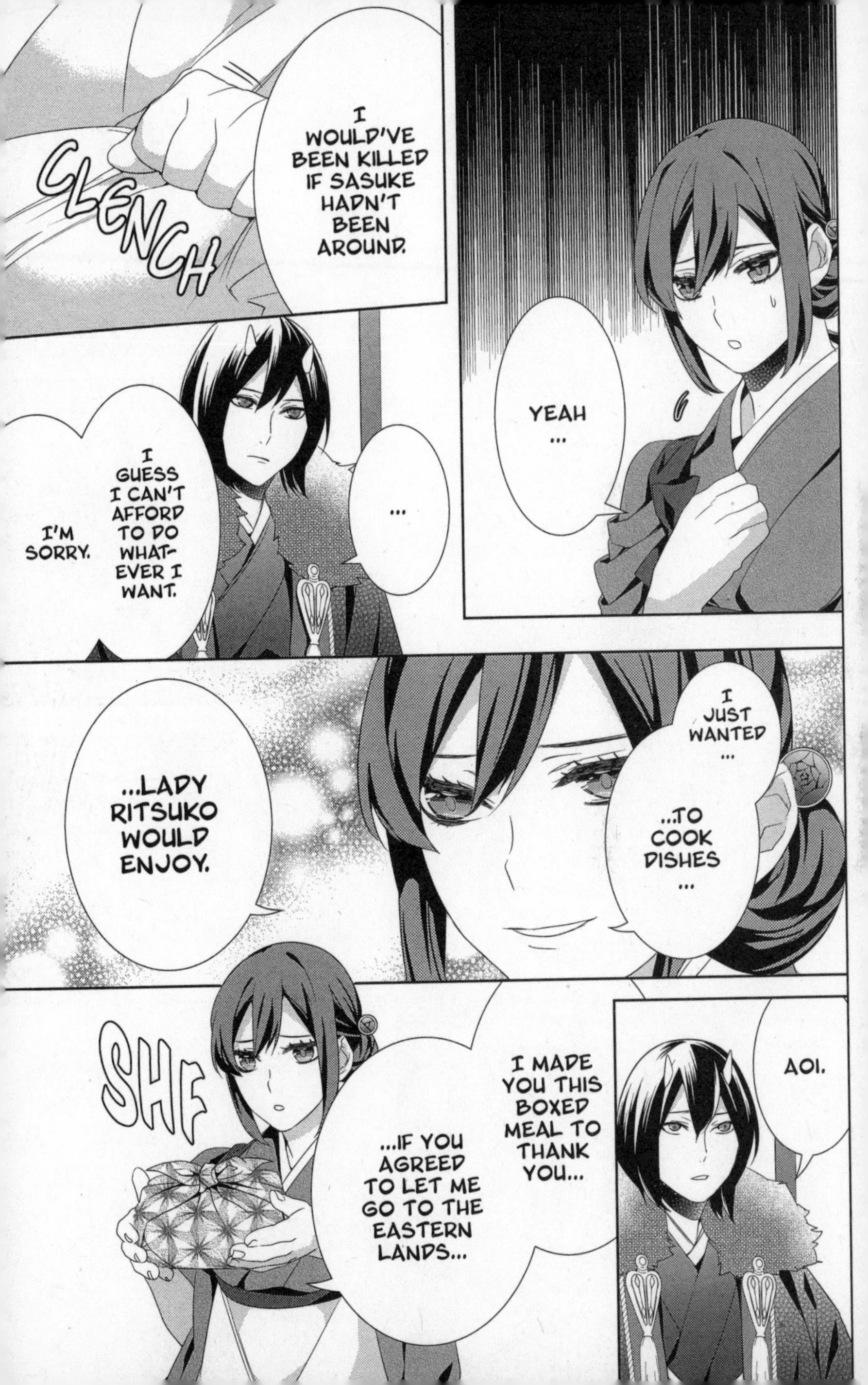
YEAH ...
CLENCH
I WOULD'VE BEEN KILLED IF SASUKE HADN'T BEEN AROUND.
...
I GUESS I CAN'T AFFORD TO DO WHATEVER I WANT.
I'M SORRY.
I JUST WANTED ...
...TO COOK DISHES ...
...LADY RITSUKO WOULD ENJOY.
AOI.
I MADE YOU THIS BOXED MEAL TO THANK YOU...
...IF YOU AGREED TO LET ME GO TO THE EASTERN LANDS...
SHF

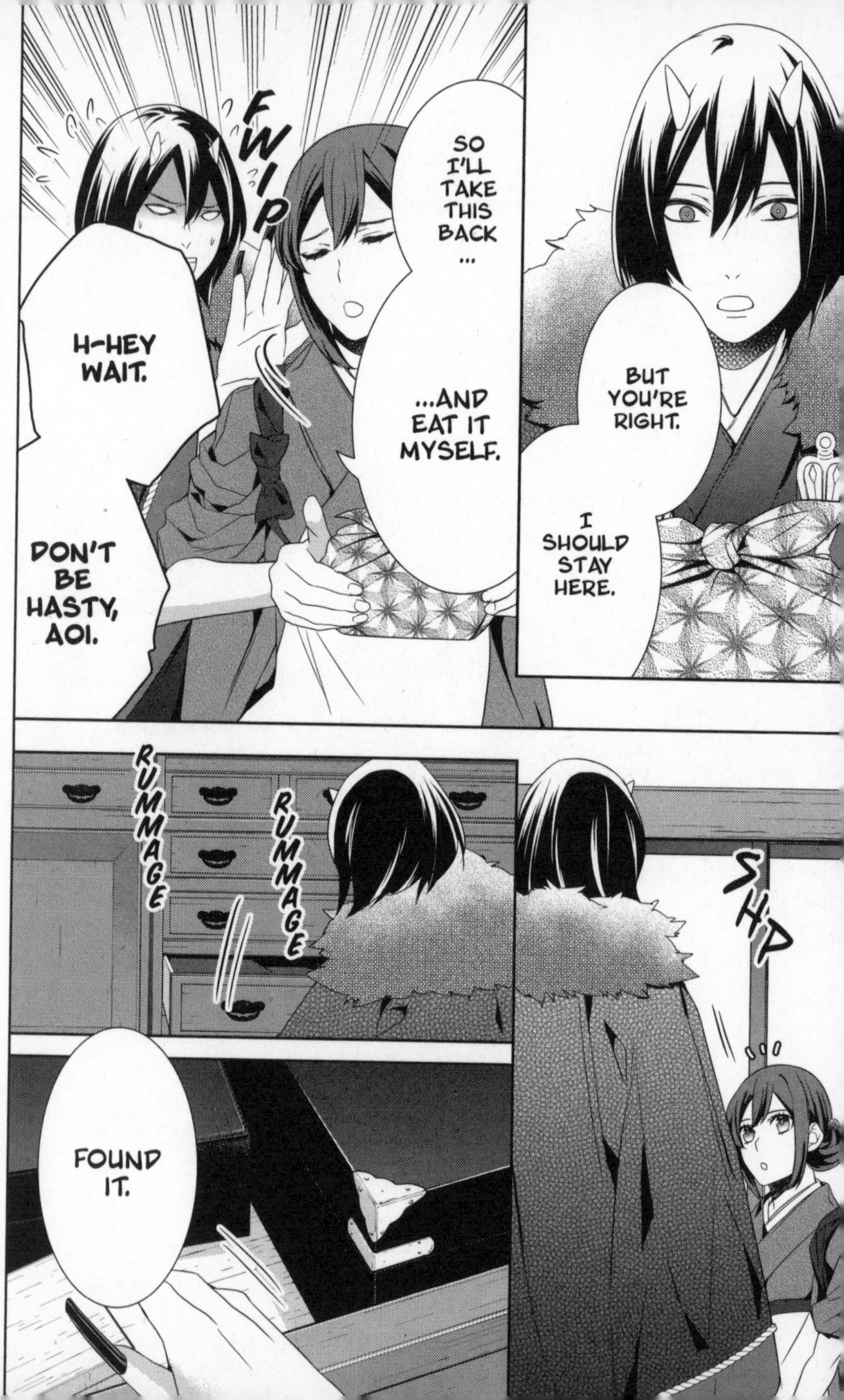
BUT YOU'RE RIGHT.
I SHOULD STAY HERE.
SO I'LL TAKE THIS BACK...
...AND EAT IT MYSELF.
FWIP
H-HEY WAIT.
DON'T BE HASTY, AOI.
SHP
RUMMAGE
RUMMAGE
FOUND IT.

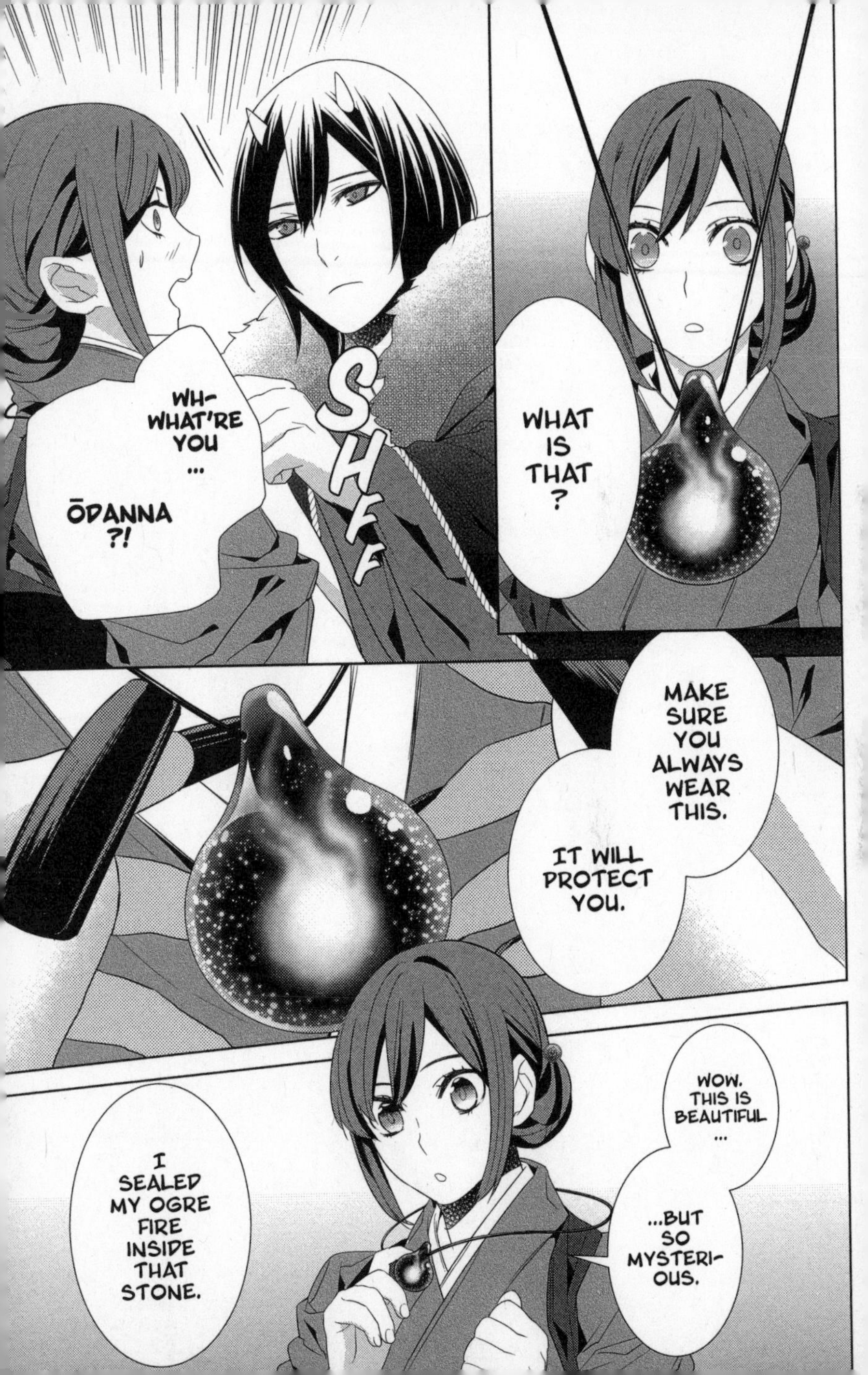
WHAT IS THAT?
WH-WHAT'RE YOU... ŌDANNA?!
SHFF
MAKE SURE YOU ALWAYS WEAR THIS.
IT WILL PROTECT YOU.
WOW. THIS IS BEAUTIFUL...
...BUT SO MYSTERI-OUS.
I SEALED MY OGRE FIRE INSIDE THAT STONE.

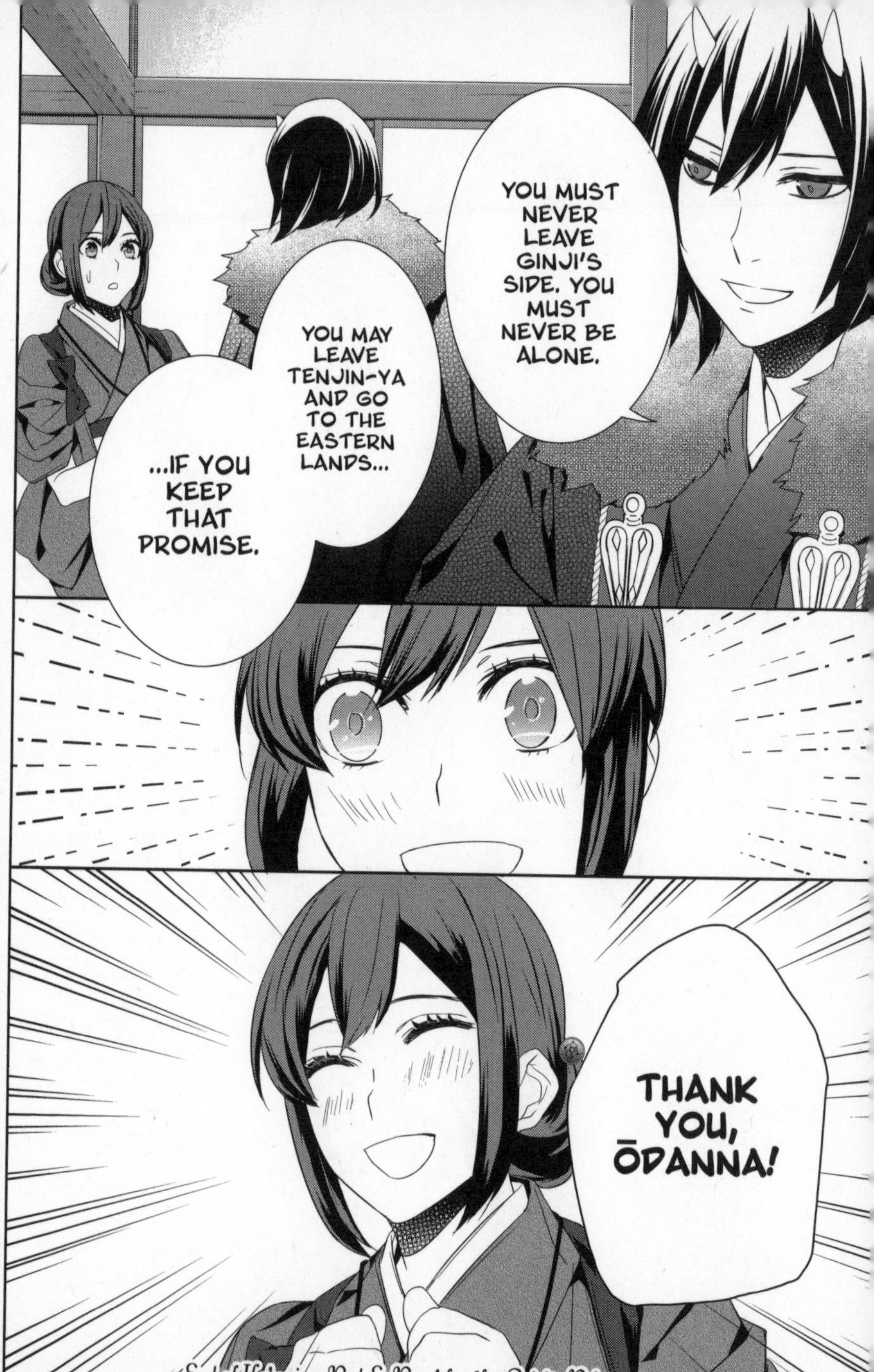
YOU MUST NEVER LEAVE GINJI'S SIDE. YOU MUST NEVER BE ALONE.
YOU MAY LEAVE TENJIN-YA AND GO TO THE EASTERN LANDS...
...IF YOU KEEP THAT PROMISE.
THANK YOU, ŌDANNA!

End of Kakuriyo: Bed & Breakfast for Spirits Volume 5

Kakuriyo
Bed & Breakfast
for Spirits

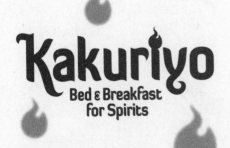

END NOTES

PAGE 57, PANEL 2
Cow demons
Cow demons, or *gyūki*, have the head of a cow and the body of an ogre. They appear near deep water and waterfalls and devour humans.

PAGE 59, PANEL 1
Kanten
Kanten is a gelatinizing agent made from seaweed. It is similar to agar, but creates a firmer texture.

PAGE 71, PANEL 3
Opens in the evening
Yūgao is a plant that blooms early in the evening and wilts the following morning.

PAGE 76, PANEL 1
Fortune Spirit
Fortune spirits take the form of little girls or boys in kimono with bobbed black hair. The houses in which they dwell will prosper, but become ruined when they leave. People used to offer red beans and rice to the fortune spirits living in their homes. They are considered to be spirits rather than ayakashi.

PAGE 126, PANEL 5
Western-style dishes
Japanese recipes derived from western dishes that were introduced after Japan opened its borders in the Meiji era (1868–1912 CE).

PAGE 29, PANEL 3
Shabu-Shabu
A hot pot dish of thinly sliced meat and vegetables boiled in water.

PAGE 30, PANEL 4
Daruma
Round good-luck dolls made in the shape of the Buddhist monk Bodhidarma. They're usually red.

PAGE 32, PANEL 3
Badger demon
Mujina in Japanese. These ayakashi look like young Buddhist priests. They are also shapeshifters and tricksters.

PAGE 38, PANEL 4
Mizuna leaves
Also known as Japanese mustard greens. They have a sharp, spicy flavor.

PAGE 55, PANEL 2
Anmitsu jelly
Syrup-covered kanten jelly with sweet red bean paste, topped with fruit.

PAGE 55, PANEL 3
Cream anmitsu jelly
Anmitsu jelly with whipped cream or ice cream on top.

Kakuriyo
Bed & Breakfast for Spirits

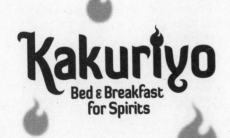

Kakuriyo
Bed & Breakfast for Spirits

5

SHOJO BEAT EDITION

Art by **Waco Ioka**
Original story by **Midori Yuma**
Character design by **Laruha**

English Translation & Adaptation **Tomo Kimura**
Touch-up Art & Lettering **Joanna Estep**
Design **Alice Lewis**
Editor **Pancha Diaz**

KAKURIYO NO YADOMESHI AYAKASHIOYADO NI YOMEIRI SHIMASU, Vol. 5
©Waco Ioka 2018
©Midori Yuma 2018
©Laruha 2018
First published in Japan in 2018 by KADOKAWA CORPORATION, Tokyo.
English translation rights arranged with KADOKAWA CORPORATION, Tokyo.

Printed in the U.S.A.

Published by VIZ Media, LLC.
P.O. Box 77010
San Francisco, CA 94107

10 9 8 7 6 5 4 3 2 1
First printing, September 2019

viz.com   shojobeat.com

Snow White with the Red Hair

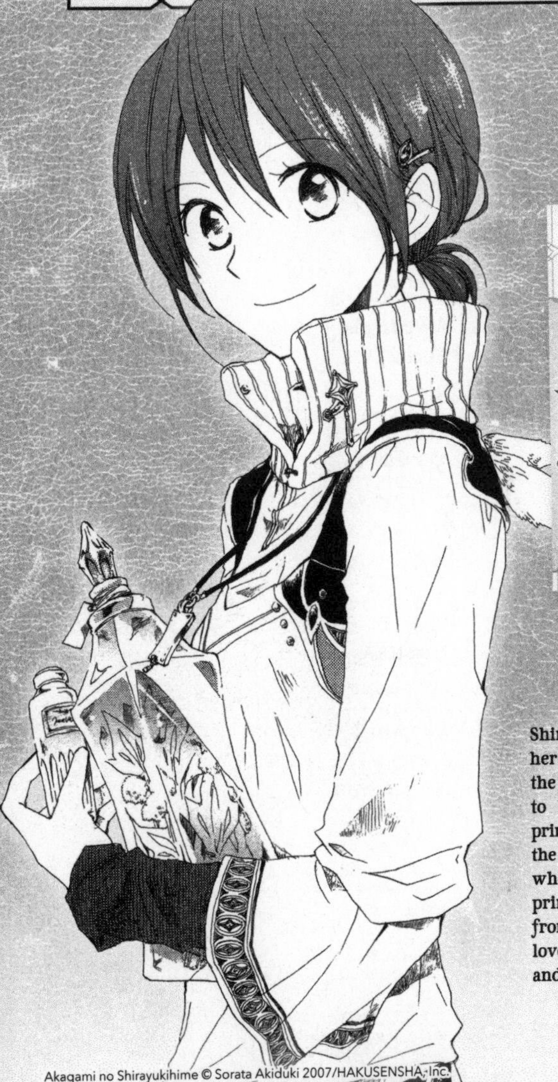

Inspired the anime!

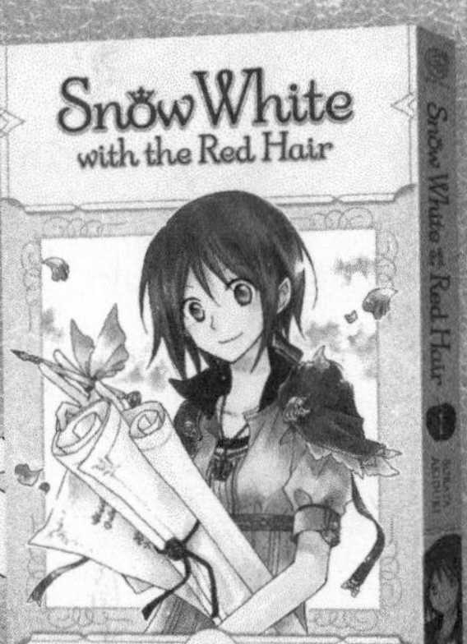

Snow White with the Red Hair
Snow White with the Red Hair
Sorata 1 Akiduki
VIZ

STORY & ART BY

SORATA AKIDUKI

Shirayuki is an herbalist famous for her naturally bright-red hair, and the prince of Tanbarun wants her all to himself! Unwilling to become the prince's possession, she seeks shelter in the woods of the neighboring kingdom, where she gains an unlikely ally—the prince of that kingdom! He rescues her from her plight, and thus begins the love story between a lovestruck prince and an unusual herbalist.

RATED T TEEN

VIZ

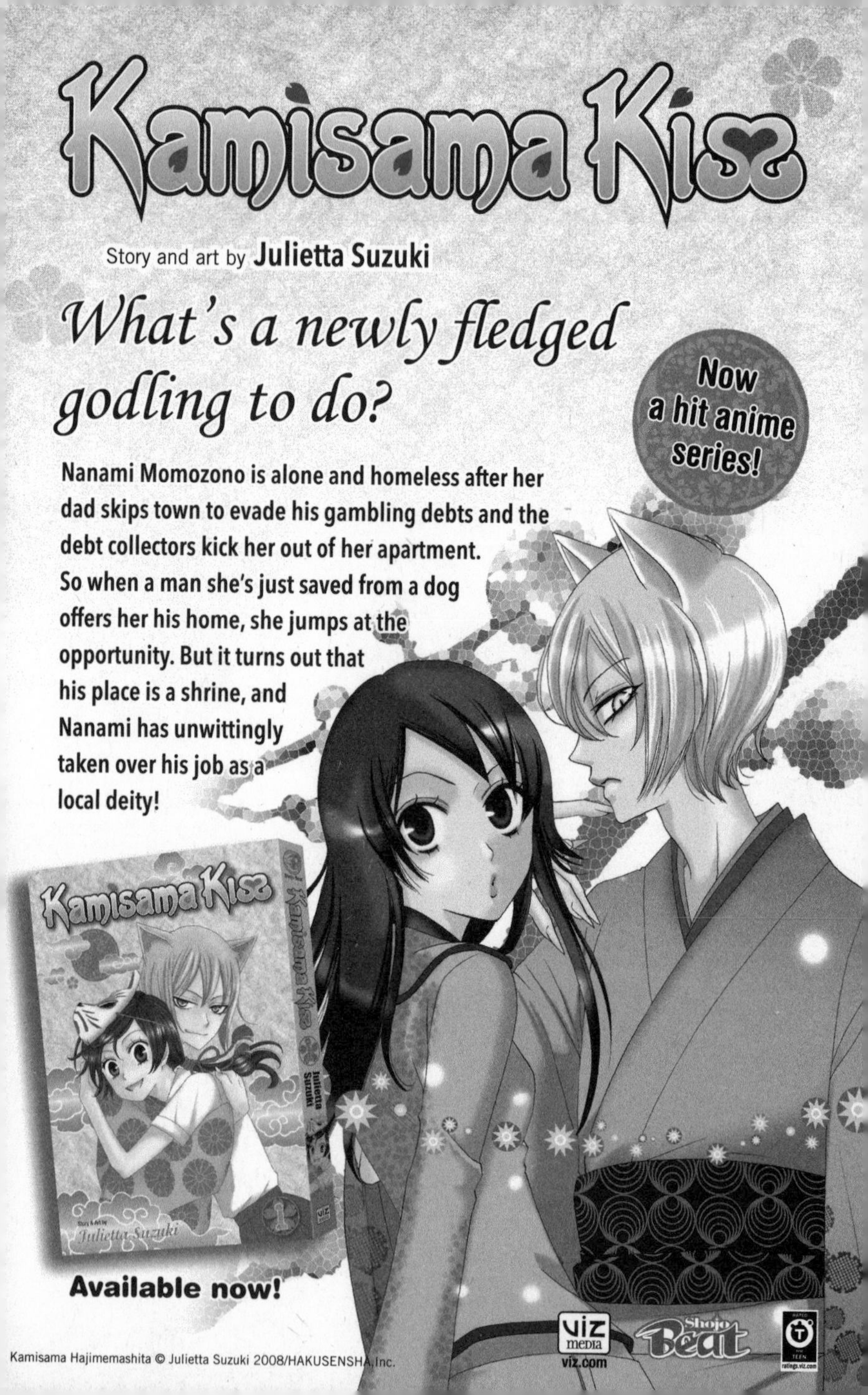
Kamisama Kiss
Story and art by Julietta Suzuki
What's a newly fledged godling to do?
Now a hit anime series!
Nanami Momozono is alone and homeless after her dad skips town to evade his gambling debts and the debt collectors kick her out of her apartment. So when a man she's just saved from a dog offers her his home, she jumps at the opportunity. But it turns out that his place is a shrine, and Nanami has unwittingly taken over his job as a local deity!
Kamisama Kiss
Julietta Suzuki
Story & Art by
Julietta Suzuki
Available now!
viz media
viz.com
Shojo Beat
Kamisama Hajimemashita © Julietta Suzuki 2008/HAKUSENSHA, Inc.

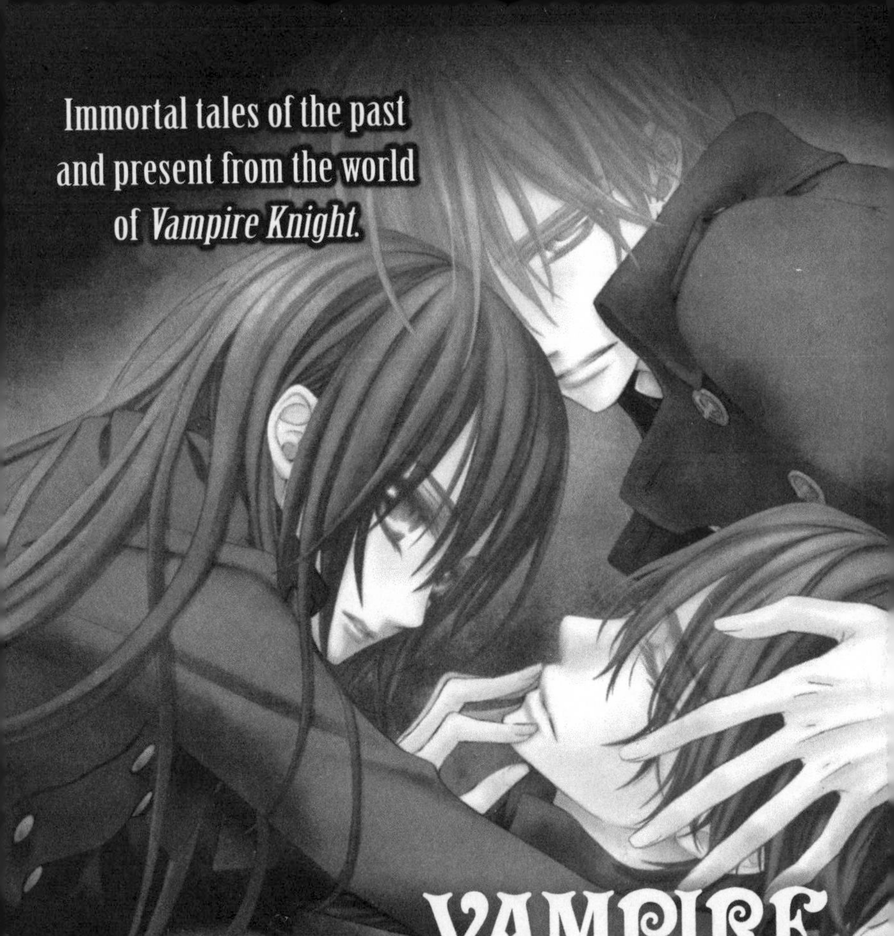
Immortal tales of the past and present from the world of *Vampire Knight.*

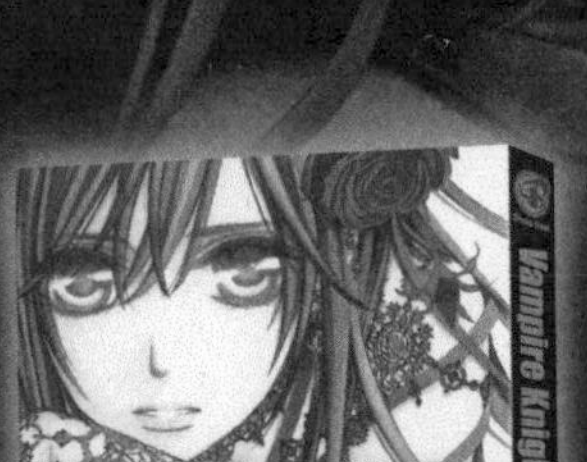
VAMPIRE KNIGHT
MEMORIES
1
Matsuri Hino
Vampire Knight MEMORIES 1
Matsuri Hino

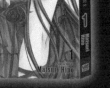

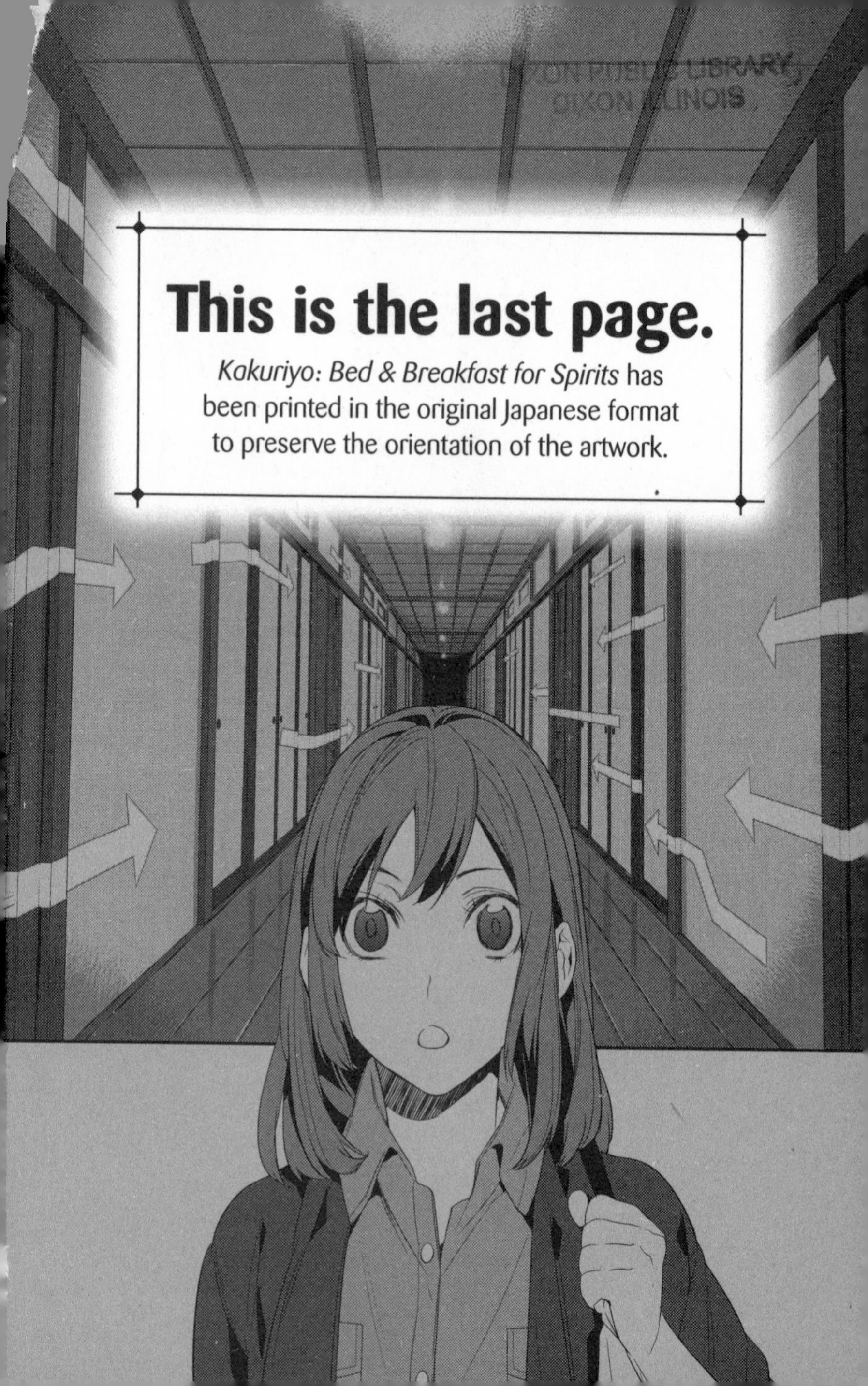

This is the last page.

Kakuriyo: Bed & Breakfast for Spirits has been printed in the original Japanese format to preserve the orientation of the artwork.